fearlessly yours
best friends book club

jennifer chipman

Copyright © 2023 by Jennifer Chipman

All rights reserved.

No part of this book may be reproduced in any form or by any electronic or mechanical means, including information storage and retrieval systems, without written permission from the author, except for the use of brief quotations in a book review.

Cover Art © @alfromnowhere on Instagram

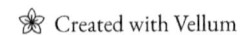

❦ Created with Vellum

*To the real Gabbi,
I hope he loves you like Hunter loves (his) Gabbi.*

Playlist

Spotify Playlist

1. The Very First Night - Taylor Swift
2. The Night We Met - Lord Huron, Phoebe Bridgers
3. Dear Reader - Taylor Swift
4. Stuck with U (with Justin Bieber) - Ariana Grande, Justin Bieber
5. Can I Call You Tonight? - Dayglow
6. Do I Wanna Know? - Arctic Monkeys
7. Gorgeous - Taylor Swift
8. Kiss Me - Ed Sheeran
9. Wildest Dreams - Taylor Swift
10. Yellow - Coldplay
11. This Side of Paradise - Coyote Theory
12. cardigan - Taylor Swift
13. Love Somebody - Maroon 5
14. Fearless - Taylor Swift
15. Little Things - One Direction
16. Slow Dancing - Aly & AJ
17. So Close - Jon McLaughlin
18. They Don't Know About Us - One Direction

19. She Looks So Perfect - 5 Seconds of Summer
20. Starving - Hailee Steinfeld
21. Sweet Nothing - Taylor Swift
22. Road To You - Five For Fighting
23. Golden Hour - Kacey Musgraves
24. Keep Driving - Harry Styles
25. invisible string - Taylor Swift
26. Sunlight - Hozier
27. Everything Has Changed - Taylor Swift, Ed Sheeran
28. Tattooed Heart - Ariana Grande
29. ivy - Taylor Swift
30. pov - Ariana Grande
31. Is This Love? - James Arthur
32. Call It What You Want - Taylor Swift
33. Daylight - Taylor Swift
34. sex - EDEN
35. Falling Like The Stars - James Arthur
36. Bags - Clairo
37. august - Taylor Swift
38. Photograph - Ed Sheeran
39. Forever Winter - Taylor Swift
40. Say Something - A Great Big World
41. Out Of The Woods - Taylor Swift
42. Comeback - Jonas Brothers
43. Ours - Taylor Swift
44. Until I Found You - Stephen Sanchez
45. You - A Great Big World

Table of Contents

Prologue	1
1. Gabrielle	9
2. Hunter	18
3. Gabrielle	25
4. Hunter	37
5. Gabrielle	48
6. Hunter	55
7. Gabrielle	63
8. Hunter	72
9. Gabrielle	83
10. Hunter	90
11. Gabrielle	100
12. Hunter	108
13. Gabrielle	119
14. Hunter	126
15. Gabrielle	134
16. Gabrielle	149
17. Hunter	156
18. Gabrielle	163
19. Hunter	174
20. Gabrielle	184
21. Hunter	192
22. Gabrielle	201
23. Hunter	209
24. Gabrielle	219
25. Hunter	227
26. Gabrielle	237
27. Hunter	244
28. Gabrielle	251
29. Hunter	259
30. Gabrielle	265

31. Hunter	274
32. Gabrielle	281
33. Hunter	292
34. Gabrielle	300
35. Hunter	305
36. Gabrielle	312
37. Hunter	325
38. Hunter	333
Epilogue	340
Extended Epilogue	346
Acknowledgements	353
About the Author	355

Prologue
GABRIELLE

October

O I pulled the sweater onto my body with a huff.

I was late, and it wasn't like I even had a good excuse. None of the costumes I ordered were right.

I hated that I'd ended up as the fifth—or sometimes even seventh—wheel in my friend's relationships. It wasn't like I wasn't used to being single—that spark hadn't been there with the last few people I'd gone out with, and Hannah, my ex... Well... Was it too much to ask that I found someone who loved me for being me? I wanted someone who wanted to go through life hand-in-hand, who I could share everything with. And the moment I was unsure or felt their feelings falter... I bolted.

So where did that leave me?

Alone, getting ready for the Halloween Party where my best friends would all be bringing their dates. Sure, only one of them was in a real relationship—Noelle and her professor boyfriend, who were hosting the party at his house near our old campus, but I knew from how Angelina talked about her friends-with-benefits hookup, Benjamin, that there was something more there. It was so obvious, especially with how they were sneaking around the office, trying to keep people from finding out.

And then there was our fourth best friend, Charlotte, who was also best friends with Angelina's older brother, Daniel. Leaving me completely alone.

It was fine. I looked at the pile of my favorite books, the ones I kept on my nightstand because I liked to reread them over and over, and sighed. What was a good, last-minute costume? I rifled through my closet, trying to find clothes that made me feel confident, maybe even sexy. I wasn't even doing it to pick up a guy—almost everyone at this party would be in a relationship anyway—but because I needed to feel more like myself again.

I was in a love rut, and I was definitely letting it affect my life.

I pulled on my favorite pencil skirt and white button-up, leaving the top few buttons undone as I tied a cardigan around my waist and slipped on my reading glasses. I finished the look with a swipe of lipstick and one last coat of mascara, my favorite pair of heels, and a tote bag full of books.

My backup plan if I got bored was to hide in a corner and read.

I locked the door to my apartment, giving my little black kitten, Toothless, some head scratches on my way out before I headed downstairs towards my white Mazda.

"I'm here!" I called out twenty minutes later as I entered Noelle and Matthew's house. They'd covered it with decorations, and it felt like I was the last person to arrive when I trudged into the dining room and found all my friends talking.

Charlotte giggled, looking at my arms. "Please tell me you did not bring a stack of books to the party."

"Well..." I tried to act coy and brush it off, even though I could tell they all saw right through me. "They *are* part of the costume."

"Sexy librarian?" Angelina asked, raising her eyebrows. "Did you bring Hannah?"

"Nah. That's over." I shrugged, not wanting to talk about her anymore. "Also," I pointed at my outfit, "not a sexy librarian. Just a regular librarian who enjoys a good romance book." Brushing the hair away from my face, I gave her a bright smile. Hopefully she wouldn't see through it.

"So, basically you on an average day?"

"Shut up," I huffed, shoving at Angelina's shoulder lightheartedly. "Everyone else had someone to match with. I didn't have any good solo ideas." I didn't mention that I'd tried on like ten different outfits before settling on this one.

"It's okay, Gabs," she said, slipping my arm through hers. "Let's get a drink and plot out how we're going to find someone for you."

"No, no. I'm fine by myself. Promise." I didn't think I wanted to date for a while. Every time I let someone in, only for it to not work out, I felt like I needed a few months before I'd be ready to be vulnerable with someone again.

I caught the glance Angelina threw at Benjamin—as if checking he was okay without her—before she steered me into the kitchen. I was glad, because God, I needed a drink. Especially watching the tension pouring off those two.

All my friends had ended up in couples' costumes, even Charlotte and Daniel, who had dressed as Sharkboy and Lavagirl. I snorted, wondering how Char had gotten Angelina's quiet brother to dress up like that. Matthew and Noelle were Kristoff and Anna from Disney's Frozen, and they'd even put reindeer antlers and a bell collar on their dog, Snowball, who looked completely content with all the belly rubs she was getting.

"Thank god you're here," Angelina said, dressed in her tight leather suit.

God, I was so going to tease her she was matching her *not*-boyfriend. He was wearing a Batman costume, which seemed too nicely detailed to be just a cheap costume he'd purchased, and Angelina had dressed as Catwoman, complete with a set of black claws.

I laughed, nudging her on the shoulder. "Still just friends, huh?"

"Shut up," she muttered.

I sipped on my Halloween cocktail—I was pretty sure it tasted like candy corn, but I wasn't complaining—and then moved to the dessert table to plop a pumpkin cookie in my mouth.

Angelina was staring across the room, and when I looked up, I saw Benjamin approaching us. Following behind him closely was an even taller man with brown hair, a touch of a shade lighter, and a nice dusting of stubble on his face. He was bulkier than Benjamin, and I was trying not to appreciate the sight of his arm muscles through his doctors' get-up.

I resisted the urge to snort over his basic costume. But also, why hadn't I thought of something like that? Scrubs seemed comfortable. One of my brothers was a vet, and he always wore them to work. No such luck working in HR for a Tech company—I was in dresses and heels more often than I was in leggings and t-shirts.

Benjamin looked at the three of us. "Hunter," he started, waving a hand. "You remember Angelina." His eyes filled with heat as he looked at my best friend. "And this is her best friend and roommate, Gabrielle."

Right, that was me. I tried to tear my gaze away from his friend, but I was having a hard time not ogling him.

"Angelina and Gabrielle, this is my older brother, Hunter."

Oh, my god. His brother? I was checking out Benjamin's *brother*. I was trying to figure out why the universe would be so cruel to me—to drop the perfect man in front of me, and then say *"Jokes on you! Because you can't have him."*

"You didn't tell me your brother was going to make it," Angelina said. "It's nice to see you again."

Hunter's rigid posture loosened up a bit, and he gave a small smile. *Wow.* The sight of it... It lit up my insides. "I didn't know if I was going to come until the last minute. I just got off work."

"Gabrielle," Benjamin asked, "Do you mind if I steal Angelina away for a moment?"

I couldn't help but give him a thumbs up, chuckling at them. They kept insisting it was casual, nothing serious, but there was no way to deny it when you saw how they looked at each other. How much trust and care they placed in each other?

I wanted that, too. More than anything. Someone to look at me like I was their universe, the way Benjamin looked at Angelina. How my dad looked at my mom.

As soon as Benjamin and Angelina were gone, Hunter turned to me, an eyebrow raised. "What are you supposed to be?" he asked, crossing his arms over his chest.

He was asking me that—*really*? Mr. Scrubs over here was judging *me*?

I forced my face into a deadpan expression as I lifted the book in my hands. "I'm a librarian."

Hunter snorted.

What the hell?

"What?" I almost sneered, my tone coming off more aggressively than I intended.

"Nothing."

"Are you making fun of my costume when you picked the most basic thing of all time?" I narrowed my eyes. "Is this even real, anyway?" I grabbed the stethoscope from around his neck, popping it in his ears before I tapped on the diaphragm.

Hunter grunted, almost like I annoyed him, but he didn't take it back like I thought he would. He didn't remove the hand I'd placed on his chest, either. Instead, he covered my hand with his own and placed the piece on *my* chest as our hands remained connected.

"That's how it's supposed to be used."

I blinked up at him. What was happening right now? I couldn't stop my heart from beating faster, almost racing as he stared down at me.

Was this my meet cute?

How was it that this man—who was absolutely the most gorgeous person I'd ever seen—was now looking at me like I intrigued *him*? Like he was maybe even interested in me?

But he didn't avert his eyes. He listened to my heartbeat with an emotion I couldn't place in his eyes. Amusement? I liked to think it was that. "Strong."

"Wh-what?"

"Your heart."

I didn't think I had any words left. Maybe I looked like a gaping fish, my mouth opening and closing as Benjamin's brother forced out a sigh. "Dr. Hunter Sullivan. It's nice to meet you, miss..."

"Oh. Gabrielle Meyer." It surprised me how much I missed the warmth of his hand when he removed it from my chest and placed the stethoscope back around his neck. "But my friends call me Gabbi. Or Gabs. I always thought Elle would be a nice nickname, too, but I could never quite get that one to stick." God, I needed to shut up. He didn't care that I wanted my friends to call me Elle. I didn't need to talk his ear off and run him off like I'd done to people before.

"I work in Pediatrics up on Hospital Hill. Just got off." Well, that explained the scrubs. And the Dr. Title.

And shit, he was a *sexy* doctor, like God had taken pity on me and served him up on a silver platter.

I bit my lip, feeling guilty for assuming. "I'm sorry—I didn't mean to imply..."

"That I wasn't actually a doctor?" Hunter almost chuckled, the corners of his mouth tilting up in the second closest thing to a smile he did all night. "It's alright. I'll give you a free pass since it's Halloween."

Hanging my head, I fiddled with the bottom of my cardigan. "Thanks. And... I'm sorry. This is just my costume, so I shouldn't have..." Assumed. You know what they say about assumptions. "I'm not really a librarian." I winced. *Duh, Gabrielle. Of course, you're not.* "Obviously. I just like reading. Mostly romance novels, but I dabble in fantasy too. Although mostly it's fantasy romance. Sometimes I'll throw in a few other genres too, but..." God, I was babbling. Why was I babbling? I blushed. "Sorry. I really like books. I don't mean to talk your ear off about it."

He shook his head, but I wondered if he was trying to fight off a smile. Either way, his response was gruff when he finally said, "It's okay. I don't mind listening. What do you do if reading books all day isn't your actual job?"

I think I might have beamed. "I wish it *was*. Honestly, I would kick ass at it. But no, I'm in Human Resources at Willamette Tech. That's where I first met your brother. Angelina's been my best friend since college. They're…"

I looked for Angelina and Benjamin, wondering where they'd gone off to, but I didn't see them.

Hunter chuckled, bringing my body to attention at the sound. Something about the deep rasp of his throat—it was doing something to me. "Seems that they disappeared on us, haven't they?"

He leaned in closer to me, and I wasn't sure if I wanted to step back to keep my body from burning up at his closeness or step in and inhale his smell.

All I knew was that every part of me was screaming out for him to touch me. And the way he was looking down at me, grinning like the devil, I knew it would be a mistake.

And as much as this man in front of me's body promised a good time, I wasn't a one-night-stand kind of girl. I wanted to find romance and love. Someone who was going to love *me*. I wouldn't sacrifice that, even if I needed to get laid… badly.

CHAPTER 1
Gabrielle

APRIL

"To Benjamin and Angelina!" The crowd cheered as my best friend and her *Fiancée*—that was still crazy to me—held up their glasses in celebration. Of their engagement, specifically.

It had been almost a month since they had come back from their whirlwind Paris trip, the one Benjamin had asked me to help him plan out some of the smaller details, and it felt like almost everyone we knew had crowded into the upscale Portland restaurant. Angelina and I's coworkers, some other friends from college, and of course our other best friends—Charlotte and Noelle, and Noelle's boyfriend, Matthew. We were all standing around a high-top table by the bar as everyone continued to congratulate the happy couple.

"They look so happy," Charlotte sighed dreamily, staring up at them.

I rolled my eyes. "You say this as if we haven't heard her threaten to punch him in the arm multiple times over the past week."

"You're just grumpy because you're alone," she pouted.

Was I? I didn't think so.

"I'm perfectly happy the way I am. Thank you very much."

Noelle snorted, her boyfriend's arms wrapped around her waist. "That's what they *all* say till you find the right person." She looked up into Matthew's eyes with so much love, and I took another gulp of my drink.

"*Sure.*" Maybe I was a little allergic to love right now. How was it just my luck that I'd lost two of my best friends to the *love bug* over the last year?

Clearly, love wasn't the plan for me right now. But that was okay—I had my book boyfriends, and my best friends, and that was enough. It would have to be. If not, well... I always had the *little friend* I kept in my nightstand drawer.

"I'm gonna go get a refill," I said, holding up my tequila on the rocks that was now unfortunately empty. "Be right back."

Did I need the refill? No, but I was still getting one.

"I'll come with you." Charlotte brushed her hands down her dress, a pretty shade of bubblegum pink as usual, but this one was more fitted than usual, paired with a gold glittery pair of heels.

"Where's Daniel?" I asked, surveying the room for Angelina's brother and Charlotte's best friend.

"He's trying to keep the peace with their parents. Their mom brought her new husband and things are... tense. I'm surprised Angelina even invited her, honestly." She looked across the room and sighed.

I raised an eyebrow. Honestly, we'd all teased her enough about Daniel over the last year, and it didn't seem to have done anything, so I didn't see any point in continuing to prod about that.

"Don't give me that look," Charlotte frowned.

"Mmm. You have any luck on that dating app lately?"

"No." She rolled her eyes. "I've about given up. Every first date I've been on in the last six months has also been the *last.* I'm getting so sick of this, honestly. And Juily wants me to take on more work at the dance studio, since she and her wife are talking about having a baby, so I don't have time to go on dates." Charlotte groaned. "Plus, the dress commissions keep me busy enough as it is. Something's gotta go, and you know it won't be my books."

"Charlotte." I shook my head with a smile. "You're insane."

We both got the bartender's attention and ordered our drinks before continuing our conversation.

She twirled a blonde hair around her finger as she pondered something in her mind. "I'm trying to meet *the one*, you know? When I meet him, I'll know. Like somehow I'll be able to feel it, deep in my bones."

It was a sweet dream; I had to give it to her. But this wasn't a romance novel, and soulmates weren't real. Neither was the perfect book boyfriend. Tall, dark, and handsome, who wanted to worship me on a pedestal? Ha. Must be nice.

What *would* it be like to know you'd met the right guy instantly? I wished I knew. For a few moments there on Halloween, I thought I *had* found the man of my dreams. Tall, with the perfect amount of scruff detailing his jaw, and those piercing green eyes that had held me hostage from the very first moment.

Somehow, this man could reduce me to a blubbering idiot without even trying. I didn't know where all of my ability to use the English language went when he was around, but most of our conversations ended up with him grunting and me rambling to fill the silence. I couldn't help it. It was like word vomit, tumbling out of my mouth before I could stuff it back in.

He was like all the traits I loved in my book boyfriends rolled into one, and yet...

Despite all of my daydreaming and fantasizing, this was no fairytale romance. He was my best friend's boyfriend's brother. Her soon-to-be brother-in-law. No way was that happening. Not on several fronts. I wouldn't risk my relationship with my best friend for a stupid fling.

The worst part? I was pretty sure the shade of his eyes was now my favorite color green.

I could probably attribute my word vomit to the fact that I'd grown up with two older brothers myself, and life in my house had always been chaotic and messy–sometimes it felt like I couldn't get a word in edgewise, so if I managed to get attention all my thoughts would come tumbling out at once. Still, I loved my family and missed them often, but I'd made a life for myself here in the Pacific Northwest, and I didn't want to go back to Boston.

I turned my eyes back to her. "Yeah. But we're not living in a romance novel, Char. Your perfect man isn't going to come sidling up next to you and whisk you away for a dance."

"You never know," Charlotte said, wiggling her eyebrows as she sipped on her vodka cranberry.

"What'd I miss?" Daniel asked, nudging in between us at the bar.

"Gabbi thinks I should get back on that dating app," Charlotte said, completely throwing me under the bus.

"Hey! I did not."

Daniel frowned at her. Huh.

I often wondered if there truly was nothing going on between them, how they could have been friends since our freshman year and not even feel a smidge of affection for each other. But what did I know? I'd always made a point of not falling for my best guy friends throughout high school, and in college, well, I'd ended up with the three girls as my group. They were basically like my family out here, considering my actual family was on the other side of the country from me.

A fact I didn't like to linger on for too long.

"Hey," came a deep, smooth voice, and I didn't have to look up to know who it was. I was pretty sure I'd never forget that voice again for the rest of my life. Damn.

"Hunter, hi." I couldn't even help the warmth that spread over my face. Hunter Sullivan, Benjamin's brother—in the flesh.

It almost wasn't fair how handsome he was. It also definitely *wasn't* fair how perfect he was—in every way but one.

He didn't want me. Not like I wanted him.

"You look lovely today."

I tried my best not to blush. I appreciated his compliment, but I hated when I turned into that girl around him. The bumbling, blushing fool who couldn't shut up.

I took a moment to admire my favorite emerald green dress, remembering how confident I felt in the mirror before I left. My hair was swept into a braided crown up-do, with a few tendrils hanging out in the front. I wasn't one to dress up often, choosing leggings and a comfy crewneck when I was off the clock. Most of the time, if I wasn't leaving the house, I didn't even do my hair or makeup, but tonight... tonight I felt good

I gave him my best small smile and took another sip of tequila. "You too. Erm. I mean, you clean up well."

He chuckled. "I promised you I don't wear scrubs all the time." It felt like in the six months I'd known him, I'd seen him in something other than his scrubs less than a handful of times, one of which was New Year's Eve. A night I tried very hard not to think about.

I hummed in response. "So you did."

I admired his well-trimmed beard, wondering, like always, what it would feel like to run my fingers against it. God, I needed to stop thinking about him like that.

Hunter looked between me, Daniel, and Charlotte, before announcing, "Mom wanted to take a few photos of the bridal party before anyone tries to sneak off. Namely, the guests of honor."

Charlotte giggled as we watched Benjamin tug Angelina closer to his side. "Should we make bets on how long they'll last?"

"Like my mom will let him leave," Hunter grumped, tugging at the burgundy tie that he'd worn with a sharp gray suit. "She already made it explicitly clear to me—I'm not allowed to go until every single present is in *my* car."

I laughed, picturing all six-foot-four of him and those muscular arms he'd built—bossed around by his mother, but he stared back at me.

"What?"

I shook my head, hiding my small smile. "Nothing. Let's go take pictures."

We stopped by our table, dropped off our drinks, and dragged Noelle with us over to Angelina and Benjamin.

All eight of us bridesmaids and groomsmen were gathered together.. For the girls, Angelina had asked me to be her maid of honor and Charlotte, Noelle, and Benjamin's sister Emily to be her bridesmaids. Benjamin's side was, no shock here, his brother Hunter, Angelina's brother Daniel, his good buddy Liam, and Nicolas, who was Angelina and I's friend from college, the new CEO of the company we worked for, and now one of his closest friends.

But that was a story for another time.

"Enjoying your party?" I smirked at Angelina as we all got arranged for the picture, and she rolled her eyes at me, brushing her long, dark curls off her olive-skinned shoulder. She'd worn a white sparkly a-line dress with a pearl headband, and she looked radiant. Unlike me, who had a tanned complexion practically year round, even during the Portland winters, Angelina's skin fluctuated, thanks to her Italian-American heritage.

Either way, she was gorgeous. I'd always admired her tall stature and the way she'd carried herself, even back when we'd been awkward eighteen-year-olds sharing our first college dorm and all of my romance novels. And yet, if it was possible, she was even more beautiful now.

"You know me." Her eyes sparkled. "I do my best work in the spotlight." She winked. Angelina had always thrived in settings like this, where her hair was perfectly done and her red lipstick paired perfectly with the diamond pendant looped around her neck and the red-bottom heels she'd worked so hard to afford.

I found I was in my element when I simply tossed my hair

into a braid and had my camera or a book in hand. They were both hobbies, sure, but they were the things that I loved.

I laughed. "That's my girl. Did I tell you earlier that your legs are killer in this dress?"

"You did," she grinned back. "Twice."

"Smile!" the photographer called out, interrupting our whispered conversation, and I turned to the lens and for the first time in months, I truly wasn't faking the dazzling smile I gave the cameras. Because at that moment, I had my girls by my side, and I was happy.

Angelina laughed as we all pulled apart. "God, this is crazy, isn't it? I never thought I'd be the first one out of us to get married. But he's my best friend, and, as much as I hate to admit it—" She made a little vomiting sound as Benjamin rolled his eyes —"I love him." She kissed his cheek.

I knew she did. It had been obvious, watching her deny her feelings as the two of them hooked up, but they complimented each other better than anyone I'd ever met.

"I know." I patted her hand. "Let's go get another drink."

I needed it if I was going to keep my lack of a filter in check around Hunter, or I had a feeling I was going to be putting my foot in my mouth *way* more often than was socially acceptable.

∼

"So, is everyone excited about their *big announcement?*" Harper, who worked in marketing for our firm, asked the crowd. "I can't wait to find out what it is!"

"Oh, yeah," I said and took a sip of my wine as Nicolas raised an eyebrow at me. "I'm just *dying* in anticipation." Nic rolled his eyes after I gave him a wink.

I already knew what it was. Angelina had planned their wedding as soon as they got home from their engagement, and after they'd found a weekend available at their *dream* venue this summer, they'd booked it. The only other people who knew about it were the wedding party—and their parents.

You could see our efforts strewn all over our apartment—Angelina wasn't one to skimp on any details. We'd spent hours poring over wedding magazines and Pinterest, and I knew more now about types of flowers and cake than I'd ever thought possible.

The best part? *Destination wedding!* Our planning had reminded me how desperately I'd wanted to travel. It was perfect. I'd hardly been able to go anywhere since college, even though my passport was waiting for stamps. Not that I didn't have trips *planned*—I could find a million excuses why I didn't go, but part of the problem? I didn't have anyone to go with me. It made it hard to justify a thousand-dollar plane ticket to get anywhere outside of the country, knowing that I'd be going alone.

Nicolas cleared his throat, turning to me and changing the subject. "Do you think there's cake?"

I couldn't keep in my laugh.

I'd met Nicolas during my freshman year of college—he was a year ahead and lived on the floor above us in our co-ed dorm. He reminded me of my brothers, so it made sense that we'd make such fast friends. When I graduated with my communications degree, not knowing what I wanted to do, he helped me get a job with his father's software company. The one *he* was now CEO of.

Nicolas was running the company, Angelina was the Chief Marketing Officer, her husband-to-be was the Chief Financial Officer, and I was fine with my position as an HR Manager. Wasn't I? Sometimes when I'd dreamed about my life, I always thought there would be... more. I'd get over that feeling eventually, right?

Angelina tapped the side of her wineglass with a knife to get everyone's attention. "Hi everyone," she grinned, her black curls spilling over her shoulder as she turned to look at her fiancé. "I know you're all waiting with bated breath for our announcement, but I wanted to say a few things about this guy right here before we get to that." Benjamin slid his arm around her waist as she rested her other hand on his chest.

"When we first met in person, I hated him. I'd convinced myself he didn't like me, and that he was nitpicking every little thing that I did, and it drove me *insane.*"

Benjamin chuckled at her side, and she shot him a look.

"Little did I know that deep down, underneath all of that, was a guy who would treat me like a princess and make me feel like I was *actually* worthy of love. So, I want to say thank you to the man who's going to be my husband, even if you're infuriatingly perfect ninety percent of the time and I think about throttling you daily, you're also my best friend, and I love you so much." The crowd laughed, and Angelina turned back to the crowd, her eyes dancing between all of us. "Finally, I hope you'll all join us this August for our wedding—in France! Everyone's invited, but we know that it's far, so we'll also be having a little party once we get back to celebrate as well." I could feel the excited buzz in the room, the chatter that was already beginning between all the guests.

Benjamin smirked. "Once I can pry her away from our honeymoon, that is."

She flushed, her cheeks pinking in a way they never used to—not before meeting him. "Anyway, thank you all for celebrating with us, and we appreciate you all for being here tonight."

He pulled her tight, placing a kiss against her cheek. "I'd like to thank this wonderful woman for agreeing to marry me, even though we both know she could do so much better."

She rolled her eyes, swatting at him, even though I could see the laughter on her face. "That's it! Get back to enjoying the party!"

I turned back to the group, giving Harper a satisfied smile, before excusing myself and heading to the bar to get a drink.

"Aren't you glad you don't have to keep that secret anymore?" That deep voice I love asked when I finished ordering my drink.

CHAPTER 2
Hunter

I raised an eyebrow. "Dude, you're whipped."

They'd just announced to the entire room where their wedding would be, and I'd said the same thing when he first told me.

Benjamin scratched at the back of his head. "Listen, it makes her happy, and that makes me happy. Plus, we were looking at some Chateaus available as venues, and it's really—" He waved a hand. "Not important. But, I know you have a bunch of PTO you haven't used since you haven't taken a vacation in like six *years*, man. Why don't you take the month off and travel afterward?"

It wasn't a bad idea. "Hm." I frowned. When was the last time I'd done something for myself?

"What?"

"Just marveling at you having a good idea."

"Which one? Proposing to Angelina, or you taking time off work?"

We both laughed.

"Both. You did good, Benjamin."

I looked over at our mom, who was standing at Angelina's side, clearly so happy to have another daughter to add to the family. Benjamin's eyes trailed over mine, and I couldn't resist teasing him. I may have been in my thirties, but there was no expiration on poking fun at your younger siblings.

"You know she was interrogating Angelina at Christmas, right?"

He groaned. "Yes. We'd been officially dating for like *a week*. Sometimes I'm surprised that didn't scare her off."

I snorted. "Yeah, well, luckily she'd already fallen in love with you, dumbass. But you might tell mom to lay off baby talk for a while." Knowing her, she'd be waiting for grandkids as soon as the wedding night was over, but I was pretty sure my brother and his bride-to-be weren't in a rush.

Benjamin shook his head. "Any chance you want to take one for the team? I *am* getting married first, after all."

"And have a kid? With my schedule? Hell no." I took a sip of my beer. "Mom needs to accept that she's getting grandkids when she gets them, and that's that." If at all, but I hadn't said that to her. I wasn't sure I ever wanted to have a family after watching so many of them fall apart in my hospital rooms. "Besides, I'm very much happy with being *single*. I want mom to stop trying to set me up with someone." I narrowed my eyes at him. "And don't tell me my solution is getting a girlfriend *again*. Not happening."

"I'm just saying..." he started, and then shook his head. "If you want her to get off your back, maybe you should get a girlfriend."

"You say it like it's so easy. Like you didn't pretend to not be in love with Angelina while you were sleeping together for *months*."

He shook his head. "It's not the same."

"Oh?" I raised an eyebrow. "Enlighten me how it's *not*?"

He clasped a hand on my shoulder. "Either way, we're getting married now, and it all worked out the way it was supposed to."

"Well, cheers to that," I said, clinking my glass with his as I tried to avoid my mother's stare from across the room.

I'd never realized how unfortunate it was to have my mother

in town, practically breathing down my back, until now. While I figured she would have laid off me with the whole, you know, my brother getting married *thing*, it was the opposite. It was so much worse.

I was pretty sure she'd tried to give three different women my number during the course of the day. Of course, she'd been insistent on coming with me *everywhere*. I was happy she didn't insist on coming to my hospital this trip, because for all I knew she would have tried to set me up with a patient's mom or one of my fellow doctors, and that was drama I didn't need.

But despite my mom's nefarious intentions to get me married off, I loved having all of my family around. I never felt like I got to see my sister Emily enough, since in addition to her *jet-setting* around as a Social Media Influencer, the only time I made it home to Montana was during the holidays.

It was still strange to think that less than eight months ago, my brother and I barely talked. Sure, we'd both been busy with our respective careers, but our relationship *had* suffered from distance. But everything changed after he met Angelina. He'd called me, and we'd rebuilt our relationship stronger than ever.

Tonight, at least, we were all in one place. As soon as she'd heard the two were engaged, my mom started planning this party. Our extended family—the ones who were close enough—had all come, as well as many of the people Benjamin and Angelina worked with at Willamette Tech.

But, staring across the room, I didn't care about saying hello to any of them as I stared at the green dress that wrapped around Gabbi's body and looked like *sin*. I couldn't think about anything else when she slipped away from her table, except I needed to be next to her.

I'd been trying not to focus on it all night, especially when we took pictures all together and I was close enough where I could have pulled her in. My feet were moving before I could stop them, and I didn't care where the thought came from.

Only for a voice to stop me in my tracks. One *very* specific voice.

My mom's.

"Hunter!" she called again.

I turned around, trying to will my face to not look as annoyed as I *felt*. Sure, she'd knocked me out of my trance-like state, but at what cost?

I sighed. "Yes, Mom?"

She'd gone over the top with this whole thing, but the event screamed Benjamin and Angelina: elegant, *classy,* sophisticated.

But if it was me? I'd rather be celebrating with my closest friends at a bar. Just me and my girl. Even though *that* would never happen.

"Oh, good. I wasn't sure you'd heard me."

I gave her a small smile. "What's up?"

"Isn't this all lovely?" She said with a sigh. I knew what was coming before she even said it. "Don't you want to do this yourself?"

I groaned. "I'm a doctor. I don't have time for dates and all of this."

Being single made me content. Most women wouldn't want to put up with someone who puts their job first, anyway. Especially when we saw some awful things. The things I've seen kids go through, how strong they were... And how their parents fell apart when the worst happened to them—that could fuck you up easily. It was why I tried not to get attached to anyone. I knew how easy it was to lose someone. Car accidents, cancer... There were so many ways life was determined to knock us down.

"I'm just saying, I was already married with kids when I was your age, and you're not getting any younger."

I frowned. Sure, she and my dad had gotten married during medical school, and she'd had us during her surgical residency, but how many times had we wished they were home more? I didn't want to do that to a kid. I'd seen enough neglectful parents while working in pediatrics that I'd vowed to never be like that.

"What about Angelina's sweet friend? Gabbi? She seems nice." My mom perked up.

Gabrielle? Oh, god. She wanted me to date my sister-in-law-to-be's *best friend*. Did she not see all the things that were wrong with that picture?

I crossed my arms over my chest. "I can't date her, Mom."

She fluttered her eyelashes at me like she was trying to be sly, but I knew what she was doing. "Who said anything about a date? I'm just saying you could get to know her, and who knows..."

"No. And I'm fine the way I am. I promise."

She sighed, shaking her head, but I gave up on telling her the same thing I'd already said *again*. I was pretty sure she would never listen to me, anyway.

My eyes trailed over to Gabrielle, laughing with her friends. She shone so brightly whenever she was around her friends—like the moon on a clear evening. Like a bunch of stars, the constellations painting the sky like those little freckles that dotted her nose and cheeks.

I couldn't stop thinking about what my mom had said. Was she right? Should I go for it?

No, I thought to myself, trying to get those stupid ideas out of my brain.

You don't have time for a relationship, and it would never work out. And then when it didn't, you'd have to see her for the rest of your life, and it would be miserable. This was why the only women I ever slept with were one-night, no strings attached sorts of things, and never people I worked with.

I walked away, heading towards the bar. I needed a drink. And I'd already spotted the brunette in the little green dress who headed that way.

"Aren't you glad you don't have to keep that secret anymore?" I asked her.

Who was I keeping it from? My only friends outside of work either didn't know them or... were standing inside this room. Angelina roped me into becoming friends with her little brigade of book lovers. Maybe I'd just wanted an excuse to talk to her.

She turned to look at me. "Oh. Hey, Hunter." The little blush had already spread over her cheeks, making the little freckles on her nose more noticeable.

"Hi, Gabrielle."

I ordered another bourbon as the bartender slid Gabbi a tequila on the rocks.

"Hi." She winced. "I already said that. Ignore me." She glanced between me and Angelina, who was currently leaning against Benjamin as she sipped on her wine.

"So, I, uh... You're the Best Man," she said, stating the obvious—as if we hadn't taken wedding party pictures forty-five minutes ago. As if we both hadn't known this for the last three weeks.

I nodded. "And you're Maid of Honor."

"Well, it's... It'll be fun. Guess it makes us partners of a sort."

Why was I thinking about the other ways we could be *partners*? Partners in the sheets? I wasn't supposed to be picturing her like this. Especially not at Angelina and Benjamin's engagement party.

"Mhm." I cocked an eyebrow. "I suppose it does."

"Are you excited to see your brother get married? Or is it weird that your younger brother is getting married first? I mean... that's presuming you even want to get married, you know." She made a face before looking up at me. "I don't even..." her voice grew quieter, trailing off, "... know that you do," she mumbled under her breath, so low I could barely hear her.

"Right..." I blinked. I always felt a little lost for words when she talked to me. No matter the endless stream of chatter that she presented me.

I opened my mouth to talk, yet nothing came out.

Did I want to get married?

I'd thought about it before, sure. The idea of having someone to come home to was nice, but then I thought about all the hours

I worked. Of the times when I'd wished my parents were home more when I was growing up and they were both surgeons. I wouldn't wish that on anyone, not a wife or kids. "I'm not sure."

"Okay... Well..." Gabrielle shrugged, turning her attention back to the rest of the room. "I'm just gonna go..."

"No." I begged her with my eyes. "Please stay. I..."

"Sorry?"

"I don't know anyone else here. And all these girls here..." I winced. Some girls my mom invited already tried hitting on me before the announcement, and I knew they were only interested because I was a doctor, like they were seeing dollar signs by looking at me. But Gabbi... she'd never cared about that. "You're much better company," I finished.

Gabrielle raised an eyebrow, muttering something under her breath.

"What?" I asked.

"I thought... Never mind."

"You're different."

"Oh, gee, thank you. Just what every girl wants to hear." She rolled her eyes.

I huffed. "That's not..."

"I think I see Angelina calling for me, so... I'll see you later," Gabbi said, forcing a small smile.

Fuck. How was I constantly fucking things up around her?

I ran my fingers over my jaw, smoothing my beard down as I tried to figure out how to keep myself from screwing everything up—again.

CHAPTER 3
Gabrielle

Around the time I finished washing my hands, I heard Benjamin's voice whispering outside the door. Peeking out, I tiptoed closer, knowing I shouldn't eavesdrop, but I couldn't help myself. I'd always been a little nosy.

The voice was gruff, and the sound of it sent heat to my core, and I recognized it instantly.

Was that... Hunter?

"God, she's so *ridiculous*," I heard Hunter say as I rounded the corner, pressing my body up against the wall as I caught their conversation. "I don't think she could be any more annoying if she tried."

I peeked around the corner, seeing Benjamin's furrowed brow.

"Come on, Hunt. Gabrielle's just—"

Gabrielle? I stepped back. *Me?*

He was talking about me? There was this sinking feeling in my gut, and I didn't even know how to feel. Sure, he normally didn't say too much to me—the occasional overly flirtatious line, which I generally brushed off, but this?

I thought maybe things would be different. But maybe I'd been making up the way his eyes kept drifting over to me. After our conversation earlier, maybe I was delusional—I'd convinced myself that there was something there because I was a little too infatuated with him.

But now? I was done.

I didn't even want to know what Benjamin was going to say—even if he was attempting to stand up for me, I couldn't listen to it. Hunter bad-mouthing me wouldn't make me listen. I wished this damn restaurant had another way I could go, but unfortunately, to go back to the party, I had to walk right past the two of them.

"Excuse me," I muttered, shoving past them to find Angelina.

I debated if I should tell her I had a headache or something, and dip out early, but I knew she would interrogate me till she found out the truth. Angelina raised an eyebrow as I came back to stand beside her, but I shook my head instead. I wouldn't ruin this day for her. I wouldn't tell her about the way my stomach had dropped hearing the guy I'd had a massive crush on for months talk about how he didn't like me. I was going to get over it, kill him with kindness, and get through the end of this wedding.

Because it was *fine*. I'd get over this stupid infatuation I had with Benjamin's idiot brother, and then we could just be friends. Really, what did I care if he thought I was some silly young girl? I didn't.

With that, I decided my favorite thing about this party was the excuse to dress up *and* the free alcohol, courtesy of Benjamin's parents. I ordered a shot of tequila from the bar, threw it back, and then willed myself to forget what I'd heard—at least for the rest of the night.

"What's wrong?" Angelina asked, frowning.

"It's nothing," I said, shaking myself out of my funk and preparing to order another shot when Angelina just shook her head. "Really. It's fine. I don't want to ruin your night, so let's go celebrate. We have to celebrate the future Mrs. Sullivan, after all."

I threw my arm around her shoulder, pulling her back towards the festivities.

I planned to dance until my brain shut off, and hoped that when I woke up tomorrow, I'd have forgotten everything that slipped out of Hunter Sullivan's lips.

～

"No. Definitely not." Angelina was staring at herself in the mirror, smoothing the front of a fitted, white dress, face twisted up like she couldn't quite place what was wrong with it.

We'd all agreed to go dress shopping the day after the engagement party since Benjamin's mom and sister were both in town, and I was very glad I'd stopped drinking when I did last night. I enjoyed alcohol in moderation, but sometimes when it was a celebration I liked to go a little crazy. I'd done another tequila shot after Hunter's *confession* to his brother, and luckily, Angelina had stopped me before I'd thrown back two more. Still, I'd successfully made it through the rest of the night unscathed, and ignored Hunter's presence as best I could.

We'd been to a few shops before this one, and while we'd come up with several options at some of the bridal boutiques, but there was nothing Angelina *loved* yet. Now, we were a few mimosas in, draped across the white leather couches of the current dress store.

"It's too plain," Charlotte popped up. "Especially for France. You need something… *more*."

Angelina nodded. "It's not *me*." She looked at the girl who was helping us, and the two of them moved back into the fitting room so she could try on the next one.

"I still think I could make her one," Charlotte pouted.

Noelle nudged her side. "Aren't you already busy enough between the dance studio and the dress commissions you have? And the wedding is in four months, which doesn't give you much time."

"I know," she sighed and looked at Noelle. "When you get married to Matthew, I'm going to disown you as my best friend if you don't let me make your dress." Charlotte narrowed her eyes. But it was a little like seeing a baby animal trying to act ferocious: she'd always been all bark and no bite. Char was the quietest and shyest of our friend group, so it always made me laugh when our tiny innocent blonde threatened anything.

Noelle gave her a sheepish grin. "I think you've got some time before that, anyway, Char."

"What about your own?" Angelina said, coming out in another dress that she adjusted in the mirror, fidgeting with the lace skirt.

"*My* wedding dress?" Charlotte laughed. "I'd have to find someone to get married to first." It was so weird to think that she and I were the last two single ones in our friend group.

"What about you, Gabrielle?" Benjamin's mom asked from the couch next to mine.

I think I choked on my mimosa, because the only thing that came out of my mouth was, "W-what?" I straightened up and spoke again. "What about me?"

"Are you seeing anyone?"

I took a deep swallow. "Nope. Just me and my cat, Mrs. Sullivan." God, did that sound pathetic? Maybe I was a little pathetic.

"Please, you can call me Molly," she gave me a small smile. "I told Angelina the same thing when we first met. Besides, we're going to be family, right?"

"Er... I guess." If you count me being Angelina's best friend as being her family, sure. I'd never quite been comfortable calling my friend's parents by their first names, but I supposed now was as good a time as ever to get used to it.

I looked up at my best friend, who shook her head in the mirror before turning to us. "I'm gonna go try on a different one." She was a perfectionist, I swear. I knew every little detail was going to have to be perfect for this wedding or she would go crazy.

When Angelina came out in a lace-sleeved dress with a structured corset-style bodice and a long-flowing a-line skirt with a long train. The skirt was a soft chiffon fabric, and when she turned in front of the mirror, she was *glowing* in it.

"That's it," I gasped. *"That's* the one."

"She's right," Emily agreed.

"You think?" She did a little turn, inspecting herself in the mirror, but I could see it in her eyes. She loved it.

"Definitely." We all confirmed.

"Good, because I think..." Angelina's eyes sparkled as they tucked a veil into her hair. "I think it's perfect," she said, touching the delicate detailing on the lace.

"Oh, honey," Benjamin's mom said, tears pricking her eyes. "I'm so happy to have you join our family. You and Benjamin make the absolute perfect couple."

"Plus, it's nice to have another girl in the family," Emily bemoaned. "You can finally help me gang up on them."

A few months ago, I might have wondered what it would be like to join a family like that too—no thanks to my stupid crush on Hunter—but now, I was content to be here and watch my best friend.

"So, that's the one?"

Angelina nodded. "This is the one. This is my dress." We all cheered, and after Angelina admired herself in it for a moment longer, she wiped her eyes and gave her attention back to the rest of us. "Okay, let me take this off, and then you can all try on some bridesmaid dresses." She grinned. "Then the fun begins."

Angelina left to go take the dress off, and Noelle and I moved over to the rack of colored gowns. The girl helping us had let us know we could get most dresses in any color, so it was deciding what silhouettes we all liked.

Noelle was thumbing through our options when she looked at me. "Did you ever think that Angelina would be the first of us to get married?"

I shook my head. "I thought it would be you for a while."

"Pff." She held up her hand. "I don't even have a ring yet. Besides, Matthew and I are in a good place. And I think he's always had these fears that if we get married—when we get married—that something will happen to us after he lost his parents in college."

"And?"

"And it turns out getting him to go to therapy was harder than I thought it would be." She giggled. "But it's better. So I'm not worried about it. He's stuck with me at this point. I'm too attached to his dog for him to leave me." Noelle grinned. "What about you? I know you haven't dated in a while. Aren't you lonely?"

I shrugged. Sometimes it felt like something was missing in my life, but was I? "I have you guys. And at least Charlotte and I can be single and forever alone together."

"You're ridiculous," Noelle said, rolling her eyes.

Charlotte scoffed as she pulled a light pink dress out. "Besides, if I'm still single in two years, I'll be begging my mom to find me an arranged marriage. *Seriously.*"

"What happened to the solidarity?" I frowned.

"I want to have a family." Charlotte's expression was wistful, her near-constant smile forming into what almost looked like a frown.

Noelle pulled a green dress off the rack, holding it up to her body. "I feel like it's always so hard to find dresses that are flattering on me," she groaned, pulling out a dress and then shoving it back on the rack. "It either doesn't fit my hips or it doesn't cover my chest."

I would never fit into anything less than a size 10, so I understood where Noelle was coming from. Unlike Angelina, who was tall and lean and all legs, or Charlotte, who had the body of a lithe ballerina, I had hips, and I *certainly* hadn't had a flat stomach since middle school. But I'd never hated that about myself.

Angelina joined us, back in her knee-length dress, as we continued looking through the options for bridesmaid dresses. They were available in a wide variety of styles and colors, but they'd let us know we could order almost any style in any color, which was nice. She pulled out one and then made a face. "I was thinking maybe you could each pick the dress style that flattered you the best, and then all get the same color?"

"I love that idea," Charlotte agreed. "What color were you thinking?"

"Maybe like..." She ran her hands over the dresses, pulling out different fabrics and colors. "This?" She held up a silky champagne color, elegant and perfectly fitting. "I was thinking floor-length, but the rest you can decide. I want everyone to like their dresses *and* feel amazing in them."

"Smart." I grinned. She'd always been the most practical one out of all of us, a trait she had kept even after she'd stopped *pretending* to be cold-hearted and incapable of love.

"*Oh*, I like this one," Emily, Benjamin's sister, said, pulling out one with flowy cap sleeves.

We each found a few options that seemed like they'd flatter us, and spent the rest of our visit laughing, trying on dresses, and drinking the mimosas that were now mostly champagne.

"Do you know the problem with you reading so much?" Angelina rolled her eyes at me as I slid another book around, reorganizing my shelves as she sat on my couch.

What used to be *our* couch, except now she was *abandoning* me and moving out of our apartment to move in with Benjamin. I couldn't be mad at her for it, I really couldn't—I was glad she found her person. But damn, I didn't want to lose my best friend and the only roommate I'd ever known.

I frowned at her after I flipped another book out and placed my hands on my hips. "What?"

There was probably a myriad of things wrong with me, and that didn't even account for the dark romance kick I'd been on last year. But reading in my free time? That wasn't one of them.

"You have too *high* of expectations."

"Please. Like you were any better before you met Benjamin. And might I remind you, you didn't even *like* him at first?"

She *might* have had a point, though. Maybe standards for love were a bit... okay, *way* too high. And who was going to meet those expectations? None of my exes had. Of all the partners I'd ever had, I'd never felt secure in the relationship like I'd always longed for.

It was probably why I'd ended almost every relationship I'd ever been in. My split with my last girlfriend hadn't *exactly* been amicable. We didn't even need to talk about my last *boyfriend*.

Maybe I was always looking for more, always reading too much into it, but I knew what I wanted... and what I didn't. I wanted *my* love story, that whirlwind romance, the feeling like I couldn't live without the other person.

Angelina waved me off. "I still stand by hating him. He was an asshole at first."

"You're marrying him!" I said, laughing, plopping down on the couch next to her. I had some holes on the shelves now—partially because she was leaving me all the furniture in our apartment, and I didn't need as many bookcases for my own collection as we had for both.

I *was* very sad about the contents of our once-shared book collection, and seeing how empty it was now made me resolve to fill it back up again. But that was fine—I was already plotting out the books I wanted to buy.

We'd lived together since our first year of college, that fateful random roommate that somehow ended up becoming my closest friend and like a sister to me. I'd miss living together more than I could properly express, coming home to snuggle on the couch and watch a romcom together or our reading marathons where we certainly got more talking done than reading, or our Netflix binging as we ate takeout. *New Girl* was on in the background as we packed, and it felt fitting to watch one of our shows as we said goodbye to this chapter of our lives.

"Anyway, back to my point. You need to get back out there. It's already been what... four months since your last date?"

I bit my lip. Had it been that long? I'd gone out with this girl—Hannah—and everything seemed just fine until I started doubting myself. That fear ate away at me until I was canceling plans left and right, and nothing felt right anymore. And afterward... It was always so hard to put myself back out there again.

"Yeah." I sighed as I collapsed against her shoulder.

I had always thought I'd meet the person I was going to marry in college—like, we'd meet on the first day and they would whisk me off my feet and we'd be together for the rest of our lives. No such luck. Any boyfriend or girlfriend I'd had never worked out. Some of them it was probably for the best. And afterward, it took me months before I wanted to open up to another person.

That was probably why I'd stuck with her and Charlotte and Noelle—who lived across the hall from us freshman year—for so long. Because they were my people, and I never wanted to lose their friendships.

But my best friend? She was *literally* living the plot of a romance novel after she got stuck with her office nemesis at a work retreat. Sure, it was partially because of my meddling. It was obvious from the beginning that he was head over heels for her, but with her stubbornness, it took me and our friend Nicolas to force them together for a week. Somehow, it worked out, and Angelina and Benjamin had fallen for each other.

"I thought maybe..." She hesitated.

"What?"

She shook her head. "I just thought maybe there was something between you and Hunter."

I wrinkled my nose. "Between me and Hunter? Ha. Hardly." I resisted rolling my eyes. "Besides, he thinks I'm annoying. I can't seem to shut up around him, and it's always accompanied by that scowl of his." I mocked Hunter's grumpy expression, throwing in a grunt for good measure. "That's what he's like."

She couldn't hold back her laugh. "Oh, god. Is not. He's not that bad."

I couldn't help but think about my conversation with him on New Year's Eve. Sure, we had hung out since then, but *that* was the moment I knew nothing was going to happen between the two of us. My little crush on him? Doomed to fail. Clearly, yet again, I'd picked the wrong person.

Noelle and Matthew had been all flirty, as usual, and I covered my eyes as a joke.

"Gross! Come on! See what I mean? Can't a single girl have one moment of peace around here?" I remarked, even though I didn't mind that much. *I enjoyed seeing my best friends happy—I just wished there was somewhere out there for me, too. And after meeting Hunter at that Halloween Party... I'd been hoping maybe it was him.*

He looked straight at me, smirked, and said, "I might know where you can get some peace," *and then took a long sip of his beer as held eye contact with me, and I couldn't look away.*

It was like a hyper-beam pulling me in. Those damn green eyes and that expression on his face... Finally, escaping his spell, I blinked, then narrowed my eyes at him. "I don't need that sort of peace, thank you."

He gave me another look, one that had me blushing over the insinuation, but I couldn't stop imagining what it would be like. His bedroom, just the two of us, with that powerful body that looked so dashing in a suit?

But... Angelina told me Hunter wasn't looking for anything serious. And I didn't know what hurt worse—the thought that I could be another one-night-stand for him or that he would flirt with me so shamelessly when we both knew nothing could ever come from it.

I leaned against Angelina's shoulder, needing to get him off my mind. "I can't believe I'm losing you to a *man*. Even if you picked a good one." I was so glad Angelina had finally let herself fall in love and realize she deserved someone like Benjamin, who wanted to put her first and treat her like a princess.

"You're not losing me, babe. You'll always be my best friend."

"I'm going to miss having you here so much," I said, pouting at her. "And so is Toothless."

When I said her name, I heard a little meow and the jingle of a collar, which made me smile. I hadn't planned on getting a cat, but last year, while Angelina was at her work retreat—the same one she'd met her husband-to-be at—I'd found her sitting in a shop window, a tiny little black kitten, and I knew she had to come home with me. The second they put her in my arms, she cuddled against my chest, purred, and fell asleep, and I knew she was mine.

I wasn't even a cat person until that moment.

But Angelina was. She rubbed Toothless's furry little head when she jumped up in between the two of us. "I know, huh?" She was talking to my cat, who meowed back at her. "Tell your mommy that I'm going to be back over to visit all the time." Angelina brought her attention back to me. "Plus, if you think you can get rid of me that easily, you're deranged."

"Nah. Benjamin knows he can't steal you from me that easily. I'd fight him for it."

"Good." She cracked a grin, knocking her shoulder against mine. "Now, come on, let's get the rest of this stuff packed up before the guys get here."

"Or... I could unpack the boxes and keep you hostage here *forever*."

Angelina laughed, and when Benjamin and Nicolas came to grab her stuff, I didn't even know what I was so worried about. So what, I was living on my own for the first time. Nothing was going to change, not really. I'd still see her all the time, and we still worked at the same office.

"At least you'll never leave me, huh, Toothless?" I said once I was alone, scratching her black fur around her neck. She purred, curling up into a ball on my lap, effectively ending my inability to use my laptop. Which was fine.

I had a billion things I could have been doing anyway, instead of just staring at Pinterest and an open Google Doc with places I wanted to travel. I was excited that I'd finally be able to this summer, with Angelina's wedding in France.

I needed to focus on that, instead of all of my feelings about Hunter Sullivan, this attraction that just wouldn't go away no matter how hard I tried.

CHAPTER 4

Hunter

I was sitting in my office, staring at my computer monitor, when there was a knock on my door. "Hey," said my favorite nurse to work with—Kaitlin, who was now happily supporting a shiny rock on her left ring finger. Her fiancé worked for the Portland Trail Blazers, and on top of being one of the hard-working nurses the pediatrics floor had, she also had no interest in me. It was refreshing.

Partially, because I'd decided a *long* time ago never to sleep with anyone I worked with ever again. Since then, I have had rules: no one at the hospital, and never more than one night. I didn't like it when they got attached. I couldn't give them what they wanted, anyway, so why bother trying?

"Lizzie's asking for you, Dr. Sullivan." Kaitlin was wearing a pair of lilac scrubs today—a lot of the nurses, and even some doctors on our floor liked to wear bright colors and fun prints to make the kids smile. It was a fun touch, I thought, even if I rarely took part.

I shrugged my lab coat over my navy scrubs, admiring my name embroidered on the stark white fabric as I always did. It might not have been the path my parents thought I would take, but I loved working with kids. They might have both been surgeons, but while I admired how committed they were to their careers, I'd taken my life in a different direction. I still worked crazy hours, especially when I was working the night shift, covering for my fellow doctors, or on call, but other than that, it was a much calmer schedule than my parents ever had.

"Thanks, Kaitlin."

I saved the task I was working on, getting ready to get up and make my rounds, visiting patients, and checking in where I could since I didn't have any new consultations left for the day. Working in a Children's Hospital meant seeing a variety of cases, but I'd helped treat kids fighting cancer, ones who needed surgery for epilepsy, brain tumors... The worst cases were the ones where we did everything we could, but it still wasn't enough. I carried those failures with me, trying to push aside the anger and sadness that always followed me.

I smoothed my hand over my face, hoping today would be a good day.

Knocking on the door, the little girl's face instantly lit up as I stepped into the room. "Dr. Hunter!" She held up her coloring book, trying to show me what she was working on.

"How are you feeling today, Lizzie?" She'd had a heart defect, and she'd had minimally invasive surgery, but everything was looking up.

"She's mostly good," her mom answered for her as she continued to color in her book. "Still a little tired, and the incision site was bothering her, but that's nothing we didn't expect."

"Right. Mind if I take a look?" I asked her, and the little girl shook her head. I gave her a quick check-up and then gave mom the thumbs up. "Everything looks great."

She breathed a deep sigh of relief. "Thank you. We appreciate you so much."

"Just doing my job, Mrs. Grey."

"Oh, stop it. You're the best doctor we've had."

I offered her what I hoped wasn't an awkward smile. "Thank you."

"Do you have a girlfriend, Dr. Hunter?" Lizzie popped up from her coloring book.

I chuckled, sitting on the edge of her bed. "No, Lizzie, I don't."

She looked up at me with her big blue eyes. "Hmm... Will you be *my* boyfriend, then?"

Her mom sat in the corner, trying to hold in her laughter as I looked at her six-year-old daughter. I shook my head. "I don't think that would work out, sweetie. I'm too old for you."

She frowned, like the thought hadn't even occurred to her yet. "But you're all alone!"

"Hmm." I pretended to think about it. "You've made a good argument, but there's one thing you haven't considered."

"What's that?"

"You're going to find the perfect guy out there, and you'll have completely forgotten about *me*."

She gave me a big, toothy grin. "You think?"

"Oh, I know."

"Thanks, Dr. Hunter," she said, and I laughed again.

"Get some rest, and hopefully you can be out of here soon." I gave her a fist bump before standing up and giving them my goodbyes before slipping out into the hallway.

Her mom hurried out behind me. "Oh, Dr. Sullivan!"

I looked up from the nurses' station, where I'd stopped to jot down some notes. "Sorry, Mrs. Grey," I said.

"Savannah." She shook her head. "And actually, it's just Ms... Lizzie's father left us when she was a baby. It's been... We've been alone a long time." She gave me a hopeful smile. "I know this is probably wildly inappropriate, but would you maybe want to grab a drink sometime? After Lizzie's discharged, of course. I just..."

She looked at me, curling a blonde strand of hair around her finger, but all I could think about was the brunette with amber eyes and freckles on her nose who'd looked so... angry when she bumped into me towards the end of the engagement party. What had she heard to make her like that, anyway? I needed to find out; because I couldn't have her be mad at me.

"I'm sorry, Ms. Grey, I can't. Patient's parents and co-workers are off-limits."

"I understand," she sighed. "It was worth a shot. Well, I'll... see you around, then." She gave me a sad smile, hurrying back into the room with her daughter.

The rest of the day, I felt like I was going on auto-pilot.

And yet... I couldn't stop thinking about Gabrielle.

Finally, my shift was done, and I was getting ready to head home.

"Going home already?" The nurse sitting at the reception desk asked me. I looked up from the phone in my hands, finding the small nurse with reddish brown hair, Sophia, sitting there.

I grunted in acknowledgment but then thought better of my surly attitude. "My brother and his fiancée invited me over for dinner, so I'm actually on my way there." I needed to drop by the store and grab something to take, plus change out of my scrubs, and I was going to be late if I didn't hurry.

"See you tomorrow?" Sophia asked.

I hummed in response, giving her a small nod before heading out the door and towards my car in the parking garage. I loved my trusty convertible Jeep, even if it was too cold out to have the top down, thanks to spring in Portland being as cold and drizzly as the rest of the year.

It might have been wet and gray outside, but I couldn't deny that I was in good spirits leaving work. Maybe there was a certain brunette I was looking forward to seeing again. I'd talk things out with her, and we'd be fine. Not that I was going to let anything happen, of course, but seeing her would be enough.

I needed to get my shit together before I did something stupid —like fuck up everything completely.

"Hunter!"

The door opened to Angelina holding a glass of wine, her red lipstick somehow still perfectly applied. Angelina always presented herself perfectly, even for all of us over to celebrate them officially moving in together. She'd practically been living here for the last few months anyway, but I knew Benjamin was happy to have her with him all the time.

"Looking good, Lina," I said, leaning in to hug her. I still couldn't believe she was my brother's fiancée now—that they were tying the knot. I'd liked Angelina for him since the beginning—even when they were both trying to sneak around and deny the fact that they were in any sort of relationship. The first time I'd met her, they'd insisted they were *just friends*.

Just friends, my ass. I smirked at the thought.

Pulling out a bottle from behind my back, I extended it out to her. "I brought this for you."

"Oh, you didn't have to do that. Just you coming was enough. I know how much you work." She took the bottle of red wine from me before urging me inside their cozy apartment.

"I couldn't miss celebrating my little brother and you moving in together," I said.

Her lips tilted up. "Everyone else is already in the kitchen. Come on."

She ushered me into the room, and I tossed my coat over one of their barstools and marveled at the scene. The entire group had gathered around the kitchen island.

Six months ago, I'd never met most of them, but now somehow I'd become ingrained with Angelina's friend group. But I couldn't complain. Angelina, my brother's girl, definitely brought out the best of him, and all of her (book-obsessed) friends were warm and welcoming.

Noelle and Matthew were both by the stove, the former leaning against the counter with a glass of white wine in her hands and a red glow spread over her face—probably from something that her boyfriend had said to her. Somehow they'd convinced Matthew to cook for the evening, and he'd pulled a white apron over his button-up and sweater combo that somehow communicated his college professor status. They'd been dating since last spring, and happily lived together in a little house right off the college campus.

It was obvious how much they cared for each other, and sometimes I felt a brief pang in my heart that I'd never experienced that. Not that I had time for it, anyway. And who wanted to be with someone who was on call 24/7? I couldn't think of anyone who'd be so willing to live a life like that. It was a wonder my parents had even had three kids when they were both surgeons who practically lived in the OR.

Charlotte was sitting on a barstool, while Angelina's brother Daniel was talking to Benjamin off to the side of the room. I gave them all a small hello as Angelina placed the bottle of wine I'd given her on the counter and moved to wrap her arms around Benjamin.

The only one missing from the current scene was Angelina's best friend, Gabrielle.

"Hey, Hunter," my brother said, grinning at me as I nodded hello to everyone.

Before I could even utter a word back, I looked up, and something quickly overran any thoughts of responding to Benjamin. Gabrielle.

Her presence caught me off guard, as it always did. There was an electric buzz in the air anytime I was around her, and it took everything in me to ignore it. Fuck, she was pretty. And double *fuck*, she was off-limits.

Maybe my mom was right when she said I should go after her, but... I wasn't a relationship guy, and there was no way I could have a one-night stand with my eventual sister-in-law's best friend without regretting it for the rest of my life. So, as much as I found her to be intriguing and enticing, she wasn't for me.

I knew it, but I couldn't help but let my eyes wander over her as she returned to the room, tugging down the sleeves of her black turtleneck top that she'd tucked into her pair of jeans that hugged every curve of her body. I was pretty sure it should be illegal how good her thighs looked in denim.

Her eyes caught mine, and she stopped dead in her tracks, deer in the headlights. "Oh. Hi."

"Hello, Gabrielle."

She looked down at the floor, rubbing her arm.

"Is everything okay? Did I say something to offend you the other night?"

"What?" She whipped her head up, looking me straight in the eye. "Did you... No." Her face formed into a straight line. "No, you were the perfect *gentleman*," she said, but I caught the sneer in her tone.

I frowned. "I can't fix it if I don't know what's going on, Gabrielle."

She crossed her arms over her chest, attempting to keep her voice low so the others wouldn't hear. "I don't need fixing, Hunter, and I shouldn't have to tell you what's wrong. You should already know." She turned around, whirling on her heels, and slid into the kitchen.

I smoothed a hand over my face before plopping down on a barstool next to Charlotte as I watched Matthew frying a pan of vegetables at the stove.

"Beer?" Benjamin asked me, moving to the fridge to grab a bottle. I nodded in response, and he tossed me one too.

Charlotte rested her head on her hands as she stared over at their red-headed friend. "So, Noelle, how's the next book coming along?"

"It's good. You know, I'm just trying to get it all edited before it's ready to go out into the world. I still can't believe I've finished another one. Feels a little surreal sometimes." She blushed.

Gabrielle smiled, seemingly already in a better mood now that she wasn't talking to me. What the hell had I done that was so bad? "Look at our best friend, a big hotshot author."

"Oh, stop that. I barely have any readers. If it ever comes to the point I make more from selling books than my actual, full-time job, then we'll talk."

Matthew placed a kiss on her forehead as he moved around her in the kitchen. "Yes, and if my wonderful girlfriend is ever that wildly successful, you bet I'll be the first one to scream it from the rooftops."

"Thanks, babe." She stole a green bean out of the pan, plopping it in her mouth.

"Anytime." Matthew gave her a little wink.

"Did you see the cover for the next one yet?" Angelina said, pulling out her phone and scrolling through it. "I think it's even better than the first."

She passed her phone to Charlotte, who squealed, and then showed it to Gabrielle, who'd stood beside her.

"Oh, Angelina," Gabbi gasped. "This is amazing. Really. And Noelle, I can't wait to share it on my account."

She blushed. "Stop. You're going to make it go to my head."

"Nooo," Charlotte protested. "You're amazing. Stop being so hard on yourself. I'll get everyone to read your books, even if I have to force them myself."

"Anyway, Gabrielle, how is your bookstagram going? I know you said you were working on some new stuff," Noelle asked, deflecting the attention off herself.

"Booksta—*what*?" I repeated. Sometimes I felt like a fish out of water around the four of them.

Gabbi bit her lip, looking over at me. "It's an Instagram account dedicated to books. I started one last year to talk about all the ones I've read, and Angelina has helped me with some graphics, too. There is this one thing I'm excited about, but I don't want to bore the guys with it."

Matthew raised an eyebrow as he turned away from the pan. "You think we don't all hear about the four of your smutty books regularly, anyway? Lay it on us, Gabs."

"Oh." Her tanned cheeks looked a little pink as she covered them with her palms.

As if she didn't realize that Angelina and Noelle might share their reading habits with their men. Truly—I didn't think any of us minded. Who knew about how Daniel felt, but I had a feeling Charlotte wouldn't talk about romance novels with him, anyway. I had this gut feeling that she'd turn the color of her shirt at even the slightest mention of that with Daniel.

But what did I know? They were best friends.

I turned my full attention to Gabrielle, watching her lean her body weight against the island. "Well, I had one of the big publishers—Red Reading Publishing?—reach out to me, wanting to send me some books. And I have a few other collaborations shaping up now that I've gained more followers. It's really cool."

"Think you'll ever want to do that full-time?" Daniel asked, ever the practical one. "I think all of you pursuing your hobbies are amazing. You should all be proud of yourselves."

Charlotte rolled her eyes. "You're only saying that because you won't share your awesome musical talent with the world."

"I'm not..." Daniel sighed. "I'm not even that good, Char." He scratched the top of his dark hair, almost the same shade as Angelina's.

"I'm just saying," Charlotte sighed, and then turned to me. "What about you, Hunter? Have any fun hobbies that you're hiding from us?"

"Uh..." I looked over at Gabrielle, and if I was mistaken, she'd almost... perked up? Was it me, or did she look interested in hearing my answer? That was weird, especially since twenty minutes ago she'd seemed determined to hate my guts. "I like to cook. And when I have free time, I like to go hiking. Benjamin and I have done a few of the trails around here."

Matthew perked up. "I like to go run Forest Park, so if you ever want to join, I'm always down."

"Yeah, actually. That sounds... nice." It had been a long time since I felt like I had any friends outside of work, let alone guy friends, and I knew I'd take him up on the offer.

"*Oh*, you know what else we should do sometime?" Gabrielle

spoke up. I enjoyed hearing her talk like this—her voice was full of passion and excitement. Talking about something she was interested in seemed to make her unfold like a flower—a beautiful rose unfurling its petals. "There are so many waterfalls around here that look so beautiful. I'd love to go take pictures, but I never want to do some of those long ones by myself."

"You like to hike, too?" I asked, surprised that it hadn't come up yet. Benjamin and I had gone a few times, and occasionally he dragged his girl along, but they'd never mentioned Gabbi.

"Well... Yeah. I don't get to do it very often, but I love the outdoors."

"I still think you would have enjoyed that work retreat more than I did," Angelina muttered, and Benjamin smirked at his fiancée.

"I think you enjoyed it fine, Angel. Besides, you got me out of it, so are you complaining?"

She narrowed her eyes. "Yes. You made me go canoeing. And there were so many bugs."

"I didn't hear you complaining when you st—mph!" Benjamin said, muffled as Angelina slapped her hand over his mouth to shut him up.

"Ew!" Angelina pulled her hand away. "Don't lick my palm, you freak."

"Do I need to remind you that you're marrying me?"

"I'm regretting saying yes," Angelina said with a roll of her eyes.

Watching the two of them bicker always made me smile—and laugh—if only because they'd both found someone who could match their wit and so perfectly complement them.

"Anyway, I'm always down for a group hike," Benjamin said. "Even if I have to carry this one down on my back."

Noelle groaned. "Every time Matthew drags me out, I regret my life fifteen minutes in. Even if I have Snowball walking with me." I was pretty sure that Snowball, their giant white Samoyed, was 75% fur.

Matthew kissed her on the cheek. "We'll pick an easy one, sunshine."

"Okay, but only because I really really *really* like you," she said, giving him a little wink before shimmying past him.

I winked at Gabrielle. "Well, I'm down if you are."

She gave me her same hardened stare, something in between a frown and a glare, and I didn't know what else to say.

"Alright! Dinner's about ready if everyone wants to move to the table."

The girls grabbed their wine glasses, moving over to the dining room table, thankfully with an extra two chairs added so all eight of us could fit around the table, and the guys all grabbed the dishes of food to bring them over as Matthew finished taking them out of the oven or off the stove.

We all slid into the open seats, and I didn't miss how I ended up sitting right across the table from Gabrielle, who was still looking at me with a look of frustration on her face.

I'd known her for months, but somehow, it felt like something had changed between us, something I didn't understand, and something that felt like it would be a cataclysmic event if I gave into the pull I felt between us.

Mission number one: get back in Gabrielle's good graces.

Mission number two: ignore how pretty she looked tonight.

One of them might have been easier to accomplish than the other.

CHAPTER 5
Gabrielle

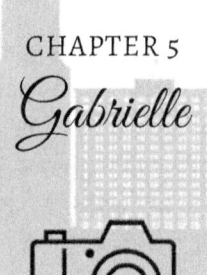

He was so handsome. So frustratingly, effortlessly handsome, even in the blue jeans and dark gray button-up shirt he was wearing. And was I more frustrated that I noticed how attractive he was because he was also infuriatingly *intolerable*? Maybe.

After we finished eating dinner—Matthew had really outdone himself this time, and everything was *delicious*—we'd all moved into the living room, staring out the windows of Benjamin's high-rise apartment. I couldn't believe they were going to leave all of this behind soon when they moved into the new house they were having built, but it all made sense. Angelina never was one to do something small. It was big or nothing.

I refilled my wine glass as we made our way back to the living room. I'd purposefully taken the couch cushion as far away as possible from Hunter. Honestly, I was still trying to figure out what the hell I'd done to make him react like he had at the engagement party, because aside from talking too much, I didn't know what I'd done to be labeled as *ridiculous*.

Angelina was talking about some of the wedding details she'd planned out, and when I finally zoned back into the conversation,

I realized there was a key aspect that we hadn't discussed yet. "Hey, what are we thinking about for the bachelorette?"

"Oh, we were thinking maybe we could do a joint party with both the girls and guys? That way, we can all celebrate together. Neither of us wants the bar and strippers thing." She wrinkled her nose. "So maybe... something a little more *low-key*? We're fine with whatever you and Hunter plan. I'm sure it'll be great."

You two. *Ah*. I glanced at Hunter. Wasn't this *lovely*? Forced to plan a trip with a guy who clearly couldn't *stand* me? But I wouldn't voice those concerns. He was Benjamin's brother—I'd just have to do my best to get along with him.

"Of course, Ang. We can do whatever you want."

I meant it, too. I'd do whatever I could to make sure it was a success. Even if that meant putting up with Hunter Sullivan. I gave her my sweetest smile and tried to ignore the way Hunter was frowning at me.

Yeah, asshole. I heard your conversation, I thought, narrowing my eyes at him.

"You know, we've been talking about going somewhere for months... what if we did a little trip?" Noelle asked, perking up.

"If it's after May, we'd both be free," Matthew confirmed. "I'm not teaching summer semester this year and Noelle should be able to take time off fairly easily as an Academic Advisor."

"Oh yes, I love the sound of that," Charlotte agreed.

"What do you think, Angel?" Benjamin asked, looking over at her.

She nodded. "But if anyone tries to make me go hiking, you're all dead."

"No hiking," I laughed. "Got it. We will keep it as opposite of hiking as possible."

"Perfect." We shared a conspiratory grin, and when I looked over at Hunter, I caught him staring at me. I held his eyes for a moment and then frowned, wondering why he could affect me this much.

I turned back to the girls. "Spa day?"

"Oh, I'm so in," Charlotte said, giving a little sigh.

"Sounds great to me," Benjamin chimed in. "We'll find a few dates that work and then see who else wants to come in the next few weeks."

"Perfect." I gave them both my best smile, ignoring the headache that *was* coming on now. I yawned, standing up from the couch and grabbing my car keys from the table. "I think I'm gonna head out. Early day tomorrow and all." I said my goodbyes, and as soon as I slid outside the door into the cool night, I breathed a sigh of relief.

I'd escaped, except—the door opened and closed behind me, and my heart beat a little faster in my chest when I found myself chest to chest with Hunter.

"I, um..." My eyes were wide, trying to figure out how to escape this.

"Why are you acting weird?"

"What?" I frowned, crossing my arms over my chest. "I am *not*."

He raised an eyebrow. "You've been ignoring me all night. Every time you make eye contact with me, you frown, as if I did something terrible to you. We have to work together for this party now, not to mention the fact that we see each other almost every week, so will you please talk to me?"

"There's nothing to talk about."

"Really? Because I feel like that's the opposite of the truth."

I pursed my lips. "Can we please do this another night?" I rubbed at my temples. "I'll text you."

He sighed, clearly frustrated as well. "Fine. I'll talk to you soon, then."

"Yep."

I left that night with a head full of ideas, a sinking feeling in my gut, and a headache that would not go away.

THERE WAS nothing like completely throwing yourself into work—or books—attempting to forget the *other* things going on in your life. Or rather, one very specific man. It'd been almost two weeks since I spoke to him, but I knew my avoidance was only going to last so much longer. Besides, my rage had simmered out, leaving me with questions and no answers, and that might have been the worst thing of all.

Unfortunately, as much as I'd wanted the distraction, work was slow, especially given that I worked in Human Resources for a big tech firm, and you'd think that at least something out of the ordinary would go on during a day-to-day basis.

Sometimes I wondered if I had looked into my future in college if I still would have chosen this life when I picked Communications as my major instead of going into something else. I enjoyed it, sure—I loved working with people and helping to solve others' problems. Every once in a while, I felt like maybe I wasn't living up to my full potential. Whatever that *was*. I loved graphic design and photography as much as I enjoyed fixing people's problems, but I wasn't sure if the latter was even fulfilling me enough anymore.

So instead of focusing on my job, I was *trying* to create yet another travel itinerary for Europe that seemed as equally unlikely to happen as the last few. The problem was, I couldn't decide where I wanted to go after the wedding. I was pretty sure I could get at least a week off after, but maybe if I played my cards right with Nicolas—being friends with the CEO had to mean *something*, right?—then I could take an extra week off, giving me a full three weeks in Europe.

I liked to think I had three passions in life: books, photography, and traveling. So, maybe it was *okay* that work was a little slow right now because I had my hobbies to distract me.

Like the dozens of trips I'd planned while no one was around, and everything was quiet. Or my Bookstagram account, where I shared photos and reviews of my favorite books. I'd gotten pretty good at graphic design for it, too, though sometimes I'd pester

Angelina for help with art—and I always loved it when she'd draw fanart of our favorite characters and couples. That was one perk of being best friends with an artist. Of course, Noelle benefited from Angelina's talents the most—since she drew the covers for Noelle's self-published romance novels.

I sighed in happiness, thinking about all the history, the beaches, and the things I wanted to see. I'd dreamed about something like this for so long, and now it was so close, I could almost taste it.

My notebook was open, a list of cities and countries staring back at me. London. Amsterdam. Rome. Salzburg. The French Riviera. Mont-Saint-Michel, the tidal island that the Kingdom of Corona in Disney's *Tangled* resembled. Neuschwanstein Castle in Germany. There were so many places and not enough time. I'd have to pick where to go from my list since there was no way I could hit all of them. I wouldn't be able to go everywhere, but with two weeks off after the wedding, hopefully at least I'd be able to check a few things off my bucket list. Places I'd always dreamed about seeing. I wanted to go to the places that inspired some of my favorite movies and books, though, because they meant so much to me.

Thinking of the trip made me think of the wedding, which turned my thoughts back to one infuriating doctor. Hunter. Something still frustrated me with what he'd said the other day, but I still didn't even know what had caused him to say that about me. Either way, I owed him an explanation.

After all, he owed me one too, didn't he? It wasn't like we wouldn't be spending a lot of time together for the rest of our lives, since Angelina was basically a sister to me and she was marrying Hunter's brother. Maybe we'd never hung out *alone* before, and I had a feeling that my imminent forced proximity to him wouldn't be all sunshine and rainbows, but... something was different.

I couldn't decide if not knowing was worse than this worry that had built in my chest. Did he really not like me that much?

Why did I care, anyway? He'd long since proved he wasn't the man for me, even when I couldn't help but wonder differently. Even when I couldn't help but picture those bright green eyes and his brown curly hair when I closed my eyes, thinking about what it might be like to see him *really* smile at me.

And the way he'd looked when he asked me what was wrong, if there was something he'd said... The pain in his eyes was clear. I was protecting myself, but was I being too harsh on him without letting him explain? God, maybe I was being a bitch over nothing.

I didn't like when someone was mad at me and I didn't know why, but that was what I'd done to Hunter. So maybe it wasn't fair, not entirely. And maybe if I wanted something to change, I needed to be the one to act first. To reach out.

And we still needed to plan this weekend getaway together, since I'd be damned before I did all the work myself. So he didn't like me? He better suck it up, because I would be dragging him kicking and screaming until he helped me. I gave myself a satisfied nod as I closed out of my google doc and pulled out my phone to send him a text.

GABRIELLE
Hi.

It's Gabbi, FYI, just in case you didn't have my number saved.

HUNTER
I knew it was you, Gabrielle.

Oh. Right. Well.

What's up?

I thought maybe we should talk sometime soon about all the wedding stuff, and this party we have to plan.

> Maybe you can come to the hospital for lunch one day this week? I normally get about an hour.

> Oh. Sure. I guess that works.

> Great. Wednesday?

> Yeah, that's fine. I guess I'll see you in a couple of days.

"Great," I huffed to myself, tossing my phone aside and looking across the mostly quiet office, wondering if Angelina would be in her office so I could go talk to her instead of wallowing in my self-pity about one Hunter Sullivan.

Sighing, I stood up and made my way to find her.

CHAPTER 6
Hunter

MAY

> **GABRIELLE**
> Wedding Countdown: 14 Weeks!

> **HUNTER**
> Is there a way to unsubscribe from this countdown reminder?

> Hush, you. We're still on for later, right?

> Yep.

> Okay. I'll text you when I get there.

I shoved my phone back in the pocket of my scrubs, throwing myself back into work for the next few hours so I wouldn't think about the fact that she was coming here. It wasn't like I didn't have patients to check up on or reports to write and a million things to do, anyway.

And if I was excited to see her? Well, I wouldn't analyze *that*.

I steered myself into the cafeteria when I got her text that she'd parked and was on her way in, and found us a table by the large windows that overlooked the city where we could talk.

Gabbi showed up bundled up in a white knit top and a chunky tan cardigan with her hair tied up in a topknot. And there were those jeans again. I completely *hated* the way they hugged her waist.

"Hey," I called out from my table in the cafeteria, waving her over to me. "What's that?" She had a cooler draped over her shoulder.

"I wasn't sure if you'd eaten anything yet, so I brought food."

I eyed the cafeteria behind us, but really, I couldn't argue against not eating the hospital food.

"You didn't have to go through all the trouble to make food for me," I grumbled. Didn't she have work today too? And she'd brought *me* food?

Gabbi laughed as she started pulling out containers. "No. I can't take the credit. I can pretty much only make mac & cheese and chicken nuggets, so don't get your hopes up here, mister. That being said, I *am* great at ordering takeout."

"You don't know how to cook?" I asked, raising an eyebrow. It was surprising, with as long as I'd known her, that I didn't know this about her. Normally, when I tagged along to the girl's hangouts, we'd either gone out to eat or one of us guys had cooked, letting them talk about books while we drank beers in the kitchen.

She opened the containers, revealing still steaming Chinese food, before offering me a shrug. "Not really. My mom was always saying she would teach me, but then I came to college in Portland, and I decided on staying here, and she's all the way in Boston, so..."

"I could teach you," I offered, surprising myself.

"Really?" She looked shocked.

I nodded my head, pulling a container of broccoli beef towards me and sticking my fork in it. "Sure." I opened another one, looking to see if she'd gotten fried rice. When I found the container, I picked it up victoriously, shoveling a bite into my mouth.

Gabbi sat frozen, staring at me as I dug in. "Huh."

"What?" I stopped eating, wondering what was up with her.

"I'm just surprised."

I wanted to wipe that look off her face—the look of confusion, the way she furrowed her brows in consideration... "That...?"

"You *want* to spend more time with me?"

"Why would I not?" Sure, we'd never spent time alone together before, but that wasn't because I hadn't wanted to. We'd never had a reason to. Seeing her every few weeks with her friends was enough to remind me of all the reasons I couldn't *like* her.

"What?"

Gabbi shrugged. "We've never spent much time alone before. I didn't think..."

"Hmm?"

"Never mind." She muttered something else under her breath.

"Gabbi."

"It's just... I didn't think we were friends."

"Aren't we? Why would you think that?"

She didn't answer me, picking up the container of sweet and sour pork and shoving a bite in her mouth.

"Okay. So, can we get back to the more important conversation here?" Gabbi pulled out a yellow notebook from her bag and flipped it open to a blank page.

"You don't think us being friends is an important conversation?" I narrowed my eyes at her.

"Well, it's just... We really need to plan this bach party out. It's not that far ahead, and if we don't want to do something in town..."

"We're friends." I grit out.

"Okay," she said, sounding like she was mostly trying to placate me. "We're friends. Now back to the trip—"

"No," I gruffed. "I mean it. We're friends. Why do you think I always talk to you when we're all hanging out?"

"I figured... I was like your pity conversation." She winced. "Now that I'm saying that out loud, I can see how it sounds bad. It's... Well, Matthew and Noelle *are* Matthew and Noelle. And then Benjamin and Angelina have each other, and even if Charlotte and Daniel aren't dating, they're best friends... So I felt like I was the leftovers you got stuck with."

I didn't like that she thought that about herself, but all I could do was shake my head. "I didn't get stuck with you. Okay? I need you to know that."

She nodded. "Alright." She held eye contact with me for a moment and then plunged back into her notebook. "So, I've been brainstorming, and I think if we're going somewhere, we should do something classy. Like, everyone goes to Vegas for bachelor parties. That's lame."

"Okay. So something that is *not* lame? Any ideas?"

"Well... figuring we'll stay on the west coast, there's Seattle, or... Central Oregon? California has some options too... maybe Napa?"

"Napa is nice."

"You've been?"

"Yeah. It's been a few years, but there are some nice places there. Seems like it'd be classy enough for you?" I smirked.

"The land of wine? Hell yeah."

She quickly jotted down a few notes on her paper. "We could rent a house for everyone. That way, the girls and guys don't have to split up, and then we can plan one or two activities apart."

"Seems reasonable to me."

"Did Benjamin tell you who all they wanted to come? I'm assuming it won't be a giant party."

"With those two?" I laughed. "I think they'd kill each other before they had a bunch of people they didn't *really* like."

"True." She looked contemplative. "I'll start looking for places once we figure out everyone who is coming then. What do you want to take care of?"

I scratched my head. I'd never been in charge of party planning before, and I had to admit, I didn't know the first thing about putting together an event like this. I'd had a few friends get married, sure, but their bachelor parties had been a night at a bar or a strip club, not a weekend out of town with all of their couple of friends. "Uh, I don't really know what I can help with—"

She looked resigned. "It's fine. I can figure it out on my own."

"No. That's... That's not what I meant," I huffed. "I've never planned something like this. What all do we need to figure out? Food? Activities? Cars?"

She nodded. "Maybe we could both come up with some ideas of things we think would be fun to do with the group and then get back together?"

"Sure." I grunted. "Your place?"

She blinked. "Yeah, I... That works."

"Good. I'll cook."

"You don't have to do that."

"Maybe not," I smirked, "But I'm going to. And you're going to help. I'll teach you." She looked skeptical, but I reassured her, "It'll be fun, I promise."

"Okay," she finally relented, and I nodded, satisfied.

We both returned to eating our food, having only taken small bites here and there while we were talking, and I gobbled down the Chinese food. Wherever she had gotten it from, it was *delicious*.

"What are your plans for after the wedding?"

"After?" she questioned, looking up at me. "Why?"

"I've been thinking... Benjamin made a good point to me at the Engagement Party. I haven't really taken any time off in years. I have a bunch of time off accrued, and the hospital's agreed to give me almost the whole month off, so I'm thinking of maybe doing some traveling. And... Angelina mentioned to me you might do the same."

Her jaw dropped open, and she moved to close it so quickly. "You want to travel?"

"Is that... so surprising?"

She waved a hand. "No. Of course not. I have two weeks off after the wedding too." She bit her lip. "I've been trying to plan out my itinerary for the last few weeks. I need to book flights soon, but..."

"Me too." I looked at her, and a thought popped into my mind. "Why don't we fly together? Then we don't have to be alone, and we can get a car to the hotel together, since it'll be a bit of a ride."

Gabbi furrowed her brow. "I mean..."

"Come on. It'll be better if we're not alone, won't it?"

She poked me in the biceps. I'd worn long sleeves under my scrubs like usual, and it made me think about the fact that I'd hardly ever worn anything around her where she could see my bare arms. Hm. Interesting. I'd seen her tattoo, the one on her inner arm, but I didn't think she'd ever seen mine.

"You're being weird."

Did I space out for too long? Had I been staring at her too intently? Shit. I couldn't stop wondering if she had any others hidden on her body.

"Why?"

"The Hunter Sullivan I know would frown at forced proximity with another person. And you're signing up for 18 hours sitting next to me on a plane?"

Maybe I wouldn't hate it if it was you, I thought, but I didn't say it. Instead, I grumbled under my breath. "Yes."

"Well. Um."

"You don't have to decide right now. I'm not saying you have to change your plans for me. If you've already got an itinerary—do it."

"Alright," she breathed out. "Maybe."

I flashed her a grin—maybe was good enough for me. I'd wear her down later.

We finished eating, and Gabbi had gone back to writing notes and ideas on her notebook when a familiar head of hair came into the cafeteria. "Dr. Hunter!" Lizzie's voice shouted, and I gave Gabrielle a look of apology before Lizzie's mom wheeled her over in a wheelchair.

"Look at my favorite patient, up and rolling around," I said, giving her a smile. "How are you feeling today, Lizzie?"

"Good," she nodded. "Mommy said that if I'm *really* good, she'll let me buy a new doll when we get home."

"Oh, is that so?" I raised an eyebrow, and she nodded, giving me the biggest grin. They had pulled her platinum blonde hair up into two high ponytails on either side of her head, and I reached over to tug on one of them.

"Who's this?" She asked, clearly having noticed that I was sitting at the table with someone else and I wasn't alone for once.

"This," I said, looking over at Gabrielle, who had an amused expression on her face, "is my friend, Gabrielle. Her best friend is marrying my brother."

"Ohhhhh," Lizzie said, as her mom gave me an apologetic smile. "Well..." She cocked her head, looking at the two of us. "What about you two? Are you going to get married, too?"

Gabbi choked on her food, and for a second I thought I might actually have to give her the Heimlich before she coughed and took a sip of water. *You okay?* I mouthed to her. "Wrong pipe," she rasped.

I turned back to my patient, who clearly missed my whole *I'm single* thing from a few weeks ago. But before I could answer, Gabrielle did for me. "We're not—"

"Oh, that's—"

"That would *never* happen." Gabbi finished.

"Oh." Lizzie looked dejected, but her mom leaned down and asked if she wanted ice cream and after a resounding *yes,* they were off.

As soon as they were gone, I raised an eyebrow. "Never?" I

rested my head on my palms as I looked at her. "Why exactly are you so vehemently against us, Gabrielle?"

She furrowed her brows. "There are a thousand reasons, Hunter. I'm afraid it would take me all day to list them all."

I gave her a little smirk. "Oh, yeah?"

"Mhm. Now back to the topic at hand—"

I glanced at my watch. Somehow we'd already been here for forty-five minutes, and even though I was supposed to get back to work soon, I couldn't help myself. "Do you want to come somewhere with me?"

"What?" Gabbi raised an eyebrow. "Don't you have to get back to work?"

"Just trust me." I extended a hand to her to help her up.

We quickly cleaned up the remnants of our food, throwing away the trash before she placed her hand back in mine and I led her out of the hospital and to my favorite place.

"Well, what do you think?" I stood back, letting her take in the courtyard.

"Oh..." she gasped. "Hunter, this is beautiful."

The courtyard was bursting with color, filled to the brim with flowers, benches, and little interactive things for the kids.

"I like to come out here sometimes," I said, surprising even myself that I was sharing the information so willingly. "It helps during the long days." I swallowed roughly.

She wandered through the flower beds, sitting down on one of the brightly colored benches. "I bet."

I sat down next to her, letting my eyes sweep over the brightly colored plants. Even the constant Portland drizzle couldn't dim the brightness of this place.

"They built it a few years ago to help cheer up patients, but a lot of the doctors will sit out here too. And the parents who have other kids will bring them out here while they're getting treatments."

Gabrielle nodded, resting her head against my shoulder.

CHAPTER 7
Gabrielle

I was crazy. That was the only answer for why I'd agreed to this. His stare had worn me down and his nonchalant offer to teach me to cook had somehow taken away my annoyance.

GABRIELLE
Are you sure about this?

HUNTER
It's only dinner. It's not a big deal.

But still... I feel bad. You don't have to cook for me.

I'm not cooking for you, remember? I'm teaching you how to cook.

Same difference.

Also, fair warning, I'm pretty sure Toothless will be all over you. She is always all over Benjamin. I hope you like cats.

They're okay.

> Dog person?

> Sure. If I had time for a pet, I'd like a dog someday.

> Some day?

> Work keeps me busy.

> I see.

> See you soon.

I pulled open the door, surprised to find that I was actually a little nervous for him to come over. Sure, I'd brought people back to my apartment before, here and there, but it was never like this. Purely platonic. Because we were friends, weren't we? I mean, we always had been, but now it was... different. Easier.

"Hey."

"Hi." His eyes brushed over my baby blue t-shirt dress. "You look nice."

I turned my head to hide my blush. "Thanks. Come on in."

He held up the bags and a bottle of wine. "Let me put all of this away and then we can get started."

Toothless meowed, coming out of my room to see who was there. She was one of the most vocal cats I'd ever seen, and she wanted attention from everyone. Honestly, I loved having such a lap cat, because she'd come to cuddle up with me on the couch when I was reading.

"Hello, there," Hunter said, crouching on the ground with his hand out as Toothless walked over to him, curious. "So, you're the famous cat, huh?" He scratched her head, and she brushed against his leg a few times, happily enjoying his touch.

I watched quietly, amused that despite saying he didn't really *like* cats, he was still showing mine love and affection. It made my heart flutter, and I had to will the sensation away. I was trying so hard not to like this man; it wasn't even funny.

"So what are we making?"

"Chicken Cordon bleu."

"What?" I raised an eyebrow. This was the first thing he was going to teach me how to cook? Wouldn't it be more helpful to start with something... easier?

"It's—"

I interrupted him before he could correct me. "No, I know what it *is*, but isn't that a little too... complicated?"

"Complicated?" He laughed. "No. It's easy, you'll see. Plus, there are a lot of different components that I think will help you learn how to cook."

"Alright. Well, show me."

Hunter was an outstanding teacher. He was incredibly patient, walking me through all the steps as we filled the rice cooker with ingredients, showing me the best ways to cut the fat off the chicken, and when he handed me the mallet to pound the chicken flat, a smirk spread across his face. "Mom always liked to say it was a great way to get your anger out after a long day."

I laughed. "So what you're saying is it's a great stress reliever?"

"Absolutely."

Perfect. I picked up the meat tenderizer and went to town.

"Jesus. Why are you hitting that so hard?" He asked as I pounded the breast flat.

"I'm just imagining it's your face." I batted my eyelashes innocently, expecting him to laugh, but he frowned.

"Do you really dislike me that much?" I swallowed as he stepped in closer, almost caging me in with his arms on the counter. I hit it once more for emphasis as we maintained eye contact, not letting a single emotion show on my face. *Did I?* It felt like I was lying to say yes. I'd never really disliked him, anyway.

"No," I muttered.

Hunter shook his head, pulling the flattened chicken from my hands and into the pile I'd made.

"So, um," I said, changing the subject. "Should we keep going with these?"

He placed a plate in front of me full of sliced cheese and ham. "Each one gets rolled up with a piece of cheese and meat."

"Easy enough." *Maybe* this cooking thing wasn't so bad, after all. Why had I been making such lazy meals or ordering takeout for so long, anyway? I made a mental reminder to ask my mom to teach me her favorite recipes the next time I was home in Boston.

"What's next, chef?" I said after we'd wrapped all the pieces of chicken.

He assembled three bowls—eggs, flour, and bread crumbs—and then showed me how to dip them. First, the egg, then the flour, and finally rolled in the breadcrumbs before plopping it into the pan.

"Your turn," he gestured, and I grabbed one piece of chicken we'd rolled and followed the steps he'd done.

He was watching me like a hawk, and I couldn't help myself. I dipped my fingers in the flour and threw it at him.

"Oh, it's *on*, little fighter," he exclaimed, picking up a handful.

"No!" I shrieked, and he chased me around the kitchen counter before wrapping his flour-free hand around my waist and dumping the flour over my head, the white powder dusting over my face

"This means war, Hunter Sullivan," I said, narrowing my eyes as I tried not to inhale flour.

He chuckled. "You're feisty tonight, Gabrielle. I like it."

"Well, maybe you would have seen this side of me sooner if you'd gotten to know me," I said, and I surprised myself with how much of my tone sounded like a sneer.

He froze as I scooped up another handful of flour, leaving two perfectly placed handprints on his dark gray t-shirt, right over his pecs. "Well, now you've crossed a line," he growled, and I gave him a little flirty smile as I danced around him, somehow more interested in this game we were playing than the meal we were making.

"Maybe I want to get to know you better," he whispered into my ear as his hands tightened around my waist, before he let me go, and this time it was my turn to stare stupidly at him.

"Alright, what's next?" I asked, hands on my hips, fully aware that there was flour *everywhere* on me, and deciding I didn't care one bit.

I sort of wished I'd had his hands on me to mark me like mine were on him.

We brushed up against each other as we tried to move around my tiny kitchen, me to open the oven and Hunter to grab a clean washcloth out of the drawer.

"Come here, sweetheart," he murmured after he'd gotten it damp, and when he started running the warm towel over my face to clean up the residual flour dust, my heart skipped a beat in my chest. I was pretty sure he could hear how loud my heart was beating with how close he was standing to me, but if he did, he said nothing. It reminded me of the Halloween party when he'd listened to my heart with his stethoscope after I'd accused it of being fake.

He made another pass over my nose and cheeks with the washcloth, and I looked up at him.

"There. Good as new." He patted me on the head and the warmth spread across my cheekbones, and I was *way more affected* than I should be from a cloth wiping over my face and hair.

"Now, let's make the sauce, shall we?" He pulled out the rest of the ingredients we needed and then pointed at me with the spoon in his hand. "But you stay over there. You've lost your cooking privileges, sweetheart."

I pouted. "It was just a little flour."

He looked down at his t-shirt as if in explanation. My handprints pressed against his chest, and I sighed, hopping up on the counter to watch him as he explained what he was doing.

I fidgeted with my necklace, running the charm back and forth across the chain.

How was this so *effortless*? Spending time with him was easy.

It felt like we'd done this dozens of times before, instead of this being the first time. He fit so seamlessly here, and not for the first time, I couldn't help but wish for something more. For something that couldn't happen—wouldn't happen. Because he'd made it clear exactly how he thought about me that way, hadn't he?

"Um... Do you want a clean one?" I looked at his shirt.

He frowned. "It's fine. Besides, you probably don't have one that fits me anyway—"

"I think I..." I cleared my throat. "I have one of my old boyfriend's shirts around here somewhere, actually. It would probably fit."

"What?" He gritted his teeth. "Why the fuck do you have that?"

I stepped back, startled by his tone. "I don't know. He left it here, and it's soft, so I just kind of... stole it. It's not that big of a deal. I can throw yours in the wash."

We stared at each other until he shook his head. "No, it's... It's fine. Come on, let's finish dinner so we can eat."

I nodded, but for the rest of the night, all I could focus on were all the reasons Hunter might hate me for still owning one of my ex's shirts. None of them were good for my poor heart.

∽

GABRIELLE

Wedding Countdown: Thirteen Weeks!

I STUCK my phone back in my pocket after sending my countdown text, not bothering to wait for a response from Hunter—who was probably working anyway—and headed inside to meet the girls.

"Hey." I slumped down onto the couch at our usual coffee shop, surprised at how busy I was with everything going on. A stack of travel books replaced my usual fantasy or romance ones. I had some both for the joint bachelor/bachelorette party I was planning with Hunter, and the European trip I was trying to plan for myself.

"You look exhausted," Angelina pointed out.

"Don't remind me." I groaned. "Work has been crazy, and I feel like I'm being pulled in six million different directions."

Charlotte plopped down next to me, placing a croissant in front of me and grabbing her coffee—almost white, so it barely even counted as caffeine with all the milk and syrups she had in there.

"So how's it going with Hunter?" Angelina asked.

"What?" I blanched.

She raised an eyebrow. "With planning the Bach party together...?"

Oh. Right. "It's good," I nodded, taking a big bite of my croissant so I didn't have to answer for a few moments. "Everything's coming along great." We booked everything, and we were finishing up plans. Thankfully, Hunter took a lot of responsibility into his own hands, insisting on booking the Airbnb and the activities we'd picked. I thought I was going to have to do it all by myself, so it was a pleasant surprise.

"That's it?" Was it me, or did Angelina seem... disappointed?

"Yes, *Mom*. Nothing new to report."

Noelle nudged Angelina on the side. "Lay off of her."

She huffed. "Fine."

I glanced at Charlotte, hoping to get her to back me up, but she shrugged.

"Did you all already book your hotel for the wedding?" Noelle asked us, changing the subject. She was such a mom friend sometimes, reminding us of all of the things we needed to do, as well as making us matching shirts and bags like she didn't have a care in a world who saw them.

I nodded. "Yup. All ready to go. I just have to book flights. What about you?"

"Matthew wanted to go to Sweden and maybe Norway before the wedding since that's where his family is from. I know it's been hard for him ever since he lost his parents in college, so we're figuring out details for that right now. What about you? I know you've been talking about a Europe trip *forever.*"

This seemed like a dream coming true because I had wanted to travel so badly. "I have. I do. Honestly, I'm almost overwhelmed at all my options," I laughed. "But I think it'll be good, a little cross-country voyage. Just me and a backpack and some hostels." I sighed, dreamily.

Charlotte picked up her coffee and sighed. "I wish I didn't have to get back so fast after the wedding. I can't take more than a week off from everything." She waved her hands in the air as if to encompass all the things she did. I understood—she was trying to run her own business, sewing handmade gowns and dance costumes, as well as working part-time at a dance studio as an instructor and choreographer. She loved those kids and would do anything for them, and I could tell her heart ached for a family of her own.

Angelina leaned her head back against the headrest of the couch. "We booked the honeymoon, and it's a month long and somehow that still feels like it's going to go by so fast."

"How'd you get that much time off?"

She gave me a little wink. "It helps when you're friends with the boss. Plus, we figured we could work remotely a few times a week to check in with our teams. It's not ideal, but... It'll be worth it."

"Yeah." I nodded, sipping my coffee. It would be worth it.

Charlotte looked at Angelina. "Have you two talked about kids yet?"

Angelina almost spit out her coffee.

I knew she hadn't been sure if she wanted to have kids in the past, but when she'd gotten together with Benjamin, he'd told her he'd stay home and be a stay-at-home dad if that was what she wanted so she could still have her career.

I thought that was the best of both worlds. Plus, it wasn't like they couldn't work from home. Plenty of people in our company started working remotely, so much so that we were considering downsizing our Downtown Portland offices.

"Not anytime soon," she finally said. "I'm staying on birth control for a few more years. Besides, we're only 27... What's the rush?"

Charlotte nodded, but I noticed she seemed a little more sullen, and withdrawn. I'd have to ask her what was wrong later.

Having kids... I tried to imagine it myself. I'd never been with a partner long enough to dream about having kids with them, and I wouldn't lie, the idea of childbirth made me a little queasy, but if I met the right person...

Everything would be different, wouldn't it?

CHAPTER 8
Hunter

We finalized everything for the bachelor party over the last two weeks, and now, with it slowly approaching, all we had left to do was wait for the day to actually arrive.

I smiled as I got Gabbi's weekly text with the countdown to the wedding. It had annoyed me at first, but now I looked forward to her texts, if only because I could talk to her. What the fuck was wrong with me to be feeling this way?

GABRIELLE
Wedding Countdown: 10 Weeks!

HUNTER
Everything all set for the trip?

Yes, Hunter. *rolls eyes*

Okay. Great.

I was thinking we should continue our cooking lessons.

Dinner tonight?

I sat there, looking at the screen, for far longer than was probably acceptable, waiting for her to text me back. I wasn't sure *why* it was so important to me, but I wanted to see her. Ever since she'd come to the hospital to have lunch with me and we'd cooked together at her house, something felt... different. And sure, I'd see her next weekend, but that would be with all of our friends around. And for whatever reason, I wanted to spend time with her, just us.

> Are you sure? You're not too tired from work?

> No. Come over.

> Please?

> Well, if you insist... But you better make me something good.

> We'll make something good together.

> Here's my address.

When she knocked on the door, slightly out of breath and her cheeks pinked with exertion, I gave her a small smirk. "In that big of a hurry to see me, sweetheart?"

"What?" she said, sticking her bag on the dining room chair as her breathing returned to normal. "No, I just—took the stairs. Trying to get in better shape for the summer." She blew a hair off her face, turning to pull some things out of her tote and piling them on the table.

"What's all that?" I asked, eyeing Gabrielle's pile of books.

She gave me a sheepish grin. "I'm trying to plan my trip for after the wedding. It's been so long since I've traveled, and I finally get to again, but it's so overwhelming. There are so many places I would love to see, and—"

I picked up one of the travel books. She had added tabs, and as I flipped through, they seemed to mark some cities and places she wanted to go to.

"You want help?" I asked, raising an eyebrow as I placed it down and picked up another.

"Mmm. Maybe."

London. Paris. Amsterdam. Rome. Madrid. Munich. She had books for a handful of the biggest cities in Western and Southern Europe, and I quirked an eyebrow at her. "Sweetheart, if you want to hit all these places, you're going to need a lot more time than two weeks."

She groaned. "I know. It's impossible. It's not fair that the world is so big and I've seen so little of it. I want to do it all, see —everything."

I knew what she meant. Sure, I'd been lucky enough to travel during high school and college, but there *was* so much of the world out there I hadn't seen. "You're Belle," I muttered, and she blinked up at me.

"Like... the Disney Princess?" She blinked.

"Mhm," I grunted. Maybe I was exposing myself right now, but she'd always been my favorite growing up. "She wanted to see the world, and she loved to read, and she didn't care what people thought about her. Like you." *And you're beautiful*, I thought. That brown hair and those enormous amber eyes got me every time I looked at her, like it drew the breath from my lungs. For a little while, I'd been able to ignore it, and then after the engagement party... I couldn't anymore.

"I care what people think about me," Gabrielle whispered.

"You shouldn't," I all but growled, trying to rein in the frown on my face. I shouldn't be this possessive of her feelings. Shouldn't have wanted her to know how goddamn perfect she was, but I *did*. "You shouldn't have to apologize to anyone for being exactly the person you are."

"I... Do you want to start dinner?" she asked, changing the topic away from her.

I'd let her, for now, but it was getting harder to resist the temptation. I wanted to talk about her. Ask her what her tattoos meant. Ask her every little thing that made her brain tick.

I stepped away from the table and moved into the kitchen. I'd already laid out all the ingredients for dinner—much simpler than last time, though I had a little something up my sleeve to teach her.

"What are we making?"

"Garlic pork tenderloin, roasted potatoes, and homemade rolls."

"Yum." She leaned up against the counter next to me. "What's first?"

I pulled out a mixing bowl, grabbed the flour, and looked at her pointedly. "No flour shenanigans this time," I said, looking pointedly at her as she gave me an innocent smile.

"Who, me?"

I grabbed an apron, slipping it over her neck before moving behind her to tie the back.

"Oh. Thank you." She blushed a little as I tied on my own.

"Okay, let's start," I said, walking her through it. She looked so focused, her expression one of pure concentration as she measured the flour, and I didn't miss the way she stuck out her tongue in concentration.

If I was being honest, I really didn't mind another flour fight, but I was wishing this one would end up *much* differently, and that wasn't a thought I should have about my brother's fiancée's best friend. Not at all.

After she finished mixing the dry ingredients, we measured and added the wet ones, left with a sticky ball of dough.

I spread flour out on the counter, scooping the ball out of the bowl, and then turned to her. "And now we just need to knead it."

"Like this?" She asked, a smirk on her lips as she massaged the dough with her hands.

"Mmm, close, but..." I stepped close behind her, my arms coming around hers as I wrapped my hands on top of hers, guiding the movements myself.

It felt so right to stand here, holding her like this, that I almost lost myself in the idea. Maybe my brother knew what he was talking about when he said he wanted to come home to Angelina every night. Having someone like this, well... It might not be so bad.

We both stayed like that for much longer than was probably acceptable, partially because I didn't want to step away. When we'd finished the dough, Gabrielle spun around, still caged in by my arms, and looked up at me.

"And then?" She whispered, her lips half an inch from mine, and I couldn't move. All I could think about was her lips. I wanted to kiss them so badly. I wanted to know how it felt to have her lips pressed against mine. But I couldn't. We—I needed to control myself.

I moved my head, shaking the feeling off as I stepped away from her. I cleared my throat before speaking, still aware of how rough it sounded. "Now we put it back in the bowl and cover it with a towel, and let it rise."

She nodded, and I tried my hardest for the rest of the night as we made the pork and potatoes not to stand too close to her. Not to soak in her presence because I didn't know how to live without it anymore.

～

"OH MY GOD. That was so good." Gabbi groaned, shoveling her last bite into her mouth.

I smirked. "See why I enjoy cooking so much?"

"I think I'm going to gain fifteen pounds if we keep doing this every week." Her face flushed. "Not that... I think we're going to or anything, but—"

"We should. Why not?"

"It doesn't take too much time for you?"

"Honestly, Gabrielle. I pretty much go to work and then come home, maybe catch a sports game or two on TV, and relax.

Occasionally I'll go to the bar after with work buddies, but other than that... No. I'm not too busy."

"Okay." She nodded and then bit her lip. "Were you serious earlier when you said you'd help me plan? Because I could use help to make some decisions." She pulled her laptop out of her bag and those travel books were once again spread out all over the table as we began thumbing through them.

"You know, I think I have a map..." I said, muttering to myself as I went into the other room to look for the Europe map I'd bought the other day to plan my itinerary. It seemed silly for us both to plan separate trips, but we weren't close enough that I could suggest we go together... were we?

"Have you booked your flights yet?" Gabbi asked me, chewing the end of a pen as she sat in front of her laptop, a search screen open with flight options. "I know we talked about flying together, but I figured it would probably be easiest to book them when we were both together. You know, to save time..."

I shook my head. "What are you thinking?"

She clicked a few buttons and then showed me the flights. "These are the cheapest for the days I was thinking. You could book different return flights, of course... You probably need to get back home sooner after the wedding—"

"I don't."

She jerked her head up, her eyes meeting mine. "You don't?"

I shook my head. "I got all the time off approved. Two weeks, just like you." I grinned at her.

"Oh. Perfect. I don't know if you want to fly in and out of Paris, but that's what I was thinking since these flights are pretty affordable..."

I looked over the webpage. "That works for me. Let me grab all my information so we can link our accounts."

"Okay. Do you want to book them right now?" Her cursor hovered over the button.

"Sure." I hurried to find my passport and airline number so we could book them, and when we got to the seat assignments section, she looked over at me. We were almost thigh to thigh, crowded over her laptop, and I tried my best not to let my leg touch hers. It was a temptation I couldn't let myself indulge in to let us touch.

"Fair warning... I do plan on taking the window seat," she said, selecting the window and aisle on one of the sides. Our flight from Portland to Atlanta had 3 across, but the one to France was two, four, two.

I chuckled. Honestly, I expected nothing less from her. "I'm not going to fight you for it, little fighter. The aisle is fine with me."

"Oh. It's just I like sleeping against the window, and—"

"Okay."

She nodded, as if she expected more pushback, and let out a breath. "Alright. Booked."

"Perfect." And I meant it—it would be perfect.

∽

JUNE

"I can't believe we finally made it!" Gabrielle squealed with the other girls as we all gathered in front of our Airbnb for the long weekend. After she'd spent so much time making sure everything was perfect for the weekend, I couldn't help but marvel over the house she'd found. We'd ended up with an entire group of us for the festivities, and thankfully everyone had taken an extra few days off work so we could make the whole thing into a long weekend.

The house we'd rented felt more like a mansion, and even though some people would have to share rooms, it felt so spacious. I was skeptical at first when Angelina and Benjamin had thrown out the idea of doing the party together, but I had to admit, this wasn't bad.

Some of Benjamin and Angelina's friends from work had

come, too—Nicolas and his assistant, Zofia; Liam, the redhead who was giving my little sister a little *too* much attention; Noah, the quiet brunette one; and Naomi, the software engineer who was sporting a leather jacket.

I was happy that Harper turned down the invitation to come, mostly because I was pretty sure she was into me, and I had no interest in *her* like that.

The rest of the usual suspects were all here too, of course: Benjamin and Angelina, all wrapped up in their cozy love cocoon until they bickered about something; Matthew and Noelle, who'd thankfully been able to come since classes were out for the summer; and finally Charlotte holding her pink luggage and Daniel, who was always hovering around her.

Everyone had flown down to Oakland and then we'd rented cars to get us all here, but we'd made it in one piece. Mostly.

"I can't believe they lost my luggage," Emily moaned. Of all the people who could lose their clothes, I thought Em might be the worst. She'd worked her butt off to become an influencer on social media, posting pictures and filming her daily life, and I'd never known someone so obsessed with her closet, but I was proud of her for making her dream work. Even if my parents had a heart attack when she told them she was going to drop out of college to share her life with the internet. She'd secured a few big brand deals, and ended up with tons of packages from companies of clothing to wear and other products to sponsor, but the only ones she ended up featuring on her page were things she actually used and loved.

"It's okay, Em," I reassured her. "They're going to find it and we'll get it back."

"In the meantime, you can always borrow something," Charlotte chimed in. "I'm sure one of us can find you something that fits."

Emily, resigned to her fate, nodded, heading into the house as she tapped on her phone screen.

"Wedding countdown: eight weeks," Gabbi whispered in my

ear as we followed everyone else inside, pulling in her suitcase behind her.

"Here," I grunted, taking it out of her hands, "let me carry that."

She frowned, crossing her arms over her chest and stopping in her tracks. "I *can* take care of my own luggage, you know, Hunter."

"I know you *can,* Gabrielle, but that doesn't mean you should. Besides, I like to do nice things. Now hold the door open for me, sweetheart."

She rolled her eyes, but I noticed how she didn't shut the door in my face, and when we got inside, her hand wrapped around mine on the handle, and she whispered a quick *thank you* before heading off in search of her room.

That was fine, because I need a moment away from her so I could stop thinking about the way it had felt when she'd put her hand on top of mine.

We rejoined the group after everyone had settled in, lounging on the couches in the giant living room as we waited for our first activity of the trip to start. We'd filled our three days here as much as possible with fun things to do, but we had also scheduled some downtime to hang out, since it felt like we so rarely got to all do that these days.

I looked over at Gabbi, looking so fucking beautiful in her sunshine yellow dress, and I couldn't help the warmth that spread in my chest from looking at her. It'd always been like this, ever since she tripped all over her words in front of me that very first day.

Matthew had once said that Noelle was like the sun—the center of his universe, so full of light that his life orbited around her. I liked to think that Gabbi was like the night sky—so fucking beautiful to look at. Even when you didn't see her, she still somehow affected you, just like the moon and the tides.

Fuck. Where were these thoughts coming from? I needed to

rein it in. And stop fucking staring at her like I couldn't get enough—even though I couldn't.

Benjamin grabbed my arm and tugged me away from the group and outside onto the patio.

"*Don't*," Benjamin warned, distracting me from the sight of her.

"What?"

I didn't think I'd ever heard him so cold before. "Don't touch Angelina's best friend, dude. Don't touch her, or fuck her, or even *think* about her like that."

"I wasn't." I shook my head. Sure, I'd noticed her—I always fucking had. But that didn't mean I was trying to get in her pants. Well—not that I'd mind. But I knew that one night wouldn't be enough with her. There was no way. Especially after I'd gotten to know her over these last few months.

He sighed. "She's her *best friend*. In girl land, that means she's going to be around forever. If you mess with her…"

I held up my hands. "I'm not going to sleep with her and dump her or anything like that. We're all friends, right?"

If they kept inviting me to hang out with them all the time, what did they expect? Of course, I was going to befriend the one single girl. And sure, Charlotte and Daniel weren't together, but they spent all of their time with each other, so what difference did that make? I didn't want to be the third wheel on any couple.

Besides, I didn't even need an excuse to like her. Gabrielle was more than beautiful, or fascinating, she was also simply incredible.

She liked to talk about books a *lot,* which was great because I liked to listen to her. I hadn't even told her yet that I also liked to read. Sure, maybe not as much as she did, and often it was only a book or two a year if I was lucky, but when I was younger, I had sat and binged all the Lord of the Rings books one summer. It was still one of my favorite series of all time, and sometimes I liked to sit down and do a giant marathon of all the extended cuts of the movies.

When was the last time I'd ever done something like that? I couldn't even fucking remember. In some ways, I'd become such a shell of the person I used to be before my job took over my life. And it was okay, and I had let it because I really fucking loved my job. I loved working with those kids. I loved seeing their smiling faces when they got to leave the hospital, healthy and whole, and it broke my heart when that wasn't the case.

And if the hospital staff thought I was grumpy because I didn't spend all of my time flirting with nurses or other co-workers, who was I to blame? I wasn't there to find a wife or a girlfriend.

Benjamin was looking at me like he didn't believe me, and I sighed. "Look. I know she's off-limits. Even if Mom thinks she's a nice girl and I should go out with her, I know all the reasons it would never work." I pinched the bridge of my nose. "I can't fucking commit to a relationship, man. You know how busy my schedule can be."

"Okay. Just making sure."

I eyed the group, everyone still inside and laughing. "I'm really glad we're doing this, Ben."

"Yeah, me too, Hunt. Me too." He gave me a grin before heading back inside to find his wife-to-be, and I stood at the balcony for a moment longer, looking out across the golf course the house was off of.

I ran my fingers through my hair, separating the curls, and let out a sigh.

What was I getting myself into?

And how much longer could I keep lying to myself about it?

CHAPTER 9
Gabrielle

"So," Angelina nudged me as she plopped down on the chair next to me, her nails freshly done. "You and Hunter seem to get along well." We'd already got massages when we arrived, and then had moved to get our nails done—both manicures and pedicures.

"Uh-huh," I said, trying to decide how much I could reveal about how it really *had* been going with Hunter. All of our dinner dates. We'd had a few more since the first one, and I'd started looking forward to seeing him. How badly I'd wanted to kiss him the other night when I'd gone to his place.

Nothing had happened, and yet, it almost felt like something else had shifted between us. We'd gone from being a little more than acquaintances to friends, and I was trying to ignore the butterflies in my stomach when he looked over at me with those serious green eyes.

All of it made me want to throw up, honestly. It made me more nervous than I'd ever been. I would have picked at my nail beds had it not been for the girl currently painting them.

"Come on, babe! You gotta give me more than that."

"I feel like we had this exact conversation in reverse last year," I said, rolling my eyes. "Except, this time, I really have nothing to share. There's nothing going on between us, Ang. We're just friends."

"Hmph," she muttered under her breath. "Between you and Charlotte, I'm not sure which one of you is worse."

I turned my head to look at Charlotte, who was in the pedicure chair with Noelle next to her. "What do you mean?"

Angelina shrugged. "Just more of the same with Daniel. I swear, they drive me *crazy*."

Zofia sat down on the other side of me. "What are we talking about?"

I rolled my eyes. "Men."

"Oh, tell me about it," she laughed.

"How's everything been working for Nic?" I asked. "I miss you being right next to me." Zofia used to work in HR with me before she became Nicolas's assistant. And now it felt like I hardly ever saw her.

"I'm constantly having to chase him down to get things done, but you know... the usual."

"You know, I'm not sure he's changed in that regard since college. Honestly, I've never met a man so much like a golden retriever." Angelina laughed.

"I think he's... well..." Zofia looked off into the distance. "Never mind. It's not important." She shook her head, fixing her attention on the woman in front of her.

I sensed there was something she didn't want to talk about, but I wouldn't push too hard. "What color are you getting for your nails, Zo?"

"I was thinking like a pale green," she said, studying her bare nails. "It always looks nice."

I had to agree—I'd seen the pale green Sari she'd worn last year for the holiday charity gala that the company had put on. The color looked absolutely gorgeous with her warm brown skin.

"Good choice," I agreed. I studied my hands, the bright yellow I'd picked for them making me smile.

If nothing else, I could count on the sunshine-y color to

always improve my mood. It was probably why I loved the color so much. Originally, I'd thought about painting them green, but I decided maybe that was a little too on the nose. They matched the dress I was wearing, too, the yellow eyelet sundress perfectly complementing the extra warm glow my skin had as the days got warmer.

Angelina's nails, for probably the first time in her life, were a shimmery white, the perfect color for the bride-to-be. I'd seen her so often in red or black that it was almost strange to see her in white, but she looked positively ethereal.

What? She mouthed at me as she caught me staring, but I shook my head with a smile.

"So, what do we think the guys are up to right now?" Emily said from across the walkway, where a woman was working on her nails.

"Probably doing boring man things," Angelina scoffed, rolling her eyes. "*Golf*, right?"

"I dunno," I snickered. "I bet Benjamin would really enjoy it if you put on one of those tiny golf skirts and went with him."

She narrowed her eyes at me. "Don't you dare encourage him. I absolutely do not need to be forced into one more outdoor activity!" Angelina muttered something under her breath, which sounded a lot like, "*Besides, he gets to see enough of that at the gym, thank you.*"

Noelle laughed. "I used to say that about running the trails with Matthew and Snowball, but now I kind of enjoy it."

"You know, I'm kind of thinking of getting a dog myself..." Charlotte said as the girl painted her toenails a bright shade of pink.

"Really? You?" Noelle asked her, raising an eyebrow.

"Well... I'm still single, and I live alone, so I thought maybe it would be a good idea."

"What does Daniel think?" Angelina asked, bringing up her brother.

"What?" Charlotte's cheeks pinked.

"Isn't he over at your place all the time?"

"Oh. Mm. Yeah. We're best friends, after all."

"Come on, guys," I said, sighing, "leave Charlotte alone." Her eyes flashed to mine in a thank you, and I turned back to Angelina. "You still thinking about getting your own cat? I know Toothless misses you."

She grinned conspiratorially. "I have a plan. Benjamin doesn't know it yet, but after the wedding, I'm planning on getting one."

I laughed. "How do you think that'll go?"

She shrugged, looking at her nails. "If he wants me to have his children one day, he can let me have a cat."

"Fair enough." I chuckled. She'd make him work for it, that was for sure. Still, I was pretty sure whoever those kids were, they'd be damn lucky to have Angelina Bradford—Sullivan, I supposed, as their mom.

Emily and Naomi were chatting over in the corner, and I loved watching everyone interact with each other. We'd only just arrived, but this was already shaping up to be a glorious trip.

∽

"WE'RE HOME!" Emily sang out as we danced through the front door. I'd lost count of the number of mimosas I'd drank while we were at the spa, and after being pampered completely from head to toe... I think it was safe to say we were all feeling *completely* relaxed and slightly buzzed.

"That was *so* nice," Charlotte said, admiring her sparkly pink nails against her pale skin. She'd pulled her blonde hair up off her shoulders today and into a claw clip, twisting it at the nape of her neck, and yet she still somehow looked like a picture-perfect ballerina, even in her regular clothes. "I don't take enough time for myself anymore," she sighed. "Plus, the nails don't always work when I'm sewing all the time. But dang, they're pretty."

"I can't believe we're back first," Emily complained, collapsing on the couch with her arms up. "I'm starving. What time was dinner again?"

I didn't even have to pull out my itinerary with our plans to give her the answer. "The chef is coming over at 5:30 to prep and he's supposed to start cooking around 6. But I have no idea exactly what time we'll be eating. Hunter and I ordered some snacks that should be in the pantry, though."

"Oh, Hunter and I, hmmm?" Angelina asked, elbowing me in the side as she slid in past me to grab a soda from the kitchen.

"Shut up," I said, rolling my eyes. "You know it's not like that. Besides, he's one hundred percent not interested in me. There's no way. You should have heard him at your engagement party, Ang."

I'd ended up spilling it all to her after she cornered me at the end of our last coffee date, if only because I was truly incapable of keeping anything from my best friend. Sure, I hadn't told her how I felt about him, but that was only because I hadn't sorted out my own feelings, right? So if I wasn't telling her about the dinner dates or how he was teaching me to cook or the way I was pretty sure we almost kissed the other night, that was just fine.

"I'm just saying you should have seen the way he was looking at you earlier. Damn." She fanned herself. "I was like, is it hot in here, or is it me?"

"To be fair, it *is* hot in here. It's June in Central California, Angelina."

She glared at me. "You know what I mean."

"Nope. I absolutely do not. He doesn't look at me any specific way. You're delusional."

"The delusional one here is you, Gabs." She patted my head. The con to being the shorter friend was that I was always in reach for her to do things like that—or to use me as an armrest. I didn't really mind being one of the shorter ones in our friend group, though. I liked my height the way I was, even if I wasn't a leggy goddess like Angelina was at five foot ten inches. My five foot six was *perfectly fine*, thank you very much.

And sure—my brothers were both over six feet, and somehow all the men my friends and I spent our time around were over six feet, but I never really felt short until Angelina did something like this to me.

I rolled my eyes. What are best friends for?

"So, do we have any plans while we're waiting for the guys to get back?" Zofia asked, perched on the edge of the couch, her warm brown skin popping against the white fabric. She'd dressed in a pretty cotton maroon wrap dress that showed off the lines of her body, perfectly accentuating her waist.

I swear, if Nicolas Larsen doesn't date you, he's an even bigger idiot than I thought, I thought to myself. I'd noticed the way he acted around her, and she was constantly dancing around any deeper conversations with him, but I didn't think I'd missed the spark between them.

"Nothing specific, but there is the pool out back—" Hunter and I had booked a house with one since we were here in the summer, and when we'd all wandered through the house earlier, I had seriously wanted to strip down to my underwear and get in.

"Wait, wait. I just had the best idea." Angelina whispered conspiratorially, filling us in.

"Oh my god." Zofia laughed. "*Yes.*"

Emily groaned. "Do not get Benjamin and Hunter started. We'll be in prank war for the rest of *time.* I can't tell you the things they did to me when I was younger."

"Plus, we don't even have anything good to prank them with," I said, thinking back to all the things I'd done with my own brothers when I was younger. Emily and I were both the youngest, with two older brothers, and even though she was a few years younger than me, it made me realize how much we had in common in that regard. While *her* brothers had become a doctor and a businessman, I had a professional NHL hockey player and a veterinarian for mine. I thought her brothers and mine would get along pretty well.

Not that they probably ever would. I normally saw them once

or twice a year, if I was lucky, when I went home for the holidays or the occasional birthday, and I didn't even remember the last time they'd all come with me.

I shook the thought out of my head, a devious grin filling my face instead. "What if, instead of a prank..." I trailed off. "I have a better idea. Come on, let's go get changed."

I explained my plan to them, and we all agreed to meet back downstairs in 15 minutes once we'd changed.

"You know... Matthew shares his location with me. I could probably stalk it so we can find out what hole they're on." Noelle said, whipping out her phone.

"Smart thinking," Angelina agreed. "I have Benjamin's as well. And I can pull up the course map, so I bet we can figure out exactly what hole they're on and how much longer they'll be there and how long it will be before they get back."

"Perfect," I grinned. "Let's do it."

CHAPTER 10
Hunter

Since Gabbi and I had planned out the itinerary ahead of time, we'd purposefully chosen a time for the girls and guys to do their own thing at the beginning, and then we'd do dinner tonight as a group before hitting all the wineries tomorrow.

I'd chosen for the guys to all go golfing, which is how I found myself in the middle of the green with Benjamin, Nicolas, Liam, Daniel, and Benjamin's other friends.

We were on our thirteenth hole, enjoying the game, when we got a text from our group chat with the girls.

ANGELINA
We're back. Where are you guys??

She sent us a selfie of them all lounging at the pool in their bikinis. Gabbi was in a green high-waisted one. Honestly, I didn't even notice the rest of them. Goddamn. Was it possible for her to be any more perfect?

"Fuck," Matthew muttered, shoving the phone back into his pocket. "That's just cruel." He looked over at me. "Think we can skip the last five holes?"

Benjamin snickered. "I'm sure they'll still be out there when we get back. Come on."

He patted Matthew on the shoulder before they looked over at me. "Hunter! Your turn. And put your phone away!"

The heat prickled the back of my neck. Why was I embarrassed that they had caught me with the photo still open on my phone?

I wasn't the only one who had said nothing. Daniel was massaging the back of his head with his hand, and I was seriously glad the girls had only sent it to our group chat of us eight. There was something *good* about knowing that all the other guys besides the four of us didn't have a picture of our girls on their phones. Not that she was *mine*, but—

I grabbed my driving iron and moved up to the tee, doing my best to focus on the shot instead of Gabbi's glowing skin, but it was no use.

"You'll get it next time, bro," Benjamin said, slapping me on the back.

"Yeah, whatever," I muttered. I suddenly didn't care one bit about the rest of the game or hanging out with my brother. I just wanted to go back to the house, throw a t-shirt over her, and steal her away so no one else could look at her. Because if I noticed her, then surely the others had as well?

And there was something completely unsettling in that fact.

I didn't enjoy thinking about someone *else* looking at her. I'd noticed over the last few months that her friends had teased her about ex-boyfriends, but she'd never mentioned anyone else. The relief I'd felt each time had been immense, but I knew how men were. I *was* one, after all.

And thinking about Gabrielle's tits in that tiny green bikini... I had to adjust myself in my pants, trying to will the thought away of how mouthwatering she looked.

Fuck.

THEY WERE, in fact, *not* still lounging by the pool when we got back. It might have been the most disappointing part of the whole day, even surpassing my losing streak after the thirteenth hole. Thinking about Gabrielle in that tiny green bikini, her cleavage in that damn top, and how angry it made me to think about someone else seeing it had distracted me entirely.

I needed to get a grip. Perhaps it was a *good* thing that they'd already gotten out, dried off, and changed into nice outfits for dinner as if we weren't staying in to eat, because I didn't know how I would have reacted if I had seen her out sunbathing in that damn thing.

Gabbi was in the kitchen when I got back downstairs from my shower. I hadn't wanted to stay in my sweaty golf clothes for one more moment. Plus, if I was being honest, I'd needed the cold shower to get my mind off of something else—*someone* else.

She'd thrown on another one of her t-shirt dresses I'd noticed she favored, this one a dark gray.

"So, what'd you all do while we were gone?" I slid in next to her, grabbing a beer from the fridge as she popped a cheese cube into her mouth.

"Oh, you know, the usual. Pillow fights, showed each other our tits, played *Never Have I Ever*, talked about or—" I frowned, and Gabbi rolled her eyes. "We were reading."

"All of you?" *Sure, they were* 'reading.' And we'd been on Mars. And I wasn't still thinking about the way tits sounded coming from her lips.

"Did you miss the whole *Best Friends Book Club* thing? We *do* like to read."

"No, I, uh... I thought it was just the four of you who did." I scratched my head, separating the still-damp curls.

"It is. Sometimes we all read the same book, but mostly we like to talk about the ones we've read and suggest them to each other." She perked up, looking over at her friends and all the girls. "And, *occasionally*, someone else comes along who asks for a recommendation, and somehow, between the four of us, everyone is now reading something." Gabbi winked.

"Wow. Color me impressed." I was trying to figure out how they'd all managed to bring so many books in their luggage. I leaned in really close and lowered my voice, practically pinning her in place as she leaned against the counter. "Do you remember when you dressed in that sexy librarian costume?"

"Not a sexy librarian, a regular one." She protested, crossing her arms over her chest like she knew what I was picturing. "But sure."

"Say what you want, but that was definitely one sexy librarian. And she absolutely knows her stuff about books. Why don't you do something with all that knowledge of yours for a job?" I tapped on her forehead, that big brain of hers hiding underneath.

"It's..." She bit her lip, as if wondering how much she would reveal to me about her life. "I love it now, but what if that changes because of a job? And then there's always the risk..." Gabrielle shook her head. "Sure, I don't want to live, eat, and breathe Human Resources, but it's a pretty sweet gig. And I'm sure I won't stay there, anyway. Not long term."

"Is there something you want to do?" I pressed.

She looked up at me, amber eyes wide. "I don't know. I guess I haven't really..." she trailed off as I stepped in closer to her, setting my can down on the counter. "Thought about it," Gabbi finished in a whisper as my fingers trailed over her chin.

I knew I shouldn't be doing this, that I shouldn't be touching her, but I couldn't help it. And when she looked at me like *that*, all I wanted to do was lean down and take her mouth. To see what it felt like with those soft lips pressed against mine.

"Hunter..." she said, her eyes heated with desire. The liquid honey pooling in her eyes was dragging me in, and I couldn't look away. Couldn't move away, either. She'd caught me in her tractor beam, and I couldn't have escaped even if I wanted to.

The shoulder of her dress slipped down, exposing her bare shoulder and the green strap of her bikini.

I groaned. "Sweetheart," I said, tracing her bare shoulder. "You're killing me."

I couldn't stop touching her. Wouldn't, except anyone could come in here and see us like this, standing so close together, my hands trailing down her sides till they came to rest on her waist.

"I know," she murmured.

I swallowed roughly, leaning down, but—

"We can't," she whispered, placing her hands against my chest as if she was going to push me away. "We're—We're the best man and maid of honor. Hunter, we can't do this. What would our friends think?"

I frowned. "If I kissed you?"

She shook her head. "If we hooked up."

Knowing that was in her mind as much as it was in mine made my blood heat, but I knew she was right. Nothing could happen between us. Benjamin had told me that earlier today, hadn't he? For fuck's sake, why was I ready to throw everything away for some girl?

Except, even as I thought about it, I knew it wasn't true. She wasn't just some girl.

"I'm sorry," Gabbi said, before she turned around and walked away.

I was too.

~

WE HAD dinner at the house, a delicious Italian meal we'd had a chef come prepare right in front of us, the perfect culinary experience plus incredible wine pairings.

"Woo!" Gabrielle said, holding up a glass of wine. What was that? The third—or *fourth*?—that she'd had. "I still can't believe you're getting married!" She cheered at Angelina, the group of girls laughing at the giant table in the kitchen.

We'd moved onto dessert, and thankfully we didn't have anywhere to go tonight, so there was no *real* reason to stop her. I wasn't in charge of her, nor was I going to be the one to make her stop, but I couldn't stop myself from keeping an eye on her. I'd learned a long time ago that you couldn't *make* Gabrielle do much of anything she didn't want to do, anyway, and it made me smile. She always dove in to any situation head first, and I liked her little spark of independence.

We'd all changed before dinner, although we were eating in the house, the girls all putting on fancier dresses and us guys in slacks and button-ups. Thankfully, we'd all forgone the jackets and ties, but even I had to admit we made a pretty sharp group when we were all dressed up together.

The girls wouldn't know what hit them when they saw us all in our tuxes.

In a lot of ways, I'd gotten used to hanging out with all of them. Maybe it was because Benjamin had brought me into the little group, but hanging out with him, Daniel and Matthew felt like our own little group, and even better than anything, we all understood what was going on with our girls.

I had to stop thinking of her as mine, but I couldn't help it. Over these last few weeks, spending more and more time with her, the attraction had only grown. I liked her way more than I should have, and I knew letting myself really *see* her was only going to make that worse. But what else could I do? I didn't want to stop spending time with her. I wanted to keep giving her cooking lessons, even if they ended up with us both a mess and her having learned nothing—at least we had a good time.

I wandered outside, finding Gabbi standing on the balcony, staring up at the stars, her wineglass still in hand. Everyone else was still in the living room, laughing and drinking, so I knew we were likely to remain alone out here.

It was dangerous, after earlier in the kitchen, but I couldn't help it. I wanted to be in her presence, wanted to soak it into my very being.

"Hunter!" she exclaimed. She'd popped her foot behind her as she rested her torso on the railing. "Look how pretty the stars are out here." She sighed. "They're never this bright in Portland."

"Light pollution," I muttered with a frown, coming up to stand beside her. But I didn't have to look at the stars to know what was in front of me. "Very beautiful," I agreed.

I was still looking at her.

Gabrielle finally turned her head back, her eyes finally meeting mine. She swayed a little on her feet, and I couldn't help steady her with a hand on her waist.

"Sweetheart," I muttered, closing a hand around her wrist and trying to pull her back onto the wooden bench on the deck. "You should sit down."

"I'm fine," she insisted, even as I steered her over to the seats. I sat down, but...

"Oof!" she muttered as she tumbled into my lap, wiggling to get off. I held her hips, effectively pinning her in place.

"Hey. little fighter. That's not helping anyone," I breathed against her ear, trying to get her from grinding down on me again. To say she was doing things to me—she *always* did things to me—was an understatement.

Her eyes were big and wide as she turned to look at me. "Oh. Oh god."

I was trying to ignore her pressed up directly against my dick, but when she basically straddled me, I couldn't help but let out a moan. "Gabrielle—"

I could hear the hitch in her breath when she looked up at me, and I froze in place. "Your eyes are *so* green," Gabbi said, her hands cupping my cheeks. I knew she'd had too much to drink—I'd tried to stop her before she downed the last glass of wine, but it was no use. And now she was hanging off of me like a monkey at the zoo, but I wasn't doing anything to stop her.

"You're drunk, sweetheart." I said, running my hands over her loose, unbound hair. She'd put some loose waves in it for the evening, and it surprised me how different it looked from her normal, straight hair.

She frowned. "No, I'm not."

I smoothed a strand of hair back over her face. "Yes. You are."

"No." She hiccuped.

I chuckled. I loved her feisty spirit when she bickered with me. "Here, drink this," I said, handing her the cup of water I'd brought outside with me.

She pouted at me, and fuck, the sight melted my heart a little, because she was so damn endearing when she looked at me like that with those big honey-colored eyes of hers. "I don't want it," she said, pushing the cup away.

I sighed, looking around the room. "Gabrielle. You need to drink it, sweetheart."

The groan she let out went straight to my dick, and she wrapped her delicate hands around the cup, tipping it up to her lips and watching me as she drank.

"Happy now?"

"Very." I took the cup back, placing it on the table beside us, but she made no move to get off of me.

Gabrielle's fingers danced across my chest, as if she was tracing the pattern on my printed shirt. "So, I was thinking..."

"Mhm?"

"I think you should kiss me," she whispered, a seductive breath against my ear as I fought every rational thought. I wanted to kiss her. I wanted to kiss her so badly. But—"Don't think about it. Just... Please."

She wrapped her hands around my neck, her fingers tangling in the curls at the nape of my neck. I'd always kept my hair a little longer, especially since it had those little ringlets my mom had loved so much as a kid, and suddenly, I was even happier as she scraped her freshly painted sunshine yellow nails down my neck. She might not have been wearing that little yellow dress anymore, but I couldn't get it out of my mind, anyway.

Her head tilted down towards mine, and before I could think, before I could even breathe, I obeyed her, as my lips pressed against hers. Or maybe it was hers against mine. I wasn't sure who really initiated the kiss, but holy hell.

I pulled away to look at her, satisfied that her eyes were less dilated and she honestly seemed like she'd already sobered up a bit. "I'm sorry—" she said, moving to get off my lap, but I didn't let her.

A growl ripped through my throat, and before I could stop it, I was kissing her again, rougher this time, as if I couldn't get enough of her. Maybe I couldn't. Maybe I never would.

There was no air, nothing in this world but her and me as I gave in to what I needed. When she whimpered against my mouth, tightening her grip on my hair, I opened my mouth for her, letting her tongue meet mine. She tasted sweet and tart—like citrus and wine and that lemon cake she'd had earlier.

When we finally broke apart, it took everything in me not to take her lips again.

"You have no fucking idea how long I've wanted to do that, sweetheart." I placed a kiss behind her ear, trailing down her throat, wishing I could pull down the top of her dress right here and taste her sweet little tits on my tongue.

But I wouldn't do that. Not around all of our friends. This was already so wrong. I shouldn't have been kissing her.

"Fuck," I grumbled. I didn't have any business being out here alone with her. I shouldn't have caved to the temptation, even if I wanted her.

"Come on, we need to get you to bed." I stood up off the chair, still holding her against my front, and set her down. Maybe I could have carried her into the house like that, fucking bridal carry and all, like I didn't have a care in the world, but I was trying to control myself.

Plus, I needed to not have her core pressed against my strained erection for one minute longer, because I was pretty sure I was going to explode from one touch, from one kiss.

Fucking hell.

I kneeled down in front of her so I could carry her on my

back, letting her climb on. Even like this, I tried not to think about how satisfying it was to have her legs wrapped around me.

I took a moment to adjust her, grabbing onto her thighs, as she settled her head against my shoulder.

"Onward, noble steed," she joked.

"Glad to see you still have a sense of humor even when you're tipsy," I laughed.

She poked my cheek. "Well, of course, I do. *I'm* fun. I don't know why you don't like me."

The wind got knocked out of me. "Who said I didn't like you?"

Her nose nuzzled against my neck, but she didn't answer.

"I'm trying not to be so annoying," she said, her statement punctuated with an enormous yawn.

What? Who told her she was annoying? Did she really think I thought she was? Fuck. I needed to have a conversation with her about this tomorrow when she was completely sober.

We'd probably also have to have a talk about that kiss. Ugh, that *kiss*.

"I'm gonna take you to your room," I muttered as I opened the sliding door and walked into the house, and she poked at my cheek, causing me to turn my head to look at her, seeing the pout she'd plastered back onto her face.

"Can't I just... stay with you?"

"I don't..." I swallowed roughly. "I don't think that's a good idea, sweetheart."

"Why not?" Gabbi frowned. "I don't want to sleep alone, Hunter." Her voice sounded so dejected, so terrified of rejection, that I couldn't help it.

"Okay," I breathed out, aware that it was the dumbest fucking decision I could make, but I made it anyway. And I carried the girl I wanted so badly, yet couldn't have, into my room.

CHAPTER 11
Gabrielle

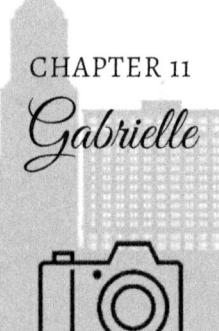

There was one thing I was keenly aware of as I woke up: there was a weight across my abdomen that did not belong there. And I was *warm*, much warmer than usual, pressed up against a hard surface that smelled like spice and something fresh, like...

My eyes opened in a flash. I'd recognize that scent anywhere. And that weight on resting over my stomach was clearly one muscular, tattooed arm. Had I always thought forearms were this attractive? God. I let my eyes trail up to one enormous body that I'd clearly cuddled against—bare chest and all. And to make things even worse, in the middle of the night, my leg had ended up thrown over his.

Oh my god. We didn't—?

I picked up the sheets, peeking underneath, grateful to find myself mostly clothed. At the very least, my undies were on, and I was pretty sure I was wearing *his* shirt, but I didn't think we did anything. *Did we?*

I tried to remember what exactly happened last night after dinner, when I'd been up on the deck and he'd come after me, but...

"Good morning, little fighter," he muttered as I tried to extract myself from his arms

"We didn't—?" I asked, looking at him, wishing the entire world would open up and swallow me whole.

Hunter shook his head. "No. You think I would take advantage of a drunk girl like that?" He frowned at me. "No, Gabbi." His hand reached out like he was going to touch my face, but then he dropped it into a fist at the last moment.

"Oh. Okay. Well, good." Why was I disappointed that nothing had happened between us? That he sounded so resigned to that fact? "But why exactly am I wearing your t-shirt?"

It was soft, cozy, and *huge*. But that still didn't explain why I was wearing it or in his bed.

He rolled his eyes. "You were going on and on about how you were uncomfortable, and then you took off your dress and threw it on the floor. I figured I'd cover you up so you wouldn't be embarrassed."

I cleared my throat. "And, um, why exactly am I in your bed?"

He gave me another frown. "You don't remember?"

I shook my head. There were bits and pieces, sure, but...

"I said I'd take care of you, Gabbi." He smoothed the hair down around my face. "I meant it." *Oh*. He'd brought me back here to monitor me. I felt like the best friend's little sister all over again—obviously, I couldn't take care of myself. Obviously, I *needed* someone to take care of me. It'd been like this my whole life, and I was so sick of it. I gave an outward sigh, trying to push myself away from him so I could escape. I wasted my efforts when he tugged me in closer to him. His face was only inches from mine when he said, "Besides, if we ever fuck, I promise you'd remember it."

My body grew hot at the idea, just thinking about what it would be like to be with him like that. I was certain that he would *ruin* me. Suddenly, it all came rushing back to me—falling on his lap. Sitting on him, straddling his hips. That kiss. Oh, god. It mortified me. I'd begged him for it. And he'd let me kiss him. But he'd enjoyed it too, hadn't he? I was pretty sure he had. I was pretty sure I wanted it to happen again.

"I gotta go," I mumbled, getting out of the bed and not even bothering to find my dress or shoes. Hopefully, everyone else in the Airbnb would still be asleep, and I could escape back to Charlotte and I's room unscathed.

I noticed Zofia sneaking out of the room I was pretty sure was Nicolas's—still in last night's clothes—and I wondered if I wasn't the only one who made a terrible decision last night.

Sure, we hadn't actually *done* anything, but why did I still feel like I was sneaking around?

I tiptoed back into Charlotte and I's room without waking her up, and slipped under the covers, hoping to get another hour or two of sleep before I had to get ready for the day.

∼

CHARLOTTE NUDGED me as we got ready for the events of the day. "Where were you last night? I woke up at like two, and you still weren't in here."

"Oh, I... fell asleep on the couch."

She raised an eyebrow. "Really?"

"Mhm." I really hated lying through my teeth like this, but what else was I going to do? Admit that I'd fallen asleep in Hunter's bed? That I'd stolen his Glacier National Park t-shirt and left my heels and dress in his room because I was too busy trying to escape?

Hell no. For several reasons, I wasn't admitting that to anyone.

Charlotte swiped a coat of glittery pink gloss over her lips as I twisted my hair up and pinned it in place, leaving a few strands in the front out.

I'd packed a shirred seersucker teal tank dress and a cute straw hat to pair with my white wedges for the day, and even though I felt way girlier than normal, I thought I looked cute.

I'd done minimal makeup—because who had time for an entire eyeshadow look? (Charlotte, that was who), and had finished securing the necklace I wore every day when I heard a knock on the door.

"Coming!" I announced, rushing to open the door, and when I whipped the door open, there was Noelle. She'd dressed in a cute little yellow number while Angelina was in a white sundress. "Hi," I smiled, glad to have a moment for the four of us. I loved that we'd expanded our friend group to include their boyfriends —and somehow, the guy I now couldn't get off my mind—but sometimes I missed when we'd spend more time alone.

Everything was changing, and even though I didn't want to freeze time or for things to stay the way they were, I liked it best when we were just us.

"Who's ready for another day of drinking?" Noelle asked, plopping down on my bed, and I groaned.

"Don't let me drink as much as I did yesterday."

"No?" Angelina smirked. "But you're so fun when you're drunk."

"I wasn't drunk," I muttered. "Just tipsy." Sure, I'd had *quite a bit* to drink yesterday, but I wasn't *drunk*. I'd definitely known what I was doing when I asked him to kiss me. And then I'd thought he didn't want it, didn't like it, but... I couldn't have been more wrong.

Charlotte wrapped a finger around a blonde curl as she stepped out of the bathroom in her pink dress.

I wished I could talk to them about this. Goodness knows I'd interrogated the hell out of Angelina when she told me about Benjamin. I had a personal stake in their relationship, anyway—and I was invested. He'd needed a little help to get her attention, so...

In the end, everyone won.

Well, except for me. I was sitting here at her bachelorette party thinking about her soon to be brother-in-law in a very *un*-friend like way. And if what I'd felt while sitting on top of him had been any sign...

I swallowed roughly, internally screaming at myself to get a grip.

I needed to survive spending the entire afternoon in close contact with him. There was no use thinking about anything else that might complicate things like *that*.

~

THERE WERE two things I was absolutely sure of: one, drunk Gabbi was most undoubtedly not to be trusted. And two, well... this wine train may have been the best and worst idea of the trip. Because I'd been stuck in an enclosed space with Hunter for the entire *day*, and I was still trying to avoid the fact that I'd woken up pressed against his bare skin.

Never mind the fact that he'd pressed his thigh up against mine.

I felt like my skin was on fire, and I couldn't stop picturing his firm arms roaming all over my body, exploring me... I squeezed my eyes shut. *No way* was I going to let myself daydream about that right now.

Our group had a huge booth for the duration of the ride, and we got to stop and get off the train to go to each winery along the way. It was the perfect way to experience all the vineyards of the Napa Valley, since we didn't have to drive and could taste as many as we wanted.

Except I was trying my hardest not to drink too much again, because drunk Gabbi? I didn't trust myself. I was pretty sure I'd jump him again if I was anywhere remotely close to that.

I'd survived the first few stops by sitting next to the girls, but this time, when I'd slid into the booth, I'd looked up and Hunter was crowding in beside me.

I groaned internally, even as I felt the warmth of his body pour into mine.

"Are you avoiding me?" He whispered into my ear as a waiter topped my wine glass off.

I crossed my arms over my chest. "No."

"Then why have you not said a single word to me all day?"

"That's not... I-I just..." I stuttered, but I couldn't really *deny* that I had been avoiding talking to him.

"Gabrielle." His voice was low, stern. I would have liked to say it didn't affect me, but it did. After last night, well... "Is this because of last night?"

I didn't respond, too busy focusing on ignoring the heat I felt from his thigh pressing against mine under the table. After I downed another glass of wine, maybe I'd feel better.

"I crossed a line last night, Gabrielle. I didn't mean to make you uncomfortable. I wanted to make sure you were okay. It was... fuck... I didn't..." He shook his head.

"It wasn't that." I shook my head as I took another gulp of my wine, praying that the next stop would be sooner rather than later so I could make another hasty exit—it was concerning to me how many of those I was turning out to need today.

He said nothing else, evidently waiting for me to continue, but what was I supposed to say? When we stopped, I tried to linger at the back of our group to get off, but Hunter did too, which is how we found ourselves walking side by side down the aisle, apparently not speaking.

I was still feeling awkward from earlier, and still a little mortified from last night.

One of the other passengers smiled at us as we shimmied past her. "Oh, you make such a beautiful couple!"

"No," I stammered. "We're not—" I looked at Hunter, who looked amused.

The lady gave me a wink. "I can just tell these things, honey. No need to be embarrassed."

"I—" But I couldn't say anything else, because she was gone, already in the next cabin.

Hunter stood there, staring down at me as I narrowed my eyes at him. "What?" He laughed.

"You didn't correct her."

He grunted, turning away from me and muttering something under his breath that I didn't catch.

"What was that?"

"It was nothing. Come on, we should get out there." He cleared his throat, looking up and down my body.

"Seriously. What did you say?" I poked at his chest.

"You look beautiful."

I rolled my eyes, poking at him again. "That's not what you said."

He huffed out a breath before he crossed his arms over his chest, blocking my fingers from poking him again. "I'm not telling you what I said if you can't even tell me what you're thinking."

"Hunter…" I shook my head. "I can't do this. We can't do *this*. You know that."

"If we both know that, how do you explain last night?" He said, and I couldn't help but think about the way his lips had felt against my skin. Wondering what it would feel like to have him whisper filthy words to me, to praise me for being so good for him, and it was all too real and vivid and definitely not good. "Do you regret it?"

"It… That was a mistake," I said, swallowing roughly as I imagined him pinning me against the train car wall and kissing me again. "I shouldn't have done it. We're supposed to be friends, and—"

"You're right." He agreed, but I saw the anger flash through his eyes. "It was a mistake, and it won't happen again." Hunter stepped away from me and off the train, leaving *me* frustrated and confused, and trying to figure out why I already felt an absence of heat from where his body had been moments before.

What the hell just happened?

"It *was* a mistake." I breathed to no one but myself, hoping that maybe if I stayed away from him long enough, I'd actually believe the words I told him.

Wasn't it? Because I knew we shouldn't be together, but I couldn't help but want it, too. I'd wanted it since the first day I ever laid eyes on him, and I'd known I couldn't have him even then.

But fuck—kissing him might have been the biggest mistake of my life.

And even so... I wanted him to do it again.

CHAPTER 12
Hunter

I didn't like that she was avoiding me all day, or that any time we'd made eye contact she'd look away too quickly.

For a split second, when she'd woken up in my bed, I'd let myself imagine what this could have been. If she hadn't been drunk the night before. If she'd wanted me the way I wanted her.

But then she'd left, and I was pretty sure I'd fucked everything up between us. How could I even fix that? I didn't know, but I was going to try.

We still had one winery left on the train before we'd head back and she still wouldn't meet my eyes. Sitting next to her earlier and when some other guest on the train was the closest I had got, even though she'd been right to push me away.

What would our friends say if I had kissed her right there like I wanted to? We'd had too many close calls.

Too many moments where I'd wanted more. I'd had to keep reminding myself of all the reasons we couldn't. But that still didn't stop my eyes from seeking her out, from wanting to flirt with her every chance I got. I wasn't going to go there, though—right? I needed to stop this thing before anything else happened, and yet—all I wanted to do was scoot in next to her, to have her laugh because of something I said, to watch her light up while talking about something that she loved, and I hated she was doing any of that with anyone but me. Even if she was talking to Benjamin's friends, I couldn't stand it.

"Dude," Benjamin said, pushing against my shoulder as he caught me staring at her again. "You good?"

I nodded. What else was there to say? *No, I'm crushing on your fiancée's best friend?* That would go over well after he told me not to touch her yesterday.

"I'm gonna go get another bottle of wine," I muttered instead, not even waiting for someone to come back over to order it.

We had the rest of the day, and then we'd be heading home after brunch tomorrow. How was I going to get us back to the way things were? At least before—before we'd kissed, before we'd woken up together—she'd been talking to me. Did I need to reassure her we were friends and nothing more? That last night was an accident, but it wouldn't happen again?

Fuck, I hated even the thought of uttering those words to her. Because I wanted... I didn't even know what I wanted, but I know I wanted her.

"What are you doing?" Emily muttered, sliding in next to me at the bar that was at the front of the train car.

"Hm?" I turned to look at my sister.

"You're an idiot." She crossed her arms over her chest, leaning against the counter.

I raised an eyebrow. "Gee, such loving words from my little sister."

Em rolled her eyes. "What's up with you?"

I glanced back across the train car at Gabbi in that little striped dress that somehow made her skin look like she was glowing. "Nothing." I frowned. "I need to get something out of my head, is all."

Emily sighed. "You *may* be more hopeless than Benjamin was."

"Hey." I scratched at the back of my head. "Not fair."

Benjamin might have once thought he was the family disappointment by not becoming a Doctor, but I was pretty sure *I* was even despite that. Because all our mom really wanted for any of us was to be happy. Now, Benjamin was marrying his dream girl. Emily was a successful social media influencer (whatever the fuck that meant, because I was pretty sure I only understood twenty percent of it), and I was... stuck. Maybe I'd been stuck for years, in a rut I didn't know I was even in. I didn't know how to get out of it, because I'd been living in it for so long.

But... my eyes trailed back to Gabbi.

It was worth getting out of it, wasn't it? Maybe someone like her... Maybe it would be worth it.

Emily patted my shoulder and then grabbed a bottle of wine from the bartender. "I'm just saying. Sure looks to me like something's going on inside that big ol' head of yours."

I couldn't help but grumble all the way back to our table, holding the bottle of red wine I'd acquired, and when Gabrielle's eyes met mine across the table... Yeah, I needed to sort these feelings out sooner rather than later. Because I was starting to think I'd be willing to give up a lot of things for Gabrielle Meyer.

When we finally got off the train at the last stop of the day, I couldn't help but wander over to where she was sitting on the winery's patio. She'd been talking to Zofia and Naomi, and I cleared my throat.

"Hey."

Gabrielle looked up, holding her hand in front of her face to block the sun despite the floppy hat she was wearing. "Oh. It's you."

"I... Who else did you think it would be?"

She gave a little shrug, staring into the bottom of her wineglass.

"I wanted to confirm details for tonight," I muttered, doing my best to keep my distance. If she thought last night was a mistake and just wanted to be friends, I could do that.

"Right." She nodded.

We'd planned to go to a bar that also did dancing on Saturday nights, which felt like the perfect conclusion to the day. Sure, we'd all already had plenty to drink over the weekend, but the dancing would be fun.

For the people who loved to dance, of course. I'd always preferred sitting on the sidelines, anyway. I didn't need people to watch me attempt to dance. It wasn't like I was uncoordinated—I'd played sports growing up, and still liked to throw around a ball every so often, but I felt awkward when I had a bunch of people watching me.

Slow dancing was more my speed, and yet... when was the last time I'd done it? My senior prom? Maybe once or twice at a wedding? I'd hardly had any long-time girlfriends since college—once I'd gotten to medical school, that had basically taken over my life.

And now—I hardly felt like dancing. Hardly felt like participating in the activities, after she'd told me the last night was a mistake. I'd basically all but admitted that I would have fucked her if she'd been sober, and then she threw it back in my face as if it was all an accident. Well, fuck that. I wouldn't sit there and listen to her tell me I was some big mistake.

Even though I hadn't been in many serious relationships lately, I knew I was worth more than that. I'd been trying to take care of her—I'd been trying to watch my alcohol intake all weekend, because I tended not to drink too much *anyway*, because if anyone needed medical care, well... I *was* a doctor. Plus, I'd been taking care of people my whole life. Benjamin, Emily, and now... I sort of felt responsible for *her*, too. Maybe it had been all the time we'd been spending together lately, but I'd liked it.

And now... she'd thrown it all back in my face.

"Everything's all set for the limos to pick us up at 8. So we should have enough time once we get back for everyone to get ready before we go." I did my best to keep my expression neutral.

"Amazing."

"Great."

"Perfect."

"Are we done listing off adjectives now?" I asked. "If not, I know a few more. We can throw fantastic into the mix."

Gabrielle scowled at me. "No. I think—I think that's good." She waved me off.

I nodded. "Good."

"Great." She seemed to realize what she was starting again, and changed the subject, looking back at the others sitting at her table. "I'm going to go get another refill." She held up her wineglass. "Anyone want anything?"

I watched her walk away, wishing that my brain and my heart could get on the same page.

∼

THE GIRLS all had little sashes on over their party dresses—Angelina's said *Bride to Be*, of course, and the rest all said *Team Bride*. They were all giggling as they crowded into the back of their limo—we'd rented two, so somehow we'd agreed that the best decision was to separate, girls and guys, and show up to the bar separately. I'd called ahead of time to let them know we'd be coming, since we had a large group, and they'd assured me we'd have a space blocked off for us to sit.

The girls had gone all out in short, glittery dresses, while the guys were all in suit pants and button-up shirts. I'd left the top few buttons undone since we weren't wearing ties, and really, it wasn't surprising that a group of young professionals like us cleaned up so nicely.

I climbed in the limo after Benjamin, sliding into the back seat as we drove to the bar.

The limo was fully stocked with alcohol—sure, I'd technically paid for it with the rental fee, but we might as well take advantage of it, right—so we all took a shot. "Cheers, man," I said, as we clinked our shot glasses together. "To a long and happy life and a *very* happy wife."

Benjamin laughed. "Amen to that."

Nicolas was next to me, and I turned to look at him. Maybe *I* was acting weird, but he looked... I nudged him. "Everything okay?"

He looked up at me. "What?"

"I know we don't know each other very well, but you seem... off." Benjamin and Nicolas had gotten pretty close after he'd started dating Angelina, enough that he'd asked him to be a groomsman, so I knew from association how he was normally always happy and joking around with everyone. Today, he looked contemplative, almost... nervous?

He swallowed. "I think I fucked everything up."

"What do you mean?"

Nicolas dropped his head into his hands. "I crossed a line I shouldn't have crossed."

Oh. I *did* sort of know how he felt. I was sort of in the same situation—everything between Gabbi and me definitely felt fucked up. "You mean... with Zofia?"

"Yeah. I'm... I don't think I could live without her, man. She keeps my head screwed on straight, and with everything at work..." He sighed.

"But it's more than that?"

Nicolas scratched the back of his head, fingers combing through the blonde strands. "Yeah. It is."

I grunted in response, wishing I could get the brunette girl in the dark blue dress out of my mind. "I'm sure you'll figure it out, Nic."

He sighed. "I hope you're right."

Benjamin leaned over. "What are you two gossiping about?"

"Nothing," I said, waving him off. I didn't want to confess what I was feeling, and I wasn't sure Benjamin wanted to broadcast his feelings about his assistant, either.

He frowned, but turned back to Daniel, who he'd been talking to for most of the drive.

"We're here," our driver announced, letting us out at the curb of the bar, and I thanked him as we got out, giving him a tip and letting him know I'd text when we were ready to leave.

We all piled out onto the street, looking for the girls, but they must have already gone inside, so we headed in after them.

Liam slapped Benjamin on the back before heading to the bar, obviously intending on ordering drinks, and I scanned the bar, looking for our girls. They'd evidently commandeered the giant booth in the corner, one the employees had put together so all of us could fit at it, and as I headed over there, Gabbi started passing out straws to the girls.

Angelina was laughing at her curly Bride straw, which looked like the most useless thing I'd ever seen, but if it made her laugh, then I guess that was a good thing. The rest of the girls had pink heart straws, which they were apparently going to drink their cocktails out of. I rolled my eyes, knowing that they were going to be absolutely worthless in absolutely anything except making them suck *really* hard.

Do not think about sucking, Hunter, I scolded myself, not sure where the thought had even come from.

"How'd you get here so fast?" I asked Gabrielle, sitting down on the end next to her. She turned her head like it surprised her I was even talking to her.

She smirked at me. "I tipped your driver extra to take a few wrong turns so we could beat you." She sipped her Piña colada up her silly straw.

I snorted, leaning an elbow on the table as I watched her. "Not fair."

She batted her eyelashes. "No one ever said we had to play by the rules, Hunter Sullivan."

"You're going down, Gabrielle Meyer."

She laughed. "I'm going to go dance with the girls. Catch you later?" She gave me a little wink before she was sashaying across the room, the sequins on her dress catching the lights as she swayed her hips to the beat. She knew what she was doing when she moved like that.

I couldn't fucking take my eyes off of her, even when Liam came over with a pitcher of beer for us, and even when Benjamin sat down next to me. I kept watching her dancing with her friends, them laughing and spinning and grinding against each other, and it felt like there was some magnetic pull that kept my eyes trained on her as she danced. She'd left her brown hair down, flowing around her shoulders, those blond highlights her hair naturally possessed stood out in the bar's light.

I wasn't lying earlier when I'd told her she was beautiful. She always was—even in a t-shirt and jeans.

"They're quite the group, aren't they?" Liam asked, and my eyes wandered over to where the girls were dancing—Emily and Zofia had joined the rest of them after finishing their drinks. Matthew was stuck to his girlfriend's side, like always, close enough to hold on to her waist, but still dancing with the girls.

I made eye contact with my brother, who raised an eyebrow, and then turned back to Liam. "Our little sister is off limits," I barked at him, knowing that of all the girls here, well... She was the only one unspoken for, it seemed. Sure, I was pretty sure Zofia and Nicolas hadn't made anything official, even if they had done something that crossed the line between boss and assistant, and Daniel was definitely going to be pining after Charlotte for the rest of his life if he didn't make a move soon, but the others... Naomi was married, though her wife hadn't been able to come because she was busy with work.

He threw his hands up, acting all innocent. "*Hey*, I'm not looking. I promise." He cleared his throat and said, "I'm actually... I've kind of been talking to Harper. She couldn't come this weekend, so..."

Benjamin raised an eyebrow. "You *have*? When were you planning on telling your *best friend* about this?"

Liam shrugged. "When we made it official. It's only been a few dates, but we get along really well."

"That's great, man," I said, breathing in a sigh of relief that someone our age wouldn't be trying to get with our twenty-four-year-old sister. She might have been an adult, but she was still ours to protect, and I sure as hell wouldn't let anyone touch her who didn't deserve her.

Nicolas tipped back his drinks, draining it to the dregs, and then stood up. "I think I'm gonna go out there and dance. Anyone want to come with?"

I shook my head and watched as Nicolas trailed over to Zofia, looking like a lovesick puppy. He grabbed her arm, and I didn't miss the little smile she gave him as he pulled her into his arms, moving them with the rhythm of the music.

"I should go dance with my wife-to-be," Benjamin said, finishing his drink as well before getting up and giving us a quick nod.

"I'm going to go call Harper and then get another drink. Anyone want anything else?" Liam asked, but neither Daniel nor I wanted another drink, so he headed towards the door to go outside.

"And then there were two." Daniel looked at me, and I shook my head in exacerbation.

"Are we pathetic or what, man?"

"Hm?" He traced the rim of his empty glass with his finger.

"They're all dancing out there, having a good time, and we're sitting here moping like idiots instead of being out there with them."

"What's your excuse?" He muttered, staring into his empty glass.

"What?"

"I've been around them all a very long time, you know. I've seen the guys Gabrielle has gone out with. She's clearly into you, isn't she?"

I looked at Gabbi. "It's... I can't." She said we couldn't do this. It was a mistake ever kissing her to begin with. "Benjamin would kill me. If anything happened..." I frowned. If we slept together, and then things fell apart? I'd have ruined my relationship with my brother and the rest of the group.

"He'd get over it," Daniel chuckled. "Besides, if you're really that worried about it, don't tell him until after the wedding. And you know Angelina would absolutely be in heaven if her best friend ended up as her sister-in-law."

My eyebrows furrowed. I didn't want to talk about Gabrielle and me right now. "Well, what about you? Why haven't you made a move? I know everyone thinks you two will end up together."

Daniel took a deep breath. "It's not that simple for me. We're... We're *best friends*, man. We've been best friends since she was eighteen, and I just... I can't ruin that, on the off chance that we'd work out. I can't jeopardize our friendship."

"So you're going to watch her marry someone else?"

"What?" His head jerked up. "Who said anything about anyone else? Is she dating someone?" He almost growled. "Angelina didn't tell me she was seeing anyone again."

The corner of my lips tilted up into an amused expression. "Can't risk ruining it, huh?"

He groaned. "You're going to be a real pain in my ass for the rest of our lives, aren't you?"

I smirked, holding up my beer glass. "Absolutely, that's the plan."

"Don't look now, but I think someone's getting handsy with your girl."

"What?" My head jerked over to where the girls were dancing, and I saw Gabrielle had gotten pulled away from the group. I turned back to him. "And she's not my girl."

Daniel rubbed his forehead, that tiny crease in between his eyebrows. "What part of *don't look now* did you not understand?"

Sometime while we'd been talking, another guy had danced up next to her, placing his hands on her hips. I shot out from my seat. I knew I shouldn't have done it, but in that moment—I didn't care what anyone said—what we'd said, literally only hours ago; she was *mine*, and I'd be damned if she danced with someone else.

I shot through the crowd, surprised at how easily I could maneuver myself in front of them.

"Don't you dare fucking touch her," I growled at the guy, my expression one of cold fury. She looked startled by my tone, but I shook my head, glaring until the guy sulked away.

"What the hell, dude? What gives?" Gabbi said, putting her hands on her hips as she scowled at me.

"I didn't like the way he was touching you," I muttered, looking away.

"Well, if *you* won't touch me, maybe I'll find someone who will," she grumbled.

I moved in closer to her, enough to bend down and whisper in her ear. "I'm trying so hard to be your friend, sweetheart."

"What if I don't want to be just friends?" She breathed, uncrossing her arms from her chest and looping them around my neck. "What if I want *you* to touch me?"

"No. We can't. I..." I stopped mid-sentence, knowing nothing good was going to come from me finishing that.

I can't touch you, because if I do, I know I'll ruin myself for anyone else. I can't touch you, because I want you so badly I can't even bear it. I can't touch you, because you're everything that's pure, and good, and perfect, and if I touch you, I'll taint your shine. I can't touch you, because I won't want to stop. Because you said it yourself, it was a mistake.

"That would be a mistake."

She looked up at me, those amber eyes reflecting the lights of the bar back, and I could read the entire expression on her face from her eyes alone.

The song changed to a slower one, and when I heard the first notes play, I held her stare. Took a deep breath. "Do you want to dance?" I murmured instead of acknowledging that question in her eyes, and when she nodded, I wrapped my arms around her waist, letting us sway in a circle across the floor.

Maybe it was a mistake, but fuck, I was an idiot for her.

CHAPTER 13
Gabrielle

We danced in a slow circle, and I was still trying to process the fact that he was here, this close to me. Things had only gotten worse all day, and it all started when I'd fled from his room so quickly when I woke up. But what other choice did I have? If I let us get too close, things would get weird, and then when it inevitably failed, it would be so awkward around everyone else.

It'd be better to get through the wedding without addressing this stupid spark I felt between us; the tension I wanted to give in to before it suffocated me. Yet his tone, the venom in his voice when he'd agreed with me and said it was a mistake?

Knowing all of that, I still couldn't help myself. *What if I don't want to be just friends? What if I want you to touch me?* God, I couldn't believe I'd said those things, especially after I'd told him we couldn't happen. No matter how much I wanted him to kiss me again, he'd still said *no,* and I knew it wouldn't happen. I knew it, but why were those green eyes I loved to get lost in staring down at me like I meant something *more*?

Sometimes I forgot how tall he was until we were standing chest to chest like this—I was average height, sure, but standing at six foot four, he towered over me. I liked that, though. He made me feel small and dainty, something I hadn't been since I was thirteen years old, finally hitting my growth spurt. It felt like I'd gone from a zero to a size six overnight that year, and ever since then, well... I'd never been the smallest girl in class, and I was okay with that. But why did I love the way his gigantic hands wrapped around my waist? Why did I like the juxtaposition between our heights so much?

"Do you really regret it?" I whispered, finally, unable to bear not asking anymore. "Kissing me?" Why had I told him it was a mistake earlier? Why had I told him any of that?

"What?" He said with a jolt of surprise. It was like he hadn't expected that. Like he hadn't expected *me*. "Regret it? With you?" His voice was low. "I would never."

"Oh." I wasn't sure I was breathing properly. This man who had impossibly frustrated me, that I couldn't help feeling so attracted to... The way he was looking at me? I didn't have enough words.

I wanted him to kiss me again. No—needed him to kiss me again. All I wanted was to feel him against me, to know that this was *real*—that we were real, not some sort of dumb, possibly drunken mistake, and that he wanted me as badly as I wanted him.

Despite all of that...

"But... you don't want me." I tried to ignore the stinging in my eyes. We were still swaying back and forth, Hunter not stopping the movement of our bodies for one second. "You don't even like me. I'm just the annoying sister all over again, aren't I? God, I'm stupid, I've been so ridiculous—" I tried to pull away, but his arm tugged me back.

"Says who?" He leaned in so close that our noses were touching, as he hunched over me, all six feet and four inches of glorious height towering over me.

"What?"

"Who says I don't like you?" He sounded angry, and I flinched a little at his tone.

"But..." I started, my chin dropping open.

Hunter shook his head. "*You* don't get to decide who I like and who I don't like."

"But you *don't*. You don't want this, and even if you won't regret it, I shouldn't have kissed you, and I'm messing everything up—" I shut my eyes, willing myself not to cry on this dance floor. It was a miracle none of our friends seemed to be around to witness my embarrassment. That would be my luck, after all.

"No. Fuck. Elle."

My eyes flew open.

He'd called me Elle. Never, in all the years, had I imagined how much I'd like it spilling from his lips. I knew now that there was a reason no one else had ever called me it. I'd simply been saving it for him.

"Hunter..." I breathed out. Truly, something about how he looked at me made me feel special, valued, and treasured. I loosened my grip around his neck to trace a hand over his cheekbone, and his eyes fluttered as his breath caught in his throat.

He gritted his teeth. "I said we *can't*. Not that I don't want to. Okay? Besides... You're the one who said we *can't*. You're the one who said it was a mistake. And it would be. So maybe... We should keep our distance from each other."

I nodded. "You're right," I said to him. "We need to be friends. Because anything else..." I shook my head.

"Right." He gave me a curt nod. "Friends."

I pulled out of his arms when the song ended, only offering him a reluctant smile that didn't quite reach my eyes and a small, "I'm sorry," before I darted away to the bathroom.

I needed to escape for a few minutes, to sort out what was happening in his head, what was happening in *mine*. But, of course, my girls cornered me when I came out of the stall.

"What's going on between you and Hunter?" Angelina asked, crossing her arms over her chest.

"Nothing."

Noelle raised an eyebrow. "You think we didn't see you two

on the dance floor? He came to tell that guy off for touching you, and it looked like you two were having a serious discussion."

"You saw that, huh?"

"Oh, yeah. You're not pulling over a fast one on us, *missy*."

"I'm not trying to pull anything over on *anyone*. There's honestly nothing going on between us. We're... We're just friends. Honestly, I think I'm like an annoying little sister to him." I winced because even saying the words out loud hurt.

Angelina arched a brow. "You're sure?"

"I... Yeah." I resignedly spoke, and I tried to put on a cheerful smile. "Now, what are we all doing in the bathroom? We should be out there enjoying your party, Bride-to-be!" I hoped my upbeat tone didn't betray me.

Charlotte frowned at me, crossing her arms over her chest. "You know we're all here to talk if you need it, right?"

I nodded, almost not trusting myself to speak, because the love I felt for the three of them made my heart feel so full. I knew it. I really did.

We all interlinked our arms, Angelina and Charlotte on either side of me, Noelle on Charlotte's other arm—all of us ending up in one long chain. I tugged us out of the restroom and back to the dance floor. I was only a little eager to avoid the rest of the conversation.

I knew if they pressed, I'd spill everything: how attracted I was to him, and how much I wanted to give in to that attraction. The way he'd kissed me the night before.

Instead of all of that, I ordered a round of tequila shots from the bar, threw them back, and danced the night away with my best friends. I tried my damned hardest not to think about Hunter sitting at our table or the way his eyes were on me all night. They were like a constant presence, his stare burning into me, lighting me up every time our gazes connected.

It didn't matter, though. There was nothing else we could say or do.

My fork scraped the bottom of my plate, the sound grating in my ear as I pushed around my breakfast potatoes.

If I was being honest—brunch was awkward. More specifically, *Hunter* and I were being awkward while everyone else was talking and laughing as they munched on their pancakes or breakfast tacos. We'd picked a super cute and trendy breakfast place in town, and it was a *good* choice—the bottomless mimosas certainly agreed with me.

I wished the dynamic between Hunter and me wasn't so chilly. It felt like the simple relationship we'd devolved into had dissolved overnight, and I hated it. I hated that one moment of weakness had ruined the friendship we'd built up over the last two months. There were so many nights we'd spent laughing in the kitchen that it seemed *wrong* that we'd regressed back to this.

My eyes caught his for a moment, and I could see the concern that flickered in them.

Of course he's concerned, I tried to tell myself. *He's worried about you because he's your friend, and you've barely said two words during breakfast this morning.*

Because he'd agreed with me last night and I *hated* it. What exactly had I wanted him to say? I was right; he was right. There was nothing else to it.

I'd woken up early and trudged out to the deck all wrapped up in my blanket to watch the sunrise, only to find that *he* was there, too.

"Couldn't sleep?" He mumbled.

I shook my head, turning my head to the streaking in the sky. "No."

"Ah."

"What about you?"

He shook his head.

"Mm." I pulled the blanket tighter around my shoulders.

Neither one of us said anything else, even once we went inside and got ready for breakfast, but I tried not to think about how peaceful it was, even sitting in silence together. I couldn't afford those thoughts—I really couldn't.

I met his eye across the table, and he raised an eyebrow, but I shook my head.

My phone buzzed with a text, and I looked down into my lap to open it.

HUNTER
You okay?

GABRIELLE
I'm fine.

I don't believe you.

I don't care.

I turned my phone off, throwing it back into my purse, and turned to Zofia, sitting next to me. I figured I'd better make conversation, so none of the others expected something was wrong.

"Did you have fun this weekend?" I asked her as she looked down at the fruit on her plate.

She looked up at me, her eyes flickering over to Nicolas's on the other side of the table. "Ah. Yeah. It was great. I loved being able to spend more time with you and Ang outside of work."

"Agreed," I said. "You ever going to leave him and come back to us in HR?" I winked at her.

She bit her lip. "I don't—There's just... He *needs* me." Her eyes met mine as she spoke in a hushed whisper.

"Oh." Maybe when I'd seen her sneaking out of his bedroom yesterday morning, it had been what I thought it was.

I gave her a gentle nudge. "Hey. I'm happy for you, you know?"

Her dark brown eyes met mine. "Thank you, Gabs. I really

miss sitting in the cubicle across from you, but Nicolas... He's a good man. And a good boss."

"I agree." I nodded, raising my voice so he could hear me. "Even if he left me out of that work retreat last year."

Benjamin chuckled. "But it all worked out, didn't it? Because I got Angel out of the deal, and you got... a cat."

"Toothless is a very fantastic cat, thank you very much."

"Don't worry, he'll be eating his words on the cat front soon," Angelina said with a wicked grin as she sipped her morning juice through her ridiculous Bride straw.

Benjamin frowned. "We're not getting a cat. We're about to be gone for over a month on our honeymoon, plus the wedding—"

"Relax, Boy Scout. I'm not saying we're getting one tomorrow."

He muttered something under his breath, and we all laughed.

There was one thing that would always be for sure—life together would be very interesting.

CHAPTER 14
Hunter

I dropped my keys into the bowl by my front door, rolling my shoulders back, hoping to wear off some of the exhaustion from the day. There were always good days and bad days, peaceful days and rough days—today had been one of the latter. It had been long, and I'd had to give out some tough diagnoses, and all I wanted to do was distract myself from thinking about the day.

I rubbed my eyes and before I knew what I was doing, pulled out my phone and sent a text. Somehow, I looked forward to Gabrielle's silly little texts, and since she hadn't sent me one recently, I couldn't help myself. Maybe I wanted to steal a bit of her sunshine, as if I could absorb it through osmosis just by talking to her.

HUNTER
> Where's my weekly countdown, sweetheart?
> I was thinking you should come over tonight and we can keep going with our cooking lessons.

Honestly, I didn't really give a shit about teaching her to cook. I wanted to spend time with her, but I wouldn't say that to her. It had already been a week since we'd gotten back from the weekend in Napa, and not talking to her was killing me. I knew why she was avoiding me, but it still sucked.

> **GABRIELLE**
> I'm not sure that's a good idea

> Why?

> You know why, Hunter

> Gabrielle, I...
> I just want to see you
> Please?
> It's just dinner. As friends.

> Okay... As friends.

When she arrived that night, I let a few seconds go by between her knocking and me opening the door, just so I didn't look desperate to see her. Even if I was.

She dropped her bag on the chair, but I frowned as she sat there and stared at me.

"What?"

"Where are your books?"

She raised an eyebrow. "What books?"

"You... You always bring books with you," I grumbled. Travel books, the books she was reading, you name it. In the handful of times she'd come over, she'd always brought *something* with her.

"Well..." She gave me a sheepish grin before pulling one out of her bag. "I *am* reading this one, but I didn't realize you paid that close of attention."

"Of course I do." *I always pay attention to you, Gabrielle.* It was on the tip of my tongue to say, but... We were friends. So how could I ruin it by telling her how much I thought about her? I wouldn't... I couldn't.

"Okay... So, what are we making for dinner?"

"Alfredo sauce."

She raised an eyebrow. "Alfredo?"

"Sure. You can use the elements of making this to make all sorts of white sauces. Plus, I got everything to make chicken and garlic bread, too—"

"Garlic bread? Say no more."

"Next time, we'll have to do homemade pasta as well."

"Oh, next time, hm? So our dinner dates are back on?" She smirked before closing her mouth quickly. "I mean... I don't think they're actually dates, just that, I..."

"I know what you meant," I said, offering her a small smile before changing the subject as I got out the pans. "Have you decided where you want to go on your trip yet?"

She shook her head. "I've narrowed it down, but it's still... It's a lot. I've been trying to plan out a route and find hostels I can stay at by myself, but maybe the girls are right. Maybe this is too much to do all by myself."

We started the sauce; as I showed her each step. Once it was all mixed in the pan, I turned back to her.

"We could go together."

"What?" She stopped stirring the sauce to look at me, and I stole the spoon for her so I could keep it from burning as she processed my offer.

"On your trip," I added. "We should go together."

She blinked at me, like she was trying to connect the dots inside her brain or put together some sort of puzzle. "Go... together." She repeated, and I nodded at her non-question. "To *Europe*?"

"Mhm."

"Why?"

"Because." I cleared my throat. "You were planning a trip. I have a bunch of time off, anyway, so it makes sense."

"It does?"

I nodded. "Then you don't have to be alone, and we can still do whatever you want there."

"You don't have any requests?"

"Well, sure. I'd love to get a Guinness in Dublin, or go to the Coliseum in Rome, but when it comes down to it, I know it'll be fun." I cleared my throat. "Because I'll be with you. And we're already flying together. As friends."

I wished I knew what was going on in that pretty little brain of hers, but finally she gave me a curt nod. "Alright. Okay. Friends. Yeah. Let's... go together. What could go wrong?"

A hell of a lot of things, but at least I knew she'd be safe this way. I felt like she was mine to protect, mine to watch over. I wanted to make sure she enjoyed herself, that she smiled, but it was more than that, too. I couldn't bear the thought of her being all alone.

It was part of the reason I enjoyed these dinners of ours so much.

"Here, try this," I said, scooping up a bit of the sauce with the spoon up so she could taste it. She leaned in, holding my eye contact as she put her lips up to it and tasted it.

"Oh, that's good," she confirmed. "Wow."

"And you made it."

"Well, technically, *we* made it," she said, and I knocked into her shoulder playfully.

"Can't take any credit, can you?"

"What would I do without you?" Gabrielle said, and then opened her eyes wide, as if she realize what she'd implied. "Oh. I mean."

"I know," I confirmed.

Because I *knew*—and I didn't know what I'd do without her, either.

JULY

> **GABRIELLE**
> Wedding Countdown: 6 weeks!

> **HUNTER**
> Thanks, sweetheart.

> Are you still coming today?

> Of course. Why wouldn't I?

> I didn't know if you'd gotten called into work...

> I'll be there.

> You driving?

> Yes. I took the top down on the jeep and everything.

> Shotgun. *winky face*

I licked at my cookie dough ice cream as I watched the girls scream as they ran into the water. It was mid-July, sure, but the Oregon Coast was infamously cold, no matter what time of the year you went to the beach. It was a beautiful day outside, hot enough that we'd gotten ice cream to cool down, but the water was still *frigid*. Still, the four of them were out there playing in the waves as we sat on our towels in the sand.

"I can't believe they're out there in that freezing water," Daniel said, pushing the sleeves of his t-shirt up. "I put my feet in for about five seconds, and I thought they were going to fall off."

"Girls," Benjamin muttered. "They're stronger than all of us."

I laughed as I watched Matthew slather on another layer of sunscreen.

"What?" He frowned. "I'm Scandinavian—I burn easily."

I glanced at Noelle. With her freckled skin and ginger hair, both of them had the *skin-burns-easily* gene. "I think your future kids are a little screwed, aren't they?"

He chuckled, and I knew he was looking at his girlfriend. "Probably. Still wouldn't trade her for the world, though, man. She's..." Matthew sighed. "She's everything."

Benjamin patted him on the back before looking at Angelina, who was laughing as she ran through the waves, away from Gabbi. "I know what you mean."

"How'd you know when it was the right time to propose?" Matthew asked my brother.

"I guess... I'd always had the feeling, ever since we got together officially, but I knew I wanted it to be special. So then it was about figuring out the time and place. So I was talking to Nicolas, and he mentioned I could borrow his jet—and Paris has always been her favorite place, so why not?"

Matthew chuckled. "I don't quite think a foreign country is on the list, but... yeah." He shut his eyes, his lips turning up into a smile as the sun shone down on him. It lit up the blonde strands of his hair, and even when he opened his eyes, that expression didn't fade.

"You're thinking about proposing?" I asked him, and he nodded.

"Soon. We've been talking about it for a while, but we wanted some time to be together before we got engaged. I picked out the ring last week though... so all that's left is figuring out *when*. That being said, I think I already know the *how*." He grinned.

"Yeah?" Daniel asked, chiming in. "You going to let us all in on this big plan?"

"I *was* thinking I could rope you all into it if you were up for it."

"Of course, Matt. You know we're always down to help."

"I planning on doing it after we're home from the wedding, since her favorite season is fall."

Benjamin grinned. "It'll be great to have another married couple in the group."

"How is it you're not even married yet and you're already insufferable?" I groaned.

"You're sounding more and more like Gabbi daily," my brother pointed out. "Is it because you two have been spending all that time together?" He frowned. "You remember what I said, right?" His eyes were accusing.

"I don't know what you're talking about. And there's nothing going on between us, seriously. We're just friends."

Thankfully, neither Matthew nor Daniel seemed to know what he was talking about when I looked at them.

Benjamin shrugged his shoulders in mock resignation, but I knew he wouldn't give up on making sure I wasn't sleeping with Angelina's best friend. And I understood, but also—dammit, I could keep it in my pants, for fuck's sake. I wasn't some horny teenager who needed to get laid so badly I couldn't see straight.

Even though I sort of felt that way any time, I glimpsed at Gabbi in her black bikini. Her ass, the line of her cleavage on the top of the cups... It was almost too much, but I stoned myself to the sight, not letting any of them see how much it affected me.

The ice cream at the bottom of my cone was almost liquid by the time I finished it, but I sucked it down to the last drop anyway, enjoying the freshly made waffle cone it had come in.

The girls must have had enough of the cold water, because they trudged over to us, dripping wet. Noelle's hair was fully damp, like she'd fallen in to the ocean, and she made a little tsk sound when Matthew stood up to wrap her in a towel. "You okay, sunshine?"

"Y-yes." Her teeth chattered. "It's so c-cold."

He pulled her into his arms and then into his lap when they settled down onto his towel, keeping his arms around her. "Better?" He asked, and she nodded, trying to towel dry her damp red curls.

Charlotte had fared a little better, despite being the shortest of the bunch—I guessed that was because of her gracefulness in dance. I hadn't actually seen her dance, but Gabbi assured me she was an incredible ballerina, and could have gone pro if she wanted to be in a ballet academy, but she'd chosen to work as a dance instructor and choreographer for a local studio instead. Maybe it wasn't the most profitable of careers, but she was living out her dreams. And she always seemed to have a smile on her face, so I guessed she was happy.

Did I look like that at work? Did I feel like that from my job? I wasn't sure anymore. I loved my patients, kids like Lizzie, who deserved so much more than constant hospital stays and check-ups, but I knew it was my calling.

Gabbi sat down on her towel, spread out across from mine, as Angelina settled in next to Benjamin. In a lot of ways, it was funny—half of us coupled up, and the other half of us single.

"Oh, Benjamin, how's the new house coming along?" Daniel asked my brother. They'd put down money on a brand-new construction in Beaverton, and since Daniel was a structural engineer, he loved hearing the progress of the build.

"The foundation's been poured and they're working on framing it now. I think we should be able to walk through before we leave for the wedding, when the framework is all done."

"Oooh, that's so exciting," Gabbi chimed in. "I can't wait to see it when it's all done."

"Wait till you see the closet," Angelina sighed. "I'm going to have so much space for my shoes."

"They were more important than my clothes," Benjamin grumbled to me, which made me laugh.

"You know what they say, bro. Happy wife, happy life."

He turned to me, the smile clear in his eyes. "Yeah, man. It is."

I looked over at Gabrielle, who'd pulled a sleeve of Oreos out of her bag, happily munching away as she let the water drip dry from her skin. *Huh*... I wondered what a life like that might be like—with her.

CHAPTER 15
Gabrielle

> **GABRIELLE**
> Wedding Countdown: 30 days! Officially one month!
>
> **HUNTER**
> As if I could forget.

Smoothing a hand down the silky material of my bridesmaid dress as the seamstress zipped it up, I looked in the mirror, looking at the way the champagne color of the dress made my tanned skin look like it was glowing. I'd been skeptical at first, but it really was the perfect color.

I was so distracted that I didn't even hear the door chime of the little boutique.

"Hey, look who it is!" Charlotte shouted, and Hunter gave us a small wave, coming over to say hi.

We'd ended up ordering the dresses and the guy's suits from a small local shop that did both, plus alterations, so I guess it wasn't a *surprise* that he was here, but also, of all the days?

"I was picking up my tux," he said, addressing the other two, before his eyes turned to me. "Hello, Gabrielle," he murmured.

"Hi," I squeaked.

"I haven't seen you since dinner last week," he said, voice low enough that I didn't think any of the other girls would hear him. We'd made homemade pizza dough and then covered them in toppings, and it might have been the best pizza I'd ever had. But watching him leave my apartment that night had been... I didn't know how to explain it, but everything felt *right* when he was around.

"I'm sorry," I winced. "Turns out this friend thing is harder than I thought."

He didn't respond, but I could see the question in his eyes.

"Gabrielle, can we talk for a second?" He said, louder this time, and I nodded, letting him pull me into the dressing room. "Wedding stuff," he added to Charlotte and Noelle, as if that explained why we needed to be alone.

"Hunter." I crossed my arms, keeping my voice down as he stared at me. "What are we doing in here?" I furrowed my eyebrows at him.

"You look—*wow*."

"You like it?" I looked down at the dress, fiddling with the fabric in the front.

"Do I *like* it?" He muttered, tilting my chin up to look at him. "Fuck. Gabrielle. You're beautiful."

I blushed. "Angelina picked the color, but we all got to pick the style." His hand reached up, his fingers moving towards my collarbone like he was itching to touch me, but thought better of it at the last second.

"Spin for me."

"W-what?"

He took my hand and twirled me around, the bottom of my skirts swaying from the movement.

"It's perfect." Hunter cleared his throat. "I need your help."

"And you couldn't have... I don't know, texted me about this?"

"Instead of...?"

"Pulling me into a tiny fitting room?" I raised an eyebrow. "Who knows what they think we're doing in here?"

He stepped closer to me, one hand resting on my waist as his eyes flickered down to my lips and then back up. I thought he was going to kiss me, but then... "What are you getting them for the wedding?"

I—*what*? Where had that come from? "I haven't decided yet. They have their registry, and the wedding shower is next week, but..."

"Do you want to go shopping together?"

I raised an eyebrow. Did he *really* want to spend more time with me? I mean, he was teaching me how to cook, and maybe this would get our friendship back on track after the last few weeks, but still... "Sure. Okay."

"Great. I'll pick you up Sunday morning at ten?"

"Why not Saturday?" I blinked, surprised he would willingly give up his Sunday to go shopping with me.

"Don't you girls have your book club on Saturdays?"

Oh. He remembered. "I—well, yeah."

"So. You can't do Saturday. I'm not trying to steal you from the girls."

I nodded. "Okay. Sunday it is then."

My heart fluttered a bit in my chest as he gave me a cocky grin, heading out of the fitting room, and I tried to will the butterflies away.

I shouldn't be feeling them for my *friend*. Shouldn't be feeling them for the guy who was going to be my best friend's brother-in-law. But I couldn't help it. They were determined to stay there.

∽

"Four weeks," I said with a smile as I slid into his jeep that morning. I liked when I got to give him our countdown in person even more than I looked forward to our brief texts about it.

Friends. We were doing a really great job pretending that was all there was between us. We'd successfully made it through exactly two whole interactions without bringing up that kiss at the Bachelorette, and it was driving me *crazy*. And here I was, at the freaking *mall* with Hunter Sullivan, trying to find a gift for Angelina and Benjamin—what did you give someone who already had *everything?*—and the rest of the things on my list for my Europe trip.

Plus, I needed a gift for the bridal shower, but I wasn't sure I wanted to buy *that* in front of Hunter, anyway.

I figured what the heck—why not knock out two birds with one stone, right? We were already here, anyway. I'd already dragged Hunter out of the second cookware store—inevitably, we weren't even going to end up bringing their gifts with us to France, but that was a separate problem, and we were heading towards our next stop when I turned and noticed a flash of blonde hair behind us.

"Oh God, no," I muttered low, under my breath, and Hunter raised an eyebrow in question.

"Gabbi?" Came a female voice I knew all too well. Crap. She'd seen me.

Hunter looked over at me as I bit the skin around my nail. "Do you know her?"

I nodded. "Unfortunately."

"Who is she?"

"My ex. Hannah." How had it been nine months since we'd broken up and I'd barely even thought about her? This was the unfortunate thing about dating in a city like this—sure, it didn't feel small, until you ran into someone you knew almost anywhere you went.

"Hm." He looked contemplative, and I raised an eyebrow at him.

"What?"

"You should probably turn around and say hi."

"*Fuck*," I muttered under my breath before I finally stopped walking and turned around to face her. "Hi, Han."

"Oh, gosh," Hannah said, bubbly as ever. "I thought that was you! It's been so long, I wasn't sure if I was seeing things." She turned to Hunter. "And who might *you* be?"

"This is Hunter. His brother is marrying my best friend." I gave her a small smile, even though it didn't reach my eyes.

"Ohhh, the friends you never let me meet. I get it." She was so chipper, even as her voice dripped with the passive-aggressive comment. We'd dated for a few months, *sure*, but it never felt like we were quite serious enough for that. My friends were my family here, and I wasn't about to introduce people to them unless I thought it was going to last. And Hannah... We were too different. Of course, things weren't going to last long term between us. Seeing her now reminded me of that.

"It wasn't like *that*," I said to her, shaking my head. "We'd broken up before I even met him, anyway. And we were never that serious."

She shrugged. "Because you didn't want to be."

"What?" I felt my whole body freeze up.

"It's fine. You weren't ready to commit to *me*, and it would never work out between us. I get it." She looked at Hunter. "Hopefully it works out better for you than it did for me." Hannah gave me a sad smile. "I better be going, but... It was good to see you, Gabrielle."

"But we're not..." I said, but she was gone before I could even clarify again that I wasn't even dating him.

"So... You've dated girls?" Hunter said, his voice rough, and I looked up in shock. Somehow, I didn't even realize that I'd never talked about any of my exes around him before.

Did Hunter not know that I was bi? It had been something I'd known about myself for so long that I forgot it wasn't just common knowledge anymore. I'd always found myself attracted to both guys and girls—I cared more about their personality and who they were deep down than what they looked like.

Of course, it also didn't *hurt* if they were six foot four with a head of brown curly hair and forest green eyes, but I wasn't going to say that to him. Or compliment his muscles that he had all *over*, which I could easily ogle right now with the way he'd worn a loose button-up with rolled-up sleeves over a pair of shorts. On anyone else, I thought it would have looked dumb, but he made it look amazing. Plus, you could see his forearm tattoos, and good God, they were hot.

And then there was me, dressed in jean shorts, a t-shirt knotted in the front, and a pair of converse. Luckily I'd done my hair and makeup, so I didn't feel like a complete slob around him, but still... maybe I should have dressed up? I shook my head at the thought. I didn't normally put on dresses unless I was going out somewhere. And I wasn't trying to impress him. He was just my friend. A friend who didn't know I'd dated girls before. *Yikes.*

"Yeah. And what about it?" I raised an eyebrow, ready to question him, but he said nothing.

Finally, he responded with an, "Okay."

"That's it?" I placed my hands on my hips. "You don't have questions?"

"Well... Why'd you break up?" Hunter asked me as we stood there in the middle of the mall, still watching her walk away. I wondered how many of my relationships I had ended because of my fears. "If you want to tell me. You don't have to... if you're not comfortable."

"I am."

He raised an eyebrow, like my statement puzzled him.

"Comfortable with you. I... I trust you. I feel safe with you." Maybe that was why I let the truth stumble out of me, like the word vomit I could never stop around him. This time, though, it felt a little... freeing. "I don't know. Maybe I like to self sabotage relationships when they're getting too serious. Maybe I just never actually felt a spark with her. I don't know. I want someone who loves me for who I am, all of me. Who takes the time to really get to know me and cares about me. Someone who..." I turned my body to fully look at him. The look he was giving me–listening so intently, so caring–took my breath away. "Someone who makes me better."

Was I doing that with Hunter, too? Holding back because I wasn't ready to commit to someone? Or was I just scared that the moment I did, they were going to leave me?

He had this furrowed expression on his face, like he was deep in thought, and I punched his shoulder, not wanting to talk about it anymore.

"Come on. We still have to find our gifts. And I need a new swimsuit for the French Riviera. Or three."

He gave me a little smirk. "Do I get to watch you try them on?"

"No, *weirdo*." I laughed, shaking my head. "Does that sound like something a friend would do? I'm afraid they're for my eyes only."

"At least until we get there, right?" There was a gleam of interest in his eyes. "Because we are going *together*, after all, aren't we?"

"Not *together*, buckaroo, because we're not crossing a line." I crossed my arms over my chest, frowning at him. "I guess I'll just have to wear a cover up the whole time, huh?"

"Tease," he said as his mouth twisted wryly. "You wouldn't dare."

I smirked. "Try me."

He rolled his eyes, his eyes trailing over my collarbone, and the heat in his gaze almost made me blush. "You don't have this gorgeous skin for nothing. If you want to, show it off."

I poked at his chest. "Two can play this game, mister. If I'm showing off all my skin in its tanned glory, you're showing off that six-pack I know you keep hidden under your scrubs." I teased, but he stared at me. "Look," I said, dropping my voice low. "I can get really self-conscious when I try on swimsuits. I know I don't act like it, but I don't always love my body, okay? I've got a stomach, and stretch marks on my thighs, and sometimes I hate everything I try on."

"Gabbi," he huffed. "I like who you are—how you are—no matter what, okay?"

I nodded. "Okay."

"What else is on your list after that?"

I gave him an evil grin. "Lingerie."

I was pretty sure if he had a drink in his hand he would have done a spit-take, but given that he didn't, all he could do was look twice at me. "What?"

"Come on, Doctor Sullivan. Let's properly introduce you to the female anatomy." My smile was wicked as I pulled him towards the shop. Sure—I needed to pick something up for Ang, but also, it'd be fun to torture him a little, and see him squirm.

~

"WHAT DO you think about this one?" I held up a white lace teddy, and Hunter's eyes bugged out. I rolled my eyes at him. "For Angelina, not *me*."

"I don't particularly want to be picturing my sister-in-law in *anything*, let alone... that."

I smirked. "So you're saying you'd rather be picturing me wearing this?"

Hunter groaned. "You're going to kill me, little fighter."

I grabbed a few other options from the rack and pointed to a couch outside of the fitting rooms. "You wait there."

He sighed, muttering to himself under his breath.

I gave him my biggest smile. "I'd like to remind you that this was *your* idea."

"Not to be tortured," he grunted, and I whipped the curtain closed behind me, slowly inspecting the items in my hands.

Sure, I didn't really *need* to buy anything for myself, on account of the massive dry spell I was in ever since I'd broken up with Hannah and, well... met Hunter, but I wouldn't pass up the opportunity, either. I hung the lace garment I'd picked out for Angelina over to the side, leaving me with a few distinct sets and colors, including a teddy for myself. Green, blue, yellow, black... Okay, so I was *definitely* buying the green one.

I wiggled out of my t-shirt and pulled on the lace bra, admiring how it looked against my skin. I normally ended up super pale in the Portland winters, but during the summer I always got a nice tan—unlike Angelina, who normally ended up being able to keep most of her color. At least genetics had been kind enough to let me get any sort of color on my skin at all.

I tugged on the strap, biting my lip as I pictured Hunter tugging the cup down. What he'd do to me if he saw me in this. I closed my eyes, resisting the urge to moan thinking about his hands on me. I really needed to get a grip. I quickly finished trying on the others, and then figured *what the hell*—I'd buy all of them, along with the one for Angelina.

When I came out, back in my t-shirt and shorts, Hunter frowned at me.

"What?"

"Where's my show, sweetheart?" He joked.

I snorted, poking him in the forehead. "Friends don't let friends see them in lingerie."

He cursed under his breath, and I grabbed his wrist, pulling him to the register.

"Oh, are you buying these for your girlfriend?" The cashier asked him, giving him a sweet smile. "That's so sweet of you."

"Uh..."

I grabbed the one for Angelina. "This one's a gift for my best friend, actually. She's getting married."

"The rest of these, then?" She asked, addressing Hunter.

He said nothing, handed over his credit card. I blinked, staring at him. Once he'd finished paying, I paid for Angelina's gift, and she handed me both bags.

"I definitely get to see you in the green one now," he rasped into my ear on our way out.

"You wish." I taunted.

"I do."

My cheeks heated. "You didn't have to pay for those. I could have told her you weren't actually my boyfriend." I crossed my arms over my chest.

He grunted. "Why bother? It's fine."

I raised an eyebrow. *It's fine?* Why did I feel like we were toeing the line between friends and *more*? And why did I... not mind it at all?

∽

AUGUST

> **GABRIELLE**
> Wedding Countdown: Two weeks! We're in the final stretch!
>
> What are you up to tonight?
>
> **HUNTER**
> Was talking about going to the bar and getting a few beers with some co-workers.
>
> Why? You in?

Why was it so tempting? The idea of going to a bar, none of our friends around, and just being with him. Telling him I was sick of dancing around what happened at the bachelorette. It was like we were pretending it had never even happened. We'd agreed to be friends, yes, but... I was starting to forget why we'd agreed upon that in the first place. Why was it a bad idea to give in to this?

And if I hadn't felt that connection between us—if I hadn't wanted to kiss him as badly as I did—maybe I could have been stronger.

> Yes, I'm in. Text me the address.

I'd pulled on my favorite pair of jeans and a black lace top and black heeled boots, grateful for the Portland summer for being warm enough to wear a tank out and not be chilly. I'd thrown a jacket in my bag for on the way home, sure, but right now, I looked good.

As I slid into the booth, I smiled at his coworkers. I'd met some of them in the few visits I'd made to Hunter at work, so luckily I didn't feel too awkward about being here without the rest of my friends. This was my first time in what felt like forever going to the bar without them. Last fall, I used to go out more with my team at work, but that was while I was dating Hannah, and ever since Benjamin and Angelina had got back together, most of the time we went out to the bar it was with all eight of us. And if I was being honest, I enjoyed having the guys around.

"Hey," Hunter murmured, eyes flitting down over my top before he looked back up at me.

"Hi," I whispered back, looking across the table at his coworkers.

They were already deep in the middle of a conversation about something that had happened that day, so I just sipped on my beer as they talked.

Hunter cleared his throat as I continued to drink, getting everyone's attention. "Hey, guys. I wanted you all to meet Gabrielle. She's–" He looked over at me, like he still didn't know how to classify our relationship. Honestly, I didn't either. Were we more than friends? We were definitely connected by more than this wedding or Angelina and Benjamin at this point. "–A friend." He finally finished.

I hummed in response, taking another big swig of my drink. I was starting to hate that word and the frequency that we used it at. He introduced me to the rest of his colleagues–Ryan and Mason, both doctors he worked with, as well as Sophia, Isaiah, and Kaitlin, who were all nurses.

"Oh, it's so nice to finally meet you!" Sophia babbled. "He talks about you all of the time."

"He does, does he?" I raised an eyebrow at him, and he looked away, scratching his head sheepishly.

"It's great you could come tonight, Gabrielle," Kaitlin, a nurse, said with a smile. "We were wondering if Hunter was hiding a secret girlfriend because of how much time he was spending with you."

"Oh?" I looked over at him as I finished off my drink. I didn't know he'd been telling anyone about all of our cooking lessons or all the time we'd spent together. "Secret girlfriend, huh?" I laughed. "Imagine. Of all the people, it wouldn't be me, I can assure you of that."

Hunter frowned at me. "Why would you say that?"

I looked at his friends and back at him. I needed another drink if we were doing this now. The first was thrumming through my veins, but I needed some liquid courage if I was ever going to tell him the truth. "Um... Just that I feel like I could see you with a doctor or a nurse before you'd be with someone like me."

"Someone like you?" He said through gritted teeth.

"I didn't mean—" I shook my head, lowering my voice. "Can we not do this right now?"

His friends were all looking at us, and I felt like we were making a scene.

"No." Hunter tugged at my arm. "Can I talk to you over there?"

I let him pull me out of our booth, and he guided us over to the bar, placing me in front of a stool, but I held firm, placing my hands on my hips as I glared at him. "Why did you invite me here tonight, Hunter?"

"What do you mean?"

"*Why*?" I repeated myself

"Why what?" He narrowed his eyes.

"Why do you want to spend time with me? After the bachelorette, after everything—you keep pulling away, and I don't even know what to do with it anymore. I know we're supposed to be friends, but do you like me or *not*?"

"Do I *like* you?" He growled. "Fuck that."

"What?" I blanched.

"I won't sit here while you act like you don't feel this between us. I know you do. Do I like you? For fuck's sake, Gabrielle." Hunter flashed his teeth. "What if I do?"

Oh. I blinked.

"But..."

He put his finger over my lips, effectively silencing me. "That's enough, little fighter."

I went to step closer to him, but he picked me up by my belt loops and plopped me on the bar, leaning into me with that intense look in his bright green eyes.

"Hunter..." I said, voice low, and all I knew was I wanted *more*. More of him touching me. It had been so long since the bachelorette party when I'd woken up at his side. When I'd practically begged him to kiss me that night. We'd been so good, but I was so sick of it.

"Those goddamn jeans," he growled. "They've been driving me crazy for months."

And then his mouth was on mine, and he was kissing me— Hunter Sullivan, kissing *me*, like there was nowhere else in this world he would rather be, nothing else he would rather be doing. He kissed me like it was the last thing he'd ever do on this planet, and with such finesse I thought I might have swooned if it hadn't been for his strong grip on my waist, my neck, like he was keeping me held firmly against the bar.

It was so possessive, the action, and yet I couldn't stop it. I didn't want to, because somehow we were here, and his lips on mine felt so right. And when he swept his tongue into my mouth, I knew—I'd died and gone to heaven. Because this was the kiss of a man *starved,* and I was lost in it.

He pulled away, our breaths shallow and my heart beating frantically, and I looked up at him, looked up at this man that I knew I could develop feelings for if I let myself, and I didn't know what to say.

"I..." I blinked, touching my fingers to my lips.

"Next time you have to ask yourself if I *like you,* Gabrielle, I want you to think about that." He moved to walk away, leaving me sitting on the bar, but I caught his wrist.

He looked at the place where I was touching him like it was a brand against his skin. "If you keep touching me like that, I'm not going to be able to help myself. And if I touch you again... I won't be able to *stop*."

"I don't *want* you to." I said. "I want you. I want this," I uttered it against his lips, and I didn't know if it was the alcohol I'd drank that night that made me so bold, but... it was the truth.

He loosened my grip on his arm, pushing me away. "We can't, sweetheart."

"We *can*," I insisted, looking up into his stupidly beautiful eyes before I pressed a kiss to his jaw. "Just give in, Hunter." I almost whimpered at the loss of contact, at how badly I wanted him to kiss me again.

"We can't do this," he muttered again, pulling away from me.

I ran my fingers over my lips as I stared up at him. "We... can't?" It sunk in so suddenly. He didn't want this. He didn't want me. I went to climb off his lap, but his hand grabbed me, stilling me in place.

"Fuck. Gabrielle." He shook his head. "I didn't mean it like that. I want you. You don't know how bad. But I promised—"

"Fuck your promise," I all but growled.

Hunter sighed. "I can't—I can't fuck up your relationship with Angelina, and if it went bad between us..."

"Who said it was going to go bad?" I whispered. Because my heart couldn't take his rejection. "Please, don't tell me all the ways this could go *wrong*. What about all the ways it could go *right*?"

"What if I can't give you everything you want? Everything you deserve."

He shook his head, and I knew there was no point in trying, because he'd thrown back up his wall again. Why was it the same thing every time?

He'd tell me he wanted me, and then he'd pull away. But I couldn't keep doing it anymore.

"Gabrielle..."

I shook my head. "I gotta go. Tell your friends I'm sorry, and that I said goodbye."

Because if I stayed here any longer, looking into that face I'd grown so fond of, I wouldn't be able to control myself without throwing myself at him. And I knew, somehow, that if we slept together, it would ruin me. That he would ruin me for everyone else, and there was no chance I'd ever find someone who loved me.

He'd made it pretty clear that it wouldn't be him, after all. But between the planning, the cooking lessons, and those stupid not-dates... If he let himself, I was pretty sure he would be the best boyfriend of all time.

And damn, I wanted that.

CHAPTER 16
Gabrielle

> **GABRIELLE**
> Wedding Countdown: One week!

I really wasn't sure why I was continuing to text him, considering he was possibly the most infuriating man I'd ever met, and his mixed signals were making my head spin, but I couldn't exactly stop now, could I? After the bar, I was trying to keep my confusing emotions in check. Because I couldn't deny how much my body wanted him. And maybe my heart, too, if I was being honest. But I already knew that I would never get *his* heart, so I needed to protect myself.

My phone buzzed on my bed, and I rushed over to read his response. I needed to stop acting like a twelve-year-old texting her first crush, for goodness sakes.

> **HUNTER**
> You ready for the flight?

> Yup. All packed and ready to go.

> See you at the airport?

> I'll be there.

At the time, it seemed like a good idea at the time to book our flights together, so I wouldn't have to fly to Europe alone. Now... I wasn't so sure. Thankfully, we only had one layover in Atlanta, and I was checking my two bags straight through to France. One was for the wedding, and the other one had all of my clothes for traveling afterwards. My stomach was a bundle of nerves about the trip, but I knew I'd feel better once I was through security and at the gate.

I took my bags straight up to baggage drop with my passport, and was waiting for the woman to finish everything on her end when she spoke up. "Oh, Miss Meyer, it looks like you've been upgraded. Here's your new boarding passes."

"What? I don't..." I stared at the new ticket she had placed in my hand. "This can't be right," I said, but she shrugged and waved me on.

I'd never been upgraded for flights a day in my life, and yet somehow I had today? I looked at the ticket again. *First class*? My eyes bugged out.

I turned around to ask her how on earth I got an upgrade, but she'd already waved the next person over. I took my new boarding pass and hurried into the line for security, eager to be settled and waiting for my flight where I could get a few hours of reading in, as well as hopefully take a nap.

By the time I found a seat at the gate, I had about an hour till our flight took off, and I didn't see Hunter anywhere around. I looked at my ticket again, wondering what the hell was up with the upgrade, and walked over to the desk.

"Hi," I said, clearing my throat. "I had a question about my seat assignment?"

"Yes?" the airline attendant asked me, and I felt like the silliest person for saying this.

"Well, I was supposed to be in economy... And when I checked into my flight, they said I got upgraded to first class, and I was wondering how that was exactly possible?"

"Let me look," he said, taking my seat number from my ticket and tapping on a few keys. "It looks like whoever purchased your flight upgraded it, but that's all I can tell."

"What?" I blinked. Whoever purchased my flight... "But..." Hunter and I had purchased them together. He hadn't told me about this, right? I was pretty sure I would have remembered if he'd mentioned upgrading our seats before. Was this because he felt bad for me? That he felt sorry for all of this whiplash he'd been giving me lately? Well, he'd have to do a lot more than this to get my forgiveness. Probably.

"Enjoy it, honey. That man of yours must love you a whole lot," he winked.

I stumbled back to my seat, still trying to figure out why he'd upgraded our flights without even telling me. And after last week... I didn't know what, but it felt like it meant *something*.

∼

UNLIKE ME, who'd got there with *plenty* of time to spare, Hunter arrived when we started boarding, so I didn't have an opportunity to pester him about the seats while I was waiting to get on the plane.

We got to board first, of course, being in first class.

"Why did you do this?" I turned to stare at him as he adjusted his seat. I hated to admit it, but it *was* so much nicer up there than it would have been back in coach.

"Do what?" He responded, a mischievous tone evident in his voice. I didn't miss the brief hint of amusement in his eyes.

"You know what you did," I said, narrowing my eyes at him.

Ugh. He was so frustrating sometimes, I almost couldn't take it. I'd known how he acted since last October, but it still caught me by surprise sometimes. "This isn't something you'd do for a friend, Hunter." I said, crossing my arms over my chest. "And given that we're pretending we don't *like* each other..."

"*Don't we?*" Hunter asked, his voice low. Or maybe it was just the deepness to his voice. Either way, there was almost an underlying tone of seduction in his voice, and I really didn't like it. Or maybe I *did*, and that was the entire problem.

"Why'd you upgrade our tickets?" I asked, point blank, as I continued to stare at him. He ran his fingers through his stupidly pretty brown hair and turned his full gaze on me. And those eyes, those bright green eyes, took me in fully.

"Maybe I wanted to see you smile on our *long* flight to Paris, Gabrielle. *Maybe* I thought it would be better if we got to ride in style?" Ugh. I hated it when he said my full name. Why'd he have to say it like *that*?

"And *maybe*," I ground out, "I wanted some peace." I'd packed multiple books, after all. I should have been able to read at *least* three or four of them between our flight to Atlanta and the flight to France. "Maybe I need a break from *you* and all of your confusing actions."

Hunter chuckled, like this was amusing him. Somehow, it was always like this with us. Him, flirting. Me, annoyed. What gives? He was the one who kept pulling away. So why'd he have to be so infuriating when things were just the two of us?

"Things with you are always interesting."

"Hunter—"

"You can say thank you, you know. It's much nicer up here than back there." God, I hated that he'd somehow read my mind. It *was*—and that was the problem.

He waved over the flight attendant and ordered us both champagne before I protested. Drinking with him seemed like a terrible idea, especially before such a long flight. Our flight to Atlanta was six hours, followed by a nine-hour flight to Paris, and why hadn't I foreseen this being a bad idea when he'd proposed it in the first place? Especially because I already knew how attractive he was, and with alcohol... I didn't want a repeat of the bachelorette party.

He peered at me like he was thinking the same thing as the flight attendant brought us two glasses, and I knew what he was waiting for. "Thank you," I mumbled.

"See?" He grinned at me. No sight of the grouch. I thought I might kill for him to be quiet for five minutes of this flight. Enough that I could maybe get into a good part of my book. "Was that really so hard?"

"Yes."

I ignored him in favor of pulling out my book from my bag. Sure, I'd already read it a few dozen times. Sometimes when I was in a mood, comfort reading it helped calm me down. And if I got bored, I had over twenty others loaded up on my kindle. It was a win-win, really. Especially in distracting me from the man sitting at my side.

"What are you reading?" Hunter asked, peering over at the page.

I slammed the book shut and scowled. "Can you mind your own business?"

"No. I saw my name on the page. I was curious."

"Your name?" I raised an eyebrow. "There's no character named Hunter in this book." A fact of which I was very positive, because it *was* my favorite book.

"Ah, you see, I *do* have a middle name."

Oh. Oh, because of course he did. Normal people had middle names. Sure. I did too. Not that I was going to reveal mine to him. How had I gone this long without knowing his? I scanned the page, but there were only two characters in this scene, and that meant... "Are you telling me... that your middle name... is *Tobias*?"

I needed more champagne. There was no way this stubborn man had the middle name of my favorite book boyfriend. No way.

"Yup. Hunter Tobias Sullivan. I can show you on my passport, if you want."

But the thing was... I didn't need proof to believe him. I really, really wanted the universe to stop doing this to me. Because I was absolutely not supposed to be with my best friend's brother-in-law-to-be, even if it gave me about a billion signs. No way.

"I believe you," I grumbled. "Now be quiet and let me read about my favorite Tobias."

"Why bother, when you have such a fine specimen right here?" He smirked, wiggling his eyebrows. "Who would you rather have entertain you: me, or a fictional man who doesn't exist?"

"Tobias." I glared at him. "I'd pick Tobias."

He rolled his eyes at me. "Hunter is *clearly* the better choice."

"Maybe," I said, blowing him a little kiss. "It's fun to fuck with you, though."

"I'm going to get some sleep," he said, yawning. "You should too."

I shook my head. "I'm going to read for a little before I get tired. Besides, we still have our flight from Atlanta to Paris, too." It would be a long day of traveling, and I wasn't sure how I was going to get through it without thinking about that kiss on the bar at least once.

Maybe twenty times. It wasn't good for my well-being, that was for sure. Especially on a tiny airplane and being on the window seat. I didn't want to admit how easily he affected me, but I'd realized a long time ago how much this man had power over me.

I sighed, opening my book back up and continuing where I'd left off, diving back into a book about new beginnings and second chances, wondering if I'd ever get my happy ending like that.

I LOCKED my arms around his neck, my legs around his waist, as he kissed me. After I was panting, breathless, he moved down my neck, trailing kisses down my skin. I moaned as he sucked on the spot, before drawing his attention lower, to my neckline, and down, down...

"Gabrielle." His voice called, but it was louder than I expected, like it was floating all around me instead of coming from the man in front of me. "Gabbi." He was shaking me. Why was he shaking me? "Wake up, Gabbi."

I blinked my eyes open. Oh. Shit.

"W-what?" I tried to rub the sleepiness out of my eyes, forgetting I'd put on a bit of eyeliner and mascara in the morning and accidentally rubbing it up the side of my face.

"Are you okay? You were squirming a lot, and I think I heard you moan, and I figured I'd better wake you."

Oh god. He'd caught me in the middle of a sex dream. About him. Fuck fuck *fuck*. Abort mission. How did I escape this? Could I jump off the airplane mid-flight? Where were we even above right now?

"You're overthinking again," he mumbled. "But I prefer it when you do it out loud."

I definitely did not need to word vomit about what I'd been thinking. Absolutely not. It mortified me enough without sharing that I'd been dreaming about what would have happened at the bar if we'd been careless. Friends? When he could kiss me like that?

I slumped against my seat, shutting my eyes tight, hoping that if I ignored him long enough, he would go away... to no avail.

"What were you dreaming about, little fighter?" He whispered in my ear, making me jump. Hunter reached over and plucked the book from my lap, where it had clearly fallen when I fell asleep. "I think you need to stop reading your smutty books right before bed." His voice was deep and rough, the rasp going straight between my legs.

"I wasn't even to that part yet," I grumbled, but I couldn't help the warmth that creeped over my cheeks. Even if I couldn't help my embarrassment, I hoped my tan would cover my blush.

I turned back to the window, hoping if I ignored him, maybe I could survive the rest of this flight sitting next to him.

CHAPTER 17
Hunter

When I woke up from my nap, it was to Gabbi's head resting on my shoulder, even though I'd given her the window seat. But she *was* asleep, which was a good thing.

I probably shouldn't have teased her so much about her book earlier, but I couldn't help it. She'd turned her head away from me, and I'd taken it as a sign to read her book, even though it was a romance novel.

Still, it was a story about moving on and second chances and I liked the messages in it, so I was still reading it when the captain announced we were getting ready for the initial descent into Atlanta.

She yawned, stretching her arms as she woke up, before zeroing in on her book open in my lap. "What are you doing?" She asked, raising an eyebrow.

"Reading."

"My book?"

"Uh-huh. Is there something wrong with that, or am I not allowed?"

Gabrielle looked contemplative, biting her lip. "You're just... you're reading my book."

"Yes."

"My *favorite book.*" She opened her mouth but then closed it again, and I went back to reading.

When I looked up, she was peeking over my shoulder. "What?"

"Do you... like it?"

I cleared my throat. "It's pretty good so far, yeah. It's different from what I normally read, but... I really like the main character."

She gave me a hesitant smile. "Okay then, I guess carry on."

When we got off the plane in Atlanta, we went and got food before settling in at our gate. We only had about an hour until we boarded our flight to Paris, which Gabbi filled by reading another book she had in her bag (I was trying to determine if this one was worth stealing next), and I kept reading her favorite book.

Our flight was a red-eye, so I was hoping the first-class seats would help us actually get some sleep, since we'd land in the early morning, get to our hotel, and then have the rest of the day ahead of us to settle in. It might have been insane of me to upgrade our seats to first class without telling her, but I was glad I did. Our row was only us, and the extra legroom and bigger seats were very helpful when you were six four.

She furrowed her brow as she read her book, and I frowned at her. "Have you already read that one, too?"

"Oh, no." She shook her head. "I've read other books by this author, but not this one." When I said nothing else, she kept going. "They're fantastic. I mean, her world building and character development is incredible. And there's always this sense of found family in her books, which I can relate to a lot because, you know, I moved thousands of miles away from home, and they're all really..." She looked up at me, and I knew she was watching me watch her. "... Great." She finished. "I did it again, didn't I? Ugh." Gabrielle let out a groan. "I can never seem to stop myself from the word vomit around you. I'm sorry. It's probably so annoying."

I shook my head, brushing a strand of her bangs behind her

ear. "No. It's cute. Don't stop. I like when you ramble on and on to me about things you love."

"Oh." She blinked at me. "Okay."

I hummed in response, resuming reading her book, and even after we boarded our next flight and got ourselves another round of drinks, we enjoyed each other's company like that, reading in silence. Every once in a while, I'd look up, catch her eyes, and then we'd share a small smile before diving back in.

When I finally finished, Gabrielle had fallen asleep again, so I took her book, found her bookmark, and closed both of them up. After slipping them in her bag, I kissed her forehead before turning off the overhead light. Finally, after getting comfortable, I fell right to sleep.

And when she slept on my shoulder the whole rest of the flight? I didn't complain one bit.

∼

WE'D ARRANGED for a taxi to take us from the airport to our hotel that was close to the wedding venue, where the wedding party and most of the guests were staying. I couldn't wait to get in the shower and wash the plane germs off. Even though the only thing I wanted to do was go to sleep, it'd be late afternoon by the time we arrived, and I knew it'd be better for jet lag if we stayed awake and went out into town versus go right to sleep.

I'd made a list of patisseries and places within walking distance in the little town, and since we had a day before any real wedding activities began, my plan was to go into Paris tomorrow to sightsee —assuming Angelina and Benjamin had nothing for Gabrielle and I to do.

"Oh, good," Gabrielle said, looking on the verge of near collapse as our taxi pulled into the hotel. "We're finally here."

After traveling together for a good day and a half, it felt weird that I was about to have to say goodbye for the night and only see her when we had wedding stuff going on. At least until the trip started, because it wasn't like we'd booked two rooms for after...

I cleared my throat. "Listen, I—"

"Come on, let's get inside!" She exclaimed instead, excitedly opening her door before I could even get out my thought.

I sighed, getting out to help with the bags and steering hers—and mine—towards the front desk to check in. Thankfully, the hotel management spoke English, so I could get my room key and everything, and after I finished up, Gabrielle stepped up to the counter.

"I have a reservation for Gabrielle Meyer for five nights—" She had her passport in hand for her ID, but the man made a face as he started looking at the computer.

"I'm sorry, miss," the hotel manager said, his voice thick with his French accent. "It looks like somehow your room was double booked. I'm afraid we don't have a room for you. We'll refund your card for the balance."

Gabrielle frowned. "But I booked it *months* ago—the same time as all of my friends—"

She looked like she was going to panic, so I put a hand on her shoulder. "Hey. It's going to be okay. We'll figure it out."

Gabrielle bit her lip, looking up at me, but I noticed how she didn't move my hand off her.

"Maybe I can share with Charlotte." She muttered to herself.

"Isn't she rooming with Daniel?" I brought up. It was much to everyone's amusement, since the two were still firmly in the *we're just friends* boat.

Gabrielle made a face. "Right. Um." She looked up at me, biting her lip, and I so badly wanted to take the worry out of her face.

"Stay with me," I said before I could take it back. Before I really thought about it or what it meant for us—whatever we were, whatever this thing between us had grown to be. But she hesitated. "Gabrielle," I sighed. "Seriously. You can stay with me. I have two beds. It'll be fine. We don't have to—"

"I get it. *Nothing's* going to happen, I know." The bite in her voice was evident.

I raised an eyebrow at her, but I said nothing about *that*. "Come on, little fighter. Let's go drop all this stuff off."

She nodded, and I pushed her in the elevator's direction so we could head up to our room. Thankfully, the one Angelina and Benjamin had picked had stairs, so despite it being a smaller hotel, we didn't have to lug all the bags up by hand.

When we got up to the room, I dumped my stuff in the corner and went to poke around the suite. When I came back, Gabrielle was lying on one bed, her eyes closed peacefully. I watched for a few moments as her chest rose and fell, at that light brown hair I thought of so much, before I finally allowed myself to wake her up.

"Hey." I poked her face. "We shouldn't go to sleep. Come on, get up."

"What?" She groaned. "Let me take a nap. I'm *exhausted*."

"Maybe you should have slept more on the plane then," I snorted, "instead of reading your book."

"Telling me not to read on a plane is like telling me I shouldn't breathe. Or drink water. Not physically possible." She pulled herself off the bed. "Besides, you kept me awake just as much."

"Me?" I blinked, surprised.

"Mhm. With all your snoring." Gabrielle poked at my face.

I crossed my arms over my chest. "What about you?"

She gasped. "I do *not* snore."

"Mhm... Whatever you want to think."

Gabrielle glared at me, her little eyebrows furrowed so adorably as I chuckled.

"Do you... want to shower first?" She asked, stretching her arms as I picked up a bag and put it on the luggage rack so I could unzip my bag and unpack.

"Hm?" I looked up at her. "Oh, sure, that's fine."

I grabbed a change of clothes and my bag, looking pointedly

at her before I went to get in. "Don't fall asleep while I'm in there."

She grabbed something out of her backpack and then held up the book she'd been reading on the plane. "I'm going to read while you're in there, then I'll get in. Not like, get in *with* you, but —" She turned red. "You know what I mean," she mumbled.

"Mhm," I agreed, but suddenly I was picturing her in the shower with me, and I knew that was a line of thinking that had to stop immediately. At least until I was in the shower, and then I could—

I cleared my throat. "Just give me fifteen."

"Okay." She laid down, sticking her legs straight up against the headboard, cracking open her book.

I shook my head in amusement, the way she never failed to make me smile from her babbling or her unintentionally cute actions. After turning on the shower, I quickly stripped my clothes and got in, appreciating the waterfall shower and the warmth running over my muscles after a long day of flying.

I wrapped the towel around myself, about to change but thinking better of it—the bathroom didn't have a fan, and it was super steamy, so if I put my clothes on now, I'd be a sweaty mess before we even got outside. Instead, I figured I could tell Gabbi she could get in, and then get changed once she was inside the bathroom.

I walked out, towel still around my waist. "Hey, I'm d—" I started my sentence, but before I could finish it, I lost my balance, and we were both falling to the floor.

Because it wasn't a thing that I'd bumped into—it was Gabbi. Who I'd pinned underneath me, and the only thing I was wearing was a towel. *Shit.*

"Oh my god. I'm so sorry, I—" Her eyes grew wide.

Double shit. "Fuck, I didn't mean to—"

I reached down to pull my towel up around me further, only to realize it... wasn't around my waist at all. *Triple shit.*

"Sweetheart, can you... close your eyes for a moment?"

"I'm not sure I can do that," she said, swallowing roughly.

You're making it very hard to be just friends right now, Gabrielle Meyer, I thought with a scowl.

I huffed out a breath through my nose. "I'm going to stand up, and grab my towel, and then I'll help you up, okay?"

She nodded, still staring down between us. "Eyes up here, baby."

I chuckled as her eyes met mine, and she held our stare as I pushed up off of her, turned around and wrapped my towel back around my waist, and extended my hand to help her up.

Gabrielle quickly picked up the bundle of clothes I hadn't realized she was carrying, and then turned back to me.

"Sorry I saw your dick," she muttered before scurrying into the bathroom, and I slumped against the bed, wondering *what the fuck just happened?*

CHAPTER 18
Gabrielle

Someone pinch me. I must have been dreaming, because there was no way this was all happening to me. We were stuck together in one hotel room, and when he'd straddled me? Oh my *god*.

I took my sweet time in the shower, because oh my god, he was *huge*. Who knew *that* was what he'd been hiding down there? Not me. Alright, I might have guessed, from the few times I'd been pressed up against him, and was it really that much of a surprise considering how *big* the rest of him was? But shit, he was *very* well endowed.

I'd put on a pretty sundress so we could explore the surrounding town, because we couldn't go to sleep after getting here—jet lag, *yada yada*—but it turned out that didn't really matter, anyway. I was *completely* awake now, and imagining things I definitely shouldn't have been.

I was staring at him, still trying to process what was happening. There were the facts, of course. We'd shared a ridiculously long plane ride to Paris. I'd fallen asleep on his shoulder. He'd read my favorite book, which meant more to me than I could even explain. And now, we were sharing a room. I'd seen his dick, for goodness' sake.

I was pretty sure if I opened my mouth, the floodgates would burst and all the word vomit was going to come out again. Sure, he'd told me he thought it was *cute* on the plane... (Me, rambling, cute? Absolutely not.) But I still didn't like how every single thought came free around him.

After what happened at the Bachelorette and at the bar the other week... I was pretty sure I was sliding down a slippery slope with him, and I wasn't sure how I was going to recover from it. I didn't know if I even *wanted* to recover from it. Maybe I wanted to sink down deeper onto—erm, into it. Whatever *it* was.

"Are you good?" Hunter tilted his head, watching me as I applied another layer of mascara.

"You have that look on your face you do when you're overthinking."

I frowned. "No, I don't."

"Gabrielle." He sighed. "I've spent at least one day with you a week for the last four months. I think I know what all of your little facial expressions mean by now."

"I don't know what you're talking about," I said, crossing my arms over my chest, which had the opposite of the intended effect in this dress, as all it did was push my cleavage up.

Hunter's eyes flashed down before he looked back up at me, and he shook his head, like that would do anything.

"When does everyone else get in again?" I asked him.

"Noelle and Matthew were getting in pretty late tonight, I believe, and Charlotte and Daniel are supposed to land tomorrow morning."

I let out a breath. "I'm just glad we don't have to get in and go straight to the rehearsal or dinner."

"Speaking of dinner..." He held out his hand, and when I placed mine in it, he pulled me off the bed, leaving me staring up at him as neither one of us said anything. His eyes dropped to my lips, and then back up.

I cleared my throat. "Should we go?"

"Mhm." But he kept staring at me.

"Hunter."

He shut his eyes, resting his forehead against mine. "I'm just... I'm trying really hard not to kiss you right now."

"Oh. Okay." I ran my fingers over his jaw. "But you could, you know? You could kiss me... if you wanted."

He smirked, dipping his head down and lightly brushing his lips against mine.

"Sometimes... I think it's all I want," he said, a little breathless, before kissing me again. Harder this time, like he had time to make up for. I closed my eyes, losing myself in the feeling of his lips against mine, his stubble rubbing against my face. I loved his beard as much as I loved running my fingers through his hair, and there hadn't been enough time for this. Just uncomplicated touching.

My stomach grumbled, and he laughed as he pulled away. "Let's go find you dinner, hm, little fighter?"

I nodded. "I'm starving." Starving for multiple things, but I wasn't going to say *that* to him. "I think I saw a little restaurant around the corner from the hotel. We could try there?"

"Perfect." He slipped his hand in mine and pulled me out the door of our room.

And the entire way to the restaurant, he never let them drop. Not once. Just kept holding my hand, like there was nothing in the world he'd rather be doing.

Did he know I felt the same way?

∼

I SWIRLED my fork in my carbonara pasta, moaning at the first bite as the flavor of the sauce and bacon exploded on my tongue. "God, Angelina was right. French pasta is to *die* for."

He chuckled. "Wait until you try the crepes."

My eyes lit up as I took another bite. "Tonight?"

The corner of Hunter's mouth tipped up as he took a sip of the wine we'd ordered. "We'll see."

I sighed, wishing I could both inhale the entire bowl of pasta so we could go find crepes and never wanting the meal to end.

When I looked up from my next bite, I found him staring at me, with his pasta swirled on the tip of his fork.

"How is it I feel like I know everything about you and yet I feel like I learn new things every day?"

I could have asked him the same question. I knew his movements, his facial expressions. The hobbies he liked, and the things he was interested in. I knew that green was his favorite color, and the way his green henley looked against his skin was sinfully perfect.

But I didn't know his heart. I didn't have it yet, but I wanted it.

"Why don't we ask each other things then?"

He smirked. "Things you've never told anyone?"

"Yeah," I breathed. "Something like that."

"You go first," he said, gesturing to me.

"What's your favorite memory growing up?"

He ran his fingers over his beard, as if lost in thought. "Well, I think you might know I didn't have the best relationship with my parents growing up. They were constantly working, and we had nannies, but it was never the same as actually having them at home. I was the oldest, so I tried to shield Ben from it as much as possible, but..."

"Hunter..." I said, voice low. I didn't know it'd been like that for them growing up. My relationship with my parents had always been amazing—I never once doubted how much they loved me, and even when I'd told them I was moving three thousand miles away, they were so supportive, encouraging me to go after my dreams. I'd never really been able to pinpoint why I'd wanted to go to college in Portland. It was a tiny school on the opposite coast, but one look at it and I'd fallen in love. I visited during the fall of that year, and there was something about the city that clicked. And that was when I knew—*this* was it.

"It was hard, but I knew they loved us. In their own way, they cared about us. But my favorite moments were the normal ones. When we'd all sit down together at the dinner table. When they'd be home from work and we'd watch a movie together. Every once in a while, we went on a camping trip. I've always thought..." He cleared his throat. "Never mind."

"What?" I asked, resting my head on my hands as I watched him, my meal temporarily forgotten in front of me.

"I always thought if I had a kid, that I'd want to be there. That I wouldn't want to miss out on everything because I was at work all the time."

"Oh." I squeaked. "Do you... want kids?" I didn't know why I was asking.

He tsk'ed his tongue at me. "Now, sweetheart, I think it's my turn to ask a question." *Right.* "What would you be doing if you didn't work in HR?"

He'd asked me something similar before, but it was like there was a frog in my throat. The answer was a *million* things. I loved helping people, but was it enough? There were so many more things I loved to do—photograph people and things, and share books with others. Travel the world and see something new every day.

"I don't know," I admitted. "I guess I've always felt like this job—this amazing opportunity—landed in my lap, and who was I to look for something else? There are a million things, and yet..." I turned to look out the window. "The idea of doing any of them is absolutely terrifying." It felt like as much as I could handle admitting right now—both to myself and to him.

"For the record, I think you should do it."

"Do what?"

"Whatever it is that makes you happy."

I gave him a small smile as I stared into my bowl. "Yeah. I just need to figure out that is first, huh?"

He reached over the table, placing his hand over mine, the touch instantly filling me with warmth. "You will," he said, with such strong conviction that I had no choice but to nod. "Okay, your turn," he said, leaning back in his chair and looking at me. "What do you want to ask me? You gotta make it a good one."

I thought about all the things I'd wanted to ask but hadn't wanted to ruin the moment with: *what's your saddest patient story? What's wrong with Lizzie? Do you want to get married?* Did he want to be with me?

I didn't ask any of those things, though. Instead, what tumbled out of my mouth was, "What about you? If you weren't a doctor, what do you think you would be?"

That seemed safer. Less... personal. Like there was some part of me that was scared to open up my heart and give it to him, to lay myself bare in front of him.

"You know," he chuckled, "I've never really thought about it too much. I think from a young age I wanted to make my parents proud, and going to medical school always seemed like the thing to do. But I fell in love with it somewhere along the way, you know? It stopped being something I was doing for them and started being something I was doing for me. I did a rotation in peds, and that was it. I knew that was the place for me. Those kids..." He had a sad, saccharine smile on his face. "They don't deserve it. But they fight like hell, anyway."

"It's hard to watch that," I said. Not a question—a statement.

"Yeah." He nodded. Paused. "Do *you* want to have kids?" Of course, he'd ask me the question I'd asked him earlier.

I paused. "I don't... I don't know. Honestly, I always used to say no, but now... I think if I was with the right person, someone who I knew would make a really wonderful dad? I guess I'd consider it. I'm not all that jazzed about the idea of childbirth, but..." I shrugged. "What about you?"

Hunter looked away. "The idea of having someone that I could lose..." He took a drink of water, like his throat was dry. "I couldn't say."

"Well... Do you want to get married?"

He froze. "I... Maybe someday." He pushed his fork through his pasta. "If I was with the right person." He held eye contact with me as he said the last statement. "And, I believe that was two questions in a row, you little cheater." He pointed his fork at me.

"Want to get dessert?" I said instead. Maybe we'd gotten a little too real there. We weren't in a relationship. It was like we'd delicately balanced ourselves on this line between friends and more.

But I couldn't help but think... Isn't it worth it? To love and lose, rather than to never have loved at all? I didn't know. I couldn't make that decision for him. All I knew was he would be too easy to fall in love with—and the problem was, I'd known that from the beginning. Now it was just a matter of not letting myself fall.

∽

WE'D HAD DESSERT—CREPES, as promised, and I was so full when we finished, but I couldn't help but eat every last bite.

"That was *delicious*," I moaned, scooping up the last bit of chocolate spread from the plate. I'd gone basic—lemon and sugar, which was fairly traditional—but Hunter had ordered a chocolate hazelnut spread and strawberry filled one. It was to die for. I was pretty sure I could eat a crepe every day for the rest of my life and not tire of it.

After he paid the bill—which he wouldn't even let me pay my half of—my hand was firmly back in his, and he led me out of the restaurant, pulling me out towards the city center.

"Are you tired?" He murmured, looking over at me.

I shook my head. Sure, it was getting late, but it was still golden hour—that perfect period of lighting before sunset that made me wish I'd brought my camera with me from the room. Instead, I pulled out my phone from my bag, snapping photos as we wandered through the town.

It was almost nice, compared to the hustle and bustle of a big city, the quaintness of the town we were staying in. And sure, we'd be going to some of those aforementioned big cities after the wedding, but I had no complaints right now, being here with him.

I leaned my head on his shoulder, unable to stop smiling even as our walk around town ended and we ended up back at the hotel.

"Do you want to go up?" He asked, and I murmured a yes in response, knowing that I'd probably fall asleep as soon as my head hit the pillow, anyway.

He didn't stop holding my hand, even as we got in the elevator, but he didn't kiss me either. Like this was the line he couldn't cross as *friends*.

Well, *fuck that*. I was tired of being just friends. I was tired of him trying to be the good guy. Whatever he'd got in his brain—I knew he wanted it as much as I did. I'd seen the way his eyes lingered on me, even when he thought I wasn't looking.

And he was driving me crazy with his little comments and then never actually doing anything about it.

"I'm gonna change," I murmured, grabbing my nightgown out of my bag and heading into the bathroom.

When I came out, Hunter was sitting at the desk, dressed in boxers and a t-shirt, thumbing through the book I'd been reading on the plane.

"I'm all done," I said, clearing my throat. "In case you want to go brush your teeth or whatever..."

I could tell the exact moment he'd noticed my sleep apparel. To be fair... there wasn't much to it. It was a little golden silk nightgown, and I'd weaved my hair into a loose braid so it didn't tangle.

"What are you wearing?" He growled.

Why did I love that sound so much? My heart was racing as I turned to look at him. "What? You don't like it?" I asked innocently.

"Gabrielle." His voice was tight.

"What? We're just—"

"Say we're just friends again, and I'm going to show you all the ways we're *not*."

I crossed my arms over my chest, sitting on the edge of my bed. "Then why does it feel like every time we get close, you pull away?"

He stepped closer to me, pinning me between his arms on the mattress. "I'm trying so hard, sweetheart. To control myself."

"What if I don't want you to?" I said, voice breathless. I'd had enough of this back and forth. "Just let go."

Some part of me expected him to push me away, like he had every other time. It felt like it was inevitable, this push and pull between us. Neither one of us could deny the spark between us, but neither one of us seemed to be able to give into it, either. I knew it could screw up everything between us—this friendship we'd built, our relationships with Benjamin and Angelina, but I didn't even care anymore.

I pulled him down onto the bed, flipping him over so I could straddle him. I positioned my core over his lap, and I knew this was dangerous territory, but I didn't care anymore. I stared at him, watching him gazing back at me. And I knew—whatever happened tonight, it was something we couldn't come back from. Something I didn't *want* to come back from.

"Sweetheart," he murmured, tracing my jaw with the back of his hand.

"Please," I let escape from my lips. "I need you. This is what I need." I bent down, lips trailing over his short beard and jaw, before placing kisses on his neck.

He tilted up my chin, stopping me. "*Fuck*. I promised." He shook his head.

"What? Promised who?" I frowned.

He hung his head, and I pushed the curly brown tendrils away from his forehead. His hair was so soft, and I wondered what he used on it to make it so fluffy. "Benjamin."

"Your brother?" I blinked. "What does he have to do with me? With us?"

"I promised him I wouldn't fuck this up. The wedding. You. I can't... I don't want to hurt you, Gabrielle. But I'm not built for this."

"This?" I gave him a smirk. "What exactly do you think *this* is?"

"You deserve the fucking world, sweetheart. And I can't give you that."

"Why don't we just..." I hesitated. Was it wrong that I just wanted him? That I'd take him any way I could have him? Maybe he didn't see that. But maybe... "Forget about all of that for now. Forget about Benjamin, and the future, and just... have this."

I cupped his jaw. "Just... tell me. Do you want me? If you don't... just tell me, and I'll drop it. But if you do..."

"Yes." The word was quiet, hardly a sound leaving his mouth.

"What was that?"

"Yes," he said, taking my hands off his face and intertwining my fingers with his. "Yes, I want you. I want you so fucking bad, Gabrielle. You don't even know how hard it's been to keep my hands off of you." His fingers trailed up my thigh, and *yes, yes, yes...*

I grinned. "Oh, I think I do. Why else do you think I packed this?"

"This goddamn nightgown." He groaned, but I could see him pulling away. *No, no no...*

"We should go to sleep, sweetheart," Hunter murmured, tracing his fingers over my freckles as he tucked me into the comforter. "Tomorrow," he whispered in my ear. "I promise I'll make it worth your while if we wait until tomorrow." His voice was a whisper of seduction, a promise of what was to come.

"Can I... can we share a bed?" I said, looking over at his bed. Sure, we had two, but... "Nothing has to happen tonight, but I..." I squeezed my eyes shut. "I think about that night all the time, you know?"

"Yeah?"

"I'd never felt so safe as I did waking up in your arms." I

opened my eyes, looking up at him, but his face looked almost... pained. "Can you just hold me?" I whispered.

"Yeah, baby," he said, and wrapped his arms around me, holding me tight against his chest as I buried my face into his skin.

"Hunter?"

"Yeah?"

"You know you're better than any book boyfriend?" I whispered my truth, not sure why it was so easy to expose my feelings now, but it was.

We fell asleep like that, curled up in his bed, and even when I woke up in the middle of the night, still in his arms, I didn't move an inch.

For tonight, I was exactly where I wanted to be.

CHAPTER 19
Hunter

I couldn't stop thinking about her—couldn't get her off my mind. How long had it been like this, anyway? Why was it that any time she asked me to kiss her, I folded instantly?

I was trying so hard to be strong. To respect Benjamin's wishes, because I knew he was right. Gabbi was a relationship girl, but I wasn't a relationship guy. So I had no business holding her all night, or burying my nose in her hair just to catch a whiff of her coconut shampoo and that citrus smell she always had. I shouldn't have let her stay in my bed because I couldn't bear another night apart.

Shouldn't be staring at her now, wanting to pull her onto my lap and finish what we started last night. To keep going until my name was on her lips, and those little sounds that she'd been making on the airplane were coming out of her mouth. I knew she'd been having a steamy dream—for fuck's sake, I'd woke her up because if she kept doing it, I was going to be fully hard on that damn airplane, but I couldn't help but imagine what kind of dream she was actually having. And who was she doing it with? One of her damn fictional boyfriends? I hated she had all of her book boyfriends occupying her heart instead of *me*.

Dammit, I was real, and I was right here, and I didn't want to hold back anymore.

We'd spent the morning exploring the city, eating croissants and pastries before sitting along the bank of the river and watching the water flow. It was different here than in Paris—quieter, more quaint, and it felt more like a little slice of the world that was just for us. The rehearsal was scheduled for 3:00 pm, the time the wedding itself would be at, and walking around the city like that... It was fucking heaven.

I already couldn't wait for the rest of the trip, having her to myself. It was a dangerous line of thought, but maybe I didn't care anymore.

My eyes didn't drop from her frame as she paced back into the bathroom, her hips swinging back and forth in those green fucking lace panties that hugged her hips and made me want to run my tongue over every curve.

Gabrielle looked back at me and smirked. Oh, she *knew* what she was doing to me.

After yesterday—when we'd fallen to the ground, me on top of her, after I'd been in the shower and thinking about her, resisting wrapping my hand around myself and easing the ache—it was obvious that we couldn't deny this anymore. I wasn't sure either of us wanted to deny it anymore. It would have been so easy to take that strap off her shoulders last night. To suck her tits into my mouth and worship her all night long. And why hadn't I? There was nothing different in waiting till tonight.

I didn't know why it mattered, but it did.

"What are you doing to me, woman?" I growled, knowing I should get ready for the rehearsal but unable to focus on anything except Gabrielle's barely covered body. Who knew that a lacy bra could have this much of an effect on me? It certainly never had before. *She* was the only one that drove me wild like this.

"Just giving you a preview of what you can expect, you know." Her fingers danced across my chest as she walked by.

"When you finally *fuck* me." She purred, fetching another item from her bag.

"Later, sweetheart," I promised. "I'm not about to start something I can't finish."

Gabrielle rolled her eyes, "Your loss." She retreated into the bathroom, and didn't come back out until she'd decked herself out to the nines—hair curled, makeup done (I was pretty sure Em would have called it a "full glam," but what did I know? One time I'd asked her why her face was shiny, and she'd rolled her eyes at me and told me it was *highlighter*. Like I was supposed to know what that was?), and her body wrapped up in a silky sunset orange dress with straps that tied on the shoulders, fitted at the waist before it flowed down to above her knees. And then there was the leg slit, which went up to mid-thigh, and I swallowed roughly.

"How do I look?" she asked, flipping her hair over her shoulder as she slipped her nude heels on.

"Beautiful."

"Hunter..." she said, voice low, and I stood up, standing over her as I brushed her hair back before running my thumb over her lip.

"You're stunning. I—"

Someone knocked on the door.

"Later," I whispered, stepping back away from her and controlling myself. I just had to make it through dinner.

∼

THE WEDDING REHEARSAL itself went off without a hitch. They were having the wedding outside, near the Château by a stone gazebo, one that appeared to be carved out of marble centuries ago.

"They're going to decorate it with flowers, and it's going to look so gorgeous," Angelina gushed to her best friend.

Benjamin stood at my side, the happiness radiating off of him, and even I found it hard to resist smiling on a day like today.

"It's going to be great, man." I patted him on the shoulder.

"Did you bring your socks?" He whispered back.

I rolled my eyes. "Yes, I brought the socks." Benjamin was, well... He'd bought all of us superhero socks to wear with our tuxes tomorrow. Batman for Benjamin, Green Arrow for me, while Daniel got Superman, Liam had Green Lantern, and Nicolas had the Flash. Because he was a DC Comics fanboy through and through.

Apparently, that had been his one stipulation for the wedding. They had planned it together, but he'd said, "*If we're having it in France, I want to wear Batman socks for the wedding.*" Angelina had given up on saying no at that point, and I guessed it was a small enough thing that she let him have it.

We all moved inside for the rehearsal dinner, which was held in the Château's ballroom, and I could see Gabbi's eyes light up as she surveyed the room. I couldn't wait to take her around Paris and Europe and see her reaction to every little thing.

Benjamin and I's parents started the evening off by giving a speech about how proud they were of Benjamin, how much they loved Angelina and were excited about her joining the family, etc. I rolled my eyes at Gabbi, who I could tell stifled a giggle as we listened to my mom go on and on.

We were sitting across the table from each other, and I was glad we weren't sitting next to each other because I knew there was no way I'd be able to keep my hands off of her. She kicked me under the table when she caught me looking at her. I gave her my best sheepish grin.

"I'd like to say something as well," Benjamin smiled, standing up from his seat at the middle of the long table. "I know we usually reserve gifts for tomorrow, but I've been saving this one for so long, and this felt like a good time." He bent down, pulled a gift bag out from under his chair, and handed it to Angelina. "If you all might remember when we first met, Angelina hated me. Through no fault of my own," he said with a laugh, and the rest of us joined him. "I'd been egging her on, just looking for an excuse to talk to her, and that ended up in us engaging in what we could only call an email war on its best days."

"And at its worst?" Angelina muttered from his side, but even though she was rolling her eyes, her happiness was clear in them.

"There was never a worst with you, Princess." He placed a kiss on the top of her forehead before continuing. "Anyway, one of such emails was one that I printed out, and I'd look at it when I needed to smile. I thought I'd give it to her now, so when it's framed in the office of our new house that we're having built, she wouldn't think I was completely crazy."

"You did not!" She gasped, pulling the frame out of the bag and then laughing as she read the email. "Oh my god, I did not mean to send this one." She looked up at him. "This was supposed to stay in my drafts."

"Nope." He grinned. "That's why I treasured it so much, you crazy person."

"Read it out loud!" Nicolas called out, and Benjamin looked down at his wife-to-be.

"Do you want to do the honors?"

"You're the worst," she said, shaking her head at them both. "*Benjamin, you're an asshole. Disrespectfully Yours, Angelina.* God, I cannot believe that sent to you. You know I had a full draft box full of emails like these? When you really annoyed me, it was how I'd take out my frustrations."

Benjamin smirked. "How'd that work out for you, Angel?"

She punched him in the arm. "Shut up."

Angelina stood up, wrapping her arm around Benjamin's waist. "I don't have any gifts to give out, but I wanted to say a quick thank you to everyone for coming. Especially my best friends, who helped me plan all of this. I couldn't have done it without you, truly."

I watched as Gabbi and Angelina shared a whispered *I love*

you, and even when she turned back to me, the happiness didn't dim on her face.

∽

I'D ALREADY BORROWED what I needed from the kitchen, and I'd even found a blanket to spread out for us to sit on, and I tucked everything under my arm when I snuck back to Gabbi's side.

"Come here," I said, tugging her out the door. If we stayed in there a moment longer, I couldn't promise I wouldn't kiss her in front of all of her friends.

"Where are we going?"

"Outside," I muttered, still holding her hand as I led her out back and down the steps toward the garden I'd spotted earlier. I felt like a switch in me had flipped the moment we'd landed at the airport. I'd been holding her hand all weekend, and it was truly all I wanted, her hand in mine. Fuck the consequences, I didn't care.

The perks of renting out the entire grounds for the weekend? We were alone, and since everyone else was still inside, enjoying the events of the night, I knew we'd be safe from peeping eyes.

"Hunter!" She laughed. "What are we doing? All of our friends..." Her eyes grew wide.

"Are back inside, yeah?" I said, wrapping my free arm around her waist to bring her in closer to me. "We're all alone, sweetheart."

"Oh." Her eyes grew wide, and then she looked under my arm at what I'd smuggled out. "What've you got there?" She asked.

"You'll see," I said, leading her under a trellis wrapped in flowers, winding deeper and deeper into the private garden.

"This place is gorgeous," she said, her eyes wide as she captured all the details.

"Mhm," I agreed, finally coming to a stop at the little space I'd discovered earlier, before dinner. It had a bench, a nice grassy area I could spread the blanket and drop the basket I'd been carrying.

She raised an eyebrow. "Hunter Tobias Sullivan. Did you plan a picnic for me?"

"Maybe." I gave her a sheepish grin. I couldn't exactly deny that I'd smuggled out champagne and desserts, now could I?

She made a little tsk noise. "You're not just trying to get into my good graces so you can get into my pants, are you?"

I chuckled. Was I *trying* to get into her pants? No. Did I want to? Of fucking course I did. But this wasn't about that—not really. It was about doing something nice for her. Something she'd deserved since the beginning. And maybe we'd never been out on an actual date—not really—but this felt something like one.

"I still can't believe we're here," Gabrielle said, leaning back on the bench and staring up at the stars.

"In the garden?"

She laughed, taking a drink from the champagne bottle I'd grabbed. "No. Well, yes." Her eyes met mine, and I didn't miss the little blush that spread across her cheeks. "But like, in France. Today was amazing. And those two are getting married tomorrow. I never would have expected it..."

I laughed. "What *did* you expect?"

"I don't know. Part of me never thought Angelina would give anyone a chance, let alone him. But those two... They found their *person*, you know? I guess..."

I took the bottle from her, taking a long sip as I watched her face, illuminated by the starlight and the low lights from the garden.

"You guess?" I murmured, encouraging her to continue.

She shook her head before turning her whole body towards mine. "It's not important."

"No?" I whispered. "I think it is, though. And I want to know what's important to you, Gabrielle."

"I always thought that would be me, too. That I'd find the right person, and everything would work out, I guess."

"Like in your books?" I ran my thumb over her bottom lip.

"Y-yeah." She nodded. "Like in my books. But..."

"But the only thing is, your books aren't real."

She shook her head. "No, they're not."

"But *we* are real, aren't we, sweetheart?"

Our lips were only millimeters apart, and all I wanted was to kiss her again. All I wanted was to know what it was like for her to be mine. Her eyes fluttered shut.

"Mmm, Elle?"

"Yeah?"

"Can I kiss you? Please?"

Her eyes opened, and I pulled her into my arms.

I was determined for tonight to be different. No pulling away. Not anymore. I was in this. I wanted her, and I wanted her to be mine, and every other stupid reason I'd had for staying away didn't matter anymore.

It was a soft, supple kiss, slow at first, as she worked her fingers into the fabric of my lapel, holding onto me like I was the only thing keeping her on earth. She belonged among the stars, because she shined so bright, but I was glad to have her down here, anyway, where I could see her light.

I pushed my tongue into her mouth, relishing the taste of strawberries and lemon and *her*, a combination that did nothing but drive me crazy. She tugged on my jacket, pulling me tighter against her, and I wove my hands around her waist, gripping her tightly as I kissed her harder.

Gabbi let out a small moan, and that was it. How had I ever thought I could resist Gabrielle Meyer when she looked at me like *that*?

When we pulled apart, breathing roughly, she giggled before collapsing on the blanket I'd laid out.

"What?" I asked her as I stretched out my body next to hers. For some reason, I needed to be next to her, to be touching her, as if that reassured me she was still here. That this was real.

"It's just funny. In regency times, if someone caught us out here together, it'd be a scandal. We'd have to get married because we were *alone* and we *kissed*."

I poked her in the forehead. "What have you been reading lately?"

"Historical Romance," she said, reaching up to smooth a curl on my forehead. "And technically, I haven't been reading it. I've just been *watching* it." I blinked at her, and she kept going. "Bridgerton?" A pause. "Please. You *have* to know about Bridgerton."

"Nope."

"*What*? How have you not seen it?"

I raised an eyebrow. "Gabbi. I've sort of been busy, you know, being a doctor..." Okay, so maybe I'd heard some moms in the hospital talking about it, but I certainly knew nothing about it, and I definitely hadn't watched it.

"We're watching it when we get home," she muttered.

Home. The thought punched me in the gut. We'd just gotten here, and I was already dreading the idea of going home and not being able to see her every day.

"The girls and I were *obsessed* with it for a few months. Charlotte went on a serious historical romance binge."

"And you?"

"No." She shook her head. "There are no dragons. Plus, I'm not a fan of that super toxic masculinity that guys from back then tend to have." She wrinkled her nose. "I'm not anyone's property but my own."

"What?" I laughed.

Gabbi shrugged. "I read a lot of romance, sure, but my favorite books are fantasy. You know—dragons and princes and daggers, the whole thing." She shut her eyes, laying back on the blanket. "I'd love to have a dragon."

"Hence, Toothless?" I guessed.

"Mhm. When I found her—that little tiny black ball of fur who was afraid of her own shadow—I knew she had to be mine. And she reminded me so much of Toothless, so..."

"It's perfect. And I love that you have a favorite fictional dragon."

She opened her eyes, frowning at my face as I stared down at her. "And you don't?"

"Well, I don't quite think Smaug counts..."

"One, this absolutely calls for a How to Train Your Dragon marathon, clearly, and two, *Smaug?* Out of every fictional dragon, you pick the one from the Hobbit?"

"He has an entire *hoard* of gold, and literally took down an entire kingdom of dwarves, and you're telling me you think he's lame? Which one would you like me to say? Mushu from *Mulan?* Maleficent from *Sleeping Beauty?*" I bent down, tickling her side.

She shrieked, her face lighting up as she pushed me away. "Okay, okay, you win!"

I pinned her between both my arms, and she looked up at me.

One murmured "Hunter..." was all she had to say before I was kissing her again. Before I was completely losing myself in the girl in front of me.

CHAPTER 20
Gabrielle

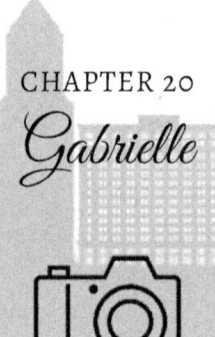

Cupping his jaw, I couldn't help myself from staring into those green eyes I loved so much. I couldn't take not knowing what it was like to be held by him, cared for by him, for one moment longer. It was something that had been building in me for so long—maybe since the first time we met, and after everything, I just... Didn't care anymore.

I gave in to the passion of his kiss, in the way his mouth covered mine hungrily. His lips were warm and soft, even as his short beard scratched against my face. But I loved it. I kissed him back with a passion that matched his, needing more, *more*, so much more. It was a kiss I'd been waiting a lifetime for. A kiss I thought I might die without. It was a kiss to rival the ones in all my books, the way he kissed me—lingering, like he was savoring every moment.

"Hunter..." I moaned, threading my fingers through his hair as I looked up into his eyes.

His lips left mine to nibble at my earlobe as I let out another breathy noise. I wasn't sure I could keep them in anymore.

"Do you want me to fuck you right here in this garden, my little fighter? Want me to take you out in the open, where anyone could see us?"

I nodded, the heat rippling along my skin at his words. I'd never done anything like this before. Never outside, and definitely not in public. But why was I so turned on just from his rasp against my skin? His lips continued to trail down my skin, like he needed to memorize my body with his touch alone.

But I was burning with need, with desire, and I couldn't take another moment without knowing what he felt like inside of me. I'd seen him naked, and now I wanted all of him. To mark me, to let the world know I was his, and he was mine. Even if just for tonight. Even if just for now.

I brought his face back down to mine, returning his kiss with reckless abandon, a series of kisses that short-circuited my thoughts.

"Make me yours," I whispered against his skin, before I pushed at his shoulder to flip us, guiding him down onto his back. I knew I couldn't make him do anything he didn't want to—not with his frame being so much bigger than mine, those powerful arms that could overpower me but never would.

He was like a gentle giant. My gentle giant. It never failed to amuse me how he could go from being so flirty and charismatic to this person who was so caring and considerate of others. And when he talked to kids, to his patients? He would be the best dad ever. I knew all of that, and all it did was make me want him more. I wanted him to be so much more than a hook-up or a fling—I wanted him to be everything.

As I climbed onto his lap, I hiked up my dress to my hips. We were in the middle of the garden and anyone could have found us, and yet I didn't care. I was too blind with lust to even notice anything else. We'd hidden ourselves behind all the hedges, and the sound of the fountain nearby would drown out any noise, so —what did it matter, anyway?

I pressed another kiss to his jawbone, and I knew he was just as affected as I was—I could feel his growing desire underneath me, and I couldn't help but rock against him, lost entirely in the moment.

His eyes met mine, and I knew he was seeking permission in his stare, so I just nodded.

"Fuck. I'm such an idiot." He slammed his mouth back against mine. "I'd been trying so hard, Gabrielle," he groaned in between kisses. "Not to touch you. To not kiss you. Not to have you like this, in every fucking way I wanted you, because I didn't want to fuck everything up. But I can't resist anymore." Hunter growled, pushing the straps of my little dress down, freeing my breasts to the air. I wasn't wearing a bra, since my dress had a low back and spaghetti straps that were tied at the top in little bows, and my nipples hardened from the contact of the air against them.

"Good," I agreed, "because I don't want you to. I just want *you*," I breathed out. "So much." I always had. And I desperately needed more of him than that first touch.

I arched my back, letting the dress fall around my waist, my tits fully exposed to the night. He bent his head down, sucking a nipple into his mouth, and I couldn't hold back a moan when he grazed it with his teeth. I'd never experienced the finesse he had with his mouth before. The way he was licking and sucking seemed to ignite a fire deep within me.

He switched his attention to the other breast as his hand moved down, lower and lower, until he was tugging up my dress, his hand dragging through the slit as it came so dangerously close to where I wanted it.

"Please," I begged, as his fingers traced patterns on my inner thighs. "Please touch me."

His fingers found the lace of my panties, that bra set I'd worn earlier just to taunt him, and he tugged them down hard, tearing them off my body. Holy shit.

I was sure I looked like a mess—ripped and torn underwear discarded next to us, dress bunched up around my waist, and his hands up my skirt, but all of that was forgotten when he finally ran a finger up my slit, running it through my arousal.

"Oh," I gasped, shutting my eyes. "Do that again."

"You're so wet, sweetheart. Did you get like this thinking about me fucking you outside?"

He pressed his thumb against my clit, and my back practically arched from the pressure. He kept it there, rubbing it in slow circles as I did my best not to shiver from the pleasure he was giving me.

"Fuck," I rasped, dropping my forehead to let it rest on his shoulder as he slipped a finger inside of me, still continuing that slow pace with his thumb.

He kept going, slipping in a second finger, until I was close to the edge, mumbling his name, and right when I felt my muscles clench, who release was *right there*—he stopped.

"Don't stop," I panted, scrambling for his hand, as if I could move it back to the place where I wanted him and urge him to keep going. To get me off.

But... He looked at me with those damn green eyes, my weakness apparently, and they were so full of lust that I leaned in, kissing him again before moving off his lap, perching on the blanket next to him.

I looked down at his crotch, where his erection painfully pressed against his suit pants.

"Let me—" I started, moving to undo his belt, but Hunter groaned before I even touched him.

"If you touch me..." He shut his eyes. Shook his head. "I want to be inside of you," he murmured.

I nodded, keeping my hands where they were, just watching him as he freed himself from his pants, the length of him escaping free.

My eyes widened at the sight. If I'd thought he was big yesterday, today, erect and fully hard? "I don't think you're going to fit," I squeaked.

He ran a hand over my hair. "You're going to take me so well, sweetheart. I promise."

"If you don't break me first," I muttered, and then gasped as he lowered us back to the ground, his body positioned over mine.

I pinned his erection between us as he kissed me again, and I was so desperate to have him inside of me, I wasn't sure I was even thinking straight anymore.

I rocked against him, eager to have him inside of me, finally, but—

"Shit. Condom? I don't—" I panted. "I don't have one."

"Fuck." His forehead rested against mine. "I have one in my wallet. Back pocket."

I reached back, pressing my hardened nipples against his chest, and found his wallet, pulling it out to grab the condom.

"It's new," he insisted, "I didn't want to assume, but—"

"Thank fucking god," I agreed, still holding the wrapper in my hands, gazing up at him from under my lashes. "Can I... put it on you?"

He nodded, and I opened the wrapper slowly, unable to resist wrapping a hand around his dick, slowly sliding up the shaft, soaking up every groan he made as I touched him. I watched his face as I rolled the condom onto him, and when he was fully sheathed, he rested his forehead against mine.

"I don't think I'm going to last very long... I want you too bad. I've wanted you for so long."

"I know," I sighed. "Me too. Longer than you've known." I cupped his jaw, running my fingers over his beard. "You'll always have round two to make it better, Hunter," I gave him a little wink.

"Fuck round two," he groaned, pinning me back to the ground. "You're coming first."

He positioned himself at my entrance, my hands still on his face as he guided his massive length inside of me, and I gasped when he pushed inside. Just the tip, but it was enough to know how much he was going to stretch me.

But I needed more. Needed him seated fully inside of me, that delicious stretch and pain telling me that this was real, and this was happening, and it wasn't just a dream anymore.

"More," I whimpered. "Please."

"You're so tight, baby. Fuck. Give me a second." He twisted his face with the effort, like he was trying so hard to make this last for me—to make it good for me—but I knew it was going to be, anyway. Because this was *him,* and he did nothing halfway. I'd seen that in the kitchen, in the way he cared for his family and patients, in the way he carried himself through the world.

"Come on, Hunter," I begged. "Fuck me. Please."

There was nothing else in this world except him and I, nestled in this small hidden corner of the garden, and I couldn't help it as I rolled my hips against him, bringing him further inside of me.

I was so close, on the edge of coming from before, and I knew once he actually started, I was going to lose myself as well. I felt too much for him not to.

I repeated the motion again, and he let out another groan before pushing in again—slamming all the way to the hilt. I pulled his mouth down to mine, needing the connection between us, and kissed him again as he started moving in earnest.

I mewled out his name as he left my lips, his mouth trailing down my body before resuming sucking on my breasts, and my eyes shut as he took the other in his hand, massaging it and tweaking a nipple.

"Fuck," I panted. "Hunter—"

"Sweetheart." He murmured, burying his face in my neck as he repeated those shallow movements of his hips. "Gabrielle."

I looked up at him, eyes shining with an emotion I didn't even know how to describe, but all I said was "*I know,*" as he kissed me again.

And when he brought his thumb back to my clit, rubbing it in circles as he thrust inside of me, hitting that spot inside of me that made a see the stars, and I was close, so close—

"Come for me, little fighter. I want to feel you coming around my cock, sweet girl."

I let myself go, tumbling into ecstasy, throwing my head back as my orgasm exploded around me, and I was briefly aware of the way I'd wrapped my arms around his neck, tugging him back down onto me as the waves of pleasure rolled through me.

I could still feel myself pulsing around him as he stilled inside of me, and I brushed the curls off of his sweaty forehead as he lost himself inside of me, finding his own climax, one that we'd been too busy chasing to care about anything else around us.

When he pulled out of me, I already missed the feeling of having him inside of me, but it was more than that. Was he going to regret this? Regret *me?* We'd just fucked in the garden, and I knew it was serious for me, but...

I looked down at my silky orange dress, wrinkled from the way we'd bunched it around my waist, and started tugging the straps back up onto my shoulders.

"Gabbi," he muttered as he pulled his pants back up, redoing his belt. I wasn't sure where he'd disposed of the condom, but I supposed it didn't really matter.

I turned away from him, pulling the fabric of my skirt back down over my knees, rubbing my hands at the sudden chill I felt.

"Are you okay?" He said, wrapping his arms around my waist from behind. "What's wrong? I didn't hurt you, did I?"

I shook my head; the words getting caught in my throat. Finally, I turned my head, seeing all the worry and concern in his eyes, and I broke. "I'm just worried you're going to regret this. Regret... us. Was this a mistake?"

He intertwined our fingers, bringing my hand up to his mouth to kiss my knuckles. "I believe you promised me a round two, sweetheart. Besides..." He reached his other hand up to my hair, brushing it behind my ear. "I could never regret you."

I gave him a little nod, but I still turned my head back to the rest of the garden, looking back to where our friends still celebrated the rehearsal dinner inside.

"Should we get back?" I asked, smoothing over my hair, hoping it didn't look like I'd just had a romp in the gardens with the best man.

Sure, I *had,* but that didn't mean I wanted the rest of them to know about it. I kind of liked that Hunter was still this little secret of mine. Sure, the girls knew we'd been spending time together, but I hadn't told them I was pretty sure I was falling for him. That these feelings went deeper than I could even explain.

And after we'd just slept together... I didn't know how much longer I could take it before I fell completely. I was in serious trouble, and I couldn't even help it. Because I couldn't stop. Not now that I knew how good we were together. Not when I saw how much potential this had to be something *good*.

CHAPTER 21
Hunter

Extending a hand towards Gabbi, I helped her up, but when she stumbled into me, I couldn't help myself.

"Woah there, sweetheart." I hoisted her up, settling her into my arms so I could carry her. My right arm was under her legs and my left under her chest, cradling her as if she was the most precious thing to me.

"They're going to know what we did," she muttered, still trying to smooth down her hair.

"No, they won't," I whispered back, setting her back down on her feet as we got back to the path.

"What else are they going to think when we disappeared for an hour and then came back like this?"

I frowned at her. "Like what, sweetheart? You still look beautiful." I reached out and plucked a stray blade of glass from her hair.

"Oh my god. I can't go back in there. I can't face them like this."

I chuckled. "They love you. Besides, did you see the amount of wine everyone was drinking? No one's going to be paying attention to your hair."

"Shut up," she groaned. "Can't you get it all out? Where did this all even come from, anyway? We were on a blanket." She did a double take at my arms. "You didn't grab the blanket?" Gabrielle frowned.

"I'll go back for it later," I whispered. "Let's go get you cleaned up."

She sighed, still talking under her breath. "This is so embarrassing. And I don't even have any underwear on now."

I did my best not to think about how she was completely bare underneath her dress, that I'd torn off those green lace panties that she'd swished her ass in earlier. But it was worth it. Fuck, it was worth it.

I couldn't believe I'd been inside of her just a few minutes before, and now we were walking back to the Château like nothing had happened. But something had. And it irreversibly changed us. At least, I knew I was. There was no way I could bring myself to regret it. Maybe the *where*, though I had to admit, losing myself in her body by only the moonlight was more appealing than I'd ever thought possible.

"What are you thinking about?" She murmured, tugging at my fingers before interlacing our hands.

"You."

"Oh." She flushed red.

"Your body under the moonlight," I added. "The way I didn't get to taste you, and that was a mistake."

Gabbi punched my shoulder, as if she was pretending to be rough, but she couldn't hurt me. God, she was so much smaller than I was, but I loved our height difference, her five foot six to my six foot four. I loved the way she had to stand on her tiptoes to get closer to me, and how I could pick her up so effortlessly.

I kept my hand in hers till we slipped inside the back door, towards the bathroom, when she dropped them, as if she was worried about someone else seeing. I helped her pick the rest of the grass out of her hair, and then she brushed off my suit jacket, and when we both looked like we were back in proper shape, I spun her around to look at herself in the mirror.

"You look so gorgeous freshly fucked, my girl." Her eyes met mine in the reflection, and I followed the movement as she swallowed. "Be a good girl, and I'll fuck you again when we get back to the room. Maybe I'll even put my mouth on you this time," I whispered into her ear, before I dropped my hands from her.

Our eyes stayed connected the whole time I backed away from her, and I could see the renewed lust that lit inside them at my promise. I slipped outside the door, going to rejoin the party, and I knew that neither one of us was going to last the rest of the night before we could have our hands on each other again.

More than anything, I was pretty sure I'd just created a monster, only I didn't know who's it was—hers, or mine—or both of us.

Either way, watching her talking to the other guys for the next few hours drove me crazy. She was laughing, and all I wanted was to be the one by her side, to be the one she was laughing at.

I wanted my cum to be dripping down her thighs, so she knew who she belonged to. Fuck. I shut my eyes. What was wrong with me?

Benjamin came and found me at the bar, drinking another whiskey, and raised an eyebrow. "Where'd you disappear to earlier?"

I shook my head. "Nowhere."

He looked at me, and then looked over at Gabbi, who was smiling at Emily as they drank from their wineglasses, and I looked away. "Sure."

I cleared my throat. "You ready for tomorrow?" I looked over at Angelina, who was wearing a stunning white dress that hugged her hips and stopped right above her knees.

He nodded at my side, and I knew he was looking at her too. "Honestly... I've never been more ready. I can't wait for the rest of our lives."

"It's good to see you so happy, Ben."

"Maybe you should try it," he smirked.

"Marrying someone?"

He shook his head. "No. Just being happy."

I frowned, but maybe he was right. I might have been holding myself back from happiness for too long. But maybe I could find it again with her.

Maybe I already had.

∽

I SAT her on the bed, loosening my tie as I watched her, those eyes of hers roaming over my body, filled with desire. I could feel my blood pumping just looking at her, already wanting her again. I couldn't believe that we'd lasted so long at the party, but when I'd caught Gabbi yawning, I'd all but scooped her up, gotten us a cab back to the hotel, and brought her up to our room.

"Come here," I said, and she turned to reveal her back to me, moving her hair away from the zipper so I could unzip her dress and get it off of her. "Let's clean you up, sweetheart." We'd gotten all the grass out of her hair earlier, but she still had a lot of pins in her hair keeping her up, and there was nothing I wanted more than to get her into bed, but I wanted to take care of her first.

I unzipped her and then started pulling the pins out of her hair, letting the rest of the curls fall down. I ran my fingers up her scalp, massaging it lightly.

"Mhm," she said, stepping out of her dress as it fell to the floor, landing in a puddle of orange against the carpet, deliciously bare in front of me. She hadn't bothered to put her panties back on after we'd left the garden, and I groaned when she reached out, cupping me through my pants, half-hard again already. It'd been hard enough watching her after we'd come back, but now…

I guided her into the bathroom, unbuttoning my shirt with one hand as we went, turning on the shower water before she took over undressing me. She shoved my shirt off my shoulders before her hands moved down to my belt, unbuckling it before pushing the button out of the hole and the whole garment down my legs.

"Impatient, are you, little fighter?"

"Shut up," she mumbled, and I finished by forcing the boxers down my legs, eager to pull her into the shower with me.

"Let's get this hairspray out of your hair first," I said, grabbing her shampoo bottle from the ledge and squeezing a bit into my hands.

She tilted her head back so I could lather it up, eyes closed as I worked the product in. Gabrielle moaned from my touch, and I tried not to let it affect me. I wasn't going to fuck her in the shower, not yet, no matter how much I wanted that. This was still new, so new, and I had so many plans for us. After her hair was appropriately clean, I let the shower water run through her hair, rinsing it all out before repeating the process with her conditioner.

After I'd gotten her hair clean, she turned to me. "I want to do you," she murmured, taking mine from the ledge. I bent down a little so she could have easier access as she massaged the product into my hair.

I shut off the shower after mine was clean, and Gabbi looked up at me with her amber eyes I was so obsessed with as I wrapped her in a fluffy towel.

"I need to take my makeup off," she mumbled, and I nodded as I wrapped a towel around myself, watching her take her makeup off with a cloth.

Bare-faced and wet hair dripping down her back, I thought she'd never looked more beautiful.

"What?" she asked me, raising an eyebrow as she dried her face with a towel.

"You're stunning."

"You're just saying that," she said, looking away.

I wrapped an arm around her middle, bringing our bodies flush together. "I would never lie to you, Gabrielle."

She turned around, wrapping her arms around my neck. "Well, I hope not, since you promised me you'd use your mouth..."

I smirked, hoisting her into my arms. "You'd like that, wouldn't you, my fighter girl?"

She nodded. "Please."

"Well, since you asked so nicely..." I carried her over the bed before dropping her down on top of it, the towel falling open around her.

She gave a little shriek as I pulled her closer to me, running my finger over her slit.

"You're so fucking wet for me, aren't you? Naughty girl."

She nodded, looking down at me as I wrenched her thighs apart.

"Only for you, Hunter," she said, and somehow, my name on her lips like that—so sweet, caring—was my downfall.

I bent my head down, licking a line up her entrance, and she squirmed against my tongue. I put a hand on her stomach to pin her in place, and then I took my time tasting her, thrusting my tongue into her sweet cunt over and over until she was crying for more, needing pressure and *more, please, Hunter*—

All I could do was comply. I moved from her pussy to her clit, sucking it into my mouth, giving it the attention it deserved as I slid a finger inside her, working her with one, then two fingers, and each moan she illicit was like a reward, like a trophy that only I could earn, like I was the only one who could ever make her like this. Sure, there'd been others, but fuck if I'd ever let anyone else touch her ever again.

I didn't know where the possessive thoughts came from, but she was mine, and it made me go red with rage when I thought about someone else having their tongue on her.

"Hunter," she cried. "I'm so close. Just a little more—"

I gave it to her, as much as she could take, switching to fucking her with my tongue as my thumb rubbed her clit, and when she came on my mouth, I lapped up every drop before I sat back up on my heels, staring down at her.

She was still breathing heavily, her breasts moving with the motion as her wet hair spread out over the pillow. How had this beautiful specimen of a human decided she wanted me? I was a fool for her, and I didn't deserve her.

I didn't, but I couldn't survive without her.

"Come here," she said, holding out her hands like she wanted me inside of them, and I slid into her arms, my hips nestled between her thighs. I kissed her like that, trying to ignore how hard I was as I intertwined our tongues, taking her mouth roughly. I couldn't get enough of her.

"Can you taste yourself on my lips, my sweet girl?"

She nodded and groaned as I rubbed against her entrance. "I need you inside of me, Hunter. Please."

"Of course, sweetheart."

I pulled a condom out of the nightstand and rolled it on. I'd never been with anyone without one, but I was pretty sure I'd have done anything she asked, even that. But not this time.

I was harder than I'd ever been, and I knew she was waiting for me to slide inside of her, but—I laid on my back, pulling her onto my lap.

"I want you on top this time, baby. Want to watch your tits bounce as I fuck you."

I ran a finger over her freckled nose as she nodded, but I could see all the thoughts swirling in her pretty little head as she looked down at me.

"Fuck, Hunter," she groaned as she wrapped her hand around my cock, lining me up with her entrance. She got the tip inside, and then wiggled down another few inches, as if she was going to take me just like that, little by little, as I adjusted to the feeling of being buried inside her. "You feel so good inside of me."

"Jesus, Gabbi. You're killing me," I said as she seated herself on me, taking all of me in, and placed her hands on my chest.

"You're s-so big," she moaned as she moved her hips, rocking against me, and I couldn't help myself as I wrapped my hands around her waist, helping guide her as she rode me. Each time her clit ground against me, I could feel the way her body shuddered from the movement.

"Look at you, sweetheart, how pretty you look while riding my cock."

She shut her eyes as she moved up and down on my dick, my hands helping guide her as she pulled off of me almost to the tip before slamming back down.

"I'm so close," I whispered, but damn if I wouldn't make her come again with me.

I moved a hand down to her clit, applying pressure the way I knew she liked, and she cried out.

"Hunter, I-I can't."

Her nails dug into my chest, and I kept up the pace as she lost herself in the rhythm, in the movements as she chased her orgasm.

"Shhh, you can. Come for me again, Elle. You're taking me so good." I gave her the encouraging words I knew she needed as she cried out, as I gave her the pressure I knew she craved. "Good girl."

The way she was riding me, her perky tits so close to my face as I watched her get herself off? It was too much. I shut my eyes, trying to hold myself back until I felt her pulse around me, like she was squeezing me, and then I let go, finding my release.

∽

"Well, what did you think about round two?" I said, smoothing out her hair as I gave her a little smirk.

She smiled up at me, well fucked and sated. I liked that look on my girl's face. I was pretty sure I'd do anything to keep it there. We'd moved to the other bed after we'd finished and I'd gotten rid of the condom, cuddling into each other as if neither one of us wanted to lose the contact.

"Mmm," she hummed, burying her head into my chest. "But I have some notes for round three."

"Round three, eh?" I couldn't help my amused grin. "You already wanting me again?"

"Always." She didn't even blink as she looked into my eyes. "I always want you, Hunter."

I cupped her cheek before brushing my fingers along her jaw, but I couldn't take this anymore. How long had I been lying to myself? I wanted her—wanted everything with her.

"You can have me," I promised. "You have me." I kissed the top of her head, wondering if it was this good with her... how had I wasted time with anyone else?

And why would I want to be with anyone else ever again?

CHAPTER 22
Gabrielle

I woke up nestled into a sturdy pair of arms, vividly aware of the hardness nestled against my ass. Turning around, I stared up at his face, admiring his sculpted jaw. I brushed my fingers against it, and he pulled me tighter against him, my nipples pressing up against his, the scrape almost instantly making me wet again. I held back the moan, and he chuckled as his eyes opened.

"Good morning, sweetheart." he said, before tilting his head towards mine and taking my lips in a soft kiss.

I pulled back. "I should go brush my teeth, I probably have morning breath—"

"No way," he said, his enormous hands wrapping around my waist. Sometimes it felt like he could contain all of me in those hands of his. When he'd cupped my breasts last night, I'd almost come just from the sight of him worshipping them so reverently, with so much care. God, if he could get me off that easily, it was no wonder there was a delicious ache between my legs.

I moaned as our skin rubbed against each other again, and Hunter chuckled, slipping his hands between my legs.

"Already wet for me again, hm?"

"Hunter," I whimpered as he brushed his fingers against my

entrance, my clit. I was coming alive from his touch, burning inside out from that little of contact.

"Does my little fighter need to come, hm?"

I nodded. "Yes, yes, please,"

"Good girl," he purred, "begging for what you want."

Hunter reached over into the nightstand, pulling out a foil square, and I was instantly glad we'd had more. Last night in the garden had been a close call, but I was so desperate that I probably would have let him do me bare if he hadn't had it. I was on birth control, anyway, and I knew I was safe with him, but still—that felt like some big scary step. I'd never not used condoms with any of the guys I'd been with, but with him...

He rolled the condom down his cock as I watched, licking my lips as he squeezed the tip.

My mouth was watering, and I think my brain short-circuited when he flipped me over, burying my head in the pillows as he palmed my backside. I could feel his dick pressed against my ass as he rubbed against me, so hard and ready for me, and I moaned into the pillows.

"I want to feel you like this," he whispered into my ear, voice rough. "Want to feel your tight pussy squeezing my dick as you take me from behind, my fighter girl, and make you come on my cock. Do you want that?"

"*Yes,*" I agreed, arching my back as I thrust my hips farther into the air, when he guided himself into me. My fingers clutched the sheets as he slid inside, inch by inch, filling me up completely. He stilled once I was taking all of him inside of me, and closing my eyes as I gave into the way he was stretching me, filling me up. The fullness that I'd never experienced before him.

"Fuck. You feel so good." His hands reached up, cupping my breasts, and I rocked my hips back against him. He pulled back before thrusting inside again, pushing me up on the bed, but I needed more pressure. Hunter tweaked my nipples, and I let out another cry.

"Hunter, more, *please*," I begged. I was already so close, just a little more—

A knock came from the door. "Gabrielle?" Charlotte's voice called out.

"Oh, shit," I whispered under my breath as Hunter froze, stilling inside of me.

I looked over my shoulder at him, his eyes strained as he looked towards the door.

"Hunter..." I murmured, finally catching his eye as he looked down to the place where our bodies connected, and he winced.

"Dammit." He shut his eyes as he slid out of me, and I already knew that I was going to ache all day. I could already feel how sore I was from yesterday.

I whimpered at the loss of contact.

Hunter shook his head before I could get out of the bed, wrapping his hand over my mouth.

"Don't," he whispered.

She knocked again, but then I finally heard the footsteps walking away from the door as she gave up.

"Fuck," I groaned, collapsing against the bed. "How could I be so stupid? I'm an *idiot*."

"Baby, you're neither of those things." He caressed the side of my face, running a finger over my ear.

I brought my knees up to my chest, not even caring that I was still naked and in bed with him.

What was I even doing? Sleeping with him last night had been... crazy. Passion and lust were on overdrive, and we were both tipsy. But this morning?

What excuse did I have for us having morning sex? That the first thing I'd thought when I woke up with him pressed against me was that I wanted to have him inside me again?

Like I needed to get my fill of Hunter Sullivan before he realized what a colossally stupid idea sleeping with me was again.

"Gabrielle. Your brain is going a million miles a minute." He grit his teeth. "Talk to me."

I shook my head. What could I say? "I just... This was a mistake. We should just... pretend it never happened and move on."

"A mistake?" He growled, pinning me against the bed with his arms. "Like fuck, it was a mistake. Why are you pulling away from me now?"

"You mean like you do every time?" I groaned in frustration. "You can *fuck me*, but you don't want me. That's what this is?"

"I never said that." He shook his head. "I told you—you have me. What are you so scared of, Elle?"

That name again. I shut my eyes. Did he know what it did to me when he treated me like this? I wasn't sure if all of his words from yesterday had been sweet nothings in the spur of the moment. How could I believe that I actually had him? That this was real?

He smoothed his hand over my hair. "But maybe... we should keep this to ourselves for now."

"A secret?"

He nodded. "Let's get through the wedding, and once we get home—then we can figure it all out. But why complicate this by getting all of our friends involved?"

"I... I don't want to be your dirty little secret, Hunter. You can't just fuck me and then pretend like it didn't happen."

"You think I want that, Gabrielle?" His voice was low, almost a growl. "You think I don't want to tell everyone that you're mine?"

I jerked away. "I feel like I have whiplash with you. One second, you're telling me you like me. And the next, it's like you've withdrawn back to that cold place again, repeatedly. I've never asked for more than you're able to give, but somehow it's still too much. I can't... I can't do this if all I am to you is some hookup. That's not who *I* am. And I know you're not a relationship guy, but I'm not trying to change you, okay?"

Eyes squeezed shut, I shook my head. I couldn't look at him if he was going to do this again. If he was going to break my heart.

"I don't know if... We can be *together*, Gabrielle. I can't... I can't hurt you. And you'll end up getting hurt."

"Why? Why are you so sure that this—us—that we're doomed for failure? I'm with you, here and now, because I choose to be. Hunter, I want this. I want us. Don't you have trust in *us*? I can see it. I can see how good we could be." My eyes prickled with more tears, and I hated him for making me cry. "Why can't you?" I whispered.

He crossed his arms over his bare chest, over the dabbling of chest hair I'd ran my fingers through last night. I liked that he wasn't bare or waxed. I liked every bit of him, but I couldn't take his softness if it was going to end the same way it always had.

One step forward, three steps back. I moved away from him and pulled the sheets back, not even caring that I wasn't wearing anything as I got out of his bed and back into mine. It was cold, and I didn't have his arms to hold me close, but fuck him. I didn't need this.

I shut my eyes as I sat on the edge of the bed, wishing everything was different. Wishing he wanted me, and fuck the consequences. The tears started dripping from my eyes before I could stop them, and a set of warm arms wrapped around me. When I looked up, his eyes were shining into mine.

"I *do* want to be with you," he whispered.

"What was that?" I'd heard him the first time, but I wanted to hear him say it again.

He swallowed roughly. "I want to be with you. I'm just terrified, sweetheart. That I'll screw everything up, and that I'll lose my best friend, and the only girl I've ever cared about."

"I am?"

He nodded against my shoulder, resting his head against my skin. "I'm going to keep fucking things up, because I don't know how to control myself around you. I never have. But if you can give me a second chance—"

I snorted. "Second?" I wasn't sure what number we were on

anymore, but I knew that I'd give him another try. I probably always would.

"Third?" He raised an eyebrow and then shook his head. "I promise I'll do my best not to let you down. But you'll have to be patient with me. I haven't... God, the last time I did this was in college."

"This?" I raised an eyebrow.

"Been in a relationship. I just..." He smoothed a hand over his face.

"Hunter." I cupped both of his cheeks with my hands, forcing him to look at me. "We don't... Let's take this slow. We can see how things are at the end of the trip, and if things haven't changed, we can call it off, okay?"

He nodded and leaned forward, kissing me gently.

"Okay," I finally agreed. "We'll be a secret. Get through the wedding, and then we can figure it out."

I looked at my phone, which had 15 unread text messages from the girls, and groaned. "Unfortunately, we don't have time to finish what we started earlier. I gotta get down to the girls." I winced.

He smoothed a hair back on my head. "It's fine. Go be with your girls, sweetheart. We'll finish this later." He leaned in close to my ear. "It's not like we don't have two weeks together after this."

My cheeks flushed, and I gave off a little squeak as I quickly got up, got my stuff together, and then jumped in the shower.

Completely by myself, because I was pretty sure if this morning was any evidence, we couldn't keep our hands off of each other. Even when we were stuck in this stupid cycle, I still wanted him.

More than I'd ever wanted anyone before. And maybe that was what scared me the most.

AFTER I'D RUSHED downstairs and to where all the girls were meeting with my bag in hand, we took a limo to the venue and promptly rushed into the bridal suite to get our hair and makeup done for the day. Emotions were high, but we were all so excited, even Emily, who was practically bouncing on the balls of her feet over the fact that she was about to have a sister. "Finally!" She'd added.

It took a few hours, but after our hair was perfectly in place and our makeup finished—I was pretty sure the glitter would never come off my eyelids, and don't get me started on the fake eyelashes—I had to admit we looked absolutely perfect.

Our champagne-colored bridesmaid dresses, each a little different, paired perfectly with Angelina's elegant dress, which we'd had to button her into, a hundred tiny pearls up her spine.

"Benjamin's going to go crazy trying to get that off of you tonight, isn't he?"

"Oh, I'm counting on it," she grinned. "And I'm so not taking it easy on him."

The photographer was taking pictures as we finished getting ready, as I helped Ang into her bridal red-bottom heels. We snapped a few more pictures of us as a group, posed and laughing, before the photographer slipped out to go see the guys.

"Everyone ready?" I looked around at our group of girls, my best friends. God, it was crazy that we were *here*, standing in the middle of this gorgeous French villa, getting ready to walk down the aisle for Angelina's wedding. "No cold feet, right?" I asked Ang, who looked absolutely perfect in her dress.

She laughed. "Absolutely not. I mean, he drives me crazy, and I can't believe we're *actually* doing this so soon, but I kind of can't wait to be his wife." She nudged me on the shoulder. "You'll find it one day too."

"Thanks, Ang." I hoped so. I hoped I already had.

I thought of Hunter, the way he'd looked at me last night as he told me I had him, and I really wished it was true.

"Come on, let's go get you married," I grinned, and we all

headed downstairs.

Thankfully, by the time we'd all gotten down there, the guys were already in their places, which just left us and Angelina's dad waiting to go outside. The ceremony was taking place by the beautifully carved stone gazebo, with chairs set up and a white runner covered in flowers down the middle. Literally, this place was picture-perfect. I wasn't sure that I could have picked somewhere better if I had tried.

We proceeded up the aisle—Emily first, then Charlotte, Noelle, and finally, me. Once we were all standing at the front, everyone stood up to watch Angelina walk down the aisle. There was no flower girl, or ring bearer, but I knew almost everyone sitting in the seats—Angelina's family, our friends from college who had flown out, our coworkers. The few I didn't know were Benjamin and Hunter's extended family, or his friends from college.

I wondered what it might be like one day at my wedding. If I'd look out at the sea of faces and recognize everyone smiling back at me. I didn't know what it would be, but I imagined a small, intimate affair. Nothing as extravagant as this wedding, but something still just as special.

Angelina's dad, who I'd only met a few times before, was walking her down the aisle, and her mom was sitting in the front row next to her new husband—a sore subject for Angelina, but at least they were here.

I caught Hunter's eye as Angelina first came out, down the stairs of the Château on her dad's arm. I'd been trying to see Benjamin's reaction, but Hunter... He wasn't looking at her at all. He wasn't watching Angelina walk down the aisle, or the happiness on his brother's face.

Hunter was looking at me. His stare lit me up from the inside out, the way his lips tilt up into a smile when he caught me looking at him.

I looked away, doing my best from hiding my blush at the way he always made me feel stripped bare in front of him.

CHAPTER 23
Hunter

Gabrielle was beautiful—dazzling, even, in her bridesmaid dress.

I couldn't even look at the bride, at my brother's wife-to-be, because I couldn't take my eyes off of her maid of honor at her back. At the smile she gave me when she noticed my eyes on her.

Angelina gave Gabrielle her bouquet to hold as Benjamin and Angelina clasped hands, and I still stared straight past them.

"I've been told you prepared your own vows?"

They both nodded.

"Angelina, I think I knew from the first moment I saw you that I was going to love you. Sure, it took a little bit of convincing to get you to realize you loved me too—" He paused as Angelina rolled her eyes—"but in the end, I don't regret that moonlight swim with you one bit. I promise to love you, even when you hate me, and cherish you always. I vow that I'll never forget to pick up mocha ice cream when you're feeling sad. I promise that I'll give you a foot-rub any time you get home from work, and that I'll never stop supporting you in your career. I hope that I'll be able to show you, more and more every day, how much I care about you, treasure you, and that you never get tired of the way I want to worship you. I can't wait to move into our house together, and to one day have a little you running around, because I know they'd be the best of us both, but especially you. I promise that we can get a cat. I promise that I'll never stop being your best friend, even when you beat me at every video game we every play together." He took a deep breath. "I love you so much, Angel, and I'm so grateful you agreed to be my wife."

After he finished his turn, Angelina unfolded a little square of paper and read her own vows.

"Benjamin," Angelina said with a small laugh. "If you'd told me three years ago that we were going to be standing here today, getting married, I would have told you that you were crazy." She gave a small smile. "Well, maybe you are a bit crazy, because you're marrying *me*, but still. I never would have opened myself up without you, and for that, I can never stop saying thank you. You showed me that someone could love me, and you've never stopped proving it to me every day how much you love me. I promise to not be such a bitch when you're being nice to me—at least most of the time. I promise to love you even when you're wearing your Batman socks and that I'll be there for you whenever someone is—inevitably—killed off in your comic books again. I vow that I'll always love you, even when I'm pretending to hate you, and there's nothing you can do to get rid of me. Thank you for loving me, Boy Scout."

The rest of the ceremony passed quickly, the "I do's", them exchanging rings, and then we were at the end. Gabrielle had tears in her eyes as she watched her best friend squeeze my brother's hand.

"I now pronounce you husband and wife." The officiant announced. "You may now kiss the bride."

Benjamin swept Angelina into his arms, kissing her passionately as he dipped her. She was almost as tall as him in her heels, but yet he still swept her up with elegance and grace.

I watched them as they walked down the aisle, hand in hand, and then it was our turn.

I held my arm out to Gabrielle, letting her loop her hand through.

"You look gorgeous," I whispered to her.

"Thank you," she said, dipping her head as we walked back towards the Chateau. "You're not looking too shabby yourself, Mr. Best Man."

I smirked. "Thank you, Ms. Maid of Honor."

We'd have to take pictures before happy hour and the reception started, but that wasn't so bad. At least I'd have her around. At least she was smiling at me.

~

AFTER WE ALL finished taking pictures in the gardens, the wedding party was quickly ushered back to the reception area. They'd chosen to have it outside, a far cry from yesterday's dinner in the Château, but the area was now decorated with string lights, and the tables that surrounded the dance floor topped with beautiful flowers and tea light candles.

After they announced Benjamin and Angelina, we were all free to grab drinks and mingle, but it wasn't long until both Gabrielle and I got pulled to the front to give our toasts. My dad went first, talking about Benjamin and how proud he was of him and happy to welcome Angelina into the Sullivan family, and then Angelina's dad said a few words about his daughter growing up. I knew their relationship wasn't what mine was with my parents, but at least he was here, making the effort.

Finally, it was our turns, and Gabrielle stepped away from me. We hadn't been touching, but she'd been standing close enough that I could feel her body heat, and I instantly missed it when it was gone.

"I think everyone here knows me, but if you don't, my name is Gabrielle, and I've been best friends with Angelina since freshman year of college when she walked into our dorm room while I was unpacking all of my favorite books, and she's been stuck with me ever since. Later that day, Charlotte and Noelle walked in the door, and the rest, as they say, is history. Angelina has been my rock for the past nine years, keeping me out of trouble and always encouraging my endless reading habit, even when I definitely should have been studying for our history class freshman year and had no business starting another romance novel. She's the closest thing I have to a sister, and truly, I don't know what I'd do without her.

"But, you know, when I first met Benjamin, I was giving him a tour of our company offices for his first day on the job, and little did *I* know, he'd gotten a glimpse of Angelina and was desperate to find out who she was. And then he did a pretty great job at making her hate him for the next two years, because it was *Benjamin Sullivan this,* and *Benjamin Sullivan that,* but when I found out she was going on a work retreat without me last year —" She looked pointedly at Nicolas, as the crowd gasped. "I know. So I knew I had to do something, because Angelina had been purposefully avoiding meeting this guy for the entire time he worked there, and I was so tired of hearing about their email battle. So I sent him an email with her shoe size like the amazing mastermind I am, and Nicolas and I parent-trapped them into being forced to spend time together."

"Thanks for that," Angelina muttered as Benjamin laughed beside her.

"It ended up working out for the best, though, because they met and tried to deny they were dating for *months* before we almost mucked it all up for them." Gabbi gave a sheepish grin. "Sorry again for that, by the way. But it all worked out for the best, because they fell in love and now we're here in *France,* of all places. And I truly can't imagine a more perfect man for Angelina than Benjamin. He takes care of her, even when she won't let the rest of us, and he knows how to get through to her when she shuts down. Even when she's being stubborn and a little irrational, he's always willing to rub her feet or pick up her favorite coffee ice cream to swoop into the rescue. He's supportive even when we girls steal her away for an entire afternoon to talk about books, and I know I'm not the only one who feels this way when I say he's become our friend as well.

"I've read thousands of romance novels, but truly, Angelina and Benjamin are real soulmates, and I couldn't be happier that they found each other. I already know your lives are going to be filled with so much joy and laughter—and a lot of bickering—and I'm so happy I get to be a part of it. I cannot wait to see where the next few years take you, and I know all of us here can't wait for the ride.

"Here's to Angelina and Benjamin!" She shouted, holding up my glass for the toast. She mesmerized me, like I couldn't stop watching her. My eyes connected with hers, and she gave me a small smile before taking a sip of champagne.

I wondered if it would ever be *us* up there someday, listening to Angelina and Benjamin give similar toasts about us. Maybe I was getting ahead of myself, but I already knew what I was feeling was real, and it was *good*—so good. I was terrified I would fuck everything up, though.

The applause died down, and I stepped up to take the microphone from her.

I cleared my throat. I hadn't prepared a speech as long as hers was, but I knew as long as I spoke from the heart that was what mattered. "Hey, everyone. I'm Hunter, Benjamin's older brother. I'm not *quite* as outgoing as Gabrielle over here, so I probably haven't met everyone yet, but I wanted to thank you all for traveling all the way here to celebrate with us.

"Growing up, Benjamin and I often did the same things. I joined Boy Scouts, so he joined Boy Scouts. Benjamin was on the swim team, because I was on the swim team. I enjoyed reading, so Benjamin picked up books, too. Even if most of them were comics. But I never minded that he wanted to do stuff together, since I was just glad to have a younger brother who was actually cool. We grew apart for a few years after college until we both ended up in Portland, but it wasn't until Benjamin met Angelina that he reached out to me and we actually rekindled our relationship.

"Now, the first time I met Angelina was actually an accident," I chuckled. "They were out to dinner, and I totally crashed the meal, but I knew even then—when Angelina fed him a dumpling—that they were meant for each other. She balances out my brother and keeps him in check when he's acting a little cocky or egotistical, and I couldn't thank her enough for that." I paused as everyone laughed, knowing it was true. "She's already become like a sister to me, and even though I grumbled about it at first, I'm very glad they forced me to attend that Halloween Party after working a double at the hospital, because I got to meet her friends. Especially..." I tried to avoid looking at her, and I didn't know how to end that sentence, so I changed the subject quickly as Gabrielle's cheeks flushed. "Anyway, they adopted me into their friend group—why, I'm not sure, but it's been so obvious to me how much Angelina loves and cares for my brother, and I couldn't be more grateful for that. Plus, hopefully, him getting married will get our mom off my back about me getting married." I looked over at her. "Sorry mom." She gave a dramatic sigh, but then winked at me, and I raised an eyebrow back—like, what's that supposed to mean?

Still, my eyes found Gabbi's.

I cleared my throat again and kept going. "There's something to say about finding the person who you're supposed to be with, when you love someone so much that you'd do anything for them..." Gabbi's eyes stayed locked mine. "And, well, I know Angelina and Benjamin have found that person in each other. Here's to a long and happy life together, you two. Now, if you'd all join me in raising your glasses to Angelina and Benjamin," I said, raising my flute, and everyone cheered for the happy couple again, taking another sip of champagne. "Cheers."

"How'd I do?" I asked her, sliding in next to her at our table.

She nodded, putting her glass back down on the table. "Good. I mean, it definitely doesn't top *mine,* but it was good."

I scooted her chair a few inches closer to mine, hoping no one would notice the sound since we were outside, but needing to feel the closeness to her.

"You were phenomenal, my fighter girl," I whispered, curling one of her strands of hair around my finger.

"Oh." Gabrielle blushed. "Thank you."

I chuckled, and then released her, sliding away as the rest of her friend group sat down with us for dinner: Matthew and Noelle hand in hand, Charlotte and Daniel who seemed like they weren't speaking, plus Zofia and Nicolas.

It was a cozy little table of the eight of us, and we all quickly dissolved into conversation, and I was grateful for the distraction from the girl at my side.

I rested my hand on her knee under the table, and when she didn't make a move to take it off, I left it there, squeezing her thigh lightly.

Her eyes met mine in a silent plea, and I was pretty sure I knew what she was asking without me even having to say anything.

I've got you, I hoped my eyes said.

There was nothing I wouldn't do for this girl. I hope she realized it. I hope she knew how my brother felt about Angelina was how I was feeling about her.

She might have thought it was a mistake, that I was going to pull away again, but I was going to show her exactly how much she meant to me.

I leaned over, watching as she picked at the food on her plate, and dropped my voice into a low whisper. "Make sure you eat up, sweetheart. You're going to need the energy for later." I winked at her, and she flushed red, shoveling another bite into her mouth.

"That's my girl," I said, and she gave me a warning glance as she looked at the rest of her friends, who hadn't even noticed us.

They were all too busy wrapped up in each other, except Charlotte, who was determinately studying her plate, and Daniel, who was rubbing at his temples.

"Later," I promised again.

We had to get through this wedding, and then I intended to show—no, tell her—exactly how I felt.

○

I EXTENDED A HAND, watching the others on the dance floor. Even my sister was out there being twirled around, but Gabrielle and I were still sitting at our table, eating cake.

"Dance with me," I said, surprising even myself.

Normally, I hated dancing, especially at these kinds of events. However, everything was different with Gabrielle, like there were a lot of things I'd realized I didn't hate at all—as long as they were with *her*. That was what made the difference. Maybe I'd realized it a while ago, when we'd danced together before, but this time it felt like *more*. Everything between us felt like more.

"Are you sure?" Her eyes scanned the crowd, as if she was looking for our friend's reactions. "Don't you think they'll notice us? What if they... catch on?"

"We're friends, aren't we?" I thought about the last time she'd called us that, and what I'd said in response.

"Yeah, sure," she muttered under her breath. "Friends."

I smirked, knowing we were both thinking the same thing. That we weren't *just* friends anymore. We were friends who'd seen each other naked.

"Friends can dance at a wedding. The best man and maid of honor can dance at a wedding." I leaned in close. "At least do it for me, so I can see you spin in this gorgeous fucking dress again. And then we can celebrate making it through the wedding."

My girl blushed, and then let out a small giggle. "Well, the night's not quite over yet, so maybe we should wait on that last part until we leave."

I smirked. "I have all sorts of ideas for you once we leave, Gabrielle."

"Oh? And what, exactly, are those ideas?"

I hummed in response, but I didn't bother to wipe the cocky grin off my face. "But I guess you'll have to dance with me to find out."

"You, Hunter Tobias Sullivan, are insufferable." She rolled her eyes.

"Eh. You like it. You like me."

"Yeah, I do." Gabrielle laughed, but I could see the truth in her eyes. I'd been trying to hold back my crush on her for so long —could we have been like this before if I hadn't been so stupid? I hated to think that I'd robbed us of feeling this sooner. "However, I'm now thinking you might even be worse than Benjamin."

"I'll take that as a compliment. On the plus side, you've never hated me like Angelina hated him, so I think I'm still winning."

Gabrielle frowned, but quickly wiped it off her face before I could ask what was wrong. "One dance," she finally said, placing her hand in mine, and I pulled her up and into my arms so I could spin her fully.

A familiar tune came on, a slow dance to a song I was *sure* I knew, and I walked her over to the dance floor, her hand in mine, before I wrapped my other hand around her waist and she placed hers on my shoulder.

"*You're in my arms, and all the world is calm...*"

Gabbi gasped as the song began.

"What?" I asked her. "Is something wrong?"

"No." She shook her head, so much emotion shining through her eyes. "I just *love* this song. It's from Enchanted, and it's—" she stopped talking mid-sentence, and I let myself get lost in her beautiful liquid honey eyes, the ones that had captivated me with since I first met her.

I twirled her along with the music, wondering how a song could be so beautiful and yet so sad.

"*So close to reaching that famous happy end...*"

"God, I want to kiss you," I said against her hair, voice low. "Do you think anyone will notice if I kiss you right here?"

"Hunter!" She blushed, almost pushing me away, but her hands clutched at my lapels as she looked up at me. "Our friends—we're still..."

"So close, so close... and still so far."

The song ended, fading into an upbeat Taylor Swift song, but she pulled away from me.

"Gabrielle," I murmured, but she shook her head.

"I just—I need a minute."

She picked up her skirts, fleeing off the dance floor before I could stop her.

CHAPTER 24
Gabrielle

I needed to escape. Needed to pull away before everything that was boiling under the surface came free. If I stayed in there in his arms one moment longer, I'd ruin everything for us.

Nobody needs to know, I'd said, and yet, when we were dancing, all I could think about was how much I *wanted* him to kiss me out in the open, in front of everyone. Heat flushed with my body at the thought, and I wished that somehow everything had been different.

"Hey." Hunter said, stepping up beside me as I leaned against the railing of the balcony, staring out across the grounds of the Château.

Maybe fleeing up here hadn't been the *best* idea, but I could still see the dance floor, see Benjamin and Angelina laughing as they danced to the music. Of course, he'd follow me. I didn't know why I'd expected anything less. I turned and couldn't help but admire him in his tux, the way it fit his broad shoulders. He'd ditched the coat, even though it was getting a little brisk outside, and had rolled his shirt up, exposing his arm tattoos. My weakness. Somehow, I would always fold around this man.

"Hi." I wrapped my shawl tighter around my arms, grateful for the breeze but feeling exposed in the summer air.

"Everything okay?"

"Yeah, I just needed a break from all the dancing, I think." I lied to him. Before I asked him to kiss me like I knew we both wanted, in front of everyone, I needed to breathe.

I wanted that more than anything, but what were we doing?

"You sure?" His hand slid to the back of my neck, cupping it. When my eyes moved up to meet his, I saw the genuine concern and care written all over his face.

I hated what he was doing to me, making me feel these things, because how was this going to work? This was casual, and a secret, and how long could we stay in this bubble, anyway?

This *couldn't* work long term, and yet what was I doing? Crushing on this man like I was a fucking teenager, dreaming of a future that would never be.

I nodded.

"Have I told you how gorgeous you look tonight?" He said, moving to kiss my bare shoulder. He had, but I didn't care. I'd let him tell me a hundred times if he wanted to.

"Hunter…" I said, low, pleading. "Someone might see us."

"I don't care," he shook his head. "I told you—I think if I don't kiss you, I'll die."

"But…"

"It's just you and me out here, my little fighter."

"Just you and me…" I breathed. It was true—no one else had come up here, and that meant we were gloriously alone. And I wanted it too—his lips on mine. The connection that made everything feel right, in a way nothing else ever had.

"Yeah."

"So, what are you waiting for?" I whispered, and there was a flash of amusement on his face before he leaned down, and all I knew was I was glad the railing was at my back, because I'm pretty sure I would have swooned from the force of his kiss.

Was that even possible?

Sure, we'd had sex the other night. More than just the once. And this morning, I'd been on my hands and knees for him. And it had been incredible.

But this kiss? Holy hell. He dipped me down, one hand at my back as I opened my mouth for him. Something about the rush of knowing we could get caught made it even hotter.

I was pretty sure every single one we shared kept getting better and better. And I wanted them all. I wanted so much more from him than he could give me. And that was the problem, wasn't it?

Why did I even agree to keep this a secret from everyone? Maybe I didn't care anymore if someone found us like this. If everyone knew how completely I'd fallen for Hunter Sullivan. What did it even matter anymore?

I wrapped my arms around his neck, not wanting to break the connection between us as his tongue swept into my mouth, his hands cradling my jaw as if I was something special, something to be protected.

"Oh," someone squeaked, and the noise brought us jerking apart. I hadn't even heard anyone coming up the stairs, because I was so focused on Hunter. "Well, I have to say, I definitely didn't expect to find you two out here."

Oh. Fuck.

"It's not what it looks like, Emily," he said, stepping away from me.

I turned away, hiding the embarrassed expression on my face at us getting caught by his little sister.

"Sorry, I'll just... I wanted to let you know Angelina was looking for you, Gabrielle."

"Is something wrong?"

"I don't think so."

I tilted my head. It wasn't like I was the only one who could help her, or that we didn't have other friends if she needed something, so why was it the one moment I'd tried to take for myself was when she needed me? I shut my eyes, exhaling deeply.

"I'll see you both back out there," Emily said, giving us a little head nod before she headed back down the stairs, her sleeves swishing in the wind.

"I'm gonna go talk to her. Fuck," Hunter said, biting the inside of his cheek. "I'll make sure she won't spill about us to anyone else."

"Because it would be so bad if they knew?" I grit out through my teeth, not sure why I was being defensive so suddenly. "Don't worry. It's not like people would believe that you and I are together for *real*." Because he would never pick me when it came down to it, would he? From the times he'd pushed me away, I should have known that. I'd been head over heels for him ever since we'd met, but maybe I was nothing more than his brother's wife's best friend. I would pick him a thousand times over, but I wasn't enough—would I ever be enough?

"Right." Hunter clenched his jaw.

I stared at him. "What?"

"You're just..." He shook his head, like he didn't have enough words to tell me what he was thinking. "You don't even understand."

"So make me understand. Talk to me." He said nothing as I crossed my arms over my chest. "I'll see you later," I said. "I have to go find Ang."

"Gabrielle—"

"Just go. Talk to your sister. It's fine."

He sighed, but went back inside to find Emily, and I slumped against a pole for good measure.

But it wasn't fine. Nothing was fine. And I felt like, somehow, everything was about to be over before it ever really started.

∼

WHY WAS I so frustrated with him? What was wrong with me to even have said that? Maybe I was pulling away before anything had even begun. *Fuck*.

I found Angelina lingering on the side of the dance floor. "You needed me?"

"Oh, thank god." Angelina wrapped her arms around me in a hug—which, I had to admit, was a little uncharacteristic of my best friend, who hardly ever hugged. "I need you to help me go to the bathroom," she whispered. "I can't get this thing off on my own." She was a little buzzed, which I figured was a rite of passage on your wedding day.

I groaned. "I think this is more than a two person operation, Ang. Besides, why can't your husband help you?"

She looked a little sheepish. "I think," she whispered, "if we go in there, we won't come out. For a while."

"Angelina!" I slapped a hand over my face, trying not to laugh.

"*Gabbi*," she pleaded, drawing out the end of my name as she gave me her best pouty face, those blue eyes begging me. "*Please.*"

I sighed. "Okay. Let's go get you to the bathroom, your highness."

Angelina giggled. "Benjamin calls me Princess. Do you know why he calls me Princess?" I shook my head. She'd never really shared the origins of hers and Benjamin's nicknames for each other—he called her Princess, and she called him Boy Scout. I could guess, but that was all I'd ever done. "It's because he thinks I'm dramatic. But it's okay because he *likes it*."

I laughed. "Is that what he told you?"

My best friend furrowed her brow, playing with the flower we'd woven into her hair above her veil. "No. But I'm pretty sure that's it."

I waved her off. "I think you're a little drunk, hm?"

She giggled, a sound that Angelina hardly ever made. I should know—I'd been her best friend for the last nine years.

I found Charlotte, and together we guided Angelina to the bathroom, scooping up her dress and helping her sit on the toilet. Sure, it wasn't anything we hadn't experienced before as friends, but it was still not something I thought I'd be doing on her wedding day.

Angelina sighed after she finished as we helped her right herself. "Thank you. I needed that. Don't let me drink any more champagne." She groaned. "It's too good."

"We should get you a glass of water, babe," I muttered, guiding her back to the wedding, delivering her to Benjamin's arms before I went to get her a glass.

"You okay?" Charlotte finally asked, sliding back in next to me as I filled a glass with ice water.

"Why?" I frowned. "Did I say something?"

"Gabs. I've known you since we were eighteen. You're telling me you're honestly not upset at all?"

I raised a shoulder into a shrug. I couldn't tell her about Hunter, but... I wanted to. So badly.

"I think I fucked up, Char."

She shrugged a shoulder. "Want to talk about it?"

"Yes." I groaned. "But I can't."

My eyes trailed over to Hunter, who was talking to Emily, and I cursed myself under my breath. It had always been like this. I'd never been able to stop my eyes from seeking him out.

As if she could read my mind, Charlotte asked, "Is this about Hunter?"

"No." I winced. "Sort of. Maybe." I looked down at the glass of water for Angelina, and then back at her. "I just..."

"You're seeing him?"

I bit my lip. "You could say that."

Her eyes widened. *"Ohmygod.* Did you sleep with him?"

"Charlotte! Shh!" I looked around, but it didn't look like anyone had heard us. "I don't want anyone to know yet. It just happened." More than once, but she didn't need to know that. Or how he had been buried deep inside of me when she'd knocked on my door this morning.

She pouted. "Everyone's got a man except me. I'm still holding on to my v-card, for goodness sakes, and Angelina's married, Noelle's practically engaged, and now you're dating, too?"

I frowned. "Well... We're not exactly dating yet." I winced, running my fingers through my perfectly styled curls even though I knew I was messing some of them up. "It's... complicated."

"Well... *un*complicate it." Charlotte said it like it was so simple, so easy.

But it wasn't, was it?

"I can't. Benjamin doesn't want us together, and Hunter doesn't want to ruin the relationship with his brother. Especially not during the wedding."

"But what do you think Angelina would think?" She squeezed my wrist. "I think she'd be happy for you. Better than that, she'd probably be ecstatic if you ended up as sister's in law. Think about it! Married to brothers." She sighed dreamily.

I waved my hands. "Don't get ahead of yourself there, Char. No one said anything about *marriage*."

Certainly not me. Had I thought about it? Sure. Was I going to say that to Hunter, the man who I knew hadn't had a serious relationship in years? No. I was pretty sure that would freak him out. If he wasn't sure he could be in a relationship when we got back to Portland, I'd respect that.

And having him for now... it would be enough. Even if I couldn't tell anyone, even if I wanted him for life. At least I'd be able to hold on to the memories.

I looped my arm through hers. "Where's that man of yours, anyway?" I looked around the dance floor, looking for Daniel.

Charlotte blushed. "He's not my man. He's just..." Her eyes seemed to find his before mine did. "He's my best friend."

"*And*?"

"And that's that. A fairytale is just that, Gabbi. A fairytale. It's never going to happen between us."

"Sure, whatever you need to tell yourself."

She frowned. "If you're convincing yourself that this thing with you and Hunter is casual, maybe that's what *you're* telling yourself, too."

Shit. Was she right? I looked down, realizing I was still holding the glass for Angelina. "Shit. Where'd she go?"

Charlotte shrugged. "Maybe Benjamin kidnapped her and took her to the gardens? They're really beautiful, aren't they?"

My mind flashed back to yesterday, and the heat rose to my cheeks. "Yeah. Yeah, they are."

I couldn't help but think about last night—about all the things he'd said to me. I was doing a really great job of lying to myself, wasn't I? But I had to protect my heart. Because if I let Hunter have it completely, I wasn't sure where that would leave me.

CHAPTER 25
Hunter

My irritation with the situation was coursing through my veins. I ran off after my sister, trying to figure out why I was irritated with Gabbi and I's conversation. *It's not like people would believe that you and I are together for real?* What was that supposed to mean?

If it was going to be anyone, it was going to be her. I wanted her to be mine.

But how could I tell her that, when I still wasn't even sure if I could commit to that long term? Sure, there was here and now, and I was good at that. I wanted to spend every waking moment we had in Europe together, after all. But when we got home? What would happen then?

And if we told everyone about us, only to discover that it wouldn't work out, I wouldn't be able to stand everyone's pitiful glances when they saw me. And Gabbi had her friends to stand by her side. I had Benjamin, sure, but I also knew that I'd disappear out of all of their lives if it meant Gabbi continuing to be happy at her friends' sides. I wouldn't jeopardize that by sticking around, even if it killed me.

But I wanted her to be that person. I did.

I grabbed Emily's wrist as I finally caught up with her near the dessert table.

"Please, Em. Don't tell anyone." I said, my voice low.

"So you and Gabrielle... You're really together?"

I cleared my throat. "Kind of?"

"I can't believe you didn't tell me! I'm your *sister*!"

"*We* haven't even really figured out what we are yet. And if Benjamin knew—" He'd be so damn pissed at me. Especially when he'd clearly told me to stay away from her. But for some reason, I couldn't. I'd been trying for months, maybe even since that fateful Halloween party, but I always felt like her presence entranced me. Somehow, being around her felt right. "Let's just say I'm trying not to ruin the wedding, okay?"

She shook her head. "First Benjamin vehemently denied he was in any sort of relationship with Angelina—see how well that worked out, by the way—and now you're in some sort of secret tryst with her best friend? Smart, Hunt."

"Don't say it like that," I frowned. "It's not like that."

"So you're not sleeping together?"

I shook my head, but I couldn't exactly deny it, and yet I still didn't feel like discussing my sex life with my younger sister. "It's more than that. She's special, okay? And I don't want to fuck it up like I screw up everything I touch. I can't do that to her. I'd kill myself before I ever hurt her."

"And you don't think that making her keep you a secret from her friends is going to hurt her?" She snorted. "You really don't understand women at all."

"Please, Em," I begged. "I'll do anything. Just let us get home before you say anything. But please, don't tell Benjamin. Not right now, during the wedding."

"Why until you get home? What's the difference?"

I frowned. "The difference is Benjamin and Angelina deserve to have their honeymoon without wondering what their brother and best friend are getting up to." I sighed. "Just... let me tell them, Em?"

She nodded. "I wouldn't tattle on you like some kid sister. Don't worry, Hunter. I'm twenty-four, not fifteen."

I pulled her into a hug. "Thanks, Em."

"Now... You should go talk to her. I saw her talking to Charlotte, and she looked upset."

"What?" I whipped my head over in Gabrielle's direction, finding her giving Angelina water.

Fuck. I closed my eyes.

Why was I continually hurting her? I needed to get on my knees and plead for her forgiveness. That was what she deserved.

But she was standing by my brother, and his wife, and if I went over there and was my normal self, they'd see right through me. Wouldn't they?

∽

I'VE BEEN LINGERING like a sad puppy as she continued to ice me out for the last few hours of the night, but I couldn't take it anymore.

The reception was winding down, and all I wanted was one last dance before we had to go back to the hotel. I needed to reassure her, because there was no way in hell I was leaving this wedding tonight with her thinking we didn't belong together. That there was any way anyone could look at her and think she wasn't good enough for *me*.

It was the opposite—it always had been. She shone like the stars in the sky, while I was a moody asshole with attachment issues.

Even my coworkers had commented on her when she kept coming around the hospital. It had only been a few visits, plus the bar, but I was pretty sure that they could all see what I'd been trying to ignore for so long.

I wrapped my hand around her wrist. "Gabrielle." I kept my voice low. "Please." She looked at where I was holding onto her like it was a brand against her skin, and I let go. "I'm sorry."

"Don't." She squeezed her eyes shut.

"Why?" I wanted her to open up to me, to tell me what was bothering her. "Baby. Talk to me." I whispered it against her skin, and Gabrielle shook her head.

"I know I fucked up, but don't let this ruin our night. I want to make it up to you, so please. Just let me in."

She opened her eyes, that amber color rimmed in silver, and let out a ragged breath. "I'm scared."

"Of what?" I whispered back, wiping underneath her eye at the wetness that had gathered there.

"To let you in." I could tell that cost her something to admit.

I would fix it—once we got back to the hotel. Once we were away from prying eyes. Once I could use my body and my words to show her how much I wanted her to give me her heart, because I wanted to give her mine in return.

"Will you just... dance with me, sweetheart?" I begged. "One last time." Another Taylor Swift song came on—a slow one, this time—and I knew it was one of her favorite songs. I'd caught her singing it so many times. Sometimes we'd turned on music as we cooked in the kitchen. It had grown on me, honestly. There was something about being around her that was so much better than my normal silence.

"Please," I said, low enough that only she could hear. "Or do you want me to ask on my knees? Cause I will. I'll get on my knees and beg for you, my fighter girl. Just dance with me."

"Okay," she whispered, and put her hand in mine, and I held it tight as I swayed with her to the music, not saying anything but feeling everything that was unsaid between us.

Was she feeling it, too? I knew we needed to talk later—after we got Angelina and Benjamin sent off, and everything cleaned up from the wedding. Once we were back at the hotel, we'd have the conversation.

I'd tell her I wanted to be together. Whatever that meant. I'd tell her how special she was.

That I was a damn fool for her.

"Come here," I said, sitting on the edge of the bed as I loosened the bowtie from around my neck. "I want to talk about what you said earlier."

As soon as the wedding was done, and we'd helped clean up and get all the gifts loaded into the cars, we headed back to the hotel. It had been a long day, and I knew we were both exhausted, but I was going to make things right before anything else.

She quirked an eyebrow. "What'd I say earlier?" A lot of things. We'd both said a lot of things, hadn't we?

I frowned. "That people wouldn't believe we were together for real."

"Oh." She twisted away, her voice growing quieter. "That."

"Fuck, Gabrielle. Why would you think that?" I stood up, moving next to her and pulling her body into mine. "Why do you not think anyone would be lucky to have you?" I pressed my front into her back, and I circled her body with my arms.

Gabbi tilted up her head, making eye contact with me. "Well... Look at you, Hunter."

"Look at me?" *Fuck that.* "Look at *you*, gorgeous. Do you not know how fucking beautiful you are? How insane it makes me, that I can't tell the world that you're mine?"

"I am?" She blinked. "Yours?" She looked at me like she couldn't possibly believe what I was saying. Like there was no way it could be true. But it was.

"Yeah. You fucking have been for a long time, sweetheart."

"But—"

"You need to get out of that pretty little brain of yours. Tell me, what would one of your book boys do to make you stop overthinking all of this?"

She blinked. "What?"

"I've been reading your books."

"The one on the plane, yeah—"

"No." I shook my head. "I've been pilfering your bookshelves for a while now. Any time I'd come over to your place, I'd write down the names of the ones that looked the most worn, or the book you were reading at the time." I tucked a strand of hair behind her ear as I bent down to look into her eyes.

"You've been reading my romance novels?"

I nodded, still cradling her body. "So, do you get it? What I feel for you? I know we said we should keep it a secret, but this doesn't mean this is casual to me, okay? I haven't felt like this in a long time. Haven't wanted anyone like I wanted you in a long time." I leaned my head against the top of hers, inhaling that coconut scent from the shampoo she'd always used. "So don't you dare, for one second, think that you're lacking in any way."

"Okay." Her response was a whisper back, and I knew it would take more than words to get her to believe me. But I would do it. I'd prove to her how much I adored her, how she was always in my thoughts.

I slipped the strap of her champagne bridesmaid dress off her shoulder, placing a kiss to the skin there. "You." I kissed her neck. "Are." A Kiss to her jaw. "Perfect." Her lips.

She twisted around, kissing me back—deeper, like she needed the connection as much as I did. I pushed her other strap down before sliding the zipper of her dress down her back, exposing her bare skin to my hands.

"Hunter. I need—"

I lifted her up into my arms, carrying her into the bathroom. "I know."

I placed her on her feet, letting her dress fall to the floor in a silk puddle, and she looked up at me, wearing just a strapless bra and another pair of those damn lace panties. I couldn't help myself, cupping her ass with my hands and massaging it.

"I'm so fucking obsessed with this," I said as she moaned from my touch.

"R-really?"

I hummed against her skin. "I have been ever since I saw you in those damn jeans of yours. Damn, Gabrielle. You're so fucking stunning, and you don't even try."

She looked up at me, glitter still painted on her eyelids, and I couldn't help but take her lips again. I needed more of her. All of her.

I pushed her panties down to her ankles, helping her step out of them, and then hoisted her up on the counter, those sparkly high heels still strapped on to her ankles.

She looked up at me through her lashes, biting her lip as I undressed. First, I flung my bowtie to the floor from where I'd left it loose around my neck, and then my tux jacket followed. Gabbi reached out, tugging me closer by the fabric of my shirt, and then started undoing the buttons, slowly. I let her, because of the look of concentration on her face, the way her little tongue stuck out of her lips as she focused? God, she turned me on like no one ever had before.

I was already so hard, so ready to be inside of her, and even through my lust, I knew that this was more than sex or desire. We needed the connection between us.

She undid the last button, and then pushed the shirt off my shoulders, her shimmery nails scratching at my skin as I finally stood naked from the waist up.

Gabrielle reached around, taking off her strapless bra before dropping it at my feet.

I looked at her as I pushed my dress shoes off my feet before unbuckling my belt and pushing them down my legs. I kicked off my pants, knowing she could definitely see the way she'd affected me.

Gabbi laughed as she noticed what was on my feet. "Are those... Green Arrow socks?"

I frowned. "Yes. Don't laugh. Benjamin insisted."

She shook her head, her lips tilting up in a smile. "You know... Arrow is my favorite show. It's clearly meant to be."

"Oh?" I asked, a smile on my lips as I kissed her. "Good thing he was my favorite growing up."

"Very good," she whispered against my mouth, her fingers dancing over my abs. "Now, would you please fuck me, Hunter?" She shimmied out of her panties, letting them join the rest of our discarded clothes on the floor, and opened her legs wide, showcasing every inch of her body for me.

"Are you wet for me?" I asked, swiping my fingers through her before plunging two of them inside with no warning. She gasped, but I groaned at the feeling of her squeezing around my fingers.

I sucked them into my mouth, tasting her on my skin. "You taste so sweet. Fuck." I closed my eyes, and she pushed my boxers down, letting my erection spring free.

I kissed her again, and her hands wrapped around my neck.

"Please," she begged.

I positioned myself at her entrance, but—"Fuck. Elle. I don't have a condom on me." They were in the other room, and I could go get one, but—

She shook her head, pulling me closer. "I have an IUD, and I'm clean. It's fine."

"There hasn't been anyone else for me," I confirmed. "For a while, but especially not since I met you."

"For me, either. I want to feel you inside of me," she pleaded, wrapping her hand around my cock, stroking up and down with her small hands, and I had no choice but to comply.

I plunged inside of her, knowing I should go slower but unable to help myself. As I gripped her ass in my hands, I buried myself in her pussy, plunging in to the hilt.

"Holy fuck," I gritted my teeth. It had been good before, but this? I rested my forehead against her shoulder. How was this even better? I could feel every inch of her surrounding me as I plunged inside, and I almost came just from how she gripped me, how I could feel her tightening up around my cock.

"*Oh*," she cried out as I pulled out and then back in, her fingers gripping the edge of the counter as the force of my body tried to move hers across the stone countertop. "Oh my God.

Hunter." She shut her eyes, like she was losing herself in the feeling as I kept up that rhythm, shallow thrusts inside of her.

"You're doing so good, baby. Taking every inch of me," I praised her, and I could feel her tighten even more around me. I'd read enough of her smutty little books to have a pretty good idea of what got her off, and if my girl wanted me to talk dirty to her? Of course I would.

She wrapped her legs around my waist, her high heels still buckled on her legs, and somehow it was even hotter as the material dug into my skin and her nails dug into my back as I fucked her on the counter.

"Harder, Hunter," she begged. "I need more. Please."

"Whatever you need," I said, kissing her as I increased my intensity, knowing that whatever I did, it was her pleasure that came first. Her little breathy noises that she made that were spurring me on, making me even harder inside of her as she moved her hips, rocking against me as she chased her climax. I knew she was getting close when she threw her head back, her nails buried in my back like she was clinging to me with everything she had.

"Come for me, sweetheart," I instructed, and I squeezed her ass as I moved inside of her.

Gabbi moaned as I drove my dick inside her once again, obeying my command as she came around me.

I could feel my balls tightening as her orgasm caused her to pulse around me, like she was determined to squeeze out every single drop of my cum.

I knew my grasp on her cheeks was bruising, and I was sure there would be red marks from how I was gripping her, but I couldn't help it as I came inside of her, pouring my release into her body.

"Oh my god," she said, breathing deeply, and I knew what she meant.

I brushed one of her stray hairs off her cheeks. "You want to tell me again how I don't want you? I feel like a teenage boy who can't even last when I'm inside of you." I groaned.

I nipped at her neck before unbuckling her shoes from her ankles, dropping to the floor with two *thud* sounds, and then I carried us both in the shower, Gabrielle's legs wrapped around me once again, and turned on the water, even as I was still inside her. I was still half hard, even after I'd come, but I didn't want to lose this connection between us yet. I looked down at the place where I was still inside of her as the warm water hit us, and *fuck*, it was... I didn't have enough words for how much I liked it.

She whimpered as I finally pulled out, easing her back onto her feet, even as I kept my hands wrapped around her waist. I watched as our come dripped down her legs before it got washed away by the spray of the water.

"Fuck, that's hot," I muttered, grabbing a washcloth to wash her skin off. She moaned as I swiped the washcloth over her slit, washing the stickiness away.

How was it we'd been dancing around this for so long? I should have been doing this for months. All of those times we'd pushed each other away, and it could have been like this?

When we finally got out of the shower, I wrapped her up in a towel, drying her off. She stood in her towel, biting her lip as she watched me wrap mine around my waist.

"Feel better?" I asked her.

She nodded.

"Want to go to bed?"

She shook her head, giving me a wicked grin, and I scooped her off her feet, carrying her back to the bed as she laughed all the way there.

CHAPTER 26
Gabrielle

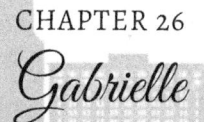

As I peeked open my eyes, somehow everything still felt like a dream. The fact that I was sleeping against a hard chest—again. Hunter's steady breaths, his chest rising and falling like the tide. That the wedding was over and we'd survived with no one finding out about us besides Charlotte or Emily seemed miraculous enough, let alone the fact that we were in bed together, and it wasn't even the first or second time.

I cuddled up against his chest, remembering last night. How he'd taken me against the bathroom counter, and then on the bed, and then from behind, against the wall, before we'd finally fallen asleep in his bed. I supposed I couldn't really call it that, though—we'd been sharing every night. At this point, it was our bed.

I'd never been one to sleep naked all the time, but last night I couldn't be bothered to put a nightgown or t-shirt on when he had me in his arms.

"Good morning, sweetheart," he said, kissing my forehead.

"I don't want this to end." I murmured, nuzzling my face against his pecs.

"It doesn't have to," he whispered against my hair, running his fingers through the silky strands. I was glad we'd gotten all the hairspray out last night, because I had no desire to spend an hour combing out a rat's nest this morning. We had to go down to breakfast with the rest of the wedding party soon, but I just wanted to stay here, in bed with him.

I looked into his eyes, wondering if agreeing to this would ruin me more than he already had. No one else was going to compare to him—ever. I was already half in love with him. "I want to believe that, but..." I sighed, biting my lip. "What does this mean for *us,* Hunter?"

"What do you want it to mean?" He pulled me into his arms, the breath whooshing from my lungs. "I told you, you have me. As long as you want me."

What did I want it to mean? Some part of me had always wanted *this.* To travel with him, to be by his side. A few months ago, I would have been naïve enough to ask for forever. To think that maybe this opportunity meant there was something more ahead for us.

Now? I wasn't so sure. I could see there was something that held him back, a part of Hunter that he didn't let anyone else see. The emotions that were kept under lock and key, and I wanted to know them so desperately, but maybe they would never be for me to know. I'd have to be okay with that, like how I'd have to be okay with only having him like this. Because he'd said to himself that he couldn't offer me more.

"Yeah," I agreed. "Okay."

He ran a hand over my back before squeezing my shoulder. "Gabrielle, I..."

I shook my head, peeling myself out of the bed and away from his ridiculously tempting body, and those mouth-watering tattoos I loved so much. I didn't even bother trying to cover up my body as I slid out of the sheets—he'd already seen it all.

"Come on, we have to get down to breakfast." I tried my best to plaster on a smile. I didn't want to talk about what would happen when it ended. Especially not now. I dug through my suitcase to grab a sundress before heading into the bathroom to get ready.

He nodded, grabbing a button-up shirt and slacks from his bag.

"We're going to have to tell them something," I said, quietly, peeking out of the bathroom while I brushed my hair out. Showering last night was probably a good idea, because at least my hair wasn't full of hairspray from my wedding updo, so it was relatively easy to pull it into a twisted ponytail.

I hated bringing it back up, but I needed to. "Em knows... and Charlotte kind of found out last night, too." I winced. "And if I'm... If we're going on this trip together, then..."

"So we tell them the truth."

I raised an eyebrow. "You want to tell our friends that we're sleeping together?"

"I'm not about to march down there and tell our friends that we fucked. No." He crossed his arms over his chest. "But I'm not going to lie, either."

"Okay, great. Glad we cleared that up," I said, rolling my eyes.

"Gabrielle." He'd buttoned his pants, but his blue shirt was still open, exposing his bare chest, as he came to stand in front of me.

"Hunter," I said back, staring into his eyes, willing to meet his challenge. I wasn't going to back down from this.

"I'm not—" he sighed. "Tell them you're coming with me. That we decided we'd go together. If you want to say that it's as friends, *fine*. If you don't want them to know you slept in my bed the last three nights and that I'd like to keep you in it for as many more days as I can have you, that's fine. But we're not fucking doing this whole song and dance. I don't know what the future holds, but I want you, okay?" He almost growled the last word.

"Okay." I had to take his word for it. Worrying was only driving me crazy. "I want you too," I whispered, as I braided my hair back to keep it out of my face.

He slipped a hand up my thigh, squeezing gently before leaning in close to my ear. "And don't put any panties on. I want to fuck you in this little thing when we get back." He snapped the strap against my skin, and it made me gasp.

"Hunter!"

He smirked as he buttoned his shirt. "Now, do you want me to go down first, or should we go down together?"

I looked up at him as I put my pearl earrings in before putting on my usual necklace. "We—together." I swiped some mascara over my eyelashes and put a dab of blush on my cheeks.

"How do I look?"

I met his eyes in the mirror.

He did a little circular motion, and I spun around for him, the skirts of my dress swishing with me.

Hunter came up behind me, wrapping an arm around my waist. "Stunning, as always." He kissed my cheek, and then released me, finishing rolling his sleeves up, letting me admire his tattooed forearms. I'd always had a thing for men with strong, muscled arms, but his were really the icing on the cake. Every bit of his body was like it had been hand-carved just for me.

"Breakfast." I cleared my throat, knowing if either of us got our hands on each other, we wouldn't be appearing at all.

"Right."

He ran a hand over his beard as his eyes bore into mine, and I could feel the heat rushing through my body just from how it felt when he looked at me like that.

"Stop it," I whispered.

"Stop being so fucking cute," he said back. "I don't think my heart can take it."

"Yeah, well," I poked at his chest. "You're going to have to be careful before I steal it from you."

"Maybe you already have," he muttered, and then he took my hand, opening the door for me and urging me towards the elevator.

I didn't utter another word until we walked into the breakfast room.

~

"Hey." I dropped into the seat next to Angelina, who looked surprisingly chipper for how much champagne she'd had last night. "How are you doing?"

She gave me a little smirk. "Great. Never better." She leaned closer to me. "I got absolutely railed last night," Angelina said with a big smile.

I couldn't hold in my laugh. "Are you still drunk?" She shook her head, and I looked over at Benjamin, who had a look of satisfaction as he stared at his wife. Angelina was wearing a loose, flowy red wrap dress, clearly having ditched the bridal whites she'd worn for most of the other wedding events. "Have you had your fill of white now?"

Angelina rolled her eyes. "I gotta admit, black is my color, but I can rock a white dress."

"How'd Benjamin do getting all the buttons undone last night?"

"Eh, he gave up halfway through." Her head tipped back, black hair flowing down behind her as she laughed. "He tore half of them off." Angelina raised her voice as she looked at Noelle. "Maybe get a zipper instead."

Matthew smirked, whispering something in his girlfriend's ear, and she turned bright red. "Matthew!" She swatted at his arm, but he just pulled her closer to him, placing a kiss on the top of her ginger head.

I shook my head. I really, really loved my friends.

Zofia and Nicolas slipped in at the end, and I didn't miss the way they looked at each other quickly before looking away. I was pretty sure the two of them had something going on ever since the Bachelorette party, but I wasn't really one to judge. And he was still her boss, so I couldn't imagine how that would complicate things if they were regularly sleeping together.

Hunter sat down next to me, holding a plate of pastries and

fruit. He placed both in front of me, leaning over to whisper in my ear, "Eat."

I blushed, and he got back up and went to the buffet table a second time without another word.

Angelina looked over at me, an obvious question in her eyes, and I shrugged. We hadn't decided what we were telling all of them. Charlotte looked at me from across the table, a knowing smile on her face, but what was I going to say?

Hunter had left that up to me. Left it in my court to decide what to tell our friends. Were we together? Sort of. But not completely. I knew there was no one else for either of us, and that this insatiable need for each other ran much deeper than just sex—the great, amazing sex, like I'd never had before—but we hadn't decided on a label.

He wasn't my boyfriend. I hadn't even told them we were traveling together. All they knew was we'd flown over together. The rest of my trip plans, I'd kept to myself. They didn't need to know that we'd booked rooms with only one bed before we'd ever even slept together. Like somehow, we had known that this would happen. That we'd break before we were ever alone with each other.

I saw him and Benjamin talking as they filled their plates, and I was still sitting there in silence when he came back, frowning as he noticed I hadn't touched my plate yet.

"Are you excited about your honeymoon, Angelina?" Zofia asked from the other side of the table, breaking the quiet that had descended as everyone went to grab something to eat.

"Oh, yeah. We're doing two weeks around Europe, and then two weeks in Greece." She sighed.

"And don't forget Italy," Benjamin said, nudging Angelina. It was easy to forget about her Italian-American heritage when she didn't talk about it much, but her mom was Italian. It was where she'd gotten her dark hair and complexion.

"Are you not hungry?" Hunter murmured, leaning over and staring at me.

In response, I picked up a pastry, bit into it and practically moaned as the flavors exploded on my tongue. "Oh, this is good."

Hunter gave me a slight nod before turning back to his plate.

"I'm so sad that I don't get to spend more time here like everyone else," Charlotte sighed. "I wish I'd had time to afford a trip."

Daniel looked up from pushing food around on his plate with a fork, and I knew there was something on the tip of his tongue, but he took another bite instead.

I looked over at Hunter, who gave me a small smile and intertwined his hand around mine under the table. "Yeah. I'm excited to see more of Europe."

"Where all are you going?" Noelle asked me. "Matthew and I leave for Sweden tomorrow."

"Paris, Amsterdam, Germany, Switzerland, and a few days on the French Riviera." Hunter answered for us, and then kissed my forehead, and everyone froze.

"We're going together." He squeezed my hand.

I looked up at him, and then at Angelina, who didn't look as shocked as I thought she would.

"Surprise?" I said, giving a sheepish grin.

Oh, I was in *deep* shit.

CHAPTER 27
Hunter

After I'd deposited a plate of food for her—pastries I'd gathered she liked after the last few months, and a plate of her favorite fruits, and then went back up to the counter to get myself food.

"You look..." Benjamin said, looking over me from head to toe as if appraising me. "Like hell."

I looked down at my attire, but I was pretty sure he was just full of shit. "Shut up," I said, elbowing him as we filled our plates at the breakfast buffet.

"Didn't get much sleep last night, *huh*? What happened after you went to bed?"

I scoffed. "Nothing." I wouldn't admit it to him, after everything we'd talked about before. Not like this.

"Sure."

"You're an asshole," I muttered under my breath as I grabbed another crepe for my plate.

"Ah, yes, but a married asshole." He grinned, proudly displaying the ring finger of his left hand, where his wedding band now sat.

"I'm trying to figure out how that is supposed to detract from your ranking on the asshole-o-meter?" I nudged him with my shoulder as I carried my plate of food in the other hand.

Benjamin shrugged. "I'm just saying, we all saw how you and Gabrielle were together on the dance floor, so..."

I glared at him. "So? We're friends. And the Best Man and Maid of Honor. Of course we danced."

"Mhm... You definitely *just* danced..."

"What the hell, man? You were the one who was so worried about me even touching her a few months ago, and now you're all over me about her?"

Benjamin sighed. "I'm sorry about that. Angelina... she kind of ripped me a new one for telling you that. Plus, I see how you look at her, man. You really like her, don't you?"

I nodded. "I've never felt this way about anyone, Ben."

"I know." He patted my back. "So don't fuck this up. Seriously. My wife will force me to kill you if you hurt her. But give me a month, because I'm turning off my phone and not turning it back on until our honeymoon is over." He rubbed his shoulders, and I knew he could use the break from his job as much as I could from mine. As the Chief Financial Officer of his company, he had a fuck-ton of responsibilities and deadlines, and I didn't envy him.

I swallowed roughly. "I won't."

"Good." He grinned, popping a piece of bacon into his mouth. "Are you going to tell the others?"

I looked at him, face tight. "That we're together?"

He shrugged as if that was a response. "Sure."

"I mean..." Were we? "We haven't really labeled it yet."

He chuckled. "Those girls might love romance novels, but if she's anything like Angelina, you're going to have to prove to her how much you care about her. So don't screw it up."

"I know." I cleared my throat. "We're traveling together."

He raised an eyebrow. "You are? How come neither one of you mentioned it?"

I hung my head. "We were sort of... keeping things to ourselves."

"Damn. I thought I was stupid agreeing to be friends-with-benefits with Angelina. But a secret relationship? That's..." He shook his head in exasperation.

"I know." I looked at my plate and back at the table. "We should get back."

He smirked. "You already missing your girl?"

I couldn't help but watch her as she talked to her friends, not even taking a bite of the food I'd gotten for her. Was she not hungry? I wanted to take care of her, wanted to make sure she was okay.

And I realized something—I wanted everyone to know that she *was* mine.

∽

"WHERE ALL ARE YOU GOING?" Noelle had asked, and I hadn't been able to resist. I told Gabbi she could tell her friends whatever she wanted, leaving the ball in her court, but the words slipped out of my mouth before I could stop them.

"*Paris, Amsterdam, Germany, Switzerland, and a few days on the French Riviera.*" I answered for both of us, and then, because I was an idiot, I leaned over and kissed her forehead.

All of her friends—everyone at the table—froze. "We're going together."

I squeezed her hand, letting her know I was there. Giving her back the reins. She could decide what else she wanted to tell them.

She looked up at me, those big honey-colored eyes full of questions, and then at her best friend. I suspected Benjamin and Angelina had figured out there was something between us a long time ago. That maybe we hadn't been as slick as I thought we'd been.

"*Surprise*?" she said, looking back at me.

"Oh, well, good." Emily sighed, leaning back in her chair. "Glad I don't have to keep that secret anymore."

"Em," I said, narrowing my eyes, but she gave me an innocent look like, *what?*

Angelina looked at us. "You're... *Really?*"

Gabbi looked at me, and I pulled her closer to my chair.

"You can tell them, sweetheart." I whispered in her ear.

Her eyes didn't drop from mine as she told the table, "Don't make a big deal out of this, please. We're just... seeing how things go."

"But you're together?" Noelle asked.

"Yeah. We're together," I answered for her, pulling her into my chest. I didn't care that we said we'd talk about what we were after the trip was over. As far as I was concerned, that was null and void. Because I had feelings for her, and fuck if I was going to let anything else take my girl away from me. And she was. She was mine, and I was hers, and I was going to make sure she knew it before we got home.

"Okay. Enough about me," Gabrielle said, waving her hands in front of her. "This is still *your* wedding celebration!" She looked at Angelina, who whispered something into her ear.

Gabbi blushed and looked back at me.

See, sweetheart? Everything is fine. I hoped she could read the thought on my face as I gave her hand one last squeeze.

Because it was. It was better than fine.

It was going to be fantastic. She'd see.

~

"Ready to go?" I asked her, surveying our room. We'd picked up the last of our discarded clothes from the bathroom since neither of us had bothered to clean up last night, and finished repacking our suitcases. Luckily, we could send the suitcase that had all of our wedding stuff back with Nicolas and Zofia, so we didn't have to cart it all around Europe for the entire trip.

That left us, our bags, and a crazy train schedule to take us all over the continent all by ourselves.

Our first stop, of course, was Paris itself—because how could we come to France and not see the city? We'd taken a train ride back into the city, checked into our hotel for the next few nights, and then I tugged her out of the door.

She'd changed into a flowy printed-skirt and white crop top, pulling her hair up into a ponytail. It was still August in France, so I understood her wanting to keep her hair off the back of her neck. I was wearing a loose fitting white button up and a pair of khaki cargo shorts. Not the most attractive outfit, but it certainly did the trick. Gabbi tucked our passports and her tiny wallet into her little crossbody purse, and gave me a brief nod as we headed out of the hotel.

"Where are we going?" She asked, wrapping her hand around mine when I extended it out to her.

"You'll see," I smiled.

She'd never seen the city, so of course we'd have to hit the big places over the next few days—the Eiffel Tower, Sacré Coeur and Montmartre, along the banks of the River Seine… There were a million places I knew she would love. But I'd also made a list of other places, too—Shakespeare and Company, the famous bookstore, and a handful of other bookstores that she would adore.

It was going to be perfect. I couldn't wait to show her everything.

We got on the train, and I was thankful that I'd thought ahead enough to have us get reception on our phones. I didn't want to talk to anyone else, so I was ignoring any texts and calls that might have come in, anyway, but I could check the maps and make sure we didn't get lost. Plus, if I lost her, I knew I'd be able to find her. And that was more important to me than anything else.

We came out from the subway station under the Arc de Triomphe, and I let Gabbi take the lead, pulling me around the thing before we came up the other side and walked along the

Champs-Élysées, poking our heads into a store every now and then just to look.

Even after breakfast this morning—how had it only been this morning, really?—we were both starving. It was past lunchtime when we found a little café to dip into off one of the side streets, and we were all too happy to drink a glass of wine as we gorged ourselves on food.

"What's next?" Gabbi asked as we left the restaurant, quickly intertwining our hands as we walked together down the sidewalk.

I knew that if we kept walking down our current path, we'd run into the Eiffel Tower, and I planned to take her up it. After that, we could stop by the Louvre, because it seemed wrong for her to come to Paris and not see the Mona Lisa—and how tiny it was. Truly, there were so many things to do and see, and we didn't even have time for all of them.

"Hunter!" she shouted, looking at me over her shoulder as she held onto her hat, leaning against a railing that overlooked the river.

I held up the two cones of gelato up in my hands in offering, and she grinned.

"Thank you, babe." She froze, like she realized what she'd said, and stared at her cone instead of me.

I tugged on the brim of her hat, getting her to bring her eyes back to me. "Sweetheart. You can call me babe if you want. Okay?"

"It's not too much?" She winced, like she was still getting used to all of this. *Us.*

I would have pulled her into my body to show her exactly how much I liked it when she called me that if it hadn't been for the gelato in our hands. "Yeah, baby," I said, clearing my throat instead.

"Okay." She patted my chest with her free hand.

I grabbed her wrist, pulling her back to me so I could fuse our mouths together.

"What was that for?" Gabbi raised an eyebrow as I swiped my tongue over her lips.

"A reminder."

"Of what?"

"That you're mine." I practically growled it. "And I'm yours. So get it through that pretty little head of yours, Elle. You can call me any name you want, because I'm the only one who gets to have you like this, okay?" I bent down, whispering in her ear. "And I'm the only one who gets to fuck your perfect pussy. But if you've forgotten... I'll remind you of that when I fuck you later." I winked at her.

Her cheeks pinked, and I kissed her again before we continued on our way.

Hours later, after running around what felt like the whole city, we'd had crepes at Gabbi's insistence, we were leaning against the concrete barrier, staring up at Notre-Dame in the distance, the sun setting in the distance, painting the sky in color.

"It's beautiful," Gabrielle said, her eyes trained on the pinks and oranges staining the sky. Her new tote bag, full of books I'd bought her—ones we'd read together, if I had any say in it—tucked under her arm, and she smiled up at me so fucking big.

"Yeah, it is." I agreed, because it *was* beautiful. The way it lit up her face? The smile that made her glow as she watched it? I could see a hundred sunsets, but it would never compare to her.

"Did you have fun today, sweetheart?"

She nodded. "This was... incredible. I'm really glad we came on this trip together, Hunter."

"I'm glad you liked it," I said, unable to keep my eyes off of her. "And you have no fucking idea how happy I am to have you by my side, Gabrielle." I meant it. Not just about the trip—in general—in *life*. I liked having her by my side, always.

She smiled, and I tucked her into my side as we continued to stand there until the sun was completely gone from the sky and the air felt a little nippy.

It was the perfect day.

CHAPTER 28
Gabrielle

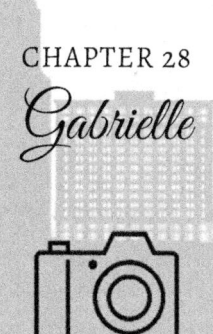

Intertwining my fingers with his, we sat on our little balcony, watching the sunset over the city. I was pretty sure I would never get used to the views. The little boutique hotel in the countryside had been beautiful, but this view of the city? Wow! I loved how green Portland was, thanks to all the rain, but the way the sunset painted the city with color, and all the history that was spread out below us... It took my breath away every day.

We'd spent the most perfect few days in Paris, soaking in as many sights as we could, and I was sad to leave, but I already couldn't wait for our next city. And knowing we'd spend the last few days at the French Riviera before flying home? Everything was amazing.

I loved our time here, but I already couldn't wait to see the other cities on the itinerary. I could tell why Angelina had her wedding in France, though. We had two more days of exploring after the first, and on top of gouging ourselves full of pastries, pasta, and bread, we'd also gotten to go to some incredible museums, Versailles, and the catacombs. But that was just the tip of the iceberg. We'd done everything we could physically do in three days.

I was pretty sure I was going to have thousands of photos on my camera when we got home, but I didn't care. I'd treasure them all. Especially the ones I took of Hunter when he wasn't looking.

I'd even gotten some other tourists to take some of the two of us, and when he wasn't paying attention, I liked to look at them. The way he looked at me gave me hope. Like maybe we could make this work even after we got home.

"What'd you think of our first stop, sweetheart?"

"It was amazing," I said, leaning against his shoulder. I'd given up on sitting next to him entirely, and instead was on his lap. Somehow, I think we both preferred it this way. "This is just..." I sighed happily. "How do you know the perfect places to take me every day?"

"Because I know you," he grunted, and I cupped his face, staring into his eyes.

A few months ago, I would have protested. Told him he didn't really know me. Maybe he hadn't then. But now, after almost five months of getting to know each other, I wondered if there was much left he hadn't learned about me. If there was anything I'd done that had truly gone unnoticed by this man. The only thing he hadn't seemed to notice was my giant crush on him in the beginning.

But now we were here, and I couldn't stop the butterflies that swirled in my stomach. "Yeah?"

He smirked. "Your favorite color is yellow, but when you wear green, it makes my heart stop. You have a favorite Taylor Swift song for every occasion, but your favorite album is *folklore*. You love otters, and I think you've got a hundred photos saved of them on your phone. Lemon desserts are your favorite, and you could eat pasta every day and never tire of it. I know your coffee order. The way you light up when you talk about books. I *know* you, Gabrielle. Like I've known no one else before." I wasn't expecting him to actually answer with *that*, but before I could open my mouth to say something else, he continued. "Elle. You have no idea, do you?"

I shook my head at him.

"The things I'd do for you. Fuck, baby. You deserve the world. I want to *give* you the world."

"You are," I whispered. Literally—he was giving me the world right now. He was showing me things I'd never seen with anyone else. Never imagined it could be like this.

"Good." He placed a kiss on the crown of my head. "Now... What should we do with the rest of our evening, little fighter?"

I had plans, but... "Why do you call me that, by the way?" I murmured. Suddenly, it was important for me to know. I didn't know why it mattered, but it did. Maybe everything he did meant something to me, no matter how big or small.

"Little fighter?" He asked, and I gave him a tiny nod. Hunter smirked back. "You're the most stubborn person I think I've ever met." He bopped me on the nose.

I crossed my arms over my chest as I scrunched it at him. "Am not."

"Are too."

"Am *not.*" Why was I so determined to win this argument?

"Do you enjoy making my case for me?"

I sighed. "Okay. Fine. I will concede that I can be a *little,* teeny bit stubborn... Sometimes."

His eyes twinkled with amusement. "But mostly, it's because I enjoy fighting with you, Elle. I like it when you don't back down." He picked me up, lifting me by the waist until I wrapped my legs around his waist and my arms around his neck. "And it's hot as hell," he said against my ear, the warm air prickling my neck.

"Oh," I said, blood heating just from the contact.

"You're so strong, sweetheart. Don't ever forget it."

"Hunter?" I said, tipping my head up so I could meet his eyes.

"Yes?"

"Kiss me, please." I breathed, and he was all too happy to comply.

"Always."

Last night, we'd been too tired after our city explorations to do anything except sleep, but I loved that I still spent every night wrapped around him. I'd stolen a t-shirt from his bag, choosing to wear that versus my pajamas more often than not.

I didn't care that it wasn't sexy, because it was so soft and it smelled like him—spicy, a little smoky, a hint of cedarwood and something else that was uniquely him. I could bury my face in his scent and inhale it for hours.

But tonight, I wanted to lose myself in him until we fell asleep, have him touch me the way that always made me see stars and make me forget, at least for a little while, that there was any chance of him going anywhere.

～

"What are you doing?"

"Hmm?" I looked up from my book from the spot on our couch to find Hunter, towel slung low across his hips after his shower. I loved him like this, with his hair slightly damp and giving me a smile that was just mine.

"Just reading," I finally said.

"Reading, huh?" He gave me a shit-eating grin, and I flushed.

"Yep," I squeaked as he plopped down next to me, looking over my shoulder at my book. "Just trying to, uh... meet my reading goal, you know?"

"Are you going to read those filthy words in front of me," he purred in my ear, "and not expect me to do anything about it?"

My breath caught in my throat as I looked over my shoulder at him, still holding my book, wishing I could hide the look on my face that told him exactly what I thought about that.

"Come 'ere, Elle." Hunter pulled me onto his lap, his fingers digging into the waistband of my little pajama shorts as I moved to put the book down.

"No," he growled in my ear. "Keep reading. I want to get my girl off as she reads her smutty little books."

Oh god. He really was every fantasy I'd ever had brought to

life, huh? His fingers dipped underneath, cupping over my panties, and I knew exactly what he was going to find there.

"You're soaking wet, aren't you, little fighter?"

"Yes," I moaned, trying to focus on the words on the page as he rubbed his finger over my slit.

"Tell me what's happening," he instructed as he moved my panties aside, teasing me with light strokes. I could feel his hardness pressed against my back, which only distracted me more.

He expected me to keep reading through this? "S-she's on her knees," I stuttered out as he plunged a finger inside me.

"And what's she doing?"

Another finger joined the first, rubbing my insides. "Sucking his c-cock." I moaned as he gave my clit attention with his thumb.

"And did that turn you on, Gabrielle?"

I shook my head, not knowing where the words were coming from, but deciding I didn't even care, as long as he kept doing *that*. "No," I gasped out as a wave of pleasure rippled through me.

"Hmm? So what made you this wet then, my dirty girl?"

I let my head fall back against his shoulder, unable to focus on anything other than his fingers plunging into me, the way they bent to hit *that* spot that he knew would drive me crazy. Somehow, having my eyes closed made it easier to admit what I was going to say next. "Thinking about you in the shower," I mumbled. "How much I wanted to do that to you, in there."

I cracked an eye open to find him looking down at me. "Is my girl telling me she wants to suck my dick?" I nodded, and his breath ghosted over my neck as he pressed a kiss under my ear. "Another time, baby."

"Yeah?" I asked, wondering how I was keeping any semblance of sanity as he kept up his pace.

"I told you, you're mine. While we're together, while we're *here*, there are..." his voice lowered into a growl. "So many." Hunter nipped at my earlobe. "Things I want to do to you."

I was trembling, breathless in his arms from his voice and what he was doing to me, "Hunter..."

"Keep reading," he instructed, and I brought the book back up, holding it in both my hands as if it was the only thing keeping me tethered to this moment. As I read the scene of him painting her throat white with his cum, I shuddered in his arms.

"I'm... so close..." I said, grinding myself down on his fingers. His thumb pressed down harder on my clit as he continued those punishing circles, and *fuck*—

But just when I was about to tip over the edge, he pulled his fingers out, denying me what I wanted—no, *needed*—most. Before I could utter a word of protest, he tapping on my lips before he popped both inside. "Taste yourself on my fingers, baby."

I sucked his fingers clean, and I groaned as I tried to focus on the words on the page—to no avail, when Hunter shifted me on his lap. When he pulled his fingers out, the saliva dribbled down my chin, but I couldn't bring myself to care.

"What're you doing?" I groaned as he pushed my shorts and underwear down my hips, lifting me slightly off his lap to get the clothing off my body. Once they joined his towel on the floor, it left us just skin to skin besides his oversized tee that I was wearing.

"You're going to sit on my cock while I make you come, pretty girl." Hunter guided himself into me, letting me wiggle down until I was fully seated on him. "Fuck. You feel so good like this."

I felt my eyes flutter shut as I gave into the way he was filling me, the possession in his grip.

"Don't stop reading," he muttered into my ear. He gripped my neck with one hand, his thumb rubbing over my lip as the other held my hip possessively in place.

"I can't—" I whined, book falling onto the floor, forgotten, as my head leaned back onto his shoulder.

"You can't what?"

I shook my head. How was it possible that he could drive me this crazy? I hadn't even moved yet, still just seated on top of him, and I was already so close to exploding. "Hunter," I whimpered. "I need more, *please*."

"More what, baby? Use your words."

He was going to make me say it. "Please make me come, *please*," I begged.

He turned my face towards his, taking my lips and inhaling my gasp as he thrust up into me again. I kissed him back as Hunter moved his other hand from my hip to right where I wanted him, rubbing my clit as I started rocking back and forth on top of him.

I groaned, picking up my pace as he continued those blissful, glorious circles, unable to stop the breathy noises as his hips thrust upwards involuntarily, driving deeper inside of me each time. I ground against him, relishing in the pressure it provided to my clit.

"Look at us in the mirror, baby," Hunter said, guiding my jaw to our reflections. "Look at how good you're taking me. How I'm fucking you."

"Hunter," I moaned, unable to take my eyes off the place where he entered me, the way my hips rocked against him. "I'm so close."

He gripped my jaw, claiming my lips roughly as I cried out, watching as his dick entered me, that steady pace as he hit the perfect spot inside of me. I'd never met a man who fit me so perfectly. He was big, that delicious stretch that never seemed to fade, but he hit all the right spots inside of me, like he was the only one suited to make me come over, and over, and over again.

I'd never been able to do it so many times in a row before him.

"That's it," he coaxed. "Be a good girl and come for me."

It felt like my body obeyed his command, tensing up before the waves of release rushed through me, leaving me boneless in his arms as aftershocks rushed through me.

I was sure I was moaning, repeating his name over and over as I came, but I was so lost in the sensations I didn't even notice.

Hunter came a few moments after me, spilling inside of me, and I looked through the mirror at his face as he lost himself to the pleasure.

Fuck, he was so handsome. And, at least for now, all mine.

As I climbed off of Hunter, I looked down at my thighs, sticky from our combined releases, and he gave me a wicked grin.

"Now I really need to shower," I groaned. "We have to catch our train in a few hours."

"I can think of another way to clean you up..." He said, pulling his shirt off my body and tugging me onto the bed. "Grab onto the headboard and sit on my face, baby."

I complied—of course I did—and Hunter went to town, licking my cunt like it was his only job on the planet.

And afterwards, we hurried to pack up our room, taking the train to Amsterdam, where we'd spend another glorious few days.

CHAPTER 29
Hunter

Traveling had never been so enjoyable before. Sure, I'd been to Europe with my family before, but seeing her exploring new cities, the radiant joy she gave off no matter what she was doing... I hadn't been able to keep the smile off my face in days. She always kept her camera on her, wanting to photograph every little thing, and I couldn't have told her no even if I wanted to. Even if she insisted on taking photos of me, and I'd have to steal it to take photos of her. And then there was that polaroid camera she kept tucked in her bag for the little moments, and I hadn't been able to stop myself from keeping one for myself.

She was fearless. That was the only word to describe her. She never failed to dive headfirst into any situation, no matter what it was or who needed help. She was the kind of girl who would dance in the rain, one worth running after in the middle of the night, one who deserved her perfect happy ending. The perfect fairytale romance, just like in those books that she was always reading.

But here? This felt like a real life fantasy. And this was coming from the doctor who hadn't believed in love for years.

My eyes couldn't look away from Neuschwanstein Castle—

the way it looked like a perfect fairytale nestled within the mountains. Gabbi had wanted to come here, so of course—here we were. I told her I'd take her anywhere she wanted, and I meant it.

She held up her polaroid camera after she'd finished taking pictures on her regular camera. "Come on, let's take one together."

"Are you sure?" I frowned. "I don't want to waste your film." We'd taken a few in other cities as we went, but every time, I felt greedy for wanting to steal them from her. Really, I was greedy for everything from her—her touches, her smiles, her kisses. All of them—I wanted all of them. I wanted to be the one to take her on hikes and take photos of her looking gorgeous, even in the morning light, when she was still asleep. I'd noticed her sneaking photos of me like that, and I wanted my own.

I couldn't imagine her sharing all of this with anyone else. Because I wanted to be the one she traveled with for the rest of her life.

I knew we said we'd wait until the trip was over to talk, but my feelings were growing stronger every day, and the more time I spent holding her in my arms, the less I knew what I was going to do when she was no longer there.

But I didn't even know if she'd want that, so I was going to soak up every single moment we had together in the meantime. I'd make her see how cared for she was. I'd put her on a fucking pedestal and worship her for the world to see if that was what it took.

Gabbi nodded. "It's not a waste. Come here."

We squeezed in tightly next to each other, hopefully in the frame, but she took two for good measure. In the second, I'd leaned over to kiss her cheek.

When the pictures turned out, I couldn't miss the way she was looking over at me in the first one.

"Can I keep this?" I asked.

"Sure. I have a ton more film left, too." Her eyes fluttered under her eyelashes. "We could take more... other places, too."

I raised an eyebrow, but I was pretty sure I knew what she meant. I was pretty sure that my dick, stirring in my jeans, knew what she meant too, and really, really liked that idea.

∼

WE'D ALREADY TREKKED through the rest of Germany, and were currently in Switzerland, sitting down for dinner. I had another surprise for her up my sleeve, and even though it wasn't quite the right day yet, tonight felt right.

"I know it's early, but… Happy Birthday, sweetheart," I said, placing a box in front of her at dinner. "I thought we could celebrate tonight."

"You… got me a present?" She sounded surprised.

I nodded. "Open it."

It was a pair of diamond studs. I'd noticed she liked to keep it simple with her earrings, and when I'd seen these… It felt right. I hadn't even thought twice about buying a pair of diamond earrings for a girl I wasn't even dating. I'd just done it.

"When did you get these?" Gabbi looked up at me. "Did you… bring this with you from home?"

I cleared my throat. "Is it too much?"

She shook her head.

"I think I knew, even then, how much you meant to me. I just hadn't wanted to admit it to myself yet."

"And now?" She asked, breathless.

"And now…" I'd told her she was mine, and I meant it. How could I ever watch someone else fall in love with the girl I'd grown so fond of? If I was being honest, the L word seemed to be right there, on the tip of my tongue. I wanted to say it so badly. When she smiled at me, it felt like everything would be okay. It settled something within my soul.

I intertwined our fingers, kissing her knuckles like I did so often these days. "You're mine." *For as long as you'll have me.*

"Yeah." She smiled, like maybe the thought was finally sinking in to that beautiful mind of hers.

Maybe I wasn't the perfect man, the perfect boyfriend, but I knew that I wanted to be that guy for her. *The perfect man?* Compared to all the books she'd read? How *could* I be? I wasn't sure that even existed, to be honest. But... I wanted to try. I wanted to be that for her. I needed to tell her so badly that I didn't want to stop this when I got home. That I didn't care what I had said before—that if it was going to be anyone, it was going to be her. That had always been true anyway, hadn't it?

And yet, here I was, only days away from the genuine possibility of letting her go. Because we'd agreed that was how this would work. That I got these few weeks with her, and then we'd go back to being friends. But how could we? How could I stop being her friend when I knew how good it was to be with her? And it wasn't even about the sex—sure, it was incredible, amazing, mind-blowing sex—but I didn't even care about that. I cared about making her laugh. Seeing her smile. Watching her face light up as we stepped off the train into a new city and losing herself in the new culture. I cared about *her,* period.

But if she didn't want me, I'd do my best to move on. Even if it hurt. Even if I couldn't hang out with my brother because she'd be there around her best friend.

But I'd do it, because I'd do anything for her.

∼

I COULDN'T STOP TOUCHING her, and I didn't even care anymore. Her smooth, soft skin was all sprawled out next to me, and every single inch of it exposed. By the time we'd made it up to the room after dinner, I'd made her come two more times, once on my tongue and once on my cock, and once I'd made sure I'd satisfied her, thoroughly, I pulled her into my arms, carried her into the bath, and let her soak all the soreness away.

Finally, we sprawled out on the bed, her damp hair spread out over the pillow, my diamond earrings in her ears.

I ran my fingers over her wrist tattoo, and she looked up at me. "Do you know why I got this?"

"No, but I'd love to hear it."

I liked that we matched. Of all her friends, we were the only ones with visible tattoos. That she liked painting her skin with the things that mattered to her.

"So..." She blushed a little, that red setting off her nose freckles like always,. "You know how much I love to read... How often I lose myself in books," she said, tracing over the open book inked onto her skin, "But it's more than that. It's reminding myself to dream. That life is an adventure—a huge one, and even if I'm just one tiny person, well... I could still ride a dragon." Gabrielle grinned as she looked at the dragon that looked like it had freed itself from the book. "I like to think my big adventure is still out there, waiting for me."

"Mhm." I agreed, kissing her wrist before moving up her body. "And what about this one?" I asked, sweeping her hair back and exposing the little twinkling stars behind her ear.

"You are stardust," she whispered, "born to shine."

And you do, I thought, *you do fucking shine. So goddamn bright.* I kissed the spot as she brought her hands to my wrist, tracing over the trees on my left arm—the forest scene that made up my half-sleeve there. I didn't fully fill it in, but I liked it that way.

"What about you?" She whispered, trailing her fingertips over my right one next. "Will you tell me what yours mean?"

"The trees... These are for my love of the outdoors. Obviously. The other side..." I grunted. I'd never shared that with anyone really before—the part of me I'd kept hidden for so long. Those little pieces of myself that I'd stored in the deepest part of my heart. "I started this piece when I lost my first patient. A little boy—Braden." My voice was rough as I swallowed. "It was cancer, my first year after medical school. It hit me harder than I thought it would. When I went into Pediatrics, it was because I wanted to make a difference for those kids. They don't deserve all the shit and pain that they go through, but they do it every day with a smile on their face. Lizzie's been in and out of the hospital for the last year, but she's got more joy in her pinky finger than some adults have in their whole body." I shook my head. "I wanted a way to remember them. The ones I lost. The ones I couldn't do enough for. So I add on to it for each one. And it's not fucking fair that they have their whole lives ahead of them and then one day—poof, it's gone. But the asshole who was driving drunk and hit their car gets to walk out of there like nothing ever happened. It's not..."

Gabrielle cupped my face in her hands, wiping the tears from my face. I didn't even know when they'd started, but I knew that with her, it didn't matter. "It's okay," she soothed, resting our foreheads together. "I'm here."

"I don't ever want to lose you," I whispered into her hair, my truth that I'd been holding onto for too long. "And I'm scared that if I let myself... if I l—"

"Shhh," she said, rubbing circles on my back. "You don't have to say it. I know." She gave me a sad smile, and I pulled her the rest of the way into my arms, wrapping my whole body around her as if I could protect her like this. She rested her head against my chest as we just held each other, needing the connection. "You'll never lose me. I promise."

Did she know how much I loved her? How terrified I was of that becoming my reality? How somehow she'd changed my life completely over the last few months?

Gabrielle placed her hand over my chest, her fingers drawing circles over my heart. "I just want..." She sighed.

My heart? You already have it. It was my turn to say, "I know, baby."

She snuggled in next to me, kissing the flowers on my arm until we finally fell asleep, wrapped up in each other, and damn. I wanted nothing to pierce our bubble, to stay like this forever.

CHAPTER 30
Gabrielle

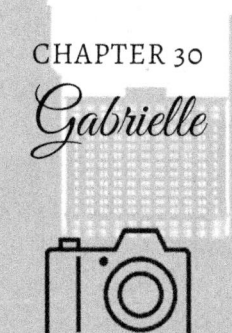

Sunlight from the early morning was streaming into our room when I woke up, a light breeze flowing in through the curtain from the open balcony door. Easing myself out of the sheets, I stretched my arms as I picked up Hunter's button-up from the night before, covering my naked body as I sauntered out onto the balcony.

Hunter leaned against the railing, staring out towards the ocean. We'd gotten to our hotel on the Riviera yesterday, and I never wanted to leave this room, this place. God, it was beautiful.

And so was he, basking in the early morning glow.

"Morning," I whispered, leaning against him, enjoying the firm shoulder I rested on.

Hunter looked down at me, clearly appraising how I looked in his clothes, and whatever he saw, he made a guttural sound of appreciation.

"Do you know what you do to me?" He groaned. "Do you know what seeing you in my shirt does to me?" He ran a finger across my exposed collarbone.

I wrapped my arms around his neck, bringing our faces closer together as he stared at the opening of his shirt, the buttons that barely covered the top of my cleavage. "Mhm?" I curled my fingers into the hair at the nape of his neck. "What do I do to you, Hunter?" I whispered into his ear.

After last night... I was pretty sure what I was feeling was real for him, too. After we'd opened up, sharing things about ourselves? It meant something. It had to.

Hunter picked me up, his fingers digging into my thighs as my legs wrapped around his back, my core pressed against his center.

"Fuck. You're not wearing any panties, are you?" He growled, and I shook my head. "Gabrielle—" he set me on the railing, and I kept my arms wrapped tightly around him as he spread my legs open with his knees. "You're gonna sit there and hold on to me while I make you come with my tongue, sweetheart."

"Oh," I squeaked as he moved my hands from his neck into his hair, urging me to grip onto the strands before he planted his hands on the backs of my thighs and kneeled down before me. "Hunter—"

"Shhh, baby. Don't interrupt me while I'm having my breakfast."

And then his tongue entered my spread pussy, his hands still pulling me apart as my bare cheeks rested on the cast iron railing. If anyone looked up off the street, they'd see his shirt covering my back, but not much else. Somehow, knowing anyone could look up and see us made it even hotter. The way he was willing to eat me out outside on our little balcony in the middle of this foreign city was making me burn up.

His nose rubbed against my clit, somehow providing the perfect amount of friction as he fucked me with his tongue. I moaned, unable to hold back the whimpers from spilling out. I'd never had this much oral sex in my life, and he barely let me return the favor. Every time we fucked, he was more worried about making *me* come first. It was *hot*.

He seemed determined to keep licking me until I came, and I tugged on his hair, bringing his face closer to me, wrapping my legs around his neck. The balcony railing was digging into my skin, but the pinch was no longer painful. It was just making me more aware of how sensitive I was right now. He flicked his tongue a few more times, and that was it. That was all I needed.

I came against his face as he sucked on my clit, my release flooding into his mouth, and he kept licking me through the aftershocks, every wave of pleasure that made my legs shake around his head.

When he pulled back, his lips shining with my release, he kissed me roughly, intertwining our tongues and letting me taste myself on his tongue.

I loosened my fingers from his hair as he stood up and pushed a hand into his boxers instead, wrapping my hand around his hardened length.

"Gabbi," he warned as I fisted him, tugging up as he gasped.

"I want you inside of me, please."

"Anything for my girl," he agreed, kissing me again as I pushed his boxers off his hips, letting his cock spring free.

Hunter ran his tip through my folds, teasing me. I wasn't above resorting to begging, if that was what it took. I gripped my hands on the railings, unable to do anything else but let him have his way with me. I'd given in completely to him, because I felt completely comfortable with him. After all, I knew he wasn't going to hurt me. He'd proven it to me, over and over.

He positioned himself against my entrance and slammed inside of me, burying himself to the hilt. His hands were digging into my ass, holding on to me so tightly to assure I didn't fall off of the narrow railing. I was pretty sure he was going to leave bruises again, but I liked the way he'd take care of me when he noticed them. How he'd fill a bubble bath for me and carry me in, letting me soak my sore my muscles before he'd take me again.

I was still so sensitive from the first orgasm that it didn't take me long to get close again, between the bite of pain from the railing and his rough movements as he rutted into me.

He leaned his head down and brought his lips to mine as he kept up that relentless pace that had me moaning into his mouth.

I came, my orgasm hitting me like waves, pulsing through my

body, and Hunter kept fucking me through it, so much that I wasn't sure if I'd lost my mind with pleasure. I wrapped my legs around his waist, as if I could push him even deeper into me, and I looked down between us to watch the movement as he disappeared inside of me, and then pulled out again.

"Fuck." Hunter groaned. "How does it just keep getting better?"

I shook my head against his skin as I rested my forehead on his pecs. I didn't know, but I couldn't get enough of him. Enough of this.

I could feel him grow even harder inside of me, his hands digging into my skin as he finally let go, spilling inside of me and making me come again.

I was still panting when he pulled out, wrapped his hands around my waist, and brought me down off the railing. My knees wobbled a little bit, and I was still a little shaky from the aftermath of the multiple orgasms, but holy shit.

"Well, that's certainly one way to wake up," I mumbled, rubbing my thighs together and feeling the stickiness from our combined releases there.

"I like you in my shirt," he smirked, tugging at the end where it rested on my thigh.

God, I never realized how much of a rush it would be to have a guy look at me like this. Not until Hunter.

"That's good," I replied, "because you're never getting it back."

Especially after he'd come inside of me while I was wearing it. I was really grateful for my IUD, because ever since that night, we'd stopped using condoms. I liked the look that spread over his face when he watched his cum drip out of me. My face flushed just thinking about it.

"Good," he growled. "When we get home, you're throwing away all of your ex's shirts." His forehead creased. "Girls or guys, I don't care. The only clothes you're wearing are mine."

I fluttered my eyelashes. "Can I wear my own clothes too,

possessive *boyfriend*?" He froze. Shit. I hadn't meant to call him that out loud. "I mean…"

"I like that." He smoothed a hair over my head. "Being your boyfriend."

"Yeah?" I looked up at him.

"But only if I get to call you girlfriend. You forget, I am a very possessive man." He nipped at my skin.

"Mmm." I swatted him away. "Down, boy. We have plans besides staying in bed all day."

He pouted. "We don't have to be *in* bed…" He looked over at the giant bathtub with jets where we'd taken a bath last night.

I laughed, flicking his nipple. "Is this why you wanted to come on the trip together? So we could spend all day in bed?"

"No." He pulled me to him, and all the words left my mouth as he nipped at my bottom lip. "Fucking you is just an added bonus, Elle."

I pulled out of his arms, heading to the bathroom and turning the shower on before turning around as I unbuttoned his shirt before letting it fall to the ground. "You coming?" I asked, raising an eyebrow as I popped a hip, knowing my ass was on full display.

He smirked and chased me into the shower, already hard again. I shrieked when he finally caught me and hefted me into the water.

It was a long time before we left the room that morning.

∽

"What's the itinerary today, sweetheart?"

I fluttered my eyelashes. "Want to go down to the beach before we go get lunch? I want to take some pictures of the town, too."

Tossing off his shirt that I'd slept in, I pulled my bikini on, shimmying the bottoms up my legs. Once I'd dressed in my sundress and floppy hat, I gathered all of my essentials in my bag. I wanted to take my camera, but I threw in the polaroid, too.

Last night, I'd let him take pictures of me with it, and they all laid scattered on the coffee table. Me in my lace teddy, me staring at him from behind in absolutely nothing... I blushed, looking at all of them, sweeping them into a pile before hiding them in my bag. I definitely did not want the maid to find a nude photo of me, even if I'd let him take them. I felt comfortable with him in ways I never had before, but... some things were way too personal to share.

"Ready?" He came up behind me, placing a kiss on my bare shoulder, and I let him pull me out of the room.

Our resort, nestled along the Mediterranean, gave us direct beach access down to the sea. Stretched out behind us was the small town, and in front of us, the beautiful blue waters. I was absolutely in love with every bit of this small seaside town. The water was calm and beautiful—I wasn't sure I'd ever been to an ocean this serene before, but the Mediterranean Sea was nothing like the Pacific Ocean.

In Oregon, the beach was cold, and even on a good day in the summer, you'd be freezing if you spent too long in the waves. When we'd gone last month, my legs had been numb after thirty minutes of jumping through the waves.

The French Riviera might have been my favorite place of the entire trip.

Sundress discarded in my bag, I went to lie down on the towel.

Hunter had other ideas. He grabbed me and threw me over his shoulder, leaving me to stare directly at his ass as he hauled me through the waves. I couldn't help but reaching down and cupping a feel for myself, since he'd left himself wide open, and he smacked my ass in return.

"Hey!" I scrambled in his grip, trying to free myself.

He glared at me. "Don't start something you can't finish, baby."

"Put me down then," I pouted, but he didn't listen to me and continued deeper into the water.

"Wait!" I shrieked. "It's too deep!" I was nowhere near as tall as him, and I had never been someone who wanted to wade in shoulder deep water in the open ocean, so I definitely wasn't about to start *now*.

Hunter adjusted me so I could wrap myself around him, clinging onto him like a baby bear on a tree. I mean, I regularly climbed him like a tree, so what was the difference, anyway?

We waded out further into the water, my arms around his neck.

"This is nice." I hummed when I finally relaxed against him.

"Yeah, you like it?"

"I've always thought I was more of a mountains girl, but I will admit, it's growing on me."

He kissed my cheek. "I'll have to take you to the mountains when we're home."

"Yeah? Already making plans for the future, Mr. Sullivan?"

"For you?" He smirked. "Hell yeah, sweetheart."

I smiled against his neck, and for the moment, I wasn't even worried about what our future might look like, because I was pretty damn certain that we'd be together.

~

I QUICKLY SENT off a photo of the beach to my friends.

BEST FRIENDS BOOK CLUB
NOELLE
> Looks beautiful. Hope you and Hunter are having fun ;)

CHARLOTTE
> Jealous. Wish I was there, too!
> Well, maybe not because I'd just feel like the third wheel again, haha.

GABRIELLE
> You're never the third wheel, babe.

GABRIELLE
Besides, what about Daniel?

CHARLOTTE
Daniel is... Daniel.

GABRIELLE
Did something happen at the wedding?

ANGELINA
OMG. Sorry, had to take a break from all this honeymoon sex to chime in. Did something happen between you and my brother??

CHARLOTTE
Well... We shared a room at the wedding.

NOELLE
And???

CHARLOTTE
And... That's it. He stayed in his bed; I stayed in mine.

I don't know. I feel like there's something on his mind that he's not telling me.

We always tell each other everything. Do you think he's seeing someone???

GABRIELLE
No way.

ANGELINA
Agreed. He'd definitely have said something if he was.

Gabs, hope you're having a wonderful sexcation!

Oops, typo!

GABRIELLE
I'm going to kill you once we're all home.

ANGELINA

No, you're not.

Because you love me.

NOELLE

And this is why I don't talk about my sex life with all of you.

GABRIELLE

Agree. Y'all are nosey bitches.

Got to go, Hunter is coming back with gelato.

ANGELINA

Tell my brother-in-law hi for me!

Actually, don't. Especially not if you're about to bang him.

GABRIELLE

You're the worst.

ANGELINA

Love you too!

I shut off my phone, smiling to myself. I missed them, but I was enjoying this thing with Hunter so much that I'd hardly had time to think about them.

CHAPTER 31
Hunter

I meant it when I told her I was already planning on things we were going to do together when we got home. She loved the outdoors and nature, and there were so many beautiful places in Oregon we could go on our weekends.

Gabbi traced her fingers over my beard as we waded in the water, hanging onto me like a koala, but I didn't mind.

I played with the ends of her hair as I stared into her eyes at the little golden flecks that surrounded her irises. I could get lost in them for hours.

"What?" she murmured as I watched her, looking away bashfully.

I ran my hand over her shoulder, squeezing it before cupping her jaw. "You're the most beautiful woman I've ever seen, my Elle."

"Don't say that," she whispered.

"Why? It's the truth."

She bit her lip, looking away from me as I tucked a damp hair behind her ear.

"Gabrielle." My voice was soft, yet commanding. "Look at me."

She looked up, her eyes shining with emotion. I felt like I'd memorized all of her expressions by now, but this one was new.

"Baby. What's wrong?"

She shook her head.

"I can't fix it if you don't tell me what's going on."

Gabrielle buried her head in my neck. "I'm scared." She whispered against my skin.

"Why are you scared, sweetheart?"

She sniffed. "I don't want to lose you. But I'm broken."

"You're not broken, baby."

She shook her head. "Maybe now. But one day... you'll realize that I'm not this perfect person who you think I am. And maybe... maybe I don't know how to be loved. I've ruined every relationship I've ever been in. Call it self-sabotage, or protecting my heart, whatever it is... I don't know, but I'm not..."

She thinks she's not loveable?

But I knew it was her deepest fear, spoken quietly against my flesh, cushioned by the slow-moving waves of the Mediterranean Sea. Like she thought that everyone she ever loved would leave her. Was that why she pulled away so early? Like she thought, *If I leave first, I won't get hurt*?

But I wasn't going to let her run. I'd protect her heart by showing her how much she meant to me. I just brushed her hair back, rubbing my thumb under her eyes to wipe away the tears.

"My little fighter," I whispered. "I'm never going to let anything happen to you. So please don't think I'm ever going to run, because the only place I'm running is *towards* you. This is what I want. I want *you*. I want the girl who cries when she reads a romance novel because she gets so attached to the characters and never wants it to end. The girl who loves dragons, because she likes to dream." I rubbed over her tattoo. "The girl who kissed me in that garden, because she knew we were worth it. And I know it too, okay? So no matter what happens, I'm here, Gabrielle. With my arms wide open, always for you. Only for you."

"Okay."

I kissed her, bringing our mouths together, and eventually her sniffles turned into little moans as I kissed the stars behind her ear, kissed down her throat, sucking a spot hard enough that I'd probably leave a mark. But I wanted to mark her, wanted everyone to know she was mine. Because I was so impossibly hers. I wanted to imprint her on my skin, so she knew how deeply she'd ingrained herself into my heart.

Our kisses turned fiercer, a clash of lips, teeth, and tongue, and when she was panting against me, I moved to carry her out of the water, unable to hide how hard my dick was against her stomach. She let out another breathy noise, and I could tell she was trying to rub against me for friction.

"What did I say about starting something you can't finish?" I whispered in her ear.

"Hunter," she groaned. "There's so many people around, but I—" *I need you.* She didn't have to say the words for me to know what she meant.

If she needed the reassurance that I was here, that I wanted her, I'd give her whatever she needed. I always would. Luckily, there weren't too many people around us in the water, but I still wasn't about to fuck her in the open ocean—I had no desire for any lingering bacteria to get in there.

But... I spied a little outcropping of rocks that was abandoned, and carried her towards it, still carrying her against my chest with her legs wrapped around my back.

"Here?" she asked when I set her down against the rock wall.

"No one can see us from the outside," I promised. "And if they do, they'll just see me. You have to be quiet and keep your voice down. Do you think you can do that, sweetheart?"

She nodded, and I moved her swimsuit bottoms to the side, baring her perfect pussy to me.

I dipped my fingers into her, barely being able to hold back my moan as I felt how wet she was. "Does the idea of being caught make you wet?" I asked her, and she nodded. "Just like when I fucked you on our balcony this morning?"

Gabrielle shivered, and I slipped my fingers inside her mouth as I pushed two inside of her without warning. She sucked on them, moaning around my skin as I scissored my fingers inside of her.

"My little exhibitionist," I praised. "Such a good girl, sucking on my fingers like they're my cock."

I crooked my fingers inside of her, scraping against that spot that I knew always set her off as I pressed my palm into her clit. Her pupils dilated as she spasmed around my hand, and I watched her saliva dribble out of the corner of her mouth as I slid my fingers out of it. I let her come down from her peak before I removed my hand from her cunt, sucking my fingers into my mouth to taste her on me.

We were in public. Sure, there was no one else around, but when Gabrielle slid onto the sand in front of me, giving me a wicked grin... I could feel my heart pounding in my chest and something about the way she was looking up at me from that spot on the floor—on her knees, for me—made my heart catch in my throat.

"Fuck. You're so pretty on your knees for me."

"I told you I wanted to taste you," she said, licking her lips as her eyes locked with mine. "Let me return the favor."

She shoved my swim shorts down just far enough to pull me out, licking her lips as her hand wrapped around my shaft. She pumped it a few times before bending her head down, wrapping her mouth around me.

"Fuck." I groaned as her tongue swiped underneath the tip, unable to control the little jerk of my hips.

She popped off, looking at me. "You have to be quiet, Hunter," she scolded, mimicking me from earlier.

I bit down on my lip as I nodded in response, watching her tongue dart out to lap up the bit of pre-cum that had leaked out, before she licked down my length, cupping my balls as she continued giving me little light touches and flicks of her tongue against my skin.

"Be a good girl for me," I ordered, tapping on her lips to instruct her to open them once she'd finished her thorough exploration of my cock. "And open up."

She obeyed, flattening her tongue against the bottom of her mouth as she allowed me to guide my cock inside her mouth.

"Tell me if it's too much, okay?" She nodded, and her eyes watered at the size, but she kept going, sliding further onto me.

I wove my fingers into her hair so I could help guide her head, trying to go slow so I didn't hurt her. But I knew she needed more, wanted me to be a little rougher with her.

I gritted my teeth, trying to hold the sensation back, but it was no use. Being inside her mouth, the sensations... When she wrapped her hand around the base to pump me, I almost blew right then.

"Gabbi, I'm going to come—" I groaned.

I poured my cum down her throat, and she swallowed every drop before she finally released my dick with a pop, looking up at me as she licked her lips. She rocked back onto her heels, looking up at me with those blown amber eyes, and I wondered if her heart was beating as fast as mine from what we'd just done.

I pulled her up to kiss me, and as she intertwined her tongue with mine, I could taste my release against her. Her hands explored my body as we continued to kiss, a punishing thing against her lips that left her lips red and swollen, and I was already rearing to go again.

Was I really going to do this? Apparently. I was pretty sure I'd lost my mind for her, because that was the only thing that made sense as I fucked her in public, not that far away from people, where anyone could have come around the corner to find us.

"Hands against the rock, sweetheart."

She obeyed me, sticking her ass out, giving me the perfect view of her delicious cheeks. I traced my fingers over the red marks on her back from where I'd pressed her against it earlier.

"Fuck, Elle. I'm sorry, baby." I kissed the marks before I

returned my attention to my throbbing cock, desperate to bury myself inside her heat.

I moved her swimsuit aside once again and pushed inside, holding onto her waist as she kept her hands against the rock. I eased in, shutting my eyes from the feeling of being inside of her.

"Oh, my—" Gabbi panted. "I can't believe we're doing this. Fuck."

"Do you like this, fighter girl?" I leaned down low, my voice gravely against her ear. "Me fucking you where anyone could find us, out in public?"

She moaned, and I wrapped a hand around her mouth to keep her from being too loud and attracting someone's attention. I rocked against her, the only sound our skin slapping against each other, our bathing suits rubbing as I thrust inside of her.

I kept going like that, fucking her with no abandon, until we both found our release and I wrapped my arms around her, pulling her upright as I kissed the back of her neck.

It was crazy how possessive I felt about her, but I didn't want her to be with anyone else ever again. I didn't want anyone else, either. It had always been her.

Ever since the first day I saw her, I hadn't wanted anyone else.

∽

HUNTER

Do you ever feel like your heart is so full it's going to burst??

BENJAMIN

You're down so bad, bro.

Maybe. Sorry I couldn't keep my promise.

Us Sullivan boys aren't very great at keeping our hands off of bookworms, as it turns out.

Enjoy your honeymoon, Ben.

> You too, Hunt.

Long after the sun went down, we were sitting against each other on the beach. We'd come out after dinner to watch the sunset, but it felt like neither one of us wanted to go anywhere. It was beautiful, and I hadn't been able to resist taking a few photos of her on my phone to save for later.

My favorite was the one of her looking out across the water as she tucked her hair behind her ear.

God, she was my favorite view of all.

"What?" she asked, catching me staring at her.

"Nothing," I muttered, and she poked at my cheek.

"Tell me."

"No."

I crossed my arms over my chest.

She gave me puppy dog eyes. "Please?"

"Can you stop being so cute?" I groaned. "It isn't fair."

Gabrielle laughed, and the sound filled my soul.

I'm so completely in love with you, Gabrielle Meyer. That's what I wanted to say.

But I didn't. I just kissed her and hoped she could feel it instead.

CHAPTER 32
Gabrielle

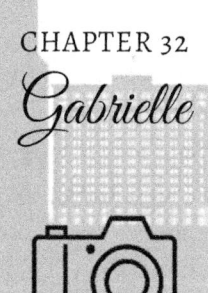

After last night, everything felt different between us, but the closer we got, the more worried I was about what was going to happen when we got home. Sure, being together just the two of us was amazing, but what about when we had to go back to work and couldn't spend every single second together? Would everything change? I didn't want it to.

"What if we stayed here? Just like this?" I wished we could.

I laid in bed, draped on top of him as Hunter drew circles on my shoulder blades. I had been snuggled against him since last night, feeling warm and content.

"Gabbi," he chuckled. "We can't. I have a job. You have a job."

"I know," I said, shutting my eyes.

How did I explain his arms felt like my home?

That this was why I never did casual relationships—because I would get attached, and if I ever had to say goodbye it was going to kill me. I'd practically cried on his bare chest at the beach about it yesterday.

Letting him know me like this, seeing all of me—it was hard to open myself up. But if I ever lost him, and then to start all over? Back to square one, dating? It would be months before I could do that. Maybe even years. I couldn't shut my eyes and picture anyone else holding me like he did. Even when he was holding back from me, not giving me all of himself... I cared about him. I think I even loved him.

And it was killing me, because I didn't want to do anything that would jeopardize this. I didn't want us to end, *this* to end. Not now, not in a week, or a month, and not in a year. I wanted to have the same happiness my friends had with him, because ever since the first time I opened my mouth around him, I'd known he was the one for me. So there was no chance I was letting him go, especially not when we got back home to Portland and everything went back to normal.

Because with Hunter... For the first time in my life, I didn't want to run. I wanted to submerge myself into his warmth. Absorb every smile he gave me, because they were rare, precious, and *just for me.*

"But we'll come back." Hunter said, as if he could understand the thoughts running through my head. He squeezed my shoulder. "Everything will be fine." He kissed my shoulder before sitting up, bringing me with him. "What do you want to do on our last day, sweetheart?"

If we had one last day in paradise, wrapped in our little cocoon, I knew exactly how I wanted to spend it. On the beach, curled up under the warm sun with a book. Yesterday had been perfect, and I loved this place so much. We also planned on exploring the market in the small town before having lunch at a café, but I didn't even care what we did as long as he was by my side.

Honestly, He'd planned the perfect trip for us, taking all of my stress away and somehow knowing exactly where I'd want to go.

"Sounds perfect," he said with a smile after we finished making our plans, and he got out of the bed, pacing over to the bathroom in just his boxers.

I watched him walk away, admiring the way his muscles flexed in his back, his shoulders, and I still couldn't believe I had him. I groaned, burying my face in my pillow before pulling myself out of bed. I'd fallen asleep naked—it surprised me Hunter let me wear any clothes during the day, honestly—and I took my hair out of the braids I'd done after my shower the night before.

I pulled on my final swimsuit I'd bought, the yellow pattern making my skin glow more than usual.

"Fuck," Hunter muttered, coming around and wrapping his arm around my bare stomach. "You look—"

I turned around in his arms, leaning up to place a kiss on his lips.

"See. Told you I'd get to see you in them." He smirked, cupping my ass with his enormous hands that knew my body almost as well as I did at this point.

I swatted him away, wrapping my cover-up dress around me. "Later, or we're never going to leave this room."

"Maybe I don't want to," he said, and I grabbed my book and beach bag off the table.

"We don't need a repeat of yesterday," I said, rolling my eyes. I'd had to go back into the water after he'd fucked me in that alcove, needing to get the stickiness on my thighs and the throbbing between my legs to go away.

"And maybe, if you're good, I'll let you put sunscreen on me when we get down there."

"Oh, if *I'm good?*" He asked, giving me a little smirk as he leaned down to my ear. "I think you're the one that wants to be a *good girl*, Gabrielle."

Fuck, he knew exactly how to make my heart beat faster now, and I felt like I was *always* ready to go. Like he'd flipped some switch in me, and I was constantly starving for him. I'd never had so much sex in my life as we'd had these last two weeks, but I'd never enjoyed it so much before, either. The guys I'd been with in the past had been... mediocre, and it was nothing like what it was with Hunter.

I shut my eyes, trying to focus on anything but his hands on me, slowly creeping towards my bikini line, and when I thought I could make it outside without jumping on him, I took a deep breath.

"Shall we?"

He hummed in response, slipping his hands in my pockets like that was the only way he could keep them off of me as we slipped out the hotel door.

Still, I slipped my arm in his, holding on tight, because I needed the connection between us like always.

∼

WE WERE HEADING BACK from lunch at a little café, planning on walking around the little town after, when it started raining. There were a few little drops at first, but I shrieked as the rain started coming down harder. Pretty soon it would soak us to our bones, but Hunter picked me up by the waist and spun me around as we laughed.

I wrapped my arms around his neck, intertwining my fingers in his curls, and brought our lips together. When he pulled away, I couldn't keep the smile off my face.

"What?" He asked, giving me a goofy grin.

"I've always wanted to be kissed in the rain."

"Well, that's good, baby, because I'm about to do it again."

He kissed me, and I swear, Taylor Swift's *Fearless* was playing in the background as he twirled me around.

"Dance with me," I breathed, and when he took my hand in his, wrapping the other around my waist, holding me tighter than he ever had before as we let the rain fall on us.

I could have stayed like that forever, but even in the warm summer rain, I was quickly getting cold. He pulled me under an awning, the water dripping off our hair and our clothes completely drenched.

"Guess this cancels our beach plans, huh?" I looked out at the rain, which was slowing, but not stopping. I shivered, and he wrapped his arm around me.

"Should we go back to the room?"

I playfully punched him in the arm. "Determined to get me back in bed, huh?"

Hunter smirked. "Or... you can read another one of your books out loud to me," he said, wiggling his eyebrows before leaning down close to me. "But either way, we'll end up in the same place. Don't forget it."

"Come on." I rolled my eyes and tugged him along, thankful that I had safely tucked all of my precious goodies from the market into my bag. I'd been trying to pick up gifts for the girls along the way, but I'd found one last thing here that I wanted to get each of them.

"Thank you," I sighed against his arm as he threaded our hands together.

"For what?"

I smiled. "Everything."

Because where would I even start?

∽

IT TURNED out he *did* plan on keeping us in the hotel for the rest of the afternoon. Even after the rain had puttered out, we were sitting on the couch; me resting my head on Hunter's lap as we both read.

I was still trying to process the fact that he would willingly read my romance novels just to make me smile, but I didn't really mind. I had a feeling it would only work out for us in the future, and if it gave him suggestions, well...

I yawned, stretching my arms behind me. "I should probably pack up my suitcase. Since we leave tomorrow. I can't believe it's already time to go home." I pouted up at him as I closed my book, setting it on the coffee table.

"We have time before we have to worry about that."

I reached up to run my fingers over his beard. "Once you get me in that bed, I'm not getting out."

He rested his hand around my neck. "I'm not *letting* you out of it, sweetheart."

"So..." I sighed.

"Fine," he relented, letting me off his lap.

I moved over to my suitcase, grabbing all the stuff I'd strewn around the room over our last few days before sitting in front to shuffle my stuff around.

At one point, after I'd finished folding everything and getting almost everything put away, Hunter came up beside me, plucked something out of my bag, and grinned down at me.

He held the lingerie in his hands that I'd taunted him with at the mall. I'd worn most of the others that I'd bought, but this was the last one that I hadn't worn for him.

"Put it on for me," he spoke low against my neck. "I want to take it off of you."

As I stood next to him, I took it from his hands.

I hummed as I held the lacy thing in my hands. "Oh, you'd like that, wouldn't you?"

"Be a good girl for me," he instructed, "and I'll give you what you want." He pressed his erection into me, and I couldn't help the whimper that escaped my lips.

I quickly scampered off to the bathroom, stripped out of my t-shirt (his) and undies, pulling on the lace that barely covered my ass or tits. Honestly, it didn't conceal *anything*, but maybe that was why I'd teased him with it in the first place.

I came out in it, hands behind my back, and when his mouth dropped open, my cheeks heated, and I dropped my gaze to the ground.

"Hey." His hand gripped my chin. "You don't ever have to hide from me, baby."

I nodded, and he took my hand, pulling me into him.

I kissed his jaw, not even caring about the scratchiness from his beard, and then his lips. It was a slow, sensual kiss, our mouths on each other as our hands explored each other's bodies, as if we hadn't been doing the same thing for the last few weeks. He squeezed my breasts, and I let out a moan.

Hunter pulled away, not dropping eye contact as he started unbuttoning his loose shirt, and then pushing his linen shorts down his legs.

When his clothes were nothing but a pile slung onto his own suitcase, he pulled me back into him, pressing his erection into my stomach before kissing me again.

"I fucking love that I'm the only one who gets to see you like this." A kiss to my jaw. "I don't want you to wear these for anyone else ever again." A nip at the ear. "You're so fucking beautiful, Gabrielle." He sucked the skin on my neck into his mouth. "So much that it makes me crazy."

He plucked at the strap of the lacy bodysuit, snapping it against my skin and making me gasp. It was a brief flash of pain, but then it turned into pleasure. He did the other one, and I gave a soft moan. My nipples hardened, and I wanted more. "Again." My eyes met his.

He smirked, snapping them against my skin again as he mouth over the lace, sucking my nipple into his mouth, lace and all.

Hunter's eyes darkened with lust, the green in his eyes almost completely gone as his pupils expanded. I could barely keep mine open as he alternated between snapping the straps and grazing his teeth against my nipple or pinching the free one with his hand.

"I love your hands," I moaned. It was something I might have been embarrassing to admit before, but I'd stopped caring anymore, giving myself into the pleasure. "They're so big, and I love when you put them all over my body."

"*Fuck,*" he gritted his teeth, foregoing the snapping altogether and pushing the strap down off my shoulder. He let it fall, and then switched to the other one, and I shimmied a little against him, wanting—no, needing—the friction from rubbing against his *very hard* erection. He was all man, and fuck, I loved that.

Hunter closed his eyes and groaned. "Baby, if you do that

now, this is going to be over before it even begins. And I want to take my sweet fucking time tonight."

"Sorry," I whimpered. I would normally have teased him for being a quick shot—because let's face it, neither one of us tended to last very long the first time—but there was something different about tonight.

Standing there in my lace teddy, straps resting on my upper arms, I couldn't miss the reverent look on his face as his eyes swept over me—my body, slowly, like he was capturing this moment, and then my face, like he could somehow memorize every inch of me. I blushed as I took his hands and put them on my breasts—still half covered in the little lace cups that I spilled out of, which made him groan again before he bent his head down and sucked one of my nipples back into his mouth.

This wasn't like before. This was a man on a mission, and that mission was to make me come. Never mind if I'd never been able to do it from nipple stimulation alone before. I was pretty sure Hunter could do anything he put his mind to, even if that meant he was being rougher than normal.

But I loved every minute. *Fuck*. My eyes practically rolled into the back of my head as I saw stars.

I still couldn't believe it was this good every time. Even when he wasn't even inside of me, he made me feel more than I'd ever felt with anyone else. Sex used to be something that was mediocre, but with Hunter... I could come just from his fingers and, apparently, him sucking on my nipples, and fuck if he wasn't the best I'd ever had.

I didn't think there was anyone else who I would have ever let touch me the way he did. It was more than trust between us that allowed us to be this compatible in all aspects—it was a deep soul bond. Because we loved each other, didn't we? We hadn't said the words, but...

I whimpered as he released me, leaving my breasts damp with his saliva but I didn't care, I really didn't care, and when he cupped my cheeks and moved me backward till I hit the wall, all I could do was give in, to give him my whole heart, because it had always been his, anyway.

Pinned to the wall, Hunter grabbed my leg and pushed it up so he had easier access to my slit, and I knew exactly where his eyes focused. I was already soaking—I always was with him, and between the foreplay and the delicious stretch my leg currently had from the way he was holding it, I knew I was helpless to him.

Hunter pressed a finger to the lace, and then trailed it up my stomach, over all the little details the lace teddy had. "How attached are you to this little thing?" He asked me, fingers running over the little pearl buttons, the bow that rested underneath the lace cups.

I shook my head.

"I'll buy you a new one," he breathed. "A thousand new ones, as long as I always get to see you in them. Whatever you want, baby, I'll buy it for you."

And then he tore the crotch open.

He ran his fingers through my arousal and rubbed it over my clit.

And then, with no warning, he plunged inside of me, forcing my back against the wall further.

He intertwined his free hand with mine, resting them against his chest as he moved inside of me.

Despite how rough he'd been just a few moments earlier, he wasn't in a rush. He kept moving in and out of me at a slow pace, short and shallow thrusts as our eyes held. I wondered if he was thinking what I was. That this was so much more than sex. That my feelings for him ran so deep, and I couldn't even say the words out loud yet.

"I feel like you were made for me," Hunter said as he joined our hands. "This pussy was made for me."

I cried his name as my body arched towards him, my nipples pressed against his hard chest, and the feeling was so much more than sexual pleasure. It was like his touch echoed through my soul, and the degree to which my body responded stunned me, even now.

"So perfect for me," he groaned. "God, Elle, if you're not careful, I swear I'm going to make you mine forever." Did he know what he was saying to me? Did he know how much I *wanted* that?

Shivers of delight spread through my body, and I couldn't disguise my body's reaction to him, his touch, the way he overrode all of my senses.

"Please," I cried, my eyes prickling with tears. I wasn't even sure which I was begging for—to come, or to be his, always.

Maybe both.

He'd drained all my doubts and fears to the point where it was just us, this, intertwined in passion and heat even as he rocked into me against the wall, my leg pinned between our bodies.

"Say it," he instructed, finger positioned above my clit.

"What?" I could barely think.

"Say you're mine."

"I'm yours," I breathed.

He finally pressed down, giving me that extra pressure I so badly needed to come.

"You're mine." He agreed, and despite his rough treatment, I could hear the importance behind those words.

"I'm yours."

I moaned as he started rubbing my clit, and as if his touch hypnotized me, as if he commanded my body, I shattered into a million glowing stars.

Hunter was close behind me, abandoning himself to the sensation as he spilled inside of me.

Still panting, he let my leg drop, and I already knew I'd be feeling it tomorrow, and then he cupped my ass, lifting me up till I wrapped my legs around him and he carried me to the bed just like that.

Like he didn't want to pull out either. Like he didn't want to lose the connection.

Sex had never been like this for me. I'd never lost myself in someone else's body like I did with his, night after night. He'd made me come more times in a row than anyone else ever had. And his confidence in the bedroom only made me want him that much more. Honestly, I was pretty sure I'd never been as turned on as he made me in my entire life.

He laid me down on the bed, and I held his face in my hands, tracing over his nose and lips with my thumbs as I rubbed his beard.

Still interconnected, we laid there, holding each other.

"Is it always going to be like this?" I asked, and he ran his fingers over my ribs, like he could play a melody on them.

"Like what?" He murmured.

"This *good*." I tilted up my chin to look at him.

"Mmm. I think so. Because it's us."

"Yeah?" I snuggled against him further.

"Yeah."

I kissed him, letting my tongue brush against his, and it didn't take long at all before he was hard again inside of me.

He made love to me in our bed, hands intertwined on the sheets, his lips against mine as I came apart beneath him, his love flowing into me endlessly.

CHAPTER 33
Hunter

You know when you know something is coming, but you dread it so much you think somehow, if you avoid it, it will never happen? I think we both knew it was coming when we got to the airport, but we'd both been dancing around it for so long that I didn't even know what to say anymore.

I didn't want that conversation to happen, though.

We'd made so much progress over the last week. And after last night? When I'd made love to her in our bed, hands intertwined as I moved inside of her? I knew what I felt, and I was pretty sure she felt the same, but we still had to say the words. I still needed to hear it from her.

I didn't think I could come back from it if she said she didn't love me.

"We should talk," I finally grunted. Why did I say it like that?

Maybe we could have avoided it for a little while longer, could have lived inside the bubble until our plane was on the ground in Portland instead of sitting in the terminal in France, but I was stupid. So stupid.

She nodded. "I know." Her eyes were shining with tears as I laced our fingers together.

"Maybe we shouldn't."

Gabrielle looked up at me. "You know as well as I do that's not going to work. We have to talk about... us. And this. Whatever it is."

"I know." I sighed. "But I don't know if I'm ready to do that."

"Why not?"

"Because everything's about to change. We've been living in this... bubble for the last three weeks. And they've been the best weeks." I looked her straight in the eye. "I haven't laughed this much in years. Haven't smiled this much, but I..." I shook my head. Not having the words.

"I know," she whispered. "Going home changes everything. But we said we'd talk about it after the wedding, and now that we're going home, I just... Has anything changed for you?"

"Gabrielle, I..." I didn't know what to say. I wanted to say yes, *fuck yes*, let's be together for real. But the words caught in my throat. How did I tell her what I was feeling? That I'd been half in love with her when I agreed to our vacation fling. I was certain I was in love with her now. There were so many things I needed to say to her, but I didn't have enough words.

"It's okay," she said, the corners of her mouth turned up slightly. But the smile didn't quite reach her eyes. "I know what we agreed to, alright?" I hated the sound of hurt in her voice, the fact that I had put it there in the first place. "It was just fun, after all."

And it might have started out that way, but now... it hurt hearing her refer to us so casually. As if it meant nothing to her. How long had it been since this had stopped being *just* fun between us? Or maybe it had never really been *just fun* in the first place, because I couldn't get a grip on my feelings for her. And every night we had been together... I'd wanted that. I'd wanted her.

So why couldn't we try? *Because that's not what you agreed upon.* Some voice in my head said. *Because that's not what she wants. That's not what* you *want.* But what did I want anymore? I didn't know.

All I knew, sitting here, staring at our gate in the airport, was that I had feelings for her. That I cared for her more than I'd ever care for anyone else.

"Just fun?" I laughed, bitterly. It was on the tip of my tongue to tell her exactly how I felt, those three words I'd never given a woman, but what would it change?

We'd made love last night—I knew we had, because what had passed between us? That was so much different from every other time—but now she was saying I was just fun? Just some silly way to pass the time? *Oh, look, there's Hunter, he's single, and he's here, so I might as well fuck him, right?* Why did all the thoughts running through my head make me even madder? She hadn't even said any of it, but it was killing me inside. I shut my eyes, trying to close out the intrusive thoughts. She wasn't one of my shitty college girlfriends who was only dating me because I was a doctor.

This was Gabrielle, the girl who's smile brightened up my every day. The girl who loved romance novels and photography and baby otters, and couldn't have cared less about my money or how. I could spoil her.

And I knew what was happening. She was pushing me away, protecting her heart before it could get hurt. And fuck if that didn't make that stupid organ pumping blood through my body clench. Because she shouldn't have had to protect her heart from me.

I wanted it. I wanted every bit. But she was pulling away. Because she was *scared*. Scared that if she gave me her heart, I'd break it. Scared that if it broke again, no one would be there to pick up the pieces.

And what was left to say?

Everything.

"Baby..." I said, voice low. "Is that's really what you want?"

She shook her head, eyes shining with tears. "No." The words were a whisper, barely loud enough for me to hear, but I did. I heard it.

"Good." I took her hands in mine. "Because that's not what I want, either." Gabbi looked up at me, and I could read the questions in her eyes. "I'm not going to let you pull away because I care about you. Because I want you. Because you mean more to me than I could ever properly express."

"What are you saying?"

"I think I'm falling in love with you, Gabrielle Meyer." I rested my forehead against hers.

"I..." Tears dotted her eyes.

"You don't have to say it back, but I just need you to know, okay? When I first met you..." I shut my eyes. "I didn't think I could have it all. I didn't think I could have my career and make time for someone else. I was terrified that the person I was with would grow to resent me when I spent all day at work, if I was home late, or if I got called to come in. But these last few months with you, even when we were just friends..." I opened my eyes and wiped her tears off.

"They've been the best months of my life, baby. I know you think you're broken, but I'm going to prove to you that you're not. Okay?"

She opened her mouth, but no words came out. Finally, she nodded, and I pulled her into my arms.

We sat like that, her in my lap, until we had to board our plane back to the states, and even in our first-class seats, we spent both flights completely intertwined. Like we weren't even two people anymore, but one entity that couldn't be separated. Two souls that shared one heart.

Maybe this was meant to be. I couldn't help but think it as she slept, her head on my lap, and I ran my fingers over the back of her head, through her hair, over and over.

As we picked up our bags at the airport, I thought about it. I thought about it as I dropped her off at her apartment and made an excuse to come inside just to spend more time with her.

I couldn't help but think about it as I went home and spent the night alone in my bed.

I loved her, and *I loved her*, and I couldn't stop even if I wanted to.

She was my everything.

My Elle. My little fighter.

~

I'D DISCOVERED VERY QUICKLY that there was no way I wanted to spend nights apart anymore. After three weeks of sharing a bed in Europe, I spent the entire night tossing and turning without her, and my bed felt too cold. Too empty. Not having her pressed up against me or her arm thrown over my body was a fucking mistake, and one I planned on fixing soon.

We were home, and even though we were *busy*, we still made time for each other. We spent every night I wasn't working at her apartment or mine, and I continued our cooking lessons. Only this time, there was a lot less teaching being done and a lot more kissing.

We'd spent two weeks in our bubble while we were in Europe, and so much had changed. This had gone from a vacation fling—if it could ever be called that—to something more. I'd told her I loved her at the airport, and it was the truth. Anything to keep her from pulling away from me, because it would hurt too damn much if I lost her.

But she still hadn't said it back. I wanted to say it, too, every day.

I love you.

How many times had I almost done it? When we were curled up together at night, when she left my apartment to go to work in the morning—I had to hold myself back. Because she hadn't said anything when I'd told her I was falling in love with her.

Because she'd cried, and I'd held her, but she still hadn't said the words.

"Fuck." I muttered it under my breath.

Benjamin slid into the booth across from me at the bar, and

I'd already gotten him a beer—our usual. One of my favorite things about Portland was all the local micro and craft breweries, and all the different IPAs they carried. I also always loved a good Porter, but honestly, I was game for almost anything.

I needed something to get my mind off of the way she kept withdrawing, even when I was over at her apartment. Sometimes I'd notice her gaze off, like she was lost in her thoughts, and she'd grow increasingly more sullen, and I fucking hated it.

I wanted my bright, happy, and babbling girl back. I even missed her word vomit, the way she'd tease me to rile me up sometimes. And I didn't even know what I'd done wrong, except to tell her I loved her.

I was sipping my beer as he looked over at me, his wedding ring glinting in the light.

"What's up?" He raised an eyebrow.

"I need your help." I swallowed roughly.

"You know I'm always here for you, but what's going on?"

"I told her I loved her."

He blinked. "Gabbi?"

"Who else?"

"I just... I didn't realize it was that serious." He scratched his head.

I frowned. "Well, it is."

He nodded. "Okay..."

"But she didn't say it back."

"What did she say?"

"Nothing."

"You know..." Benjamin sighed as we sat on the couch. "I've never seen you happier than you were these past few months, Hunter." He continued after I quirked an eyebrow. "I'm serious. My mistake was telling you to stay away from her. I shouldn't have done that."

"And?" I blinked.

"And what?"

"Aren't you going to offer me some brilliant advice, oh wise brother?"

He was the married one, after all. And how pathetic was I that I was asking my younger brother for help? I was two years older than him, but sometimes I still felt like a fucking idiot.

"Be patient. These girls..." He chuckled. "They have so much love inside their hearts, but they've all been through some shit, too. Angelina's parents fucked her up, and the world..." He ran his hand over his face. "The world isn't always nice to career-focused women. You just have to keep showing up, and she'll know that you mean it."

I frowned. "But what if she realizes that I'm not enough? That all the long hours and the overnights and being on call—what if it's too much for her?"

"Hunter." He gave me that look—one I remembered giving him before. The *you're a stupid idiot*, look. I probably deserved it, to be honest. "You'll never know unless you try."

"I don't..." I sighed. My brother raised an eyebrow, and I ran a hand over my face. "Fuck, Benjamin. I'm so in love with her. And I just don't want to fuck it all up."

"So you have to tell her."

I raised an eyebrow. "I did. That was the problem in the first place, remember?"

"No. Tell her again. The *I'm so in love with you, Gabrielle Meyer,* speech. Give her the hero's speech at the end of a romance novel." He elbowed me playfully. "I heard you read some of hers."

I shut my eyes. "Fucking hell, I'm never going to live that down, am I?"

Ben let out a roaring laugh. "I'm pretty sure we've all done it at this point. Maybe not Daniel, but you'd be surprised by the kinds of things I've learned Angelina likes because of her books." He raised his beer. "If I can make her happy, that's all that matters. Just do that. Make her happy, brother. Don't stop making her happy for one single moment."

He slapped his hand on my back, took a big pull of his beer, and I wondered if he was right.

How was I going to keep making her happy?

Now that we were home, I didn't know. But I was going to figure it out.

I had plans to make.

CHAPTER 34
Gabrielle

It had been two weeks since he'd said the words. *I think I'm falling in love with you, Gabrielle Meyer.*

And what had I said back? Not one fucking thing. We'd been home for two weeks, and I still hadn't said it. What was holding me back? I didn't know. I hated I couldn't say it. It had been on the tip of my tongue to tell him so many times, but I just... hadn't.

I was so fucking in love with him, my dream guy, this man who somehow was everything I wanted and yet still better than every book boyfriend I'd ever loved. Because he was *mine*. He was real. And he could be a little growly, sure, but I loved him, even through all that gruffness. Because he was caring and thoughtful, and he took the time to listen to me. To really know all of me.

And I loved him, I did, but why couldn't I say it?

A.SULLIVAN:
Hey. What are you doing after work?

G.MEYER:
I don't know. Probably going to go start a new book.

> **A.SULLIVAN:**
> We could go shopping, if you want?

> **G.MEYER:**
> I mean...

I pondered the thought. Sure, I had barely seen Angelina since she got back from her honeymoon, and even though we had dinner planned for this weekend, and Charlotte's birthday celebration was the next, I really missed my best friend.

> **A.SULLIVAN:**
> Come on. You know you want to.

> **G.MEYER:**
> Bookstore and coffee date included?

> **A.SULLIVAN:**
> Always.

> **G.MEYER:**
> See you after work?

"Let's go get coffee," Angelina said, sitting on my office desk even though everyone else had gone home what felt like hours ago. I felt like I was still trying to catch up on work, like somehow my responsibilities as a HR manager had doubled while I'd been gone. "And then we can go to the bookstore and go shopping."

I gave her a big grin.

"I knew that would get your attention."

"I still don't know," I huffed out, blowing a hair off my forehead. "I have a lot of work still to get done."

"Come on. You can finish it tomorrow. I miss you." She squeezed my arm. "Plus, I want to hear all the details about your trip with Hunter! And I have *so* many things to tell you about the honeymoon." Angelina closed her eyes, giving a relaxing sigh.

"Okay, okay," I laughed. "You've won me over. But what happened to the Angelina who didn't want to share details of her sex life with me?"

"First of all," she snickered. "Can you believe we're dating brothers now? Second... I'm still not giving you the dirty details, but it *was* incredible." She had a radiant smile. "I'm sure if Hunter is anything like Benjamin in that... area, that it's as good for you as it is for me." Angelina winked.

"Oh my god," I snorted, water coming out of my nose. "Please never say that again."

Finally, after saving my files and making sure I put away all of my projects, I grabbed my bag, and we headed downstairs to the parking garage, towards Angelina's parked car. I raised an eyebrow at her—she *hardly* ever drove to work. She gave me a little shrug before I climbed into the passenger seat.

She pulled out of the parking garage and onto the highway, heading out of Downtown Portland. I knew where she was heading before I even had to ask—our favorite coffee shop and independent bookstore. We'd even gone in there and convinced them to stock Noelle's first book when she'd self-published it.

"He told me he loved me," I blurted out. "Well. That he was falling in love with me. But he does, doesn't he? He loves me."

"Woah there, Gabs. Slow down. He did?"

I nodded.

"And what... did you say?"

I bit my lip. Shook my head. "I didn't."

"You just... didn't say anything?" Angelina asked.

"I was... We were at the airport, and I wasn't even sure we were going to work out. I was getting ready to pull away. You know, building up my defense mechanisms to guard my heart in case things didn't work out."

"But that didn't happen. Because you and Hunter worked out. And he sort of basically told you he loved you."

"Yeah."

"Gabrielle." She groaned. "Do you love him?"

I frowned. "Of course I do. I've loved him for a long time."

She snorted. "Took you long enough to realize it."

"How long did *you* know?"

"I suspected for a long time, but I wasn't sure, not really. Not until the wedding."

I fidgeted with my hands in my lap, trying to occupy them. "I'm sorry."

"Why?"

"I still feel like I was lying to you by not telling you what was happening sooner. That we were sneaking around behind yours and Benjamin's backs."

"Nah. I knew. I might not have known *what* you were doing, exactly, but it was there. The tension. God, every time you two were in the same room I was like *ohmygod* when are they going to fuck already?"

"Seriously?"

"Mhm. You've never acted that way around anyone, Gabrielle. Your crushes in college included. You always had this... aura. Not that you were too serious for them, because it wasn't that, but just... You were always so sure of yourself. And confident."

I snorted. "No, that was *you*. I can't tell you the last relationship I felt confident in."

Except... I could, couldn't I? Because even when Hunter and I weren't really together, weren't serious... He made me feel confident. Loved. Appreciated. I hadn't needed to wonder if this was right, if he liked me, because he never made me feel like he *didn't*. So why hadn't I been able to say I love you yet?

"I love him." I blurted out.

Angelina raised an eyebrow. "*Obviously.*"

"No, I mean... I really love him. He's the best man I've ever known. He's so thoughtful and caring, and even when he grumbles at me, I find it endearing instead of annoying. What's wrong with me to I like it when he growls?"

Angelina chuckled.

"Fuck. Angelina. I... I need to tell him. I need to tell him how much I love him." I had to tell him, before he worried he wasn't enough for me. Was I playing into his biggest insecurity, even now? "Should I call him?" I picked up my phone, looking at his contact in my favorites.

"Do you remember when you found me screaming in a pillow and living in sweatpants?"

I nodded. She'd been a mess, and I'd forced her to a "girl's night"—also known as Benjamin, waiting at a restaurant to tell her how much he loved her. And it *had* worked. She'd just been too stubborn to see it before.

"I'd say you're handling this much better than I did," she laughed. "So let's get some coffee, and new books, and maybe a killer dress so he can see what he's got," Angelina smirked, "and then we'll talk about how you're going to tell him."

"Okay," I agreed. Somehow, she always knew what to say to make me feel better. And I vowed to tell him soon. Even if that was me driving over to the hospital and collapsing in his arms to tell him I loved him. Tonight, I would do it. I'd make dinner for us, showing him everything he'd taught me, and then I'd tell him I loved him.

I dropped my head to look at my phone, wondering how many times a day he did the same thing, staring at my contact, at the last text I'd sent. I missed our constant companionship, the way we'd been around each other 24/7 in Europe, and I still, I hadn't wanted to be apart from him.

I heard the screech of tires in front of us, and I looked up, too shocked by the car appearing out of nowhere to do anything except throw my hands out and shout, "Angelina!"

The car came out of nowhere, barreling across the intersection, clearly running a red light, but there was no time to stop. Angelina had barely slammed on the brakes when we collided with the car.

The last thing I remembered was the air bag deploying and a sharp pain in my right arm before everything went black. And the one word I mumbled, like it was more important than anything else.

"Hunter."

CHAPTER 35
Hunter

Straightening my white coat, I pushed my way into the hospital room. "How's my favorite patient today?"

Lizzie beamed up at me. She was in today for a checkup, and that was a good thing. Hopefully, over the next few months, she'd have to come in even less and less until hopefully, not at all.

She beamed. "I'm great." Lizzie gave me a big smile as her mom sat in the back of the room. "Is your friend here today?" She cocked her head.

I sighed. "No. But," I looked around conspiratorially. "Can I tell you a secret?"

She nodded. "I love secrets!"

"She's not just my friend. She's my girlfriend."

Her eyes grew wide, and Lizzie gasped. "I thought she said you didn't like her?"

I was pretty sure Gabbi hadn't said *that*, but I wouldn't correct my patient. I crossed my arms over my chest. "Things change. And I'm going to buy her a big bouquet, just like the ones you get in here, right?"

She nodded. "Do you love her?"

"I do."

"Okay." She smiled. "That's good. You can do my exam now, Doctor Hunter."

"Thank you for the permission, Lizzie."

I proceeded with the rest of the check-up, letting them know everything looked fine, and once we had her blood test results back, they were free to go, and headed out into the hallway to continue my rounds.

Later, after I'd finished checking in on all my patients, I was chatting with Kaitlin about one of the treatment plans when my phone rang and I frowned.

My brother never called me during work.

"Excuse me," I said, looking down at it. "I need to take this real quick."

"Benjamin?" I said, answering my phone. "What's going on? I saw you called—"

"Car accident—" He gasped out. "There was an accident."

"Okay?" I held my breath, waiting for the sucker punch. If he was calling me, it had to be someone important. Our parents, or Emily, or...

"Angelina was driving, and—"

Shit. "Is she okay?" I immediately pictured the worst. "Where is she at? I'll be there as soon as I can."

"It's... She's going to be fine. Just a little shaken up and sore. But, uh... Gabrielle was in the car, too. She's unconscious, and—"

My world stopped. My feet were already moving before my brain could process what I was doing.

"Where." It wasn't a question, but a command. I didn't even care that I was mid-shift.

I found a nurse, letting her know there was a family emergency, and quickly grabbed my keys. I couldn't even think straight to ask him questions. All I knew was I had to get to her. Benjamin gave me the name of the hospital, and I didn't stop until I was in the car and I programmed it into my car's navigation system.

"I'm on my way. When I get there, I'll call you. I said, hanging up and throwing my phone onto the seat.

All I could think as I drove was, *please be okay. Please be okay.*

"Fuck!" I slammed my hand against the steering wheel, sending up prayers to whoever would listen. "Gabrielle, I need you to be okay," I groaned out loud. "I need *you*."

I'd known it for so long, hadn't I? But I hadn't told her, not really.

I think I'm falling in love with you? Fuck.

I'd known I was in love with her, and that was what I'd said? I'd been waiting for her to say something back, because I didn't want to say it too soon. Wanted her to tell me when *she* was ready. And I'd known it every time I'd held her in my arms, every time she'd looked at me with her big, honey eyes, and why hadn't I told her? I needed to tell her all of it, how I truly felt. I needed—fuck.

And all I wanted now was to be by her side. I was going to tell her, too—when she woke up, I'd tell her exactly how I felt about her. After that?

Good luck getting rid of me, because I was all in.

I didn't need to worry about what would happen if we broke up, because if I had my way, we'd stay together for a long, long time. I didn't want anyone else but her. I hadn't since the first moment I set eyes on her, standing in her sexy little Librarian costume with a stack of books that she'd brought to that Halloween party.

～

I DIDN'T REMEMBER parking and locking the jeep. I didn't even remember rushing into the hospital, standing there in the middle of a busy ER and watching everyone rushing around me. I'd done an ER rotation, I knew what it was like.

I couldn't focus on anything, not like this.

I was still wearing my scrubs from my hospital when I walked in.

A wrist wrapped around mine and pulled me over into a little waiting room. "Hunter." Benjamin's voice called, and I turned my head to look at him. I'd never seen him look so worried.

His wife was sitting there, a bandage taped on her temple, looking bruised and shaken, and I knew staring into his face that I looked the same way too.

"I didn't see them." Angelina shook her head, her eyes red and puffy from crying. "They came out of nowhere and I—I didn't *see* them. I should have seen them, and she's—Gabrielle—" She was gasping for breath as she cried, a state I'd never seen Angelina in before.

"She'll be okay, Angel." Benjamin squeezed his wife's hand before wrapping both of his arms around her and holding her tight. Something tugged at my heart, seeing them together, seeing how much they loved each other.

It was like that with Gabrielle and I too.

She shook her head. "It's all my fault." Her eyes met mine. "She said she was busy with work, but I talked her into it because we hadn't gotten to hang out lately. And now she's..."

My breath caught in my throat. "Where is she?"

It was Benjamin who answered me. "Surgery." He swallowed, like there was more, and he didn't want to tell me. "When they got to the scene, it was pretty bad. Her car's totaled."

"I don't give a shit about the car," I growled.

"I know. Angelina had hit her head on the steering wheel, and there were some cuts from the windshield, but Gabrielle, she..." Benjamin took a deep breath. "She tried to shield herself from the impact. And when the airbag hit, her arm..." He shook his head. "They said she was already out when the ambulance got there. I met them here, and Angelina was shaky but... She hadn't woken up yet."

"And then they took her to surgery?" I ran a hand over my face.

He nodded. "They're fixing her arm. The broken bone..." He didn't have to explain the extent of her injuries, because I understood. During my time as a doctor, I saw a lot of car accident injuries.

"I need to see her," I breathed. "I can't..."

Benjamin gave me a sad smile. "I know."

"There's one more thing," Angelina whispered, wiping her tears away. "Before she blacked out, she said..." I nodded, urging her to continue. I didn't have any words left, anyway. "Just one word. Your name. And I—I made Benjamin call you, because I know she loves you and you love her, and she needs you, Hunter—"

I shut my eyes. "I haven't even told her, not really," I muttered under my breath.

Benjamin rubbed a hand over Angelina, who was burying her face in her hands. He addressed me again. "They said they'd come out and get us when she was out of surgery."

I nodded, trying to be rational. Trying to not be out of my mind, worrying about the girl I loved. "Did you call her family?"

"I did. There were no flights for them to get on, but they're going to make it out here soon. At least she has us." She did. She had all of us, but, more importantly, she had me. Because after this, I wasn't leaving her side again.

Even if that meant moving in together tomorrow—I was ready for it. All of it.

I'd been afraid for so long—scared of losing the person I loved, scared that it would break me after they were gone—but I'd realized something from being with Gabbi. If you didn't try, you'd never know the joy of having them in your life. The laughter, the smiles, the way I felt when she looked at me... It was all worth it.

All of my fears? None of that mattered anymore. My schedule? I'd figure it out. Maybe after a few years I could switch and work at a pediatrics practice. I didn't need to be on call at the hospital 24/7 to be a good doctor.

We all sat down on the little wooden chairs, and I sat, staring at the opening to the room as I waited for a doctor to come and get us. To let us know my girl was out of surgery.

But I was terrified, thinking about all the worst-case scenarios.

∼

I SAT THERE, perched on the edge of my chair, until someone came out to let us know she was out of surgery. It was only once I knew she was going to be okay that I finally felt like I could breathe again. And maybe before it would have freaked me out, this overwhelming feeling that nothing was going to be okay without her, but now, I'd accepted the *why*. I loved her.

"You can see her now, if you want," the nurse said, and I stood from my chair without hesitation.

"Is she awake?"

"No, but you can sit with her until she wakes up. We need to continue monitoring her to make sure there isn't any sign of brain trauma when she wakes up."

I nodded. I'd treated kids who'd been in terrible car accidents, ones who had been spared terrible, life-altering injuries because they were in a car seat, but I'd also lost ones too. There was no best-case scenario here. It all sucked.

I followed the nurse into the hospital room, thanking her as she slipped out, leaving me standing in the doorway and staring at the bed.

"Elle," I whispered as soon as I was alone in the room, staring at her laying in the hospital bed. She looked so small, so still.

She was lying on the hospital bed, her brown hair laying limp around her and her right arm bandaged up in a cast. I squeezed my eyes shut, reminding myself that it could be *so* much worse. There were little nicks on her skin, sure, but she was going to be fine. She could have fractured her pelvis or had damage to her spine. And they'd brought her back from surgery to fix the broken bone in her arm, so sleeping off the rest of the anesthetic made sense.

Nevertheless, I wanted her to open her eyes. So fucking badly. I had so many things I needed to say to her.

I pulled up a chair by her bedside, sliding into it as I took her left hand into mine.

"I need you to wake up so I can tell you how I feel, sweetheart. I need to tell you what an idiot I was for not saying it before. I—I should have told you sooner. Should have said it every day, if you would have let me." I got choked up, but I kept going anyway. "You are the best thing that's ever happened to me, and I'm not going to let you go." Fuck that. I wouldn't let that happen. The universe could drag me away kicking and screaming before I ever left her side. "So open your eyes, Elle, so I know you're okay. So I can say it all to your face." I shut my eyes, resting my head on the bed as I thought about those three little words and how I needed to say them to her.

How I was going to be fearless like she always was.

Fearlessly yours, I thought with a grin as I looked at her. No matter what happened, no matter what obstacles came our way, I was going to fight for her.

CHAPTER 36
Gabrielle

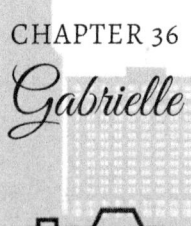

There were two things I was keenly aware of when I opened my eyes: one, the stark white hospital room, and two: a warm hand holding mine. Specifically, Hunter Sullivan's hand, connected to the rest of him sitting in a chair right by my bedside.

I couldn't have told you anything else. Knowing that he was *here* was the only thing that mattered.

"Hunter..." I croaked, squeezing his hand, and he stirred, his head jolting up and eyes flying open to look into mine.

"Elle..."

"How long was I asleep?" I was groggy, and surely I'd need to focus on the weight of my other arm later, but for now, I couldn't focus on anything but his face. The stubble on his chin, the worry in those bright green eyes—they were all mine.

He swallowed roughly, handing me a cup of water from my bedside, which I gladly sucked down. "A few hours. I should probably go let a nurse know you're awake—"

"Wait," I said, so low that I wasn't sure he'd heard me. But he had. Of course he had. This was the man who knew me so intimately, inside and out. He knew my thoughts, my feelings, and he'd explored every inch of my body. Of course, he was so finely attuned to me. "Can we just..."

He nodded. "Whatever you need, sweetheart."

I finally drew my eyes away from his and looked down at my casted arm.

"Compound fracture," he said, voice rough, explaining it to me in medical terms. As if the lack of emotion would somehow make it better. "You broke your radial bone, and they had to do surgery to fix it. You passed out at the scene."

I remembered little, but... "Is Angelina okay?"

Hunter nodded. "She banged up her head, but she'll be fine. You're both lucky to be alive." I knew how much it pained him to say those words. "They want to monitor you for head trauma for a little longer before they let you go home."

"Okay." I sucked in another breath. This wasn't what I wanted to talk about, and he knew it. "Hunter," I started, my eyes already filling with tears before I could get the words out. "I'm so sorry." I shook my head.

"For what, baby?" He squeezed my hand.

"For making you worry, for not—"

"There's nothing you need to apologize for." Hunter shook his head. "I'm just glad you're okay. But fuck, Gabrielle. I was so scared."

"But—"

"No, let me finish." His eyes pleaded with me. "I know I was stupid, ever agreeing to be anything less than yours. That I should have asked you to be mine a long time ago. Before the wedding, even. I thought I couldn't have it all—the job and the life. That I didn't have the time to offer someone I dated because I worked so much. That if I did, they'd grow to resent me and it would be over, anyway. So I just... I didn't try. I closed myself off. Sealed my heart up to love, because seeing what I see, every day—it hurt."

"Hunter..." I whispered, rubbing my thumb over the back of his hand. Not wanting to break the connection between us.

"But I was wrong. Because you..." He shut his eyes tight

before bringing our gazes back together. "You're essential. You light up my life like a thousand stars in the Milky Way. A billion. You bring all of that joy and warmth and it's fucking contagious, sweetheart, how much you make me want to smile just by being around you. When you have a camera in your hands and you focus on getting that perfect shot? You stick your tongue out to the side when you focus... And I can't take my eyes off of you for one moment. All I know is I can't let go of you." He brought our connected hands up to his mouth and kissed the back of my hand. "I can't give you up. So don't give up. Not on us. Not on this. We're more than just a trip, we're the whole damn destination.

"It was never just a fling for me, Gabrielle. I tried to ignore it for so long, because I'd told myself I couldn't want you, but I always did. From that very first moment when I listened to your heartbeat, and you accused me of not being an actual doctor." I smirked. "Even then, I knew."

"What are you saying?" I whispered. Not because I didn't know... but because I needed to hear it. The words I'd wanted to hear so badly, for so long, but I'd fooled myself into thinking I never would.

"I love you, Gabrielle."

"I knew it," I breathed, and then my lips parted and I couldn't help the grin that spread over my face.

He scowled at me. "Will you shut up and let me kiss you?"

I nodded, and he stood up out of the very uncomfortable-looking chair, cradled my head between his hands, and leaned down, placing a brief kiss against my lips.

When he pulled away, still holding my face, I gave him my truth. "I love you too, you know."

His hand smoothed down my hair, and I pressed my free hand to my pounding heart. "I should have said it before. God knows I've loved you for so long, Hunter. I was terrified that if I loved you, and you decided you didn't want this... That I'd crumble, and fall apart. And I wasn't sure if I could pick up the pieces again. Because I've never loved anyone the way I've loved you."

"Thank fuck," he said, and then he kissed me again. He was still careful, and soft, but I brushed my tongue against his lips, begging for entry, and I wouldn't have stopped kissing him then even if the world was ending. Because his lips were on mine and he tasted like home; like everything was right and was going to be okay, because he loved me, and I loved him, and nothing else mattered.

Finally, he pulled away, muttering that he should go get a doctor to check me out, and after placing another kiss against my lips, and one on my forehead, he left the room to find my doctor.

Even as they checked on me, Hunter stayed in my periphery, always making sure I was okay, asking questions, and talking about my care to make sure what I needed. I'd have my cast for at least 6-8 weeks as my arm healed, and they wanted to rule out any potential whiplash or concussion symptoms from my head hitting the seat on impact, but other than that, I was okay. It was a miracle in so many ways.

The doctor left the room, and he took my hand in his again, but instead of giving me what I wanted, he asked, "Do you want to see your friends? They want to make sure you're okay."

"They're all here?" I squeaked.

Of course, I'd figured Angelina was, but...

He nodded. "Angelina called all of them once she got cleared and they've been waiting for you to wake up. We didn't want you to be overwhelmed when you did." Hunter gave me a small smile. "But everyone's been worried sick."

I nodded. "Okay."

"I'll be right back, my fighter girl."

"I'll be here," I croaked, squeezing his hand before releasing it.

"I love you," he whispered, and then he was breezing out of the room to get the girls.

When they came in, Charlotte, Noelle, and Angelina looked worried sick, but I couldn't get past the bandage taped to Angelina's forehead.

"Are you okay?" I blurted out.

She chuckled. "Am *I* okay?" Her fingers lightly brushed over the white gauze on her face. "Just a scratch. I'll be fine. How are you feeling?"

I raised my arm as if that could answer her question as Charlotte and Noelle flung their arms around me, hugging me tightly.

"We were so worried!" Charlotte exclaimed. "Daniel and I got here as fast as we could."

My eyes connected with Angelina's, who shrugged. I'd stopped trying to figure out what was going on between them a *long* time ago.

"I'll be fine," I said, echoing the words from my doctor earlier. "I just have to take it easy for a bit."

Noelle squeezed me in another tight hug before pulling away. "We'll all let you get some rest. We wanted to check in and let you know we were here." She held up a small bag. "I stopped by your apartment and grabbed you some stuff, too."

"Oh." Tears pricked my eyes again. "Thanks. I love you guys so much."

Charlotte and Noelle left after giving me another hug each, promising to come to see me once I was home, and then it was Angelina and me.

She sat on the edge of my bed. "So I'm guessing you told Hunter?"

I gave her a small smile. "I told him. And he's here." I was pretty sure she was the one who'd made sure he got called, and I couldn't thank her enough.

"Benjamin called him." She nodded, as if in confirmation.

"Are you sure you're okay, Ang?" Now that she was closer, I could see little nicks in her skin from where the glass had shattered—I was sure there were some on my skin as well if I'd bothered to look closer.

"Do you know how many times Benjamin has seen me cry?" Angelina said instead.

I shook my head no. I'd barely ever seen her cry in our nine years of friendship.

"Less than five." She laughed. "But I bawled my eyes out because I was so worried about you. You're my best friend, and I almost got you—"

"No." I cut her off. "This isn't your fault. This is that guy for not looking where he was going or paying attention to the stoplights. You can't blame yourself. I'm okay." I held up my arm. "And look, I have a shiny new cast and all my limbs are intact." I gave her a weak smile. "We're okay."

She sighed, running her hands through her black hair. "I was so worried."

"But everything's better now." I nodded. "And I promise you're not getting rid of me that easily, okay? It'll take dragons or pirates or falling at the hand of an enemy prince, but not like that."

"The girls packed you a few books in there... if you need them." Angelina's eyes glanced towards the door. "But I'm guessing you won't."

A small smile spread across my face. "No, I don't think I will."

I opened my arms for a hug, pulling her in tight, and I didn't miss the tears that pricked her eyes when she pulled away. "I love you, Angelina. I don't know what I'd do without my best friend."

"Remember that when you're the one getting married," she winked at me.

"I think we're getting ahead of ourselves a *bit*." I rolled my eyes. "Tell Benjamin thank you?" I asked her as she stood up off the hospital bed.

"For what?"

"For bringing me the one thing I really needed."

She nodded, not saying anything else, and when her hand was on the doorknob, she looked at me. "The two of you are going to make it, you know."

Hunter and I.

I nodded, because I was going to hold on tight and never let go.

He slid back into my room after everyone else left, and I yawned. Even after being out for hours, I was still exhausted—both from the accident and the surgery, I was sure—but there was only one thing I wanted. So once we were finally alone again, I couldn't help it anymore.

"Come here, please," I said, scooting over to the edge of the bed as I held my arms open, ignoring the clunky cast on my right arm.

"I don't want to squish you," he muttered as he climbed onto the bed and pulled me into his arms, letting my head rest against his chest.

"I missed you," I said as I buried my face in his shirt, inhaling him in through all of my senses.

He chuckled. "I was only gone for fifteen minutes, sweetheart. But it's a good thing you're never getting rid of me again," he said as I shut my eyes, already drifting off to sleep, happy and content in his arms.

There were more conversations we needed to have, but we'd have them tomorrow. We had time, after all.

∽

"Alright, Miss Meyer, you're all free to go home."

Hunter stood there, holding the duffel bag of my things, looking so handsome and doting... and I still couldn't believe that *he loved me*. I'd been in love with him for so long, but to know he felt the same way... My chest fluttered at the knowledge.

I probably could have walked out of there, considering all I had was a broken arm, but everyone insisted I get pushed out in a wheelchair, just in case. Hunter scooped me up off the bed and settled me into the chair before grabbing the flowers and cards my friends had left—things I hadn't even noticed in those first few hours, because I was so wrapped up in him. I'd stayed overnight for observation, Hunter sleeping in the chair next to me—or the bed, when I could bribe him to cuddle with me—but now, I was happy to be going home.

When we got outside the hospital, it was a typical gray and drizzly fall day in Portland, but somehow the air felt fresher—cleaner. I smiled as Hunter kissed the side of my head before going to grab his car.

He pulled his jeep around to the front and then lifted me into the passenger seat before tucking a blanket across my lap. "Ready to go home?" Hunter asked.

I nodded. "Who's apartment are we going to?"

"Yours. But I'm not leaving you again," he said gruffly.

"You know... We don't even live together." I gave him a little wink, and he pinned me in between his muscular arms as he held my stare.

"Mm. We do now. And I'm going to wrap you up in bubble wrap, if that's what it takes to keep you safe."

"Hunter..."

"I meant it when I told you I loved you. I'm all in, Gabrielle. I want you in every way. If you need time, I get it, but this past month proved to me how much I need you in my life. I can't go on without you. Not anymore."

I reached up to run my fingers through his hair, pushing it back. His short brown curls fell onto his forehead, the way I loved. "I don't need time. I want to be with you, too."

"Thank fuck." He kissed me and then pulled away. "Now let's go home, sweetheart."

He closed my door, walked around to the driver's seat, and when his palm slid over my knee and he kept it like that the whole way home—touching me like he needed the confirmation that I was there, the touch of my skin to know I was here.

That I was his.

Home—that sounded pretty great to me.

He pulled me out of the car and into his arms, closing the car door with his knee.

I narrowed my eyes at him as I cradled my cast with my other arm. "You know, I *can* walk by myself. It's just a broken arm, not my leg."

He huffed. "I don't care. You're fucking hurt. I'm gonna take care of you."

The apartment was just like I'd left it—which was not surprising—it was only yesterday morning since I'd seen it last. But everything felt a little different. Like there was a different lens on the world.

After carrying me up the stairs, he promptly laid me on the couch with a blanket, where I was happily petting Toothless as Hunter moved frantically through the apartment.

"Can I help you with anything else?" he asked me after bringing me a tumbler filled with ice water.

"Do you think I could shower?" I asked, wrinkling my nose. "I feel all sticky and I want to wash my hair." He looked at my right hand and nodded, something clicking inside of him.

"Come here, you," he said, scooping me up into his arms and walking me into my bedroom, setting me down on the bed before going into my en-suite bathroom to turn on the bathtub.

"The bath?" I raised an eyebrow.

"Yes," he grunted. "I'll wash your hair."

"Oh." Did he have any idea how *much* I loved him? I wasn't sure it was possible with how much he made my heart flutter. "Okay."

He stood me up and eased off my crewneck, carefully pulling it over my cast, before unclipping my bra and then easing my leggings down my legs, leaving me completely bare in front of him except for my bright green cast. Not quite the right color, but I'd take it.

His eyes raked over my body, and my cheeks heated, but he didn't do anything else. As much as I wanted him to touch me—this wasn't the time for that.

"Here," he said, lightly lifting my arm and pulling a plastic cover over the cast, securing it at the top. It was clunky and awkward, but it would do the job, at least.

"This is going to be a long six to eight weeks," I sighed.

"Hey." Hunter grasped my chin, pulling it up so my eyes would meet his. "If I have to wash your hair every fucking day and help you shower, that's what we'll do, okay? I'm here for you. Whatever you need."

I nodded. "Every other day."

"What?"

"I don't wash my hair every day." I laughed.

He returned my grin, holding my free hand as we walked over to the tub, where he helped me in. I sank into the water as he sat on the tile in front of me.

"*Oh*," I moaned as the hot water hit my muscles. "Sorry," I said sheepishly to him.

"It's not too hot, right?" I shook my head as he pushed his shirtsleeves up, revealing his delicious forearms, and I spied a new tattoo on his arm.

"What's that?" I said, gasping as he looked down.

"Oh. I—" I traced the ink with my fingertips as he fumbled over his words. "It's for you," he finally said. I couldn't take my eyes off of the little dragon flying through the stars. "I was going to show you last night, at dinner, but..."

"Hunter..." I said, voice low, wishing that he was in here with me so I could show him just how much I loved it. "It's perfect. When did you even have time to do this?"

He gave a little mischievous shrug and then kissed my nose. "Some secrets are best kept, my little dragon lover."

"You know, all the best stories have them," I grinned. Just then, Toothless, apparently tired of being left out, scratched at the bathroom door. "Even ours."

He leaned down and kissed me again, lightly, and then ran his hand over my hair.

"I can do it myself," I mumbled, even though that was the last thing I wanted.

Hunter shook his head. "Let me," he said, taking the shampoo bottle from the ledge of the bathtub.

He dipped my head down into the water, scooping water over my scalp to get it wet, and then massaged in the product into my hair. I couldn't help the shameless little moans that I let out from his fingers working at my scalp—it felt so good, and I didn't realize how much I needed this until now.

So I succumbed to the blissful feeling of feeling cared for as he rinsed my hair and then conditioned it, and after twisting it into a bun on top of my head, he rubbed my neck and shoulders with those beautiful miraculous hands and I think I went to heaven, just a little bit.

When I was close to falling asleep in the warm water, he helped me out. "Good call," I mumbled, leaning against him, knowing I was probably getting his shirt wet with my hair but not caring anyway as I fought to keep my eyes open.

Hunter wrapped me up in a fluffy towel and dried off every inch of my body, before scooping me up and carrying me to bed without a stitch of clothing on. I was about to protest—thinking he was going to leave—until he pulled his shirt and pants off and climbed in right next to me, pulling me tight against his body.

Suddenly, every bit of tiredness in my bones was gone.

"Don't you have to go to work?" I asked, eyeing him suspiciously.

"Uh-uh. I asked Mason—if he could fill in for me today. I told him my girlfriend was in a car accident, and I needed to be here with her."

"Oh." I smiled.

"What?"

"I'm your girlfriend."

"I told you I was all in."

"I know, but... it sounds so nice, *boyfriend*."

He wrinkled up his nose. "That's so weird. Being someone's boyfriend. I feel too old to be that."

I frowned. "You're not old. You're only thirty-two."

"Thirty-three in December."

How was it possible that I felt like there were still so many things I'd left unsaid to this wonderful man? This incredible man who was now *mine*. "I can think of a few other titles if you think boyfriend doesn't suit you..." He blinked at me, but I gave him a small smile in return.

"One day," he agreed. "When we're both ready."

I intertwined our hands. "Can I tell you something?" I asked. He nodded, and I continued. "I was mad at you... for a while."

He smirked down at me. "Oh? For what?"

"When you called me annoying," I grumbled.

Hunter frowned. When he made that quizzical face, I wanted to run my fingers over the wrinkles on his forehead. "I never called you annoying."

I sat up straight. "Yes, you did. At the engagement party. I heard you and Benjamin talking about me."

"What exactly did I say?"

"Something like... *God, she's so annoying*, I think. Why?"

He chuckled, rubbing at his beard. "Elle. I was talking about my *mom*. She was getting on me about getting married again. At Benjamin's party, of all places."

"Oh." I furrowed my brows. "But Benjamin said my name—"

"Because my mom wanted me to date you, silly."

"Oh." I sounded like a broken record. "But..."

He nuzzled his head into my hair. "It was always you, my little fighter. Sure, you're a pain in my ass, but you're *my* pain in the ass."

I laughed. "Is that supposed to be romantic?"

"I can't believe you never told me. Is that why you were so stubborn all the time in the beginning?"

"Yeah," I mumbled. "I just thought you *really* didn't like me.

I couldn't fathom why you didn't. And then when you kept pulling away..."

"Fuck. I *always* liked you, Elle. I just knew I couldn't just fuck you and move on. I knew once would never be enough with you. But Benjamin told me to keep my dirty paws off you. I thought he was right. That I couldn't possibly deserve you."

I cupped his cheek. "But you do. You *do* deserve me."

"And I'm going to prove that to you every day for the rest of our lives. If you'll let me."

"That's a bit presumptuous, Mr. Sullivan."

"One day, I'm going to make you Mrs. Sullivan."

I scrunched up my nose. "That's your mom," I laughed. "And Angelina."

"And you, too... If you want." His forehead rested against mine, and I couldn't help but brush my lips over his.

Because for the first time in my life, I wanted it. I wanted to wear his ring on my finger. To have his last name as mine.

"Just promise me one thing?" I said,

"Anything. I'd promise you anything, sweetheart."

"Sometimes when I get in my head or get anxious... Can you just reassure me?" He nodded. I'd explained this before to him, so I knew he knew what I meant.

"Tell me what to do, and I'll do it."

"Love me," I said. "Just... love me."

His hand wrapped around the back of my neck, bringing our lips together.

"That, I can do," he said, and then he kissed me.

CHAPTER 37
Hunter

Just love me. She didn't know what her words were doing to me, but I intended to show her how much I loved her every day. Honestly, she didn't even need to ask. I was serious when I said I wanted to make her my wife someday. Not yet—I wanted to enjoy us being together first, but one day, I wanted to be the one at the end of the aisle that she'd be saying yes to.

I broke the kiss and rolled her on top of me, running my hands through her silky brown tresses and admiring her naked body in a way that I had tried so hard not to when I was helping her bathe. That was about relaxation—comfort. This was about something completely different, and considering I hadn't had her in my bed since we left Europe, I was dying to show her every single way I missed her.

But most of that would have to wait.

Because like it or not, she was hurt, and that cast on her arm was going to be a fucking reminder of it every single day until it came off. So I'd be gentle, and take care of her; because we both needed this after all of our time apart.

"Hunter," she pleaded as I guided her onto her back, placing her cast on a pillow and sliding my hips in between hers.

"Yes, sweetheart?" I asked, my lips just inches from hers.

"Kiss me," Gabrielle breathed out, and I was happy to oblige.

We kissed until she was a panting, squirming mess underneath me; until finally I pulled away. Watching her chest rise and fall as she breathed, I spoke the only words in my brain. "You're so fucking beautiful."

Her light brown hair was spilled on the pillows, those little freckles on her nose, her hazel eyes looking up at me with so much love—it was everything.

"I need you," she begged, reaching up for me.

I slid inside her and groaned at how fucking right it felt to be inside this woman. "Fuck, baby," I panted, burying my face between her breasts. I'd give them attention later.

"Hunter," she moaned, and I wondered if she felt it like I did. The intensity of our connection. How much I needed her, how much I never wanted to let her go.

I started moving inside of her—slow, shallow thrusts, being sure not to jolt her arm or hurt her. I needed this—we both did, but this wasn't sex for the sake of passion, desire, or heat. It wasn't some rushed labor just to get ourselves off. I wanted her always, of course, but this was different. This was *'I'm here with you, and I want to be connected to you.'* It was *'I see you, and I love you.'* It was love and happiness and feeling all wrapped into one, and my heart—the heart that had been closed off to this for so long—was overflowing at the sight of her, supple beneath me, her smooth skin and lovely curves I wanted to get my mouth on later.

That I'd never stop worshipping until the day I died.

"More," she pleaded, wrapping her arms around my neck and bringing me back down to kiss her again. "Please."

"I don't want to hurt you, baby," I said, gritting my teeth and trying to hold myself back as she rolled her hips.

"Not possible." She cupped my face with her hands. "You don't have to treat me like I'm fragile. I won't break, I promise."

I nodded, picking up the pace slightly as I slid in and out of her, as I ran my tongue over her lips and took her mouth, letting my love pour out of my body.

"Fuck, I love you."

She closed her eyes, and I rested our foreheads together.

"I love you too," she murmured.

And when we came together in something that felt a lot like *bliss* and *perfection*, I was pretty sure my life would never be better.

"Did you know otters hold hands while they sleep so they don't drift apart?" Gabbi mumbled sleepily after I tucked her into my side, completely exhausted after I'd made her come another time. I tried to go slow, but she'd practically jumped me after I'd caressed her backside, and I couldn't really complain.

"What?" I asked, tracing a finger over the tattoo behind her ear.

"I think it's cute. They don't want to be separated from the one they love, even when they sleep. Very romantic, those otters."

"Are you asking me to hold your hand while we sleep, sweetheart?"

"Mhm," she said as she burrowed into my chest, and I intertwined our free hands together.

"I'll never let you go," I promised.

"Good," Gabrielle said, closing her eyes as she finally fell asleep, nestled against my bare chest, and I knew we were both exactly where we belonged—together.

∼

THE NEXT WEEK was one of the best weeks of my life thus far. Not only because I spent every day at Gabrielle's, helping her shower and dress and losing ourselves in each other every night, but because I'd never realized how fulfilling it would be to come home to her every day.

I'd already realized that I didn't want to go back to sleeping alone at the end of this. That there was nothing more that I wanted than to move all of my stuff in with hers. I didn't want to go back to my quiet, empty apartment.

My girl kept insisting she was *fine,* that she wasn't going to break, and that I should stop watching over her like a hawk. But I couldn't help it—being a caretaker was in my blood, my DNA. She'd forced me to go back to work after the third day of following her around like a puppy dog, and even though I hated to leave her alone, I knew I couldn't follow her around every day *forever.* Sometimes I was serious about my threat to bubblewrap her, though.

Once her doctors were satisfied that there was no permanent damage to Gabrielle's brain or spine, they cleared her for normal activity. She just needed to wear the cast for 6-8 weeks. And Nicolas had given her the okay to work from home until she was feeling like coming into the office again, which was great, since I didn't have to worry about her getting behind the wheel anytime soon.

I knew it freaked her out, a little, every time she saw a car not stop at the line at a stop sign, or that looked like they might roll through a light, and it was going to take some time before she'd be comfortable again. But I'd help her through it, and I was more than happy to be her chauffeur until that point.

At the end of the week, we'd all driven to Matthew and Noelle's house for dinner, since the newlyweds were also getting ready to move within the next two months, and none of the rest of us offered our apartments. Something that I hoped to change after I asked Gabbi to move in with me. It might have only been a week since we said I love you, but fuck it. We'd already basically talked about getting married. I was pretty sure she'd say yes.

We were the last ones to arrive, on account of Gabrielle taking twice as long to get ready as normal. I was pretty sure she was going to rip her arm off before she made it the eight weeks, but I'd brushed out her hair for her and braided it—I did my best, at least.

Luckily, I'd taught myself when I was younger so I could do Em's hair when my parents had both been working full time.

"Hey." I grinned as we strolled in the front door, Matthew's dog happily coming over to say hello as I pulled the door shut. It was mid-September, but there was already a nip in the air.

I didn't let go of her hand, and Gabbi gave them all a sheepish smile. "So..." she started, watching everyone's eyes land on our intertwined fingers. "We're dating. Officially. Thought you'd all like to know."

"About damn time," Angelina said, grinning as I pulled her into me by the waist.

"Sorry for not telling you all before the wedding," she winced. "It was just—we wanted to keep it between us. We didn't know where things would go, and I don't think either of us realized how serious it was going to get..."

I kissed the top of her head, and practically she melted into my arms at the gesture.

"And she's not fucking getting rid of me. So that's settled." I grinned as we piled around the living room coffee table.

"We've all been there," Benjamin confirmed with a smirk on his face before placing a kiss on his wife's ring finger. "And look how that's turned out."

"And then there were two," Angelina said, looking over at Charlotte and Daniel, who'd been curiously quiet during the whole encounter. Charlotte forced her face into an awkward smile, her eyes connecting with his, but neither one of them said anything to deny it like normal.

I wondered what was up with them, but then again—I always did. I knew her birthday was next week, since she was the youngest of the girls, and maybe they'd figure it out before then.

"So, what game are we playing tonight?" Angelina changed the subject, already smirking at her husband.

Noelle brought out a stack of different board games and card decks. "Up for a rematch of scrabble?"

Matthew groaned. "Sunshine. Maybe let's play a game that doesn't incite World War Three?"

"Like Uno?" Angelina asked, holding up the deck.

Benjamin rolled his eyes. "I think that might be worse."

"You're only saying that because I kicked your ass last time, Boy Scout."

"I'm only saying that because you *cheat*, and you know it."

"Cards against humanity?" Daniel piped up, and Charlotte whispered something in his ear before turning bright red. "Never mind," he mumbled, staring back at the blonde. I was pretty sure Angelina's brother was majorly in love with her, but they both seemed too afraid to do anything about it.

But what did I know? I'd danced around Gabbi for months before I'd made a move. And sure, that move was kissing her, and then pulling away, but... It had all worked out.

"Oh!" Charlotte exclaimed, getting the attention off herself. "What about charades?"

Gabbi held up her cast. "Might be hard right now."

"Oh... Right. Darn."

"What about..." Matthew said, puzzling as he dug through the boxes. "A good ol' round of Monopoly?"

"We'll be here for a *week*," Angelina muttered, but Benjamin leaned over, and whatever he said to her made the flames ignite in her eyes. "Let's do it." She narrowed her eyes at her husband. "Are we doing teams?"

"I'm almost scared to find out," I said, raising an eyebrow at my brother, who smirked.

"You can imagine what it was like growing up with her," Daniel chirped in as everyone started setting up the board.

Angelina shoved at her brother's shoulder. "Shut up."

"Hey. That's my *wife* you're talking about." Benjamin leaned over to place a kiss on her jaw.

Gabrielle leaned on my shoulder, looking up at me. "Partners?" she whispered.

"Always, my little fighter."

She smiled, but I really meant it: there was no one else I'd rather have on my team.

~

"Elle," I whispered into her ear.

"Mmm."

Cuddled up against my chest, her eyes closed as she drifted in and out of sleep, and I really fucking hated waking her up. But I'd been stroking her hair for the last thirty minutes, and even though I knew the conversation with our friends would last through the night, I wanted to get her home.

"We're going to head out, everyone," I said, voice low as I lifted Gabbi into my arms and stood from the couch. "Need to get this one home and into bed."

Noelle yawned as well, cuddled up on the loveseat with Matthew, and Snowball laying directly under their feet. "G'night," she sighed sleepily. "Thanks for coming."

I nodded. "Wouldn't miss this for the world."

And it was true—Gabrielle's friends had become my friends. We were something like a little family when it was the eight of us, and I felt like we could take on anything that came our way. I'd never had a friend group that felt so special like that before. Gabbi had always talked about how the girls were her best friends, and I was realizing how much the guys were becoming mine. So I wouldn't complain.

I grabbed my girl's coat from the rack by the front door, not wanting to jostle her by putting it back on, and carried her to the car as she kept her face buried in my biceps.

When I went to slide her into the passenger seat, she whimpered as her arms slid around my neck. "Don't leave me," she pleaded.

"Sweetheart," I said, kissing her forehead. "Never going to happen. But I have to drive us home now, and then we can crawl into bed and I'll hold you all night, okay?"

"Mhm." Gabbi nodded, and I tugged one of those brown strands before she closed her eyes again, and I moved her arms so I could close the door to my jeep and get in the driver's side.

"What am I going to do with you?" I whispered, chuckling to myself as I buckled in and started driving home.

It was funny how her place had become home in a few days, but I had to admit that wherever she was—that was home.

CHAPTER 38
Hunter

OCTOBER

There was nothing like fresh air to get my mind off of everything—including the brunette who had captured all of my thoughts for the last year. Since I had the day off, we packed up my car and laced up our hiking boots, and I drove us both to Multnomah Falls.

Normally, I would have done more of a hike, but since Gabrielle still had her cast on, I'd only planned a small one for the day.

It had been a while since I'd been last, and somehow I always felt a little more at peace when I stared at the falls, and today was no different. Even though I knew everything was about to change. But I couldn't help but grin at the thought.

What I was going to ask her, officially. What would happen tomorrow, if I had any say in it. I'd already all but moved everything into her apartment, anyway. It had a bigger kitchen than mine, and even if it made my commute a little longer to work, I didn't care.

I loved her more and more every day. I wanted forever with

her, to move in together and never spend another night apart. Even if that meant waking up with a cat on my face occasionally.

"Come on, I want to show you something," I said, urging her on.

She looked so pretty all bundled up, her cheeks lightly pinked from the cold.

"Do you really think this was a good idea?" Gabrielle huffed, adjusting her giant puffy jacket over the cast again. "I really can't wait to get this thing off."

"Two weeks."

She sighed. "I know. I wish time would move faster so I could be free of this thing."

"I don't." I didn't want to lose one second with my girl.

She stuck her tongue out at me before leaning against me, resting her head on my shoulder as we walked up the trail.

When we got to the top of one of the smaller waterfalls, I turned to her, a silver key in my hands. I wasn't going to get down on one knee—not this time—but somehow this felt just as significant. The next step towards that one.

"What is this?"

"A key."

She raised an eyebrow. "Are you asking me to move in with you?"

I chuckled. "Okay, it's a *metaphorical* key. Technically, it's a key to *your* apartment. Because I know you love that place, and it's bigger than mine, and I don't want to uproot Toothless into a new home. But I am asking you if you want to move in together, *officially*, because I'm tired of going back and forth between our places."

"If I say yes, will you stop sneaking over your loads of stuff when you think I'm not looking?"

I grinned. "Deal."

"Good, because it was exhausting trying to pretend I didn't notice." She wrapped her arms around my waist. "I've been ready to move in with you since the day you took me home from the hospital. I'd love it if you moved in with *me*, babe."

"I have a third option."

She looked at me, her eyes full of questions. "You do?"

I pulled out another key. "I might have found us a house to rent. We could move in there instead. I know your lease ends soon, anyway, so..."

"Are you sure?"

"It's bigger, and there's room for you to have an entire space just for your books. We can go see it later today."

"Yes. Let's do it." Her smile filled my heart with warmth.

I kissed the top of her head. "Now that's settled, should we go get hot chocolate from the lodge? We need to plan our costumes for Matthew and Noelle's Halloween party still."

She fluttered her eyelashes. "Hunter Tobias Sullivan... Are you asking me if I want to do a couple's costume with you?"

I cleared my throat. "Yes, sweetheart."

"I think this is the most romantic thing anyone's ever asked me." Gabbi placed her hand over her heart.

"What about something with dragons?"

Gabrielle

NOVEMBER

"Look at that!" Angelina exclaimed. "She's free!" She picked up my arm, waving it around lightly, and I tried my best not to laugh.

I was finally free, though. The cast was off and my arm fully healed. I didn't have any lasting brain injuries or anything seriously wrong with me, besides a bit of PTSD getting in a car and the occasional back or neck pain. But Hunter was deliciously good with his hands, as always, and he'd taken to giving me massages almost every night.

So, I couldn't complain.

Angelina and Benjamin were celebrating moving into their brand new custom-built house with a pizza and movie night, so we were all gathered around their new *giant* kitchen after a house tour. I was endlessly in awe of the place, and I wasn't even a chef. I didn't think I'd ever be as good of a cook as Hunter was, or as much of a baker as Noelle was, but I'd learned my fair share of things in the kitchen from my man.

The man who was currently deep in conversation outside with his brother, as I turned back to my best friend. "Seriously, Ang. This place is incredible."

"I know, right?" She grinned. It wasn't anything like Hunter and Benjamin's parent's house, the giant craftsman out on a ton of land in Montana, but it was gorgeous, and had a big lot with an enormous yard, which was rare to find in the city. "Custom building it was a dream." She sighed.

"And you got your dream closet," Noelle piped up, her eyes alight with joy... and maybe a bit of jealousy?

The walk-in closet in their master bedroom came equipped with its own shoe *room*, I swear. That might have been a bit of an exaggeration, but she had more shoes than I was pretty sure a girl could ever wear. It was very *her* though, all the lace and black pencil skirts and pearls combined with the leather jacket she used to wear on girl's night out.

Noelle elbowed Matthew, her brand-new engagement ring still glittering on her finger. They'd gotten engaged before Halloween. Matthew had planned an elaborate scavenger hunt all over Portland visiting places that were meaningful to them. At the end, of course, we were hiding behind the trees, and then we'd all gone out to dinner together.

Hunter told me he'd asked the guys for help a few months back, and apparently, the four of them had their own group chat.

I'd taken his phone and renamed it to The Book Boyfriends, and, surprisingly enough, none of them had changed it back. Never mind that Daniel wasn't an official one—yet. I could tell the two of them had something going on between them, and after she'd forced my secret out of me at the wedding, I was determined to get to the bottom of it.

"Ow?" Matthew grunted, not expecting to be elbowed. "What was that for?" He rubbed at the spot, even though I knew that there was no way she'd actually hurt him. Matthew was built like Hunter—powerful, muscular arms, a wide chest, and a lot of muscle. We'd both lucked out in the looks department.

"Can *I* get a bigger closet?" She whispered loudly back, and he wrapped his arms around her waist.

"I think we might need a new house for that, baby." He whispered something in her ear, and she turned red, as always.

"Matthew!"

He grinned. "What?"

Noelle rolled her eyes. "You're gonna pay for that later."

Matthew kissed her cheek. "Looking forward to it, sunshine."

Benjamin and Hunter came in from the outside patio, a little damp from the drizzle but with smiles on their faces. He came over to me, about to pull me into his side, when I glared at him. "You're all wet."

"So?" He grinned, running a hand through his damp curls.

"So. *I* don't want to get wet," I said, pointing at my warm and toasty sweater and jeans combo. My ankle booties, coat, and scarf laid forgotten by the door, but I hadn't gone outside for a *reason*. Still, Hunter leaned in and kissed my cheek.

"Anything cool out there?" I asked him, brushing the condensation off his shirt.

"Benjamin was showing me the place he wants to build a pool."

I raised an eyebrow, looking over at his brother. "A pool, Benjamin?"

He grinned. "It'll be perfect for the kids."

I turned to Angelina, who waved her hands. "No, I'm not pregnant. I promise." She glared at her husband. "We're not even going to try until I'm thirty. At least." Angelina pointed a finger at him before turning back to the rest of us. "*But*, one day, it might be nice if we can have all our families out there. And if we build a structure over it, we can keep it heated in the winter, so it'll be usable all year round."

"I like it." I grinned.

Charlotte was quiet, but she gave me a small smile as Daniel brought her a drink.

"Hey, guys? Um..." Charlotte looked nervous, fidgeting with her clothes and rubbing her ring finger. She looked over at Daniel, who nodded at her as if he was encouraging her to go on. Giving her the strength to say whatever she needed to say. "I have something to tell you all." We all looked expectantly, not saying anything, just waiting with bated breath. Charlotte scooted closer to Daniel, who picked up her hand and wove their fingers together.

"*We* have something to tell you all," Daniel confirmed as we all watched them without saying a word. "We're... together," Daniel finally said.

"You *are?!*" Angelina shrieked, and if they thought she would react negatively, they were seriously wrong. I was pretty sure she was over the moon.

"That's not all though," Charlotte said, pulling her hand free to pull a ring out of her pocket and sliding it onto her finger. "We're getting married."

If it was possible, I was pretty sure the other six of us all collectively gasped at once. "You—*what?*"

Daniel wrapped his arm around Charlotte, pulling her into his side. "You heard her," he nodded. "We're engaged."

"Are you pregnant?" Angelina narrowed her eyes. "Daniel, you didn't get her pregnant, did you?" She looked at Charlotte. "I'll kill my brother if he did."

Charlotte flushed, her cheeks turning red. "No. I'm not pregnant. We just... realized we both had feelings for each other at the wedding, and we've been trying to figure out the best time to tell all of you."

I blinked. "Since the *wedding*? But... it's been months?"

"Sorry." She waved her hands out in front of her. "I feel like I did this all wrong. We wanted to ask all of you if you'd be in our wedding party."

"Of course!" Noelle was right there, throwing her arms around Charlotte, and then all four of us girls were in the middle of a group hug.

The guys look touched, and I knew how much it meant to Hunter to be included in this. That they all had each other.

"Oh my god, you know what this means?" Noelle said with a smile, her freckled cheeks glowing as she looked over at me. "You'll be the last two to get engaged."

I raised an eyebrow at Hunter, whose eyes connected with mine, and he gave me that dopey grin I'd found him wearing so much lately.

"I think we're good for now," I laughed. We were living together, enjoying every day as it came, and that was good enough... for now.

We'd made it through so much to be here, and I was looking forward to being blissfully happy for a while.

Life was a journey, and I knew every moment with him was going to be the best adventure yet.

Epilogue
GABRIELLE

SIX MONTHS LATER...

If you'd told me a year ago that I was going to find the love of my life, let alone that he was going to be some rugged, bearded doctor—and my best friend's brother-in-law—I never would have believed you. But that was the funny thing about fate, I guess. And I felt like I'd found the one.

Ever since that day at the hospital, true to his word, Hunter didn't let me out of his sight. But I didn't mind, not really. He'd moved into my place until my lease expired, and then we'd rented a tiny house.

Honestly, I was glad to have the bigger place, and I loved I could come home and cuddle with him on the couch after a long day of work. Sure, it was hard sometimes, with his long hours at the hospital, but he'd been looking into opening his own practice as a pediatrician. I knew it wasn't just me that was giving him cause to decide, especially after he'd come home, bone tired, and I'd hold him as he slept.

But there were also the hiking dates, and the endless group hangouts with our friends—we felt like one enormous family now, the eight of us, especially now that Charlotte and Daniel were, well... *married*. The guys' group chat name stuck, and we liked to call them our Book Boyfriends.

They were better than we'd ever dreamed of, even when we'd all thought love would never happen to us. Matthew and Noelle were engaged, happily planning their wedding for the fall, while Angelina and Benjamin were jet-setting around for work, married, and loving life. And Charlotte and Daniel's wedding in the early spring had been absolutely beautiful.

So yeah, everything was *perfect*.

I sighed, drawing in the blanket tighter around me as I watched the sunrise from our porch. It was a beautiful morning, not warm yet thanks to the dew, and I was content to just sit and drink my hot tea.

"I didn't know you were awake," came that grumbly voice I loved, shifting me on our little outdoor sofa so I could lean against him.

I shook my head. "Couldn't sleep." I tilted my head back to look at him, and I couldn't stop the stupid smile that spread over my face at his grumpy expression.

"What?" He asked, frowning, rubbing at his beard. "Why do you look like that? Your damn cat woke me up."

I couldn't help my giggle. "Toothless loves you, big man. Sorry." I patted the arm that curled around me and hugged him tighter.

"Come back to bed," he grunted, burying his face into my hair. Like he couldn't resist inhaling my scent, that coconut and citrus smell I knew drove him crazy. I was pretty sure he'd never let change my shampoo or conditioner ever again in my life.

I looked out at the sunrise instead. "In a bit."

"So, I was thinking..."

"Mhm?" I muttered, only half paying attention as the sky bloomed into color in front of me. Pinks, oranges, and blues lit up the sky. It would never get old, and that was why I always loved waking up early.

"I don't think we should renew the lease on the house."

"What?" I looked up at him, jaw dropping open. "Why? I thought you loved it here?"

"I do." He gave me a little smirk. "But I found us somewhere better." Hunter dropped a kiss on my lips, and I shook my head.

"You crazy, crazy man. This house is just fine for the two of us."

He dropped his head onto my shoulder. "Yeah, sure." Another grunt. "But what if we don't want it to be *just* the two of us?"

"What is up with you today? I'm not ready for a *kid*—"

He shook his head. "Not now. And I plan to put a ring on that pretty little finger first." He rubbed over my ring finger.

"Yeah?"

Somehow, it was crazy to me that I was the last one in our group that wasn't engaged or married.

Even Charlotte had beaten me. *Charlotte*, for crying out loud.

"Mhm. But I want it to be our place. One we build. A big house with a porch swing so you can watch the sunrise every damn morning and a big backyard so our kid can run around, and where we can build 'em a tree house or whatever the hell they want. And our dog can run around."

I raised an eyebrow this time. "You've really thought about this, haven't you?"

He nodded. "I just want to make you happy."

"You do." It was my turn to nuzzle into him, rubbing my nose against his as I moved to straddle his lap. "Every day. I'm so deliriously happy."

"Good."

"Now what was that about a dog?" I asked, laughing as I wrapped my arms around him. "We don't have a dog."

"Hmm... Are you sure about that?" Hunter asked, his normally gruff face lit up with mischief.

"*Hunter Tobias Sullivan*. What did you do?"

"Maybe you should go in the garage and find out?"

I stared at him, pulling away from his caring hold, like *what the fuck?* "There better not be a dog in the garage," I scolded.

But Hunter said nothing else, just picked me up, set me on my feet, and grabbed my hand as he started walking towards the garage, where my Mazda and his Jeep normally lived.

When we opened the door, there was a little kennel sitting on the floor, and my hand lifted over my mouth.

I knew he wasn't kidding, but... "You got us a puppy?"

He placed a kiss on my forehead. "I got *you* a puppy, sweetheart. And he can be our new adventure buddy."

"Oh." I knew my eyes filled with unshed tears, but I didn't care. I let them fall as he pulled out a tiny bundle of white, gray, and brown fur, placing the dog into my arms. The tiny thing gave me a few licks as it squirmed in my arms before settling down and staring up at me with those big black eyes.

"She's—she *is* a girl, right?" I asked. Hunter nodded. "She's beautiful. Oh my gosh."

"She's a mini Australian Shepard, but the breeder said she'd always be on the smaller side of the range, since both her parents were small."

I walked back inside our house, the puppy secure in my arms, and Hunter followed behind me, carrying in the crate and the other dog stuff he'd stashed.

"What do you want to name her?" He asked as we settled on the couch in our living room, both the sunset and going back to bed, clearly forgotten.

"I get to name her?" I asked, fiddling with the collar around her neck.

There wasn't a dog tag on the collar yet, so what was that...?

I looked down at our puppy before I looked back up at Hunter, who was down on one knee in front of the couch, wrapping his hands around the engagement ring he'd hidden on the collar as he pulled it from my fingers.

"Gabrielle Amelia Meyer. Would you make me the happiest man alive and be my wife? I want you by my side every minute of every day, and there's nothing I want more than to go on this adventure with you."

"Yes," I nodded. "A thousand times, *yes*. Life with you has been the best adventure I could have asked for."

His lips tilted up into a warm smile as he pushed the ring onto my ring finger, and then he pulled me into his arms, kissing me, causing the puppy in my arms to stir.

"Oh, sorry, puppy." I settled back into his arms, petting her soft ears. "I don't think Toothless is going to be too happy about her new friend."

"Eh." He gave me a crooked smile. "She'll adjust." He scowled. "Besides, maybe she'll stop sleeping on my face now."

I looked down at the soft brown dog, so little and loving and all *ours*. I couldn't help but inhale her sweet puppy scent again. "What about Rowan?"

"Rowan," he said, almost like he was tasting the name on his tongue. "Yeah. I think it suits her."

"What do you think, Rowan?" I turned my attention back to the dog, who barked and jumped up to lick me on the face. "Sounds like she likes it," I said, laughing.

Hunter gave me a big kiss on the side of my head. "I do too."

I shuffled Rowan into my lap to free my hands again and stared at the ring. "How did you pull this off without me knowing?" I narrowed my eyes. "And how long were you going to leave her out in the garage all alone if we went back to sleep?"

Hunter laughed as he kissed my hand, and then the ring. "I *was* going to surprise you in bed when you woke up. Little did I know you were going to sneak away from me."

I blushed. "Sorry to have ruined your plans."

"Nah. This is even better. And we can go look at the new house later today."

"Are you sure?" I blinked. "I'm okay here."

"Benjamin's been giving me grief *forever*. Besides, I thought you'd like it if you lived on the same street as your best friend."

"Really?" My eyes lit up. I'd fallen in love with their house the moment I'd walked in it for the first time, and the idea of living right next door to my best friend, and his brother... "You're serious?"

He nodded. "There are only a few lots left, and I have one on hold. The contract on the lot next door to Benjamin and Angelina's actually fell through. It's ours, if you want it. But like I said, it's up to you. I'm happy living wherever you are."

"Well, in that case..." I laughed. "I can't wait to see it."

"I can't wait to build our dream home together. And marry you. *Fuck*, Gabrielle. I can't wait to call you my wife."

As I stroked Rowan's soft brown coat, I snuggled into his chest. "I can't wait for *everything* with you, Hunter Tobias Sullivan."

He grinned. "Told you I'd make you Mrs. Sullivan."

"That is very much still yet to be seen, *Mr*. Sullivan."

Hunter placed a kiss on my nose. "Maybe."

"So, any plans left for the rest of this gorgeous day?"

"Only for you to go back to bed so I can bring you breakfast in it."

"Mmm. Breakfast in bed. What have I done to deserve this?"

"You agreed to be mine forever," he said, placing a kiss on the corner of my mouth before shifting our positions so he could get up and pad into the kitchen.

"I agreed to that a long time ago," I whispered, but I didn't move, too content to sit here cuddling with the puppy as I watched his sweatpants-clad ass bent down to grab something from the bottom cabinet.

Best view of the year right there.

I was pretty sure it would be the best view of the rest of my life, too.

Extended Epilogue
HUNTER

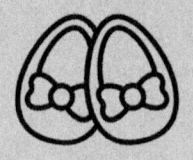

THREE YEARS LATER...

I opened the front door to our house, locking the jeep behind me as I walked inside. It had been a longer-than-usual day at work. I'd had to squeeze in a few extra patients at the practice, so I was happy to be home.

"Sweetheart?" I checked the kitchen, expecting her to be in there. She'd texted me earlier that she was making dinner, but the kitchen was empty, the only sign that she'd been in here was the oven on warm and a pan covered in tinfoil inside.

I liked to cook whenever I was home, but I was glad that I'd taught my wife enough that she enjoyed it too. We still had our weekly cooking dates, where we'd make something new together. Sometimes I picked the recipe, and sometimes she did, but even if it turned out terribly, we did it together.

I set my keys and coffee thermos down on the kitchen island.

"Gabrielle?" I called out, moving through the house.

We'd stayed in our rental for another nine months before we moved into our brand new one, the house that sat right next to my brother's home. Ours wasn't as big as theirs was, but we still had one of the biggest house models the builder had offered.

What I loved about our neighborhood was the lots were huge. Maybe not as big as my parent's house in Montana, but enough that we had some privacy in our backyard. Enough that we'd been able to fence it and put a dog door in so Rowan could run around outside.

She was a ball of pent-up energy, but that was our dog for you. Speaking of...

Normally she was by the door, waiting for me, or under my wife's feet. I paced towards the bedrooms, checking the master, Gabbi's office, and her cozy little reading nook in her library until I finally found her.

Sitting on the floor, folding socks.

"Baby." I sighed. "I could have done that when I got home."

She looked up at me with tears in her eyes. "They're so tiny, Hunter. Can you believe they're this tiny?"

Rowan was laying by her side, resting her head on my wife's thigh—ever her dutiful protector.

I nodded, taking the socks from her hand, setting them on the table, and helping her up to her feet. It was a lot harder these days, what with her giant belly. She was due last week, but we were still waiting for the baby to come. Of course, I'd find her sitting in the nursery.

"Hey." I ran a finger under her eyes, catching the tears. "It's just hormones."

She nodded. "I want her to be here already."

"I know."

"I'm tired of being as big as a house," she mumbled. "I can't even do anything anymore."

She sighed, blowing her bangs off her forehead. She'd cut her hair shorter last summer, and her brown tresses hit right below her shoulders now.

"Do you need anything?" I asked her as I guided her into the rocking chair. "Water, a snack, a foot rub?"

"Oh, the last one," she pleaded. "Definitely the last one." She moaned a little as I picked up her feet, rubbing the insole in slow circles. "And I'd also like your giant baby out of me. You did this to me. Put your mutant spawn in me, and now—you should be able to get her *out*." She huffed. "I'm going to have to push her out of me, and I will probably never be the same, so thank you for that."

I chuckled. "One more day, my love." They planned on inducing her tomorrow if she didn't go into labor on her own.

I kept massaging her like that, moving to the balls of her feet, until she sighed, closing her eyes.

I placed a kiss on her belly as Gabbi rocked back and forth in the chair. "Hey, baby girl. Come out soon so we can give your momma a break, huh?" I looked up at her to see her eyes shining with unabashed joy, and I couldn't help standing up and taking her face in my hands, placing a kiss on her forehead, then on her lips.

"I love you," I breathed.

"I'll love you more once your daughter evacuates my womb," Gabbi grumbled as I pulled away.

She was so beautiful, especially like this, and even though I'd been terrified of all the what-ifs when she'd eventually gotten pregnant, I also couldn't wait to be a dad. Sure, I was terrified of not being good enough as a parent, terrified of losing this precious life before it even had a chance to see the world, terrified that something would happen to the best gifts I'd ever gotten in life: my wife, and now our little girl.

It had taken us a little longer than the rest of our friends to get pregnant, and even if it never happened again, one was enough for us. We had enough nieces and nephews to spoil with the rest of our friends, so I knew we'd never regret our decision. But one of our own? I never could have imagined how happy this would make me. She was going to be our entire world. She was already.

I looked over the nursery, the dragon mural that Angelina had painted even when she'd been balancing a baby on her hip.

"Dinner's in the oven, by the way." Gabbi squeezed my hands. "I made Mexican lasagna. My mom's recipe."

"Sounds great." I kissed her head as she stood up out of the chair, one hand resting on her bump. "Do you want anything after?"

Her eyes shined bright. "Want to go get milkshakes?"

Who was I to deny her? "What flavor? Chocolate, peanut butter, oreo?" She'd constantly been craving sweets during her pregnancy, and milkshake runs had become a common occurrence in our house. I'd even got the other guys in on it. Since there was clearly something in the water, and three of our wives were all pregnant at the same time.

"Chocolate peanut butter banana?" She'd also taken a liking to combining as many flavors as possible. The workers at the shake place knew me by now. I think they took pity on me, so they didn't charge me for extra toppings anymore.

"You're ridiculous."

"I know, but considering I'm having your child, I think that's allowed."

I brushed the hair back off her forehead before placing a kiss there. "Yeah, it is."

She rested against me, my hand overlapping hers as we stood in the doorway and appraised the room. There was even a whole bookshelf of books, and I knew Gabrielle would start her off young. "She'll be here soon, sweetheart."

She looked up at me and sighed as I rubbed her back. "You're going to be such a wonderful dad. Look at how well you've taken care of me this whole time."

But I knew the truth—that she was going to be the *best* mom.

"Come on, let's feed you dinner and then get you that milkshake, little fighter."

"I don't think you can call me little anymore," she grumbled, staring down at her stomach.

I hoisted her up in my arms carefully, carrying her to the kitchen to prove to her she was always going to be little to me.

WE WELCOMED Quinlan Juniper Sullivan into the world on April 22nd at 2:34 am, weighing exactly eight pounds, seven ounces, and twenty-two inches long. I knew there was no one I would ever love as fiercely as our little girl or her fearless mom.

"She's beautiful," I said as Gabbi nestled against my chest, our little family all curled up together on the hospital bed.

"I can't believe we made her." Gabbi ran a finger over her cheek. "She's perfect."

She *was* perfect. All chubby baby with those long limbs she'd definitely gotten from me; because *I'd* weighed ten pounds at birth. When our friends had their kids, I'd never particularly thought they'd been very cute as newborns. Sure, they were cute now, as toddlers, but with Quin—I already loved her sweet little face.

"Our friends are all waiting outside, sweetheart. Do you want me to tell them?"

Gabbi shook her head, eyes drooping shut. "Just... want to stay like this for a bit," she yawned.

Quinlan made a little noise, and I scooped her out of Gabbi's arms, ignoring her murmurs of dissent even as she closed her eyes and rested her head against my shoulder.

"Hey, my little princess," I whispered, watching as her little hand clasped around one of my fingers. I was careful to not speak too loud, so I didn't wake her up.

"You're going to be so loved, sweet girl. And you're going to have the best mom in the entire world, and your dad is going to do his best to make sure that you can do whatever you want when you grow up. Plus, all of your aunts and uncles will probably spoil you rotten, just like your grandma and grandpa." I smiled, thinking about my parents and how much they'd been looking forward to their first granddaughter. No matter what, our house would be full of love and laughter. I'd make sure of it.

And thirty minutes later, after Gabrielle had taken what felt like the quickest nap of her life, I went out and got our friends, and for the first time, they met our daughter.

· · ·

Gabrielle

I LOOKED DOWN at our newborn daughter in her crib, wearing the green baby onesie that her aunt Angelina had bought her. Nothing but the best for my girl.

She was perfect, our little miracle. I couldn't believe that I had ever imagined a life without her, this perfect combination of my husband and I. Her soft hair was already growing in, and I hoped she'd get his beautiful green eyes.

Quinlan. I'd named her after my favorite character from my favorite book. Somehow, my husband enjoyed reading my books with me, so I'd gotten him to read them as well. He shared the main male love interest's name, anyway, so it was perfect.

"Sweetheart." Hunter's arms wrapped around my waist. "Why don't you go shower? I can take care of her if she needs anything while you're in there."

I was exhausted, and I loved he knew exactly what I needed right now. I couldn't look away from our sweet girl's face.

"Do you ever feel like your heart is going to burst just from looking at her? Like... part of it is living outside of your chest now?"

He kissed my forehead, and I knew he was staring at her like I was as he rocked me back and forth. "Yeah. Yeah, Elle. I do."

"It's been a week, and I already feel like she's grown so much." I gave a rough exhale, turning so I could bury my nose in his chest, inhaling that cedar smell he always carried around with him. Smoky and spicy, but so damn comforting. "I want to protect her all the time. Is it crazy that I want to stare at her, 24/7, just to make sure she's okay? That she's breathing."

"No." His beard scratched the top of my head as he shook his. "It's completely normal." He tipped up my chin. "But she's going to be fine if you take a shower, love. I promise."

I gave a rough nod. "Will you come with me?"

He gave a chuckled rasp. "I think we both know that's a bad idea. You've never been able to keep your hands off of me, after all."

I punched him in the shoulder playfully.

If there was one thing I wouldn't do, it was disobeying Dr.'s orders. For multiple reasons. Infection and the risk of tearing most of all. I shuddered. No thanks. Even if my husband looked increasingly sexy with those tattoos running up his arms bare to me, and my sex drive was finally coming back to me.

When I'd walked into the room earlier and found Hunter with Quinlan cuddled against his naked chest? I'd *swooned*. Even the way he looked right now with those damn Henley sleeves pushed up over his forearms was making me all hot and achy.

"These next five weeks better go by really freaking fast," I muttered to myself as I paced out of the room, heading to our bathroom to turn the shower water on, but at the last second, I turned around to look at Hunter.

He was still staring at her crib, eyes so full of love for our baby girl, and I rested my head against the door frame.

"Hey."

He lifted his head and made eye contact with me.

"I love you," I said, unable to contain the smile on my face.

"I love you too, sweetheart," he said back.

And my heart was so full.

They were my entire world. The best life adventure. One I couldn't wait to keep experiencing every single day. For the rest of our lives.

The End

Acknowledgements

To Gabbi, who inspired me to write this book and let me talk her ear off about the Best Friends Book Club characters for the past year: I love you. It's crazy to think that this book is in existence solely because of you. When I first got the idea for Disrespectfully Yours and decided to name her best friend after you, I had no idea that Gabrielle would end up becoming a main character in her own right, but I'm so glad she did. I hope you love Hunter Tobias and that he is in your top book boyfriends forever—because he's just for you.

To Meg, who kept me going even when I hated everything (true story) and yelled at me when I needed to write: thank you for your endless conversation, cat memes, and laughter. I'm so glad to have you as an author friend and to share ideas with each other.

To Katie W, my alpha reader: thank you for being such a good friend, and someone I can always count on to talk to, cheer me up, and tell me that what I'm doing isn't bad (it's very needed sometimes), I appreciate you so much. Thank you for the words of encouragement that helped keep me going as I was writing. I love you lots.

To my beta readers: Katie A, Meg, Faithlynn: thank you thank you thank you for being an extra set of eyes that was much needed! I appreciate you all so much.

To my parents, as always: thanks for being so proud of me. Thank you for telling everyone you know to read my books. I'm only embarrassed 50% of the time. Thank you for not reading them. Please don't.

Thank you to everyone who has taken a chance on my books and this world I've created. I appreciate you all <3

About the Author

Originally from the Portland area, Jennifer now lives in Orlando with her dog, Walter and cat, Max. She always has her nose in a book and loves going to the Disney Parks in her free time.

Website: www.jennchipman.com

- amazon.com/author/jenniferchipman
- goodreads.com/jennchipman
- instagram.com/jennchipmanauthor
- x.com/jennchipman
- tiktok.com/@jennchipmanauthor
- pinterest.com/jennchipmanauthor

Printed in Great Britain
by Amazon